I0662278

For Richter or Poorer

Hillbilly Hijinks

Book 4

Janet Taylor-Perry

For Richter or Poorer

By

Janet Taylor-Perry

Hillbilly Hijinks

#4

ISBN: 979-8-9853495-7-3

Dragon Breath Press
Ridgeland, Mississippi

Where Legends Begin...

Other Books by Janet Taylor-Perry

The Raiford Chronicles:

1. *Lucky Thirteen*—Semifinalist, Faulkner Competition
2. *Heartless*
3. *Broken*—Short list finalist, Faulkner Competition
4. *Whatever It Takes*

The Legend of Draconis:

1. *King Satin's Realm*—Semifinalist, Faulkner Competition
2. *Spirits' Desire*—Winner Preditor and Editor's Award, "other" category
3. *Last of an Exceptional Breed*—Semifinalist, Faulkner Competition
4. *One World*

April Chastain Intrigues:

1. *Wilted Magnolias*—Finalist, Faulkner Competition

Laura Beth Copeland Misadventures:

1. *Head Count*—Finalist Faulkner Competition

Hillbilly Hijinks:

1. *Homegrown Healer*—Semifinalist, Faulkner Competition
2. *Mountain Moonshine*—Semifinalist, Faulkner Competition
3. *Gator Aid*—Semifinalist, Faulkner Competition

Gods and Children:

1. *Ain't No Mountain*—Semifinalist, Faulkner Competition

Compiled Anthologies:

1. *Unforgettable Christmases*

2. *Tales from the Dragon's Lair*
3. *Holiday Hearth*

Anthology Short Story Inclusions:
1. *Brick Street Press: 2010 Winners*—"Internot Dating"
2. *Mississippi Profiles*—"Thibodeauxs Do Magnifique!"
3. *What Would Elvis Think?*—"Your Life Is not Over"
4. *Ordinary Miracles*—"Stomach Staples and Cyclones"
5. *Battles: Glimpses of Truth*—"Nothing in Life Is Free"

For Richter or Poorer

By

Janet Taylor-Perry

Hillbilly Hijinks

#4

Disclaimer

All entities in this story are purely fictional. Any resemblance to any party, living or dead, is coincidence.

Acknowledgments

Thanks to my plethora of author friends who continually encourage me to practice my craft. Great appreciation to my family for putting up with my eccentricities. Bookoos of gratitude to my editor, mentor, and friend, Lottie Brent Boggan for her no-nonsense approach to keeping me on track. Google her and give her books a read. Gratitude goes to my faithful beta reader, Nidia Hernandez, aka Barbra Best, author of *The Rock Star Records*, fun reads to get lost in. I can never tell Aunt Ruth Ishee how much those telephone read-alouds meant to the growth and development of my art. Likewise, although I expressed my gratitude to my daughter, Mary Catherine, before she passed away, I cannot explain how much her unwavering support meant to me. She read everything I wrote before her passing, this tome included. And no word can express the debt I owe to my fantastic cover designer, Christopher Chambers. He works magic with an idea I give him. Check out his work at juroddesigns.com. A special shoutout goes to John DeBoer, retired physician and author of multiple thrillers, for helping me with Alain's medical issue in this installment. You can find his work on Amazon. And a special note of love and appreciation to my eldest son, Matt Perry, for reluctantly posing for this cover. His face is hiding beneath the hair.

Bookoos—for those who don't know, this is a southern perversion of the French *beaucoup*, meaning a lot, much, many.

Dedication

For my youngest son, Sam. I'm glad you made me Mumzy to five. I am all the richer for having you.

And, ye fathers, provoke not your children to wrath, but bring them up in the discipline and admonition of the Lord.

Ephesians 6:4

Contents

Prologue

The small boy with light-brown hair and jade eyes winced as his obviously pregnant mother coated welts on his back with ointment while two even younger children, a girl and a boy, watched wide-eyed with fear. The mother who looked exactly like the little boy soothed, "Sh. Don't let him see you cry. It'll make him madder."

The boy whimpered, "Ma, I didn't do nothin' wrong."

"I know, baby, but he thinks you sassed him."

"He was hittin' you for makin' pork chops 'stead o' ham."

"It wudn't what he wanted."

"That don't make it right. Why don't you run away?"

"I cain't. He'd kill me if'n I left. I'd hafta take you young'uns with me. He'd track us down. I couldn't leave y'all. He'd kill *you* for shore."

"Ma, he's gonna kill us one day anyway."

The door slammed as a big burly man stomped in. "Quit coddlin' the brat," he growled.

"He's jest a baby! He didn't deserve bein' beat."

"He sassed me!" The man turned to the boy. "Quit whinin'. Git yo ass out the door and help me with these apples."

"He's hurtin'," pled the mother.

"Boy, move!" ordered the father. "Unless you want me to give you somethin' to whine about."

"Keenan, please?" the mother begged.

The man pointed at her. "You best shut up, or I'll give you some more too. You best be rememberin' you ain't nothin' but a whore I brung home to give me some young'uns to help me with this farm. You do as I say, or you can join my other four wives."

"Leave her alone," said the boy, fisting small hands.

The man slapped the child across the face and grabbed his clenched fist. "You gonna hit me? You better make it a death lick. Git up! You got work to do." The man dragged the child out the door.

1

Caveman

Possum Holler, West Virginia, was a small town well hidden from society. Most of its inhabitants never got past eighth grade, but the government did not interfere. The county sent a school bus to the town, and the children in town went to school; however, the children who lived in the outlying areas missed quite a bit, often enough to be retained. Winters made it hard to get to town and the bus.

Nonetheless, summer brought playtime even for the impoverished children of Possum Holler. The four boys splashing in the creek were great examples. Eight-year-old, brown-haired, hazel-eyed MacKenzie Reardon lived in town with the preacher, Leo Tomlin, who had taken Mac in the year before after his father died in the wake of losing all his other family members in the two previous years. Mac was one of the lucky children. Leo Tomlin made sure he got an education. Mac would be a third-grader.

Tipper Campbell was taller than the other boys, but he was only eight. He was fair and tried to stay in the shady areas. His sandy-blond hair looked like a lion's mane, and his blue eyes sparkled with mischief. Tipper was an only child whose father had died in a mining accident when he was a baby. His mother, Ina, was a single mother although she had almost married Mac's father, Ander, before he died. Tipper was currently staying with Mac and Leo Tomlin while Ina obtained a barber's license in Wilmington, the closest big town to Possum Holler. Tipper was also going to be a third-grader.

Another dark-haired, hazel-eyed boy jumped from the bank and splashed the others. Gator Jones and MacKenzie Reardon were first cousins. Gator's mother was dead, and his four older brothers had left home. Consequently, Gator lived alone with his father, Talmage, known more familiarly as Tal, on a hog farm. Gator was also eight, but he would be back in second grade because he had missed too many days.

The fourth boy had long light-brown hair and bright green eyes. Alain Richter was a year older than the others. He was tall and very thin. When he climbed onto the bank, there were visible scars on his back as if he had been beaten. His face was soft although he had suffered much in nine years. He, too, would be in second grade again due to absences since Ander Reardon had died and could no longer get him to town as he had done all four boys while he lived. Ander had somehow convinced Keenan Richter his son needed an education.

But it was summer, and the boys were enjoying some freedom. Their swim, wearing their underwear, was interrupted by giggling. Two girls stood on the bank of the swimming hole. Fay Richter, Alain's younger sister by a year, and Amy Dent, the daughter of the owner of the general store and also eight, had come to swim. Fay looked just like Alain. She wore a pair of old, ragged, cut-off jeans and a plain white tank-type t-shirt. Amy was petite. She was the only child who wore actual swimwear, a one-piece swimsuit of red with white seashells. She had her long dark-brown hair in a ponytail, and her dark eyes snapped as she teased, "Look, Fay. Four turtles are swimming."

"Be careful, Amy. They might be snappin' turtles." Fay giggled.

"Jump in and see if we bite," responded Alain. "Course, I don't wanna bite my sister."

"Well," said Amy, "gator's bite."

"Not this 'un. He ain't got no teeth," Alain shouted.

Amy laughed. "Yes, he does."

"I lost two," said Gator. "Maybe I could gum you, but I'd rather nibble Fay." Gator grinned to show both top canines were missing.

"Y'all are silly," taunted Amy.

"You gonna swim?" asked Mac, all seriousness.

"Maybe."

"Come on. Jump in," Tipper invited. "We won't bother y'all."

The girls jumped in to cool off in the sweltering summer heat and the unusually dry conditions. They frolicked and splashed until they heard adult voices from two different directions.

"Oh, shit!" exclaimed Alain. "That's Pa. We ain't back in time for chores. We gonna git whooped. Come on, Fay."

As all the children pulled themselves from the creek, Keenan Richter bulled through the thicket while Lucille Dent primly picked her way along the path. The two collided.

"Oh, get off me!" screeched Lucille, who was about five-eight with dark hair and eyes. "You are disgusting. You're filthy, and you stink."

Keenan Richter was dirty and sweaty. He was well over six feet and heavy with muscle from manual labor. He had dark graying hair and eyes bordering on honey. His face was hard and lined and covered by a thick shaggy beard. He snarled, "You ain't gotta worry, Lucille. I sho don't wanna be on you. You a snooty, hateful bitch."

"Ugh!" Lucille turned her attention to the children. "Amy Dent, you get home! What you doin' up here with all these boys?"

"I came with Fay, Momma. We just went swimmin' to cool off."

"Yes, the little Richter girl. Well, let's go. You've got a piano lesson."

"Can't I take a summer vacation from it? I'd rather draw and have art lessons."

"We'll discuss it. Let's go."

Amy grabbed one of the two towels she had brought and handed the other one to Fay.

"Thank you," said Fay.

"Is that my towel?" asked Lucille.

"Yes, ma'am," answered Amy. "I'll get it later."

"No, just keep it," said Lucille, disdain seeping from her voice as her nose wrinkled.

"We don't need yo stuff," growled Keenan.

"Well, I don't want it back after your little urchin uses it. It's contaminated."

"You mean old bat," blurted Alain. "Fay ain't got germs."

"Ugh!" grunted Lucille again as she grabbed Amy's hand and dragged her home. On the walk home, Lucille continued her critical remarks. "Amy, I don't want you playin' with those Richters. They are just nasty. Tipper and Gator aren't much better. The only child you were with today that has any potential is Mac, and only because he came to live with Preacher Tomlin. Otherwise, he'd be just as bad."

"They're my friends," argued Amy.

"Not if I say otherwise. Do you understand?"

"Why?"

"Because I said so." Lucille popped Amy's bottom. "Now, get home!"

Keenan Richter hollered at his two children. "Chores ain't done! Git yo asses home and git the strap ready."

"Please, Pa?" said Alain. "We jest lost track o' time. We'll git it all done before dark. I promise."

"Shut up! You know better. Talk back to me, and I'll give you extry licks."

Alain grabbed Fay's hand. "Come on." They ran ahead of Keenan.

"Alain," Fay whimpered, "I don't want a whoopin'."

"I'll take care of you. Don't worry, Fay. I won't let 'im hurt you."

The two got home as quickly as possible. Fay fed their chickens and milked the cow. Alain filled the buckets on the yoke with water from the well and watered the vegetables. Keenan got home and stood with a deep frown on his face and his arms across his barrel chest. Alain worked at a furious pace. As he approached the back rows of corn, he heard a whisper. "Alain!"

"Robert Lee?"

"Me and Calvin done the back ten while Pa was lookin' for you."

"Thanks."

The sun was just on the horizon when Alain dropped the yoke at his father's feet. "I'm done, Pa. It ain't dark," he declared, catching his breath in gasps.

"In the barn."

"Pa, please? I done it all."

"You shouldna run off."

"I jest wanted to have a little fun."

"Life ain't fun. Next time, you'll finish yo chores first. In the barn."

Alain walked, shoulders hunched in dejection, into the barn where Fay waited, wringing her hands. Keenan took a leather strap from a hook. He looked at the two children. "I reckon, ladies first."

Fay's cat-green eyes brimmed with tears. "Please, Pa?" pled Alain. "Don't whoop her. She's jest a little girl. I'll take her licks."

"Tryin' to be a hero?"

"No. She don't deserve a whoopin'. I lured her off."

"Alain!" said Fay. She knew Alain lied.

"Hush. Go inside."

"No," said Keenan. "Stay and see what trouble you caused yo brother. Alain, take yo shirt off."

Alain took his shirt off and leaned over a bale of hay. He knew what to expect. Keenan raised the strap. "The first five are yo sister's."

Alain's body jerked with each blow, but he refused to cry out. Keenan said coldly, "The next five are yores for runnin' off. Then, you git five for takin' yo sister."

"No!" Fay cried.

"Shut up. I ain't done with you yet." Keenan pointed a sharp finger at his daughter. "You gonna git somethin', little girl, for lettin' a *man* carry yo punishment when he don't deserve it. Matter of fact, I'm addin' five more licks 'cause he lied for you."

"Be quiet, Fay," Alain said. "Just do it!" he snapped at Keenan.

Keenan seemed to enjoy the next fifteen lashes. On the last one, Alain finally uttered a faint cry.

Baring his teeth as a wild animal, Keenan snarled, "Now, go inside and let yo ma coddle you."

Fay started after her brother. "Not you," bit Keenan. "We ain't done. You gotta learn who the man around here is."

Alain opened the door where Shirley Richter stood ready with ointment for the welts on the child's back. Some had broken the skin and bled. They heard Fay scream. Alain started back.

"No," said Shirley, clutching her son's hand. "He'll kill you."

"Ma, he's hurtin' her."

"He don't hardly never beat her."

"What's he doin' to make her scream?"

"I'm scared to ask."

"Ma?"

"If it's what I think, I'll kill him myself if I catch 'im."

"Ma, run away."

"And go where?"

"Mr. Jones."

"Tal's a good man, but I cain't put him in that situation."

As Shirley coated Alain's back, Fay ran in and hid under her mother's arm. Keenan stomped in. "Where's supper?"

"Cookin'." Shirley glowered at her husband. She was his fifth wife. All the others had died, two in childbirth and the other two of unknown causes.

A little later, Shirley put a plate in front of Keenan and whispered in his ear, "If I catch you touchin' her, I'll castrate you in yo sleep."

24

For several days Alain stayed close to the farm although the four buddies were doing odd jobs to make money. He didn't want his friends to see his bruises and scars. Keenan came in early and woke the boys. "Time for peach pickin'."

Alain groaned, "Pa, I believe President Lincoln signed the *Emancipation Proclamation.* It did away with slavery."

Keenan jerked Alain from his bed, which was an old army cot covered with a homemade quilt to add a bit of cushioning. "I said for you to git yo ass up!"

"Pa, the sun ain't up."

"You are. Git yo ass ready to pick some peaches. Don't sass me. I'll beat the hell outa you."

Robert Lee and Calvin dressed without a word. Alain followed. They ate a bowl of oatmeal with a glass of fresh milk. Alain hated oatmeal. He gagged on every bite, but he choked it down because he knew there would be nothing else until Keenan decided to break for a bite, probably some ham and biscuits and peaches, at least six hours away.

The three boys climbed the trees with baskets on their backs. They filled the baskets and climbed down to deposit the peaches in bushel baskets to be loaded onto the old truck and taken to market. Today it was peaches. Tomorrow it would be pears. All summer and fall there was fresh produce to harvest and get to market. They had peaches, pears, plums, and apples. They also grew blackberries, blueberries, and strawberries. In the vegetable gardens there were peas, butterbeans, okra, squash, watermelons, cantaloupes, peanuts, hot and sweet peppers, tomatoes, corn, egg plants, and pumpkins. They had pecan trees and walnut trees. They also had potatoes, sweet potatoes, carrots, and onions, both bulb and green. In the cooler months they would produce an assortment of greens: turnips, collards, mustard, cabbage, broccoli, cauliflower, and kale.

Richter Farms and Orchards produced good crops. Alain understood the need to help, but he also wanted to be a boy. The need to help is why Keenan resented his going to school and why the others did not go. That was one reason why Alain loved school, to escape.

A gasp caught Alain's attention. "Calvin!" he shouted as he snagged his little brother's hand to keep him from falling from the tree.

"What the hell?" yelled Keenan as Calvin's basket of peaches spilled and pelted him on the head.

"Calvin fell, Pa," explained Alain.

"Git down here, all three o' you."

The three boys climbed down and cowered in a row. "Are you stupid, boy?" yelled Keenan.

"Pa, he slipped," Alain defended the six-year-old. "He's six, Pa."

"I gathered fruit when I was six."

"He slipped. It was only one basket. You should be glad I caught 'im. He ain't hurt."

"You sassin' again?"

"No. Jest explainin'."

"That's sassin'." Keenan popped Alain.

"Why are you so damned mean?" asked Alain with tears in his eyes.

"I'll show you mean!" Keenan broke a switch from the peach tree. "Shirt off."

"No."

"What did you say?"

"I said, 'NO!' I ain't takin' no more."

Enraged, Keenan began to wallop Alain anywhere he could. Alain pushed away and ran. Keenan went after him. "I'll kill you, you little bastard!" he yelled.

Being swift and dexterous, Alain lost his father in the woods. He came out near the creek and kept following it up the mountain. He just wanted to get away. At last, he came to the waterfall.

The boys seldom climbed this far. The light caught the fall, and Alain saw what appeared to be a cave behind the water.

Carefully, he picked his way up and fell into a small cave behind the fall. There was a crevice at the back, but it was too small even for a boy.

The cave was about ten feet by ten feet. *My sanctuary, a place no one else knows.* His thought gave him some comfort.

Near dark, Alain ventured home. He knew he would receive a beating, but he had to go. Alain opened the door tentatively, sticking only half his head inside. Shirley jumped to her feet. "Where have you been?"

"Hidin'. Where's Pa?"

"Gone drinkin'."

"I *did* sass him this time."

"Baby, he's real mad."

Alain looked at his mother. "You got a black eye. Did he hit you?"

"Yeah. He went lookin' for you. He went to Tipper's and Gator's and even Mac's. He was furious when he couldn't find you. He thought I knew where you were."

"I was in the woods."

"You ain't eat nothin' since breakfast. I saved you somethin'. Eat and go to bed. Maybe he won't be too mad tomorra."

Alain got up early and woke his brothers. He whispered, "Help me pick peaches so Pa don't kill me?" When Keenan got to the orchard, the boys had almost loaded one pallet for the truck.

Keenan stared at his eldest. "Keep pickin'," Alain said to Robert Lee and Calvin. He broke a switch and handed it to Keenan. He took off his shirt and placed both hands on the trunk of a tree.

"Go ahead," Alain said. "I did sass you. It's jest that I think Calvin is more important than peaches."

"Them peaches put clothes on yo back and food in yo belly."

"Yes, sir. We've almost finished the first harvest. Please, do what you need to do, so's we can finish. Then, I'm goin' swimmin' later."

"By the time I'm done with you, you won't be able to swim."

"Yes, sir, I will."

Keenan lashed Alain's back with the switch until he brought blood. Calvin hid his face on Robert Lee who whispered, "Keep pickin'. Do it for Alain."

Even with his shirt sticking to the dried blood on his back, Alain carried food staples to his cave. He supplied it well over a period of two weeks. He took tins of saltines, canned meats, and dried fruit. He took several blankets and a pillow that Amy sneaked him without asking why he wanted a foam-rubber pillow from the store. He took a couple of lanterns, some kerosene, and a box of matches.

Alain smiled to himself. *I'll become a caveman if Pa gets too bad. Won't nobody know where to find me, not even Gator, and he's my best friend. Maybe one day, I'll show Amy. She might need a place to hide from Lucille. Lucille shoulda married my pa. They're two of a kind.*

Alain said very little to anyone. He worked with his friends and earned some money, which he gave to Leo to put into a secret savings account. He gathered the crops and started a pet pumpkin to enter in the county-fair competition. Frequently, he slipped off to be a solitary caveman.

2
Sticks and Stones

Alain Richter tended his pumpkin every day. He knew
Gator was entering his hog, Wilbur, in the livestock
competition, and Alain declared his intention to enter his
pumpkin. Keenan Richter laughed, but after a time, he checked
on Alain's pumpkin with him. "Humph!" he grunted. "I'm right
surprised. That's a nice pumpkin."

"Thank you, Pa."

"You might actually win a prize."

"Will you take me to the fair?"

"Yeah, I'll take you."

Alain started to hug Keenan the way he had seen Gator do
Tal. Keenan pushed him away. "Don't do that. You ain't gonna
be a snivelin' weaklin'. Huggin's for mas and babies, not men."

"Gator hugs Mr. Jones, and Mr. Jones hugs Gator. I seen
Preacher Tomlin hug Mac."

"Nuts." Keenan patted Alain's shoulder. "We'll pick it
Friday and take it in Friday night."

"Yes, sir."

Alain went inside and stared at himself in his mother's
mirror. "What's wrong, baby?" Shirley Richter asked when she
caught him.

"Ma, am I ugly?"

"No, baby, you a right handsome boy."

"Am I retarded?"

"No, you real smart."

"If I ain't ugly or stupid, why does Pa hate me?"

"He don't hate you."

"Yeah, he does. He don't treat none o' the others as bad as
me. He ain't lovin' to none o' the boys, but he don't treat them as
bad as me. Why?"

She released a slow, sad sigh. "He don't think you his."

"Why?"

"'Cause I worked for Fester, but he was the only man I ever lay with. He don't believe it."

"Were you pregnant with me when you married?"

"Yeah."

"Is he my pa?"

"Yes. I ain't never been with another man. I wouldn't cut out to be one o' Fester's girls even if my ma was."

"Why did you try?"

"I had to live." She shrugged.

"Who's yo pa; where's yo ma?"

She patted the side of the bed and sat down. Alain sat beside her. "My ma had some sort o' disease from bein' a whore. She died when I was about twelve. Her name was Beverly Alain. That's why that's yo name even though folks don't say it right. Fester claims to be my pa. He was right mad Keenan lay with me. Pulled a shotgun on him when I found out I was expectin'. Said he didn't want his girl with a dog like Keenan, but he was gonna make an honest woman of me."

Alain scowled. "Do you love Pa?"

"He was real charmin' when he talked me into"—Shirley sighed and shook her head—"I try."

"I don't like him neither, Ma. It's hard to love somebody that treats you so bad."

"I know. Alain, don't you never forgit that I love you."

"I love you too, Ma. Can I have a hug? Hugs ain't jest for mas and babies."

"No, hugs show love. My ma used to hug me." Shirley thought for a minute. "Even Fester used to hug me." She hugged her eldest child.

After that conversation, Alain began to wonder about his other grandparents, but he dared not ask his father.

Saturday, he decided to go into town and boldly knocked on Grandma Miriam Newton's door. She was the oldest person in Possum Holler, and Alain knew she'd be able to give him answers.

The old matriarch hobbled to her door and opened it. She gawked at the boy. "Alain, is yo ma havin' another baby and needs me?"

"No ma'am." His courage faltering, he shifted from foot to foot.

"You ain't gotta be afraid of me." The old woman took in his demeanor. "Come inside and tell me what's wrong."

Inside, the boy gazed around him. He never ceased to be amazed by Grandma Newton's house, a palace compared to his.

"Come on and sit down at the dining table," Grandma Newton instructed. She got out an assortment of cookies and poured two glasses of milk before she sat adjacent to the boy. "Now, what's on yo mind?"

Alain cleared his throat. "My ma told me about Fester and her ma."

Grandma Newton nodded. "I know Fester's your grandpa."

"I didn't 'til she told me yesterday. I got to wonderin' 'bout my other grandparent. I didn't dare ask Pa. He'd be madder than a pit viper."

A snort preceded, "I believe it. So, you want me to tell you about Keenan's folks."

"Yes, ma'am. I figured you'd know."

She sighed. "Finish that cookie and drink your milk. Then, we'll take a little walk. I think seein' will help you understand." She mussed the boy's hair.

Snack finished, the two walked to the cemetery behind the church. Grandma Newton spoke barely above a whisper. "They say the apple don't fall far from the tree. I hope and pray that ain't true for you, but I'm afraid it is for Keenan."

She led the boy to a row go crude gravestones toward the back of the property. Six blocks of concrete bore the names, birthdates, and the same date of death—all Richters.

"My last husband made these markers. Wouldn't nobody else do it. It appeared that old Coleman Richter went crazy one night and hacked his family to death. Keenan was the only child to live."

Alain scowled, thinking about the scars he had seen on his father's torso and arms.

Grandma Newton went on. Odell Dent, Royce's pa, Amy's grandpa, went to the farm to deliver saws that had come in. He found the bodies and Keenan who was about thirteen. The boy had dragged hisself out the door. Odell got him to the hospital in Wilmington, and that's the only time we ever had any police besides our constable in Possum Holler. After he killed his family, Coleman hung hisself in the barn. His autopsy—you know what an autopsy is?"

Alain nodded. "That's when they do some kind of test to tell you how a person died. But you said he hung hisself."

"Yes, but any kind of crime like that requires an autopsy. They said Coleman's brain we eat up with syphilis. Do you know what that is?"

"Not really."

The old woman wagged her head. "That's a disease you get when you bed too many folks. It can be cured if caught early, but it can kill you and sometimes make you lose yo mind if left untreated." She put a hand on his shoulder. "You remember that when you grow up. Don't be like you pa and grandpa."

Grandma Newton turned to leave. "Now you know the whole ugly story. Nobody talks about it."

"I guess that's why folks call us trash and partly why Pa is so damned mean."

Grandma Newton sopped. "You be careful with that mouth. I'm sure Keenan would cut yo tongue out if you said a word."

"You prob'ly right, Grandma Newton." Alain helped the old lady back to her house and went home with another secret. He thought to himself, *I feel ninety rather than nine.*

On the school bus Friday, Alain told his friends about his pumpkin. "It's real big. I think I might win a prize. My *pa* even said so."

"Wahtcha gonna do with the prize money?" asked Gator.

"Give it to Preacher Tomlin to put in my account."

"Yo pa'll git mad."

"I'll take my chainces. Whatcha gonna do if Wilbur wins?"

"Save it."

Alain asked, "Tipper and Mac, are y'all in a contest?"

"Yeah," said Mac.

"We are?" asked Tipper.

"Yeah, we're gonna enter the talent contest, practice for the school program in December." Mac grinned. "We'll win with our banjo pickin'."

"That's a good idea," laughed Tipper.

"How 'bout you, Amy?" asked Alain.

"I'm entering a drawing in the art show," she answered

"I hope you win." Alain smiled at the pretty girl who sat beside him.

"You too." She smiled back.

All the children entered various contests. Mac and Tipper won first place with a banjo duel. They split fifty dollars. Gator's hog, Wilbur, took first place and a fifty-dollar prize. Amy's painting also won first place and fifty dollars. Alain's pumpkin was five ounces lighter than the first-place winner, but his second-place finish netted him thirty dollars, which he gave to Leo to deposit in his secret savings account.

Alain's friends left him in good spirits. He was happy to have won a prize. However, his joy was short-lived when

Keenan Richter staggered into the produce tent several hours later, obviously intoxicated.

Keenan observed the red ribbon on Alain's pumpkin. "Hmm," he said. "Not bad for yo first try. How much?"

"How much what?" asked Alain. "Twenty-three pounds, seven ounces. First place was five ounces more."

"No, dimwit. How much prize money?"

"Oh, thirty."

"Give it here."

Alain reached into his pocket. "It ain't here."

"What?"

"I musta dropped it." Alain pretended to look around.

Keenan growled and dragged Alain by the scruff of the neck to the pickup. He shoved the boy's head against the door before he opened it and pushed the child inside. "You are a stupid little bastard. How could you lose thirty dollars?" he snarled, sliding behind the steering wheel, cranking, and slinging gravel as he sped from the parking lot.

"What were you gonna do with it anyway?" Alain pressed the heal of his hand to the knot forming on his forehead.

"None o' yo damned business." Keenan fishtailed onto the road.

"It was *my* money. I won it."

Keenan swerved across the line in the road as he backhanded Alain in the mouth. "One o' these days, yo mouth is gonna cause me to break yo neck."

Completely forgetting Grandma Newton's warning and with the bitter taste of blood in his mouth, Alain snapped back, "One o' these days, you gonna hit me one time too many."

Keenan veered into the gravel on the side of the road. He slammed on the brakes and stopped the truck. Big hands hauled Alain from the cab. The blows he gave the nine-year-old were equal to what he would have given a full-grown man in a fist fight. Alain tried to crawl under the truck to escape his father's wrath, but Keenan pulled him out by the ankles and slung him, headfirst, into the truck bed. "Stay there!" Keenan screamed. "Don't make me kill you."

Back in the cab, Keenan flew down the road; Alain was afraid to breathe. His arm hurt dreadfully. He could tell from the position of the stars that it was well past midnight by the time the truck slid back and forth as Keenan swung into their long, winding driveway.

Keenan stopped in front of the barn and staggered to the back of the truck. "I ain't done with you." He pulled Alain out by his hair. The boy could not lift his left arm to defend himself at all.

Keenan shoved him into the barn and grabbed his strap. He did not wait for Alain to assume the position for receiving licks. He hit the child wherever the strap landed.

Suddenly, Shirley Richter ran into the barn in her nightgown. "Stop it!" she screamed.

"You want some?" Keenan hollered at her. "Yo little whore spawn lost the prize money and then sassed me in the truck. His sassin' is gonna git him killed."

"That don't mean you should beat 'im like that. He's a child."

"He's a bastard!"

Shirley stamped her foot. "No, he ain't! I ain't the one that screws ever Thomasina, Dixie, and Harriet. How many bastards do you have runnin' around Possum Holler?"

Keenan backhanded Shirley. "Shut up! Go inside. On second thought, don't go inside. I'll take you right here."

Keenan forced Shirley into an empty stall. Alain could hear the struggle, but he knew his mother would lose. She would lose this time on purpose to save him.

Alain struggled to his feet. He had to get away. He started toward his waterfall hideaway, but he realized he was really hurt. *I won't be able to climb to the cave.* It hurt to move. "Gator. Gator will help me," Alain said aloud without realizing he spoke.

The two-mile walk to the Joneses' hog farm was painful and took a long time. The sky had begun to lighten by the time Alain struggled to his friend's door. He pounded as hard as he could. He heard voices, and Gator opened the door. "Alain? What?"

"Can I come in? Please? I need help bad."

"Alain, what happened?"

"My pa was real mad when I told him I musta dropped the prize money, madder than I thought he would be."

"Yo pa did this?" Gator's eyes grew wide as saucers.

Alain was black and blue. His lip was crusted with dried blood, his eye black and nearly swollen shut, and he had bruises and abrasions on his arms, legs, and torso.

Alain cried mournfully, "I gotta hide, Gator. He's gonna kill me."

"He'll come here. This'll be the *first* place he'll look. He came the last time you ran away."

"Where can I go?"

"Preacher Tomlin."

"No, Pa'll go there too. Besides, I don't think I can walk that far."

"But he could get the constable."

Alain gave a little snort. "Hill won't help. I think they drinkin' buddies."

Gator shook his head. "No they ain't. He might be scared o' yo pa though."

Alain could hardly breathe. "I won't go to Miss Ina. She ain't no match for my pa."

"But I'm more than a match for that lowlife son-of-a-bitch." Tal Jones suddenly swayed in the doorway because he had been drinking the night before. "Come to me, Alain. I'm still a little drunk." He sank into one of the chairs at the table. "June'll haunt me if I don't help you. Gator, I need some more light."

After Gator lit several lanterns, Tal looked Alain over and exclaimed, "Damn! How could he do this? Why?"

"He was mad because I lost the prize money, and I guess I sassed him when I told him it was my money anyway."

"He wanted your prize money?" Tal could not believe his ears.

"Yes, sir. Did you take Gator's?"

"No. He earned it. I'll put it in his savings account next time I go to the city. Did you really lose it?"

"No, sir. I got a savings account too. Preacher Tomlin puts money in for me when I give it to him."

"Good for you. Education and money are the way to get out. Gator, I need lots of water. Go get it." Tal got up and took his shotgun down, loading both barrels. "Take this with you. If Keenan comes up and threatens you, shoot him."

"Pa, you want me to kill Mr. Richter?"

"You're right. I'll go. Bolt the door and don't let anyone in but me." Tal stepped out. He could not believe a father could hurt his child the way Alain Richter was hurt. He wondered how the boy had enough energy to walk to his place. He came without a coat, and the air was cold. They had already had their first frost. Tal waited on the porch a second until he heard the bolt slide into place. When he heard the bolt click, he went to the well.

Gator slid the bolt into place and turned to his friend. "Is this what Uncle Ander meant 'bout yo pa hittin' you that time in the truck that day?"

"Yeah." Alain slid into a chair.

"He hits yo ma?"

"Lots."

"The other kids?"

"Sometimes, but not as bad, 'specially the girls. He's nicer to them. He don't think I'm his. That's what my ma said."

"Are you?"

"Unfortunately."

A knock at the door startled both boys. Alain grimaced when he jumped. "Gator, let me in. It's Pa." Gator released a breath he had been holding.

Tal brought in two buckets of water and bolted the door behind him. "Okay, Alain, let's get your shirt off."

Alain winced as Tal lifted his arm. Tal examined it closely. "I think it's cracked."

"It hurts bad."

"Take a deep breath so I can get your shirt off."

Alain held his breath as Tal pulled the t-shirt over his head. He blinked hard trying not to cry. "Cry if you want to." Tal soothed his hair. "We won't tell. Where's your coat?"

"I don't know. I guess it's in Pa's truck."

Tal poured water into a dishpan and washed Alain's face and other bruises. He scowled. "Well, the good news is your arm is surprisingly your worst injury, but these scars didn't happen tonight. This isn't the first time, is it?"

"No, sir." Alain looked up at his best friend's father. "I cain't do nothin' about it. He's lot's bigger'n me."

"I can."

The slamming of a car door made everybody jump. Pounding on the door made Alain cringe. "Open the fucking door!" Keenan Richter yelled. "I know the little bastard's in there. The fool was talkin' to hisself." He affected a whiny voice, "'Gator. Gator'll help me." He snarled. "Open the damned door, Tal!"

Tal pointed to the loft. Alain struggled up the ladder with one hand, but the boys made it to the room above. Tal picked up the shotgun and unbolted the door. He put the gun barrel in Keenan's face. "No, the bastard's on my porch," said Tal. "What the hell do you want?"

"My son."

"Who would that be? I know you don't mean Alain."

"Where you got him stashed, Tal? That boy's gotta learn to control his mouth."

"That boy you think isn't yours? The one you use for a punching bag?" Tal shook his head. "No, he stays here at least tonight, and if he ever comes to my door again looking like he does right now, I'll kill you. If I come to your place and see a bruise on anybody, I'll kill you. If anybody from your place should come up missing, I'll kill you. You know damned well Constable Hill would pin a medal on me for getting rid of your sorry ass. I *will* be checking on your family. You're a low-life son-of-a-bitch. That little boy in my loft is under my protection from now on."

"You're drunk, Tal."

"No, I'm stone cold sober. Seeing that child was enough to sober me. Even when I do drink, I don't hit Gator. I never hit a one of mine."

"Still they run off. Maybe you shoulda."

"Keenan, both barrels of this gun are loaded." Tal kept his voice low and controlled. "Get the hell off my property. Just for your information, Corky's now an officer, career military. The other three are in Detroit, putting together cars and making good money. I'll let you read the letters; that is, if you can."

"You've changed. You liked my company once."

"When I wasn't in control of my own emotions. June set me straight."

"Yeah, you was pussy whipped."

"Do you wanna die?"

A sneer on his face, Keenan said, "June's been gone a long time. You need a womern, or at least a lay. Ina Campbell's available. Rumor says she spread wide for Ander Reardon. And that hypocrite Preacher Tomlin."

Tal rammed the gun barrel into Keenan's gut and pushed him off the porch. Then, he fired over Keenan's head and aimed again. Keenan landed on his butt in the dirt. "That was a warning shot," said Tal. "Ander was my brother-in-law and the best man I've ever known. Leo Tomlin is a man of honor, a word you don't know the meaning of. Get out of here! I'll be taking Alain to get his arm set as soon as the sun's up. Remember what I said. You will *never* hit another one."

Tal slammed the door and bolted it again. He set his jaw in determination. He would see to it that Keenan Richter did not abuse the child he had under his roof, and the rest of the children at their home. He called, "Boys, come down."

Both boys stared at Tal once they got down the ladder. "Sit down," he commanded. He opened the cupboard and gave Alain some aspirin. "It's all I've got for pain."

"Thanks. Were you really gonna shoot 'im?"

"I will if he ever hits you again. There is no excuse for what he did. Does he beat the other children? Shirley?"

"Yes, sir, sometimes, jest not as bad as me. He don't think I'm his."

"He's a fool."

"He really made you mad, didn't he?"

"Boys, remember the Bible verse, 'A friend loveth at all times?'"

The boys nodded. Tal explained, "June was my true love. Ander was a good friend. Love like that doesn't end with death. Ander loved Ina. The filth that came from Keenan's mouth about people I love"—he nodded—"Yes, he made me angry. Friends like the two of you will go through all kinds of things, good and bad; like Ander went through with me even when I tried to push him away. He never gave up on me. Preacher Tomlin cares about every person in Possum Holler. He would even open his heart to"—he jerked his head toward the door—"that vermin. Alain, come here anytime you need to. Now we need to get a little rest before I take you to the city to see a doctor."

Tal took Alain to Wilmington the next morning to get his arm set. Dr. Gilgood, who had tried to save June Jones's life, discreetly without reporting to the authorities, set Alain's arm. He gave Alain Percocet, and the boy stayed several days with the Joneses.

On the bus on Monday on the way to school, Alain's friends rallied around him. "What happened?" demanded Amy.

"I had a fight with somebody bigger'n me."

"You obviously lost. Was it your pa?"

"You know it was," said Tipper.

"You shoulda seen *my* pa," bragged Gator.

Alain nodded. "Yeah, he fired a shot at my pa. He pushed my pa off the porch when he said ugly things about…"

"What about?" asked Amy.

"I shouldn't say."

"Did he say somethin' about my ma?" asked Tipper.

"Yeah, and Mac's pa and Preacher Tomlin. Mr. Jones knocked him off the porch and then shot at him. I'm sorry, Tipper and Mac. I love Miss Ina, and Ander was good to me. Preacher Tomlin is nice to me. My pa, well, there ain't no excuse. He's mean." His thought ran to what Grandma Newton had told him. *Still don't make it right.*

"Are you gonna live with Gator?" asked Amy.

"I wish I could, but I gotta go home soon."

"Why did he do it, Alain?"

"I told him I lost my prize money, and he got mad."

With an indignant gasp, Amy said, "It was *your* money."

"That's what I said, and he hit me."

"Dang. He's meaner'n Momma."

"Does Lucille hit you?" asked Alain.

Amy's eyes darted from one boy to the next. "Not too often. She has never left a bruise on me. Sometimes she says mean things."

"Like what?" Tipper scowled deeply at the thought of Lucille being mean to Amy.

"Like, she wishes I'd never been born. Daddy gets really mad at her. Can I tell y'all a secret?"

"Sure." All four boys nodded.

"They don't sleep in the same bed. Daddy moved into another room. I heard him tell Momma she was a cold, heartless bitch and the only reason he stays with her is because he loves me."

"I can see why he feels that way," said Alain. "Yo ma shoulda married my pa. They're two of a kind."

"Momma doesn't like any of y'all but Mac."

"We don't like her either," said Alain. "But we do like you."

"Thanks."

At school, Miss Stone, Alain's teacher, had a fit when she saw the boy. He stuck to his story that he had a fight with someone bigger than he was. She knew better, but she couldn't do anything.

Alain stayed another night with Gator but decided to go home the next day after school. Amy Dent sat beside him on the bus as soon as they got out of her mother's sight. Amy put her hand in his.

"Uh!" Alain gasped.

"Sh," whispered Amy.

Alain looked at his hand. "What's that, Amy?"

"Thirty dollars."

"Why?"

"Give it to your pa and tell him you found it. Nobody else knows. It's our secret."

"Why?"

"Because I think you're worth more than thirty dollars. Put it in your pocket."

"I'll have to let go o' yo hand to do that."

Amy smiled. "Then, wait 'til I get off the bus."

"Sticks and stones do hurt, but words hurt too, don't they, Amy?"

"Yeah. I guess we're a lot alike."

Alain squeezed Amy's hand and they both took a nap on the fifty-mile ride to school.

3

Father Figure

Alain went home. Keenan glowered at the boy but did not speak to him. Alain did his chores every day the best he could with a broken arm and his siblings' help. Saturday, Tal Jones drove into the Richter yard, scattering the clucking chickens that waddled about the mostly dirt lawn.

Keenan walked out of his barn. "What do you want?"

"I want to see all *nine* of your kids and Shirley. I told you I'd come."

"They fine." He jutted his chin out in defiance.

"Prove it."

"Hell! I ain't killed the little bastard."

"Prove it." Tal got out of his truck and leaned against the door with his arms folded across his chest, his jaw set in a firm clench.

"Shirley!" Keenan yelled.

"What?" she snapped from the door.

Keenan and Tal looked at her standing in the doorway. She was clean and dressed in a new dress of dark-green flowered gingham. She had her light brown hair twisted into a bun. Her well-defined cheek bones and vivid green eyes made her stunning.

"Where are the young'uns?" Keenan muttered.

"The two little ones are in here. The others went fishin'. Alain wants fried fish for supper."

Keenan looped a thumb in the buckle of his overalls. "Are they all alive?"

"Yeah."

Making a smacking noise with his lips, he went on, "Have I hit anybody?"

"Not lately."

"Womern!" Keenan fisted his hands.

Putting one hand on her shapely hip, Shirley said, "Not since last Saturday."

Keenan looked back at Tal. "You satisfied?"

"I guess I believe Shirley." He stood straight.

Shirley walked to the barn. Tal looked her over closely. She appeared unharmed.

"Tal," she greeted. "Where's Gator?"

"In town with Mac and Tipper. They're all sleepin' at Preacher Tomlin's tonight. Maybe Alain should join his friends."

"Oh, by all means," snarled Keenan, "take him to church too."

"Thank you. I will."

"Stay for supper," invited Shirley.

"Oh, hell!" Keenan got in his truck.

"Where you goin'?" asked Shirley.

"Anywhere but here. Fester's prob'ly. I ain't gotta worry 'bout you with Mr. High-and-Mighty here. Bet he cain't even git it up."

Keenan drove off, stirring up a whirlwind of dust that caused both Tal and Shirley to fan their faces to be able to breathe.

"Sorry 'bout that," Shirley said, coughing from the dirt in the air. "He's been in a foul mood ever since Alain come home."

"Sounds like his normal state."

"'Spose so. Will you stay and fry fish with us?"

"Your man just left." He pointed toward the lingering dust cloud.

"Yeah." She nodded enthusiastically. "We'll have a peaceful supper. You can help me slice taters and chop cabbage so we can have fried taters and slaw with the fish. The young'uns'll be back soon."

"Shirley, when was the last time he hit you?"

"Like I said. I think you scared 'im."

"Did *he* tell you about it?"

"No, Alain did."

They heard children's voices coming through the woods. Shirley laughed. "I hope they caught some."

"Ma, we got a lot!" called Alain. "Hey, Mr. Jones."

"Alain, you got enough for company?"

"Yes, sir."

Shirley said, "You boys clean 'em. Alain, you got any o' that cider?"

"Yes'm."

"Bring some in."

"Where's Pa?" asked Alain hanging a long string of fish on a tree limb.

"Bein' rude."

The boy snorted, "Oh, we don't need 'im."

"No, we don't," agreed Shirley. "Girls, wash up and help me in the kitchen. Tal?"

"I'll help the boys."

"Okay."

Tal had supper with most of the Richter family. Then, he drove Alain to town to be with his friends.

"How's your arm?" he asked as he drove.

"I can move it."

"Did you take all the pills?"

"No, sir."

"Good. Save 'em in case you need 'em."

"I will. Gator said you take some pills."

"I do. They help me stay focused without going to one extreme or the other. I'm not supposed to drink while I take them." Tal laughed. "I haven't had a drink since the night you came. I don't wanna be like Keenan."

"You had my cider."

"Only a glass."

"Did you enjoy supper?"

"It was quite good. Your ma's a good cook. Who brewed the cider?"

"I did." The boy's eyes sparkled with pride. "Did you like it?"

"Yes. Sell some."

"You think?" Alain cocked his head to the side.

"Of course. Give your pa some of the money. Save the rest."

"You think money will keep him happy?"

"Can't hurt." Tal tousled Alain's hair.

Alain spent the night with the other boys and went to church for the first time in his life, although his mother read from the Bible in her halting fashion as often as she could.

Saturday afternoon visits to the Richter place became routine for Tal. Gator accompanied him sometimes. Shirley usually invited him to stay for supper. Now and then, Keenan stayed home and sulked through the meal, but he usually left. Whenever the boys stayed the night in town, Tal took Alain to be with them.

Tal manipulated Keenan into allowing the family to go to Harvest Fest, but Keenan opted to go to Fester's. The children had fun. Shirley laughed to see her children frolic like the other children. Then she became very quiet.

"Shirley, is something wrong?" asked Tal.

"Tal, I'm expectin' again. Keenan ain't touched me since the night Alain come to you. He'll probably say this 'un ain't his."

"Is it?"

"Yeah." She looked up at him. Flabbergasted that he would even ask, her mouth fell open. "I ain't never been with nobody else."

"You deserve better than him. Shirley, is he ever tender?"

Before she could answer, the children ran up. "Ma, can we go on a hayride?" asked Alain.

"I ain't got the money."

"Yes, you may," said Tal. "Come on."

"Tal?"

"You too," said Tal.

Tal put all the children in a wagon and got Gator, Tipper, Mac, and Amy to go along. The wagon was full. "Farmer Maddox," Tal said with a laugh, "your son's bringing in a load. Take the kids on. We'll be right behind you. You big kids make sure the little ones stay seated."

"Git up!" Farmer Maddox clucked to his mule team.

Buster Maddox dropped off a load. Nobody else seemed to be in line except Lucille Dent. Tal handed Buster his and Shirley's fare. Lucille grunted, "Ugh! I ain't ridin' with y'all. What's got into you, Tal Jones?"

"Tal's a nice man," said Shirley. "Lucille, when you gonna stop puttin' on airs?"

"Shut up."

"What do you mean, Shirley?" asked Tal, quirking an eyebrow toward Lucille.

"Lucille don't want nobody to know we cousins."

Tal hooted. "Come on, Lucille. I'll buy your ticket, too."

"No, thank you." Lucille walked off.

"Buster," said Tal, "I'll take the whole wagon."

"It's on me," Buster said with a big grin on his face. "Jest to see the look on Lucille's face is worth a free ride. Hop in."

Tal gave Shirley a hand up, and Buster clucked to his mule team. Tal spread a blanket over him and Shirley.

"It ain't too cold tonight," said Shirley.

"No, it's an Indian summer, but we need a blanket."

"Why?"

Tal took Shirley's hand in his under the blanket.

"Tal, whatcha doin'?"

"Holding your hand."

"I got a husband."

"No, you have a slave master and an ogre."

"Tal, Keenan'll kill you."

"No, he won't. I'm only holding your hand."

"Is that all you doin'?"

Tal looked into the two emeralds that stared at him fearfully. "It is tonight."

"Ain't nobody never held my hand."

"Someone should. Nobody will ever know that I'm holding your hand. I swear it." Discreetly, Tal kissed Shirley's fingertips, and she started to cry. "Sh," Tal whispered. "You're a beautiful woman. Keenan is a fool."

"Tal, you scarin' me."

"I'm sorry." Tal squeezed Shirley's hand and let go. He moved closer to Buster and looked over the wagon seat to see the other wagon a little ahead. He waved at the children and received waves in return.

"Be careful, Tal," Buster whispered. "Keenan Richter is a mean son-of-a-bitch."

"Don't get the wrong idea, Buster."

"Tal, she's beautiful, and he treats her like dirt. I wouldn't blame her."

"We're friends."

"If you say so."

"I do."

"My lips are sealed. You can kiss her if you want to."

"Buster!"

"I would." He pulled the reins to get the team to turn. "I might find a way to do Keenan in. Rescue the woman and the children. They need a father figure."

"I'll keep that in mind." He chuckled. "Especially if Keenan comes up dead."

Buster glanced over his shoulder to see Tal's smirk.

"Y'all went alone?" Alain exclaimed as Tal and Shirley unloaded.

"I tried to pay for Lucille too, but she wouldn't go with us," said Tal.

Buster laughed. "The look on her face was priceless, Alain. I gave Tal and Shirley a free ride jest for lettin' me see it. Here." Buster handed Tal his fare for the children back. "I should pay *Shirley*. That made this festival for me."

Tal loaded the children in the back of his truck except for the two smallest who rode in the cab with him and Shirley. Tal took Shirley and the children home. Keenan was home.

"Oh, Lordy," sighed Shirley. "I bet he's drunk. Now, he'll want to."

"Say no," said Tal.

"Then, he'll hit me."

"And I'll kill him."

Keenan staggered out the door. "Well," he hollered, "the brood is home. Did you have fun?"

"Yes, Pa," replied Alain. "Buster Maddox gave Ma a free hayride 'cause she put Lucille Dent in her place."

"That's my girl!" Keenan kissed Shirley roughly.

Tal cringed. "It was priceless," he said to cover his awkward feeling. He looked around, counting heads. "Everybody out?"

"Yes, sir," said Alain.

"Gator, let's go. Night all."

"Thank you, Tal," said Shirley. She looked at Tal as if she wanted to crawl in a hole. Tal gave her a little wink, and she smiled slightly.

The next afternoon, Tal drove to the Richters'. Shirley came out. "Tal?"

"You okay?"

"Yeah."

"Where's Keenan?"

"Took a load o' greens to Wilmington."

"Where are the kids?"

"Off playin'. Alain's at school."

"When will Keenan be back?"

"Late, I'm sure."

"Did he hurt you?"

She rubbed both her arms in the cool autumn breeze. "He didn't hit me."

"That's not what I asked."

"Tal."

"Shirley," he took off a frayed Stetson and ran his hand through thick dark hair. "Has that monster ever made love to you?"

"I ain't sure whatcha mean."

Tal fidgeted before he took Shirley's face in his hands and kissed her. For a brief moment, Shirley tried to push away. Then, she melted into his embrace. When Tal let go of her, Shirley swooned. Tal picked her up and carried her inside where only the two youngest children slept on a pallet near the fire.

"You can put me down now," she whispered.

"Where?"

"Tal."

"Where do you want me to set you?" he asked more insistently.

Shirley pointed to the only real bed in the house. Tal laid her down gently before he found a washcloth and bathed her face. "Have you seen Grandma Newton?" he asked.

"No. Keenan won't take me into town. I don't drive, so I'd have to walk."

"Then I'll take you when the boys get home." He stood. "Rest while the little ones are napping." Over the next hour, Tal tidied the house.

Shirley came in and gasped. "What have you done?"

"Just trying to make life a little easier for you." He kissed her on the nose as he started to slip out the door to get home before Gator.

"Tal," Shirley sighed.

"What?"

"Will you come back?"

"You can count on it."

"You ain't askin' me to leave him, are you?"

"No. He'd kill you."

"If he finds out..."

"He won't. I promise. It was only a kiss and will be only a kiss."

She walked to the door with him. "Tal, ain't we sinnin'?" She stared at the bare plank floor.

"I guess if it went any further, but I won't let it." He nodded.

"Maybe it shouldn't happen again."

"Maybe. Is that what you want?"

"Ain't nobody never asked me what I want." She looked him in the eye.

"I am."

"I'm scared."

"Don't be. When Gator gets in, I'll be back to take you into Grandma Newton. Gator can stay with your little ones for a bit."

"Keenan cain't know." She put a hand to her chest. "He'd think something awful."

Tal caressed her cheek. "I'll deal with Keenan."

"Okay." She gave a deep sigh.

"Shirley, I won't hurt you."

"I know." The two napping children began to stir.

"I'll be back." Tal kissed Shirley softly and left.

Tal met the school bus on November 1st. Alain and Gator exchanged glances. "What's wrong?" Alain asked as Tal ushered him, Gator, and Tipper Campbell into the cab. It was a tight squeeze.

"Nothing's wrong." He glanced at the boys. "I just promised to run Shirley into town to see Grandma Newton when you boys got home. I figured if I picked you up today, it would save some time."

"Okay." Alain let out a sigh. "I was scared something had happened with my ma."

"I won't let that happen."

Once Tipper was dropped off on the way back to the Richter place, Alain said, "You sure about takin' my ma to town. Lucille Dent'll start some gossip."

"I can deal with her too," Tal said sternly. "After this time, I'll just be sure Grandma Newton drives out to check on her."

"Okay. I just don't want my pa..." The boy's thoughts trailed off.

Tal sighed. "I didn't do anything wrong with Shirley."

"I didn't think you did, but Pa." Alain shrugged.

"Don't worry."

Tal pulled up and let the two boys out. "Gator, stay and play a bit. It won't take long."

Shirley got into the truck and waved to her children.

Tal said once they turned onto the road to town, "Why are you so quiet?"

"I ain't never seen Grandma Newton but when the babies were born."

Tal shook his head. "She's not a doctor, but she's better than no care at all. Are you eating well? Drinking milk?" He puffed out his lips. "I remember June and the cancer. I just don't want that to happen to you. You have to take care of yourself if you keep on having babies like this."

"I appreciate that, Tal." She leaned her head against the slightly rolled-down window.

"I'm sorry," Tal said gazing at her worried expression. "I won't kiss you again. I shouldn't have done that."

A smile flickered across her lips. "I won't forget it. Maybe I can think on it when times are bad."

Tal arrived at Grandma Newton's place. The old matriarch sat in her rocking chair on the wide veranda around her home. She stood when she saw Shirley Richter get out with Tal. "What the hell's goin' on?" she demanded.

"Nothing," Tal said. "I just gave Shirley a ride into town. She's expecting again, and I wanted you to take care of her."

The old woman narrowed her eyes to slits. "This ain't no hanky-panky y'all hidin' from Keenan, is it?"

"No, ma'am!" Tal shook his head hard. "I wouldn't do that to Shirley or those kids."

Grandma Newton gave a curt nod. "Didn't think so, but I wanted to hear it from you." She waved Shirley on. "Tal, you wait here."

"I think I'll go get a root beer at Dent's."

"Fine idea. We won't be long."

Shirley nodded and followed the old woman inside. All the while Grandma Newton grumbled under her breath about Keenan dipping his wick too damned much. Shirley said, "Yes, Grandma, he does."

The old woman turned to her. "Don't he know how to pull it out?"

Shirley shrugged.

About thirty minutes later, Shirley came into the general store where Tal chatted with Royce Dent while Lucille Dent hugged the back wall folding cloth. Lucille gave a snort and went to the back of the store. Tal glowered after her. Shirley smiled at Royce. "Grandma Newton told me to get some of them One-A-Day Vitamins you have here. I'm expecting again."

Royce pointed. "Right down that aisle."

"How much?" asked Tal.

"Three-fifty."

Tal handed Royce a five and the store owner made change. He took Shirley home before Keenan returned.

During the Thanksgiving break, Tal came with Gator, Tipper, and Mac and took the three oldest Richter boys, Alain, Robert Lee, and Calvin, hunting. He showed them how to snare rabbits, the best shot to use for which game, and how to build a deer stand. Their day of hunting bagged two turkeys.

Keenan Richter scowled as the hunters returned. "Tal," he said, "you ain't their pa."

"No, I'm a friend." He gave a little shrug. "But I guess they can call me Uncle Tal. You are more than welcome to hunt with us."

"I hate huntin'."

"I recall. I got a proposition for you." He dropped the turkeys on the porch, and the children went inside.

"What?"

"You supply me with produce, and I'll supply you with pork."

"A barter?"

"Yeah."

"That'll work. Write up somethin' you think is fair."

"I'll bring it next time I come. Do you think Shirley can roast two turkeys and make a meal for Thanksgiving to feed two extra?"

"I reckon. You did shoot 'em."

"I'll bring a ham to help."

Keenan scrunched up his face. "Why ain't you goin' to the town thing?"

"Would you like me to take your family?"

"I don't give a damn. I was plannin' a trip to the city."

"On Thanksgiving?" Tal shook his head as if to dislodge something from his ears.

"And *Christmas*." He reared back. "Santa Claus don't stop here."

"Keenan!" Tal splayed his hands against the air and huffed. "These are *children*. They need a father figure."

"You doin' fine. You don't need me."

"You're their father."

"Most of 'em."

"All...of...them!"

"So she says."

"Keenan!" Movement caught Tal's eye around the corner of the house. He realized that Alain, Gator, Mac, and Tipper were eavesdropping on every word spoken.

"Tal, take 'em to the town thing and leave me in peace."

Tal got closer to Keenan and lowered his voice. "If you don't want to be a father, why do you keep getting her pregnant? Pull it out or cover it up."

"I need the help."

"Hire somebody," he said through clenched teeth.

"I ain't wastin' my money."

"Where you gonna go on Thanksgiving? Festers? I recall even *Fester* closing on Thanksgiving and Christmas."

"Nope. New place in Wilmington—Jacqui's Gentlemen's Club. You gonna play Santa like you playin' daddy?"

"I'm not *playing* anything."

"You diddlin' Shirley?"

"Keep your voice down. The boys are listening." Tal fisted his hands, wanting to hit Keenan. "Why would you say that?"

"She's been in a good mood."

"Good for her."

"Naw." He spit a line of tobacco juice that almost hit Tal's shoe. "You ain't got the balls. What would June say?"

Tal covered his mouth with his hand and spoke through his fingers. "June would probably bake you a cake with rat poison in it."

Keenan hooted. "Yeah, she mighta. She was feisty. Purty too. You was a lucky man."

"So are *you* if you'd open your eyes and notice."

"If you say so. I still got my own plans."

The boys came around the house.

"Fine." Tal raised his hands in surrender. "I give up. Alain, I'll pick y'all up early. Tell your ma to roast the turkeys, make some candied yams, and make a pot of greens. I'll bake a ham and make a pan of dressing. We'll go into town."

"Yes, sir."

"Why don't you sass *him*?" grunted Keenan.

"He ain't mean to me," answered Alain as he hung the turkeys to pluck.

"Smart mouth!" growled Keenan.

Tal shook his head. "I'll see y'all Thursday," and he took the other three boys home.

"Pa?" Gator said as they drove home after dropping Tipper and Mac at their homes.

"What Gator?"

"Do you like Miss Shirley?"

"I like Shirley a great deal. She's a nice lady."

"Are you diddlin' her?"

Tal sucked in his breath. "Do you even know what that means, Gator?"

"Not exactly, but Miss Lucille said you were."

Tal slammed on his brakes. "She said that to you?"

"No, sir. To Amy."

"That bitch!" Tal hollered as he hit the steering wheel. He did a U-turn and went back to town. He stopped in front of the Dent home and got out, slamming the truck door. Tal marched to the door and pounded on it.

Royce opened. "Tal?"

"Where's Lucille?"

"Bathing Amy."

"Amy's big enough to bathe alone. Get Lucille, please."

"What's she done?"

"You can hear what I have to say to her."

Royce yelled up the stairs. "Lucille! Come here!"

Lucille came down. "What is it?"

"Tal's here for you."

"What do *you* want?" she asked with a condescending sneer on her face.

"How dare you gossip about Shirley Richter and me?" He jammed a finger in her face. "You could get that woman killed if Keenan thought there was a grain of truth to it. I have no idea why you're such a bitter bitch, but your tongue causes nothing but misery. Shut the hell up! Those children need a father figure that doesn't beat 'em black and blue. Shirley's a good woman caught in a bad situation. Don't you say another word about her." He took a step closer. "And how could you say that to your child? Did you really think she wouldn't repeat it? That's what children do. If you don't want anybody to know what you said, don't say it in front of your child. Now, I have to explain what diddling means to my eight-year-old son. I'm sure Amy had no idea what she was repeating. Royce, I apologize for being so rude. Good night." He turned and stomped down the three steps that led to the door.

Tal could hear the argument between Lucille and Royce as he got back in his truck. He sighed as he cranked up. "Gator, diddling is an ugly thing to say. She was saying I was having sex with Miss Shirley. You know what that is, right?"

Gator nodded. "Yes, sir, I know how babies are made."

"Keenan would kill her if he thought that was true."

"Pa, if Mr. Richter died, would you be Alain's pa?"

"Yes, Gator, I would, but he's alive."

"So, you do *like* Miss Shirley."

"Yes, Gator, too much, but nothing like *that* is going on."

Despite knowing he was putting temptation in front of them, Tal took the Richter family for the town's Thanksgiving celebration. Then on Monday, he began a tree house for the children in the oak behind the house.

"Whatcha doin', Tal?" asked Keenan.

"Santa told me to build a tree house," said Tal.

"How much it gonna cost me?" He harked and spat a big glob of mucus.

"Nothing." Tal choked back a gag. "It's Santa's gift."

"Does Gator have one?"

"Yep. We built it together." He descended the tree so that he could look Keenan in the eye. "I don't have any girls, so I asked Shirley to sew some curtains to make the house look more like a real house. This is a great old oak. Why don't you at least tie a tire swing for the kids?"

"Too much trouble. I'm goin' to the field. Got greens to harvest. It's too cold to be in a tree."

"Keenan, I'm trying to help."

"Don't need yo help."

"Yes, you do. At least, the kids do. Keenan, please, be their father, not their tormentor. It'll give you joy."

"You doin' fine. Tal, I didn't want little joys. I wanted little helpers."

"She's havin' number *ten*."

"Yeah, she produces good stock."

"They're not livestock." The exasperation showed in his tone of voice and the roll of his eyes. "And she's not a breed sow."

"Tal, they don't mean much more to me. I ain't the mushy lovin' type. I ain't sure Alain's mine. Fay, well, she's right sweet." An evil smiled flickered across his face. "I ain't good at bein' a daddy like you. Maybe the young'uns can look at you like their uncle, like you said. I got work to do now."

"Go on. I'm building." He swung himself back into the tree. "I'll have to go feed my hogs before dark."

Keenan whistled shrilly with two fingers in the corners of his mouth. Fay, Robert Lee, Calvin, Gloria, and Glenda ran out with baskets for gathering greens. The kids loaded into the back of the pickup and went with Keenan to work.

"Oh," sighed Tal as he shook his head.

Shirley walked outside with the three little ones who were too small to help in the field. "I have some coffee if you wanna come in."

"Sounds good."

Tal stopped and drank coffee. He leaned against the rough-hewn table. Shirley rubbed her side as she washed dishes. "You okay?" asked Tal.

"Baby kicked."

Tal walked behind Shirley and put his hand on her abdomen. He chuckled. "Strong kick."

Shirley gazed at Tal with large startled eyes. "Keenan ain't never done that."

With a furrowed brow, Tal said, "He's never felt the baby kick?"

"No. He don't care."

"Oh, Shirley"—His voice hitched—"I wish I could take you away from this life of misery."

"Alain told me to run away. I couldn't go without my young'uns. I love 'em, Tal."

"You're a good mother. Let me get back to building. Little Joel, you wanna help?"

The little boy nodded. Tal picked him up. The boy jumped. "It's okay," said Tal.

Tal turned to Shirley. "Does Keenan hit him too?"

"Not lately. You scared 'im real good."

"I'm glad. Come on, little man."

Outside, Joel stayed next to Tal. The little boy thought he was helping as he handed Tal whatever he asked for. By the time Tal had to leave, the tree house was framed. He took Joel inside. "You need a nap. Go eat and sleep."

The little boy ate a bite and lay down. "You hungry?" asked Shirley.

"Starving, but not for food."

"Tal."

"I know." He lifted a hand like a shield. "I'm leaving." Tal kissed Shirley on the forehead and left.

Tal finished the tree house. He even painted it white and put glass windowpanes on each side of the door that had a bolt. Shirley made blue checked gingham curtains for the windows and made matching pillows for the children to sit on. The youngsters were excited to have a real Christmas gift even if "Uncle Tal" had made it.

On New Year's Eve after Gator was asleep, Tal walked to the Richter place. Keenan's truck was gone. Tal carefully picked his way around the house and tapped on the screenless window by Shirley's bed.

She raised the window. "Tal, whatcha doin'?"

"I have no clue. I just wanted to see you. You're supposed to kiss the person you love at midnight to bring in the New Year. It's gotta be close."

"Tal, whatcha sayin'?"

"I love you. I'll steal moments with you if I have to." Tal reached through the window and pulled Shirley toward him.

She put her hands on his shoulders. "Tal, you crazy. Keenan'll kill you."

"He's not here."

"No. He prob'ly won't be home tonight. He went to Wilmington."

"Maybe he'll get so drunk he'll have a wreck."

"Tal!" she gasped.

"Let me in."

"You gonna climb through the winda?"

"Yep."

She stepped back and Tal pulled himself through the window, bumping the table.

"Sh," said Shirley, waving a hand. "Tal, I'm pregnant."

"Still beautiful. Happy New Year, Shirley."

As Tal kissed Shirley, they heard a car door slam. "It's Keenan!" Shirley panicked.

"Sh. I'll go out the window."

"What about yo truck?"

"I walked." He kissed her quickly. "I love you, Shirley. Pretend to be asleep."

Tal dropped out the window, his breath frosting the air. Shirley pretended to be asleep as Keenan passed out beside her.

Spring came and then school was out. Gator and Alain were promoted. Shirley gave birth to another boy, Oscar.

Hog Rendering arrived. Tal drove his hogs to town. He added enough to take care of a freezer for the Richter family. Keenan shook hands with him. "When the crops come in, I'll take care of you."

"As agreed. Where's everybody?"

"Alain and Fay are around. The rest are at home. I didn't wanna keep up with all the young'uns. Shirley said she wudn't up to comin' yet."

"Do you mind if I take some barbeque to them?"

"Naw. I might need you to take Alain and Fay home. I'll prob'ly sleep in the jail."

"Be glad to if you need me."

Tal packed a box of food for Shirley and the children. He left Gator with Ina Campbell. "I'll be back in a bit."

"That's real nice o' you, Tal."

He sighed and shook his head.

Ina put a hand on Tal's arm. "Don't git caught."

"What are you talking about?"

"I understand."

"You really do, don't you?" He stepped back to look at the woman. "You and Ander?"

Ina gave a little nod. Tal kissed her cheek. "Thanks, but we haven't done anything wrong."

She gave him a knowing look and said, "Yet." Then she whispered, "If Lucille seen that, maybe she'll gossip 'bout you and me and leave Shirley alone."

Tal gave a little chuckle and left.

Tal drove into the yard, scattering the chickens again. The children greeted him. "Uncle Tal, whatcha got?"

"Barbeque. Are y'all hungry?"

Excited and jabbering all at once, they ushered him inside. "Tal?" Shirley said in shock.

"Hey, Shirley. I brought the party to you." He set the box of food on the table and helped her feed the children. "You look tired." He kissed her cheek.

"Fussy baby."

"Kids, all of you need a nap."

"Why?" asked Robert Lee.

"Your ma's tired. She needs a nap. Why don't y'all play in the tree house and let your ma rest? I'll clean up."

"Yes, sir." Robert Lee took the kids out.

"Lie down," Tal told Shirley.

"I'm fine."

"How old is the baby?"

"Almost two months."

"Are you still taking the vitamins?"

"Yeah. I told Keenan I was still bleedin'."

"Why?" He dipped his brow into a frown.

"I don't want him. I want you."

"Oh, Shirley." Tal pulled Shirley to him and held her close. "Have you said anything about us to anybody?" He held her a little away from him to look at her face.

"No," she said hastily.

"Ina?"

She dropped her eyes.

He assured, "It's okay. She won't say a word. She knows I'm here. You go and rest." Tal washed dishes and left.

Robert Lee watched Tal's truck round the curve in the long, dusty drive. He turned to Calvin. "I wish Pa was nice like Uncle Tal."

"M-m-me, too."

"Cal, do you think he loves Ma?"

"Y-y-yeah."

"Don't say nothin'."

"I-I-I won't. I j-j-jest wish h-h-he was my p-p-pa."

Robert Lee put his arm around his younger brother. Both knew Tal Jones would never hit a child just because he stuttered. He was a good father figure.

On the narrow country road, Tal passed Keenan and the two children that had been at the festival. Keenan honked his horn long and loud. Tal grimaced but gave him a wave.

A moment further down the road, he pulled onto the low shoulder and laid his forehead on the steering wheel. *I should go back, make sure everything's okay.*

He maneuvered the truck and went back to the Richter home. All the children were outside tending to chores. Alain approached the truck.

Tal rolled the window all the way down. "Is everything all right?"

"Pa's three-sheets-to-the-wind. He made all of us get out of the house." Alain looked at the ground. "You know what he's making Ma do." He wrinkled his nose in disgust. "He came in and sniffed the air. Then he laughed and said, 'Knew Tal wudn't man enough to take a woman, even if Lucille thinks so. But I am.' Then he yelled at all of us to get out. Ma told us to go on out and do our chores."

Tears threatened to spill from Tal's eyes. "Did he hit her?"

"No, sir, but she'll give in to him."

"I can't change that, Alain. I wish I could."

"Me too."

Tal reached through the window and squeezed the boy's shoulder. "Don't hesitate to get me if you need me."

Alain nodded and Tal, once again, went back to town to get his own son.

4

Kissing the Queen

When school began again, Alain and Gator happily went to upper elementary school. They were even happier that Miss Stone had moved up with them and had gone out of her way to have the two boys in her class again. Mac, Tipper, and Amy were in fourth grade, and their teacher was Miss Langston.

Finally able to play together at recess, the children from Possum Holler congregated. "I got a new game," Mac announced.

"What?" asked Tipper.

"The three musketeers, you, me, and Gator."

"What is it?"

"They're kinda like knights. They work for the king of France and fight for right and justice."

Gator asked, "Can Alain play?"

"Sure. Alain can be Cardinal Richelieu; he's the bad guy. He can kidnap the queen."

"Who's the queen?" asked Alain.

"Amy," said Tipper with a glint in his blue eyes.

Alain agreed with a wide grin. "Okay. I can do that".

Amy Dent readily played the queen in this new game. Alain took the rope belt from his jeans and tied Amy's hands behind her back around a tree. All the boys found sticks to use as swords. Alain tried to kiss the captured queen who screamed shrilly, and the sword fight ensued with several adult spectators. Miss Stone, Miss Langston, and Ms. Butler rushed to see why Amy had screamed.

Ms. Butler threw a hissy fit and untied Amy. She yelled at Alain, "Are you crazy, you nasty little hillbilly? Put this rope back in your pants. I see your butt crack! Where is your underwear?"

"I ain't got none."

"What were you doing?" asked Miss Stone.

Mac said, "We were playing the three musketeers. Tipper, Gator, and me were Aramis, Porthos, and Athos. Alain was Cardinal Richelieu. He kidnapped Queen Amy. We were just having fun."

Miss Stone and Miss Langston laughed. Miss Stone suggested, "You boys practice sword fighting, and next time tell Amy just to clasp her hands behind her and pretend to be tied."

"That ain't challengin'," protested Alain.

Miss Stone put her hand on Alain's shoulder. "It's challenging enough for the playground, and don't try to kiss her."

"Awww."

"Come here a minute."

"Yes, ma'am?" Alain asked after Miss Stone took him to the side.

"Were you really trying to kiss her?"

Alain looked at the ground. "Yes'm."

"Why?"

"I like her."

"Alain, you're ten, not old enough for a girlfriend."

"She held my hand on the bus." His head popped up. "It was her idea."

"Then stick to secret handholding for now. Go sword fight."

Miss Stone laughed as she came back to Ms. Butler and Miss Langston. "That child is disgusting!" said Ms. Butler.

"That child is precious," argued Miss Stone.

"I agree," said Miss Langston. "That little group will put Possum Holler on the map. You should be impressed that nine-year-olds even know about the three musketeers."

"I wish they'd stay in Possum Holler," said Ms. Butler.

"They would if they had their own school," countered Miss Langston.

"Alain Richter is repulsive. Gator's not much better. Tipper, well, he's lovable. Amy is going to be somebody if she escapes. The little Reardon boy I can stand because he's smart."

Miss Stone argued, "So is Alain if you'd give him a chance. If I could, I'd steal him away. Last year, he looked as if he had been in the ring with a champion boxer. He said he had a fight with someone bigger than him. It was his father. He's a sweet boy in bad circumstances. Gator is precious too. I would venture to say both those boys are highly gifted and would thrive and flourish in a better environment. Yeah, the other three are terrific. You need to stop being so prejudiced." She turned on her heel and walked away.

Amy chose to sit by Alain on the bus. "Sorry," she said.

"'Bout what?"

"I didn't mean to get you in trouble. I was just playin'."

"I know. What if I had kissed you?"

Amy giggled. "I would've kissed you back. Alain, do you really not have any underwear?"

"No. I outgrew 'em."

"We got some at the store."

"I ain't got money."

"What size?"

"I ain't sure. My jeans are twelves. They're big in the waist, but I'm too tall for tens."

"If I get some, will you wear 'em so Ms. Butler won't make fun of you?" She blinked innocently at the boy beside her.

"She's mean. Maybe she should be with my pa."

"She *is* mean."

"Yeah, Amy, I'll wear 'em, but I don't want charity."

She moved her pink princess backpack in front of her feet as a footstool. "Okay. Bring me some green plums."

"They're ripe now and already gone to market."

Sticking out a pouty lip she said, "Oh."

"I could bring you some o' my cider."

"Will it get me drunk?"

"If you drink too much. I could maybe sell some to Fester and pay for the underwear."

"Okay. They're five dollars, and I want one bottle for my trouble."

"You got it."

Shirley came outside as Alain loaded bottles of cider into his father's pickup. "Whatcha doin'?"

"Sellin' cider like Uncle Tal suggested. I got in trouble for tryin' to kiss Queen Amy. Ms. Butler made fun o' me for not havin' on underwear. I'm buyin' some from Amy."

"Yo pa left with buddies."

"Where'd he go?"

"I don't know."

"Well, I'll be back real soon. I'm takin' this to Fester's."

"How?"

"I'm takin' the truck."

"Since when do you drive?"

"I'll teach myself." Alain kissed his mother's cheek. "Don't worry."

For the first mile, Alain almost stripped the gears, but after a couple of stalls, he got the hang of shifting. It wasn't much different from the tractor, which he drove frequently. Arriving at Fester's, he went to the back door. He argued with Fester for half an hour before they agreed on five dollars a bottle. Fester admitted it was good cider. As Alain helped Fester bring the bottles in, he saw Keenan with two of Fester's girls.

Alain asked, "Grandpa Fester, can you keep him all night?"

"Why?"

"I hate him. He's mean, and he hits my ma."

"Does he hit you?" There was a bit of anger in the older man's voice.

"Yeah, but I'm tough."

"Jest a night's peace, huh?"

"Yeah."

"I'll keep him here." He gave a curt nod. "If he hits my daughter again, I'll kill him."

Alain jerked his head up. Fester sounded like Tal.

His grandfather mussed his hair. "Take off. Bring more next month. Five dollars a bottle." Fester and Alain shook hands like adults to seal the bargain. Alain had sold thirty bottles.

Alain got back and announced excitedly, "Ma, I sold thirty bottles, and Grandpa Fester's gonna buy more."

"I cain't believe you drove that truck."

"I'm savin' money so we can run away."

"And go where?"

"Uncle Tal."

"Alain, we done had this talk."

"That was before you fell in love with him."

"You don't know what you talkin' 'bout."

"I know how you look at him. He looks at you the same way."

"You bein' silly." Shirley shook her head.

"Don't be scared."

"You are." She pulled her sweater tighter across her chest.

"I know I'm scared, 'cause Pa's gonna kill us one day."

"Then, *you* git away."

"Not without you. He won't be home tonight, Ma."

"He at Fester's?"

"Yes'm. Grandpa Fester's gonna keep him."

"I can sleep then." Shirley kissed Alain on the head. "Git to bed. You got school."

Shirley sat at her kitchen table deep in thought before she pulled her shawl around her and left the house. She hung a scrap of cloth over her door to tell her if Keenan was home. It would fall if the door opened. The late summer full moon lit her way well. She walked the two miles to the Joneses' hog farm briskly.

Shirley stepped lightly onto the porch and knocked softly. Tal sat quietly in a chair leaned against the wall with his feet on the table, smoking his pipe before he went to bed. The gentle tap at his door startled him.

Tal cautiously opened the door. "Shirley? What's wrong?"

She flung her arms around him. With one hand he closed the door behind him as he stepped onto the porch; with the other, he pulled her close. "Are you crazy?" he asked.

"I needed to see you."

"Where's Keenan?"

"Fester's—all night."

"Oh."

"You ain't come much lately."

"I thought it best not to. Folks gossip."

"Tal, I love you."

"Oh, Shirley." Tal kissed this fragile, delicate woman who had risked so much to see him. "I love you, Shirley."

Tal took her hand and led her to his barn where the hay was fresh and clean. "I can't wake Gator."

"It's okay. Yo barn is nicer'n my house."

"It's clean."

She looked at the ground. "Tal, I gotta tell you somethin'."

"What?"

"I'm expectin'."

"You sure?"

"Yeah." She let out a long, sad sigh. "Like you said—folks gossip. I'm worried Keenan will say it ain't his."

"Oh, Lord." He put a hand to his forehead.

"Don't worry. I done told Keenan. That's why he's drinkin'. He was mumblin' something 'bout you as he went off with them Silsbee boys."

"What do you want me to do? Does he think I'm the father?"

"I don't think so. He was grumblin' 'bout you tellin' him ten was enough."

"Shirley, divorce him. I'll marry you."

"I cain't. He'd kill my kids, at least Alain. I need to go back now."

"I'll drive you."

"Okay."

Tal coasted into the Richter yard. "Is he still gone?"

"Yeah. My signal ain't fell. It's okay."

He caressed her cheek. "I wish I could take you away."

"You do every time you touch me." Tal kissed her again and she slipped inside.

On the bus the next day, Amy handed Alain a package. "That's three packs, size ten. They oughta fit."

"Did you sneak 'em?"

"No, I told Daddy."

"Amy, that's embarrassin'." He ran a hand across his face and looked out the window.

"He won't tell Momma."

"I only brought money for one pack, and I left yo cider under the doorstep of the parsonage."

"Owe me."

"I already owe you." The boy looked back at the pretty little girl.

She smiled at him. "Friends don't keep count."

"One day, Amy Dent, I'm gonna kiss you."

"One day, Alain Richter, I'll kiss you back."

"Kissin' the queen. I cain't wait!"

5

Moonshine

It became apparent that Alain was not the only one with eyes for Amy as Tipper flirted as much as a nine-year-old can flirt. He started by complimenting Amy's artwork and getting her to draw a picture of him. Amy loved the attention, but Tipper's deeper interest in Amy disturbed Mac. Without knowing why, Mac thought Tipper and Amy together was a bad idea, and he began to resent the girl.

It had turned cold fast. Mac and Tipper had a big conspiracy going and hadn't told another person, not even Gator, Alain, or Amy what was up.

Bright and early one Saturday, Mac headed to Tipper's without concern from Leo or Ina. The two boys often took off. This morning they were going hunting. Ina laughed because Tipper was not much of a hunter, but she let the boys go. Tipper took Mac to a secret place where he had a small moonshine still in operation.

"Tipper!" exclaimed Mac. "What are you doin'?

"I'm gonna be an entrepreneur—just like we studied about in social studies."

"A moonshiner?"

"One day I'll be legit. Just wait and see."

"Why you doin' this?"

"Bunch of reasons. I gotta take care o' Ma. She don't make much with sewin' and hair cuttin'. That little insurance policy was a joke. It'll take us a few more years. If I'm rich, Miss Lucille won't hate me so much. I can get Amy."

"Tipper, Amy's okay, but her ma's a bitch. You won't never be good enough for Amy by Lucille's standards. And in case you didn't notice, Amy sits by Alain on the bus."

"Well, if I won't be good enough, Alain won't either. If Lucille hates anybody more'n me and Ma, it's the Richters."

"Course, she don't like nobody. She's the reason Papa preaches on the tongue and gossip a lot."

"I know *that*. Anyway, the moonshine's gonna make me rich."

Mac reached out to touch the contraption, but Tipper pushed his hand away. "We gonna sample it?" Mac asked.

"Yeah. I got ten bottles. I'm gonna get fifty and sell 'em."

"To who?"

"Alain sells cider to Fester."

"The honky-tonk?"

"Yeah." Tipper's blond curls bobbed as he shook his head.

"Yeah. Alain gives Papa money now and then to put in his account."

Tipper set about distilling another bottle to replace the one he and Mac opened to sample. After a while, Tipper sealed the new bottle and resealed the open one. Mac had the hiccups and both boys were drunk.

"Oops!" said Tipper. "I didn't get any game. I'm not much of a shot."

Mac sniggered. "Hiccup! I got a turkey while you were workin'." Somehow Mac had managed to bag a turkey, so the boys staggered back to Ina's.

"Shurprishe!" Mac exclaimed holding the turkey up for Ina.

Ina screamed as Leo drove up because it was almost dark, and he was concerned for Mac to ride his bike back to town at night.

"Preacher Tomlin!" Ina cried. "They drunk!"

"What?"

After talking to the boys, Leo concluded they were, indeed, drunk. He demanded, "Where did you get the moonshine, and where are the other two?"

"It'sh jusht ush," slurred Mac.

Tipper said, "I shtole it."

"You got a strap, Ina?" asked Leo.

"Tipper," said Ina, "git yo belt."

Leo spanked both boys as Ina asked him to do it for her. When neither of them shed a tear, he made Tipper fetch the supposedly stolen moonshine and made the boys drink until they vomited. The next day, he made them sing an offertory for church.

At the covered dish meal, Gator observed, "Y'all look awful."

"Yeah," grunted Tipper. "We got hangovers."

"How?"

Tipper put a finger to his lips. "I got a still," he whispered. "Nobody knows. I gotta figure out how to sell it."

"Alain could help."

"I know. He hasn't been to school lately."

"Yeah, they been sick. His ma's havin' another baby."

"Damn! How many she gonna have?"

"Don't know." Gator shrugged.

Tipper puckered his lips. "You seem distracted."

"Can I tell y'all a secret?"

"Sure. You know about my still."

Gator lowered his voice even more. "You remember what Lucille said about my pa and Alain's ma?"

"Yeah. She's mean."

"I think she's right."

"Gator!" said Mac in disbelief.

"I know it's sin, but I think my pa loves her. I think the baby's his."

"You got proof?" asked Mac.

"No. I hope Mr. Richter don't. He'd kill her."

Tipper nodded. "Yeah, he's meaner'n Lucille."

The conversation changed as Amy came up with her plate. Gator never disclosed Tipper's secret, and Tipper and Mac never divulged Gator's suspicion.

Mac and Tipper discussed Tipper's plan to sell the bootleg liquor at school. "How you gonna do it?" Mac asked.

"I gotta get your pa's truck to runnin'."

"How?"

"Alain. I know he drives his pa's truck, and he knows how to use a tractor. I bet he can help."

"How you gonna ask him? He ain't been to school lately."

"I could go up there or wait."

Just after Christmas, Tipper rode his bike to the Richter place. As he pulled to a stop, he realized Keenan Richter's truck was gone, but Tal Jones's truck was there. He heard voices in the barn and found himself eavesdropping. What he heard scared him since it seemed to confirm Gator's suspicion. Tipper peeked through the crack in the door.

Tal laid a hand on Shirley's abdomen. "It's a strong kick," said Tal.

"Yeah. Seein' Grandma Newton more often makes a difference. Keenan don't like it though."

"Keenan still behavin'?"

"Yeah. He ain't been hittin' nobody. Still a grouch though."

"Are you okay? Do you need anything?"

"'Cept you? No."

"Shirley, you know we can't be together. It has to stay like it is."

"Yes, Tal, I know. Don't mean I cain't dream." She sighed. "Why didn't I meet you a long time ago?"

"I was a married man back then."

"June was lucky to have you. I cain't help but wish Keenan would act more like you. Thank you for the swings."

Tipper noticed the wooden structure with two swings on it. Then, he noticed the tree house. Of course Keenan Richter had not done that. Tal Jones had.

Tal said, "I need to get back. I just had to check on you." He leaned in and kissed Shirley. Then he picked up a crate of canned goods.

Tipper ran as fast as he could to the front door and raised his hand to knock. Shirley called, "Tipper?"

Tipper turned, not sure how to behave. Shirley came to the house as Tal put the canned fruits and vegetables in the truck.

"Alain ain't here right now," she told Tipper

"Oh, okay. I can come back. I guess I better go."

"Tipper," said Tal, "you want a ride? It's mighty cold."

"I, um, I, um…"

Shirley gasped, "Tipper?"

"I won't say nothin' to nobody ever! I swear."

Tal heaved a great sigh. "Put your bike in the back. I'll take you home."

Tipper did as Tal asked and sat quietly in the truck. Tal said, "You really will keep quiet, won't you?"

"Yes, sir, but Gator suspects."

"I figured. What about Alain?"

"He ain't said. I won't ask."

"Tipper, it's not what you think. We haven't done anything sinful. We just spend some time together, maybe kiss. She can't leave Keenan. She's too scared."

"Do you love her?"

Tal glanced at the blond-haired boy beside him. "Yes."

"Maybe…Maybe it would be better if you courted my ma."

"You want me to?"

The boy shrugged. "She says she'll never love again. It hurts too much to lose 'em."

"It does hurt. What are you suggesting?"

"She'd help you and Miss Shirley get together."

"Tipper! Ina would be appalled."

"You'd be surprised."

Tal thought about how Ina had warned him not to get caught. He realized she really did understand his heart. "I'll think about it. I'm sorry, Tipper. You're just a kid. You shouldn't have to keep my secret. Even though it's an innocent, special friendship, Keenan wouldn't understand."

"It's okay. Mr. Jones, why is love so complicated?"

"Is it?"

"Look at you and Miss Shirley. Look at Ma and Ander." Tal also realized that Tipper was quite aware of Ina and Ander's relationship, as short-lived as it had been. Tipper said, "Maybe I won't fall in love, not even with Amy."

Tal could not help but laugh. "Yes, you will."

Tal stopped in front of the Campbell house, and Ina stepped out."Somethin' wrong?" she called.

"No," assured Tal. "I was picking up some canned goods and gave Tipper a ride. That's all. Looks like snow. Too cold for the bike."

"Thank you, Tal."

"You're welcome, Ina."

"You be real careful, Mr. Jones," said Tipper as he got his bike out of the back.

"I will. Thanks."

"Thanks for the ride."

Tal waved and drove off.

The winter was brutal. School was cancelled frequently. When spring rolled around, Alain was back in school. Tipper finally got a chance to talk to him.

"Hey, Alain."

"Hey."

"You know how to get a truck runnin'?"

"Sure. Why?"

"I need to get Ander Reardon's truck workin'. I gotta have a way to make deliveries."

"Of what?"

Tipper lowered his voice. "Moonshine."

"You got a still?" Alain whispered back.

"Yeah. I thought maybe you could help me get the truck runnin' and give me pointers on how to drive and deliver."

"Got some I can sample?"

"Sure."

"Okay. Me and Gator'll come out Saturday."

"That works."

On Saturday, Alain Richter and Gator Jones drove into the Campbells' yard. Tipper bounded out.

"What y'all up to?" asked Ina suspiciously. Leo had told her he didn't think Tipper had stolen the moonshine but had a still. Ina was wary. "Where's Mac?"

"Not here today, Ma," said Tipper. "Alain's gonna help me get the truck runnin'."

"Why?"

"So I can take us places."

"You ain't old enough to drive, none o' y'all."

"Ma, if I could just run us into town, you wouldn't have to depend on Preacher Tomlin, and Miss Lucille would have less to gossip about."

Ina set her lips and crossed her arms. "Fix 'er up, boys. I'll make y'all a good meal."

"You gonna make sugar cookies?" asked Alain.

"You want some?"

"Yes'm. They're real good."

"You got it if'n you do somethin' to tie Lucille's tongue. Course, she ain't gossipin' 'bout me much no more. She done moved on to bad mouth somebody else. Preacher Tomlin let her know right quick not to talk about him and me 'cause we jest friends. No, Alain, the old bat's on yo ma. It's a good thing Keenan don't come to town often."

"What she say 'bout my ma?"

"Baby, she thinks Tal and Shirley are, you know." She rolled her hand over and over.

"Bitch!"

"Alain!" said Ina shocked the boy knew the word.

"She is, Miss Ina."

"I don't disagree. Y'all git busy. I'll make y'all some fried pork chops, mashed potatoes, and string beans."

The boys worked all morning. Alain changed the oil and rotated the tires and aired them with a battery-operated compressor. He checked the power steering fluid, the transmission fluid, the brakes and brake fluid, and the antifreeze, making sure each was safe. It took the strength of all three boys to loosen and re-tighten the lugs holding the tires in place.

At noon, Ina served the boys the meal she had promised with a plate of hot sugar cookies. After lunch, Alain gave Tipper driving lessons. "It's a good truck, Tipper. You lucky. It ain't a manual. It'll be easier to drive." Alain laughed. "I 'bout stripped the gears in Pa's truck the first time I drove it."

After several trips up and down the driveway to the Campbell home, Tipper drove a short distance on the back roads before he came home.

"You got it," Alain praised him.

"You a good teacher."

"Time to pay up."

"We gotta drive into the woods." Tipper furrowed his brow in worry.

"This truck'll go in the woods easy. It sits up high."

Tipper took his friends to his still where he gave both of them a bottle. Alain gave him advice. "How much you chargin'?"

"Five."

"Naw. Ten. I charge five for cider. It ain't as stout. Dicker. Start with twelve but settle for ten. Count yo money. Don't let 'em cheat you." With each pointer, he counted off on his fingers.

"Y'all gonna help me load?"

"Sho. Need company on yo first run?"

"Sure."

"Go to Fester's."

"Okay. I'm gonna get rich on this."

"Maybe you'll make me rich too."

"It's a deal."

The boys shook hands.

Tipper sneaked out after Ina went to sleep and picked up Alain. They went to Fester's, a frazzled-looking hillbilly with long hair and ragged beard, both mostly gray but once dark. The most striking feature about the man was his eyes. They were green as grass.

"You strikin' out on yo own?" asked Fester.

"Yeah."

"You friends with Alain?"

"Yeah."

Fester looked at the stock. "I'll give you five."

"I was thinking twelve. It's good." Tipper opened a bottle. "Try it."

Fester was impressed with the boy's spunk. He took a swig and jerked back. "Boy, where'd you learn to do this?"

"School. Science class."

"No joshin'?"

"Serious."

"Seven."

"Eleven."

Fester looked at his grandson. The eyes that met were identical. "Alain, what'd ya tell this boy?"

"I give him good advice. He ain't competition. We sell two different things. It's good, ain't it?"

"Eight," said Fester.

"Ten, fifty."

"What's yo bottom line, boy?"

"Name's Tipper. Ten, not a cent less."

"Ten? Okay. I'll take twenty-five."

"Got fifty."

"I ain't got that kinda cash."

Tipper shrugged. "Guess I can go elsewhere."

Fester scratched his chin. "It would give me somethin' over my competition. Can you deliver each month?"

"I'm small. Can't get but ten a month."

"If'n I take 'em all, will you give me exclusive? Don't sell to nobody else?"

"It would be safer for me. Yeah."

"Wait here." Fester went back inside.

"Good job!" exclaimed Alain. "If he gits shut down, you can move on."

"I can go to other counties when I get older, maybe other states. Can't get rich with just Fester, but he'll do for now."

Fester came out with a wad of money. Tipper counted it. Fester laughed. "I didn't cheat you, though some would."

"No, it's all here."

"Tipper, huh?"

"Yes, sir."

"Got a last name?"

"Campbell."

"Nathaniel's kid?"

"Yes, sir."

Fester spat a stream of tobacco juice. "He was a good customer."

"Really?"

"He wudn't a saint."

"Did he drink or visit a whore?"

Fester laughed. "Ina was his wife. He got some extry nookie here. Most men do. Keenan, lots. Don't look so shocked."

Tipper's eyes stretched wide. He asked, "What about Ander Reardon?"

"Naw. He's one that stuck to home. May musta been a good lay. Musta run in the family. Tal didn't come but once or twice with Keenan way back when. June come and drug him out after poppin' one o' my girls upside the face. Left her with a black eye. Don't never come now. Don't know where he's gettin' some. Well, Tipper Campbell, I look forward to doin' business with you."

"See you next month."

They shook hands. "Call me Fester, Fester Munro."

"See you next month, Fester."

Tipper drove in silence. "What's the matter?" asked Alain. "You done good."

"I won't be exclusive. I'll milk every cent I can from that bastard. He hinted ugly things about my ma. She deserves better."

"Sorry."

"Ander Reardon loved my ma. He was gonna marry her. She was more'n a baby factory to him. I won't ever treat my woman with the disrespect my pa did my ma."

"Yeah, I know." Alain rubbed his face with both hands. "My pa beats my ma. He don't love her. You know, she's on number eleven. Matter of fact, she was in labor when I left."

"Does Mr. Jones know?"

"Why?"

"Never mind."

"Tipper?"

"Never mind!"

"Tipper, is Tal Jones diddlin' my ma?"

"No!"

"No, it's worse," sighed Alain. "He loves her, don't he?"

"I can't say."

"Did you see 'em together?"

"I can't say."

"My pa would kill her."

"I know."

"This one belongs to Tal, don't it? Lucille Dent sho thinks so."

Tipper was quiet. He saw Alain nod. "Good for her! She deserves to be loved too."

"Tal said it didn't, that they ain't doin' that. They just good friends."

"You believe him?"

"Yeah, I do."

"Tipper, did Ander make love to yo ma?"

"Yeah."

"Tipper, when she left a while, did she have a baby?"

"I think so. She ain't said."

"I won't say nothin'."

"Me neither. Thanks for helpin' me, Alain. I promise one day I'll make you rich."

"Night, Tipper." Alain got out of the truck at the end of the path that served as a driveway to his house.

Later that night, Alain met Gator by the waterfall. They lit a lantern on the bank and opened a bottle. Alain still kept his cave secret. Gator suggested saving a bottle.

"Good idea," agreed Alain. "You ever had any?"

"No."

"You won't need much."

"You drink much?"

"Mostly cider, but I've had moonshine at Fester's."

"You go a lot?"

"Naw. He says he's my grandpa. My ma belongs to one of his girls. She died. My ma started to work for him. Fester didn't want her to 'cause he thinks he's her pa. She'd be better off there than with my pa."

"You'd rather she be a whore?"

"At least she'd git paid. My pa's jest mean."

"You love your ma though."

"Yeah." He pulled some grass. Silence ensued before Alain said, "Gator, I gotta tell you somethin', but you cain't tell nobody else. Your pa and my ma, well, I think they love each other."

"What?"

"I think you knew in your heart."

"Yeah, I guess, I did."

"Good, but we won't never be brothers 'cause my pa would kill her."

Alain opened the bottle and took a sip. He passed it to Gator. "Jest a sip," Alain warned again. "It's good. Stout. Tipper promised to make me rich when he gits rich on it."

Gator sipped and coughed. "Why would anybody wanna drink this?"

"It takes yo cares away."

"Pa says you feel bad the next day."

"If you drink too much."

After passing the bottle back and forth several times, Gator said, "I think I had enough."

"Me too." Alain lifted the bottle. "To real women, May Reardon, June Jones, Ina Campbell, and Shirley Richter." He took another swig and capped the bottle. Gator had no idea what Alain had meant by that toast, but he knew he had a deep secret to keep.

Gator said, "My head's spinnin'. I think I'm drunk."

"Yeah, you're tipsy." Alain and Gator pulled out the blankets they had and lay on the creek bank. After a time, Gator slept soundly. Alain stared at the stars. He breathed, "Oh, Ma, be careful. I love you. I love Tal. Why cain't he be my pa? Why cain't my pa love me like Tal loves Gator? God, am I talkin' to You? I don't know how. I only been to church a few times. I'm scared. The moonshine don't take the pain away. Please don't let my pa find out about my ma and Tal. Don't punish them for lovin' each other. You can punish me if You have to punish somebody."

Alain opened the bottle and took one more gulp before he slept.

6

Ms. Butler

Tal visited the Richter home Sunday afternoon after Gator told him Shirley had been in labor when he and Alain met to camp at the waterfall. Tal brought food for a couple of days. When he knocked on the door, Alain answered. "Afternoon, Uncle Tal."

"Alain. Your pa in?"

"Do you see his truck?"

"No. Who's taking care of Shirley?"

"Me. Grandma Newton jest left."

"Yes. I passed her. Where's Keenan?"

"Fester's I guess." Alain stepped onto the porch. The other children were playing on the swing or in the tree house. "Uncle Tal, I know how you feel about my ma. It's okay. You can come in. Jest don't git my ma killed."

"How?"

"It's in your eyes. You love her. I don't think Pa would notice. He ain't got no love in his soul."

"I do love her."

"I know. She loves you. Now, come on in. I'll leave you alone. I'll git the food I know you brought."

Tal nodded. "Does Gator know?"

"Yes, sir. He ain't stupid."

"I didn't mean for it to happen."

"Love or sex?"

"There has been no sex."

Alain scowled. "Swear?"

"Yes."

"Then Simon is another Richter."

Tal put his hand on Alain's neck. "I wish I was your father. I can't see why Keenan doesn't love you. You're terrific. Alain, I love you."

Alain nodded a little sadly. "I love you too. Go see my ma but know this—If you get my ma killed, I'll kill you."

Tal stepped back. Alain sounded like a grown man. "I hear you." He went in to visit Shirley.

Tal sat on the side of Shirley's bed. She opened her eyes. "Hey, beautiful," he said. "Simon is perfect."

"Mm. He's healthy. Grandma Newton said he's the biggest baby I've had."

"What do you need? I brought prepared food that will keep a couple of days, and I got you a new nursing bra."

"Tal, that's personal."

"So? Tell Keenan Grandma Newton gave it to you." He kissed her.

"Tal, Alain might come in."

"He knows how I feel about you."

"How?"

"He's smart. He didn't get that from Keenan."

"He tell you he knows?"

"Yes." He became silent.

"Tal? Whatcha thinkin'. You ain't quiet 'less you thinkin'."

"Do you want me to stay away?"

Shirley blinked back tears. "I couldn't survive without you."

"You don't have to. I already told you I'll take stolen moments. Shirley, you can divorce him. I'll hide you and the kids."

"Where? The loft?" She gave a sarcastic laugh. "I cain't leave him."

Tal scowled. "I wish he was a hunter."

"Why?"

"I'd kill him."

"Tal, don't say that. You ain't a killer."

"I love you, Shirley. I never thought I'd love again after June. You took me by surprise."

"I love you too. It scares me the way I feel."

Alain knocked. "Pa's back."

Tal squeezed Shirley's hand and caressed Simon's head. Then, he went in the kitchen and helped Alain as if he had just brought in the food.

The end of school came. Alain and Gator were ecstatic; they had been promoted. The four boys, Alain, Gator, Tipper, and Mac, fished happily as they heard Keenan Richter's voice. "Alain?"

"Shit! What'd I do now?" Alain said to his friends. "Yes, Pa?" Alain called. "What'd I do?"

Keenan came into the clearing. "Nothin' this time. I'm takin' a load to Wilmington. I want you to go with me."

"Why?" The boy tltled his head to the side, doubt written on his face.

"So you can see how to handle market. You old enough now."

"Okay." Alain gave Gator a look. Then, he said, "Y'all catch enough for a fish fry tomorrow."

"We will," assured Gator. When Alain left with Keenan, Gator said, "I gotta go, but I'll be back."

"Something wrong?" asked Tipper.

"No, I'll be back."

Gator rode his bike as fast as he could home and burst through the door. "Pa!"

"What?" Tal hollered from a pen where he made repairs.

"Mr. Richter took Alain to Wilmington."

"So?"

"Go see Miss Shirley."

"I don't think so."

"Go!"

"You sure he's gone?"

"Yes, sir."

"Okay." Tal kissed Gator on the forehead. "Go fishing."

Tal drove cautiously into the Richter yard. Keenan's truck was gone. The other kids were doing chores.

"Hey, Uncle Tal!" greeted Fay.

"Hey, Fay. Where's your pa?"

"Wilmington. He took Alain to show him how to do market."

"Oh, good. He needs to learn. I'll have to take Gator soon."

"Ma's out back washing' clothes."

"Thank you."

"You didn't bring nothin'."

"No, I just…"

"Wanted to see my ma?"

"Fay."

The girl smiled. She looked like her mother. "It's okay. We won't tell, but you owe me peanut brittle."

Tal laughed. "Small price. I'll bring double."

"I's joshin'."

"I'm not." Tal went around the house. "Shirley?"

"Tal!" Shirley smiled broadly.

"Do they all know?"

"Maybe."

Tal gathered Shirley into his arms.

Very late that night, Keenan's truck pulled up. Shirley waited anxiously as she saw Alain driving. She met her son in the yard. "He's drunk," Alain explained.

"Help me git 'im to bed."

"Did you have company today?"

"I did."

"Ma, you ain't laying with Tal, are you?"

"No."

"Okay. I jest worry 'bout"—He cut his eyes to Keenan when he moaned—"He wouldn't believe you jest special friends."

Shirley and Alain undressed Keenan in his stupor and rolled him into bed. Shirley caressed Alain's cheek and kissed his forehead. "Thank you," she whispered. "Go to bed. You need some rest."

Alain went to the area that was cordoned off as the boys' sleeping area and fell onto his make-do bed. He asked himself if his mother had done wrong today, just spending time with someone who made her feel loved. Keenan had taken him to the brothel after they went to market. The only difference between the whores at Jacqui's Gentlemen's Club and the whores at Fester's was what they charged. Oh, they looked better and smelled better, but they were still whores. Alain knew Keenan had been with at least two tonight. Alain was tall for eleven and had begun to feel the onset of puberty, but he did not want that kind of woman. He closed his eyes and dreamed of Amy Dent.

Shirley undressed herself and climbed into bed. She knew that what she and Tal were doing was dangerous, but without Tal, she would die. Keenan rolled over and groped her breasts. "No," she protested and tried to push him away.

Alain heard the struggle that ensued and got out of bed. He stood at the doorway to the bedroom holding the fire poker he grabbed on his way there. He trembled with rage. *I could jest go in and hit him a few times.* The poker clattered to the floor as Alain cried. *I ain't a killer. As much as I hate him, I ain't a killer.*

A muffled scream declared that Shirley lost the battle. She closed her eyes and tried to think of Tal and stole precious moments with him as often as possible.

The summer passed without event, but the return to school and fifth grade brought serious depression to both Alain and Gator. Ms. Butler, who hated all things to do with Possum Holler, was their teacher.

Alain plopped into the bus seat next to Amy. "I'm doomed," he moaned.

"What? Why?"

"I got Ms. Butler. She hates me."

"She hates everybody from Possum Holler. I don't know why. You just do your best and don't sass her."

"Oh, Amy." Alain sighed. "I'll try."

"What else is on your mind?"

"Ma."

"She okay?"

"Yeah. She's pregnant again."

"My momma said you Richters must fuck like rabbits the last time she got pregnant."

"What?" He sat straight up, his body tense.

"That's what she said. I don't know what she means."

"You don't know what that word means, do you?"

"No, but Daddy told her to watch her mouth. They didn't know I heard. What does it mean?"

Alain whispered in Amy's ear, "That's an ugly way of sayin' havin' sex. You do know what sex is?"

She nodded hesitantly. "You mean like we studied in science, reproduction. Mating?"

"Yeah." Alain laughed as Amy's face turned bright red.

"That's gross!" Amy exclaimed.

"I bet it's not."

"You ain't never done that, have you?"

Alain laughed. "No, I'm a kid."

"Okay. Me neither."

"I hope not! You're younger'n me. 'Sides, you gotta wait for me."

"I do?" The girl's eyes grew wide as saucers.

"Yep. One day, you'll be mine."

"You wanna do that with me?"

Alain waved his hands for her to keep her voice down when her question came out shrill.

"Not right now, but when we grow up, yeah."

"My momma would die." Amy shook her head.

"I suppose. Why does she hate me?"

"I don't know. Maybe she's kin to Ms. Butler."

"Now, wouldn't that be somethin'!" Alain cackled.

Alain and Gator worked hard in Ms. Butler's class. The woman who had despised the two boys found they were industrious and dedicated. She was surprised. When they briefly touched on plant reproduction, Alain raised his hand to her amazement for he worked hard but participated rarely unless specifically called upon.

"Yes, Alain?" she asked a little concerned.

"Ms. Butler, if I bring some seeds, would you let us plant a garden?"

"What a wonderful idea!" she uttered in astonishment. "Class, what do you think?"

The class was excited. She asked, "What kind of seeds?"

"You want winter or summer vegetables? We couldn't harvest if it was summer. How about carrots? We could grow 'em in a plant box. I bet Mr. Jones could build us a box. He's real good with carpentry. Gator, will he?"

"If I ask." Gator nodded.

"Will you, Gator?" asked Ms. Butler.

"Yes, ma'am."

"Alain, it's a wonderful idea. I think it warrants bonus points if you ever need them. Your grades are good."

"Thank you."

When recess came, Ms. Butler called Alain to her desk before he went outside. "Yes, ma'am?"

"Are you going to get in trouble for bringing seeds?"

"I hope not. I won't ask my pa. I'll jest take a few. We only need a couple of dozen."

"It's just that I remember Keenan being…"

"You know my pa?" The boy's eyes were wide with surprise.

"Yes."

"How?

"I grew up in Possum Holler until my mother ran away."

"Really? No wonder you hate us."

"I don't *hate* you, Alain. You have potential if you don't waste it."

"Someday, I'm gonna be rich."

"I hope so for you."

Alain could not believe he had glimpsed an actual human side of Daneen Butler. The next day he brought a small bag of seeds. Tal Jones visited the classroom to bring a large flowerbox. He stopped dead in his tracks when he saw the teacher, a woman a little younger than he was. He acknowledged Ms. Butler as, "Hello, Daneen. It has been quite a while. When did you become a *Butler*?"

"When we left that place," she spat.

"Okeydokey," Tal said realizing he did not want to stir up a hornet's nest. "I hope this planter is good enough."

"Quite adequate. Thank you."

"Glad to help."

Ms. Butler's encounter with Tal Jones put her in a bad mood the rest of the year though it had been quite innocent.

Winter came and both Alain and Gator began to miss days. A few times they even got to town as the bus pulled out and would not stop for them.

In the teachers' lounge one day, Daneen Butler came to make copies as Karen Stone and Lauren Langston graded papers.

"Hello, ladies," she said insincerely. "Well, I'm surprised by your pet students."

"How so?" asked Karen.

"They're making good grades. They're not downright retarded."

"No, they're smart!" snapped Lauren.

"Average. Alain did have a great idea with the vegetables. Let's hope now that winter's upon us that they don't miss too many days."

"They wouldn't if you'd help."

"How can I help?"

Karen grabbed Lauren's hand and shook her head. The two of them had padded the boys' attendance record so they would not be forced to retain them due to absences.

Lauren said, "You could make your class something they'd never want to miss. You could love them."

"Lauren, you ask too much."

"What do you have against Possum Holler?"

"I grew up there until I was twelve." She snorted with disgust. "It's dirty and ugly and poor. My mother lived there, and she made *sure* I got on the bus. She never knew which low-life, stinking hillbilly raped her, but the people treated her as if she had done something wrong. Finally, she ran away and took me with her. She scrubbed toilets in Wilmington just to raise me. I was one of those nasty little urchins, but I got out. If their folks cared for them, they'd get out." She loaded paper into one of the copier trays. "I know their parents. Nathaniel Campbell was scum. Even as a boy, he visited whorehouses. Ina Newton Campbell was decent. She never saw Nathaniel for what he really was. Handsome as the devil, but rotten to the core. That's why Tipper's angelic—Ina. It might be a good thing Nathaniel died, or he'd have corrupted Tipper. Ander Reardon and May Newton Reardon were good people, the only ones I miss in the least. Mac lives with the preacher now that his folks died, but he would probably have grown up to be a decent man."

"He does?" interrupted Lauren. "Mac lives with Leo? Maybe I should go in…"

"Yeah." Daneen stacked copies and put in another sheet and gave Lauren a strange look. "You know the man?"

Lauren just nodded as her thoughts temporarily transported back to her college days. Daneen's words cut through the foggy memories.

"Lucille Munro, I don't know why she married Royce Dent, but she did. Royce is a decent man. Not handsome, but he has a good heart. Lucille's daddy helped run one of the whorehouses Nathaniel Campbell visited. He got shot for cheating at cards. The Joneses got out and came back. How could they?" She shook her head in disbelief. "They doomed Gator. For God's sake, they named him *Gator* after Tal's dream of playing football for the University of Florida. Tal's other four ran off so I heard. Can't say I blame them."

She huffed a derisive breath. "The Richters, especially Keenan, are trash. That old goat might be my daddy as many women as he's been with, some against their will. He's at least twenty years older than Alain's mother. Can you imagine if Alain is my little brother?" She put a hand to her cheek. "Oh, God! The horror!"

"Daneen," said Lauren, "you've said way too much. It would be poetic *justice* if you are Daneen Richter! If those boys fail because of your bias, I will see to it that you get fired!"

Karen and Lauren walked out. Lauren Langston had to get away from Daneen Butler before she completely lost her temper.

She said outside, "Karen, I've never physically assaulted anyone, but I might strangle her before I leave this place." *Well, I did throw things at Leo…*

The year passed and Alain had another little sister, Yvonne, during spring break. The last day of school arrived. Daneen Butler reviewed report cards and wrote 'Passed to sixth grade" or "Retained." She looked at Gator Jones's and Alain Richter's. She mumbled to herself, "Twenty-one days, one too many. The rules tell me to retain them. Damn it! They actually made the grades, but it's the rule."

She tapped her pen on the form over and over. Taking a deep breath, she wrote "Retained" in bold letters and passed out the report cards. When Gator read his, he cried and marched to Ms. Butler's desk.

"Why?" he asked.

"You missed one day too many," Ms. Butler replied without emotion.

"But the lowest grade I had was an 86. It's not fair. Miss Langston and Miss Stone would do something."

"Gator, it's the rule. I have to follow the rules. You missed more than twenty days."

"Maybe you miscounted."

"I did not. Sit down."

Alain walked up and glared at Ms. Butler. "I thought you might've come to know and comprehend after what you told me. Gator, let it go. You cain't expect this heartless bitch to understand us."

"What did you say, Alain Richter?"

"You're mean and hateful and spiteful, and you hate us, even though, technically, you one of us. You would never go outa yo way to help us. We jest 'nasty little hillbillies that won't never amount to nothin'.' You know, payback's a bitch."

"Uh!" Ms. Butler popped Alain across the face.

Alain put his hand to his cheek. "I'm used to bein' hit." He left the room.

Ms. Butler screeched, "Come back here! You don't have permission to leave."

Alain walked into Lauren Langston's room. She demanded, "Alain, what's wrong?"

"I been retained. So's Gator."

"What? I warned her." She smacked the top of her desk.

Alain got close. "What happened to your face?" demanded Lauren.

"Ms. Butler slapped me."

"Why?"

"I told her what I thought. She didn't like it."

"What did you say—exactly?" Lauren scowled at the boy.

He looked at the floor. "I sorta called her a bitch."

"Alain!"

"She is!" he said defensively.

"That's not the point."

"You think so too."

"Come with me."

Lauren took Alain's hand and led him back to Ms. Butler's room. "Explain!" Lauren demanded.

"What?" snapped Ms. Butler. "The little heathen missed twenty-one days. He failed."

"Daneen! Count again."

"Why?"

Lauren leaned close. "To prove to the child that you're not a bitch."

Daneen Butler stood up. "Lauren, I think you've said too much this time."

"You slapped him." She stomped her foot. "That's hardly a paddling on the behind."

"Did he tell you what he said?"

"Yes, he did."

"He deserved it."

"Because he told the truth?"

"Lauren, we'll see who gets fired."

"Don't waste your time. I already signed a contract in New Orleans. I won't be here. Karen won't either. I now have my master's in English, and I'll be teaching high school. People like you who don't really care make the system fail. These two boys didn't fail. *You* failed them. It's taking every ounce of control I can muster to not slap you."

Lauren called Gator and Alain to her. "I'm sorry. I tried."

"It ain't yo fault," said Gator. "I'll miss you."

"Me too," added Alain.

"I think I'll see y'all again one day." Lauren hugged both boys. "Don't give up. If you have to, take your high-school equivalency when you turn sixteen."

Lauren Langston would see them again, nineteen years later. However, after another year with them, Daneen Butler did not want to see them again. Alain Richter made life hell for her although Gator tried his best. The boys missed more than twenty-one days the second year in fifth grade, but the attendance record only showed eleven absences. They were promoted. Daneen Butler realized that could have been her and found some compassion for the other children from Possum Holler. As she handed Alain his report card, she whispered, "I'm not a heartless bitch. I might even be your sister."

Alain started to speak. "Not another word." Ms. Butler shook her head. "Prove me wrong about you."

7

Promises to Keep

Labor Day of Alain's thirteenth year brought another trip to market with his father. The boy groaned, knowing there would be a stop at Jacqui's Gentlemen's Club and that he would get home well past midnight and still have to go to school the next day. Even before they arrived early in the morning, Keenan had already imbibed in several swigs of whiskey from a bottle under the seat of the truck. *Wild Turkey ain't moonshine.* Alain's thoughts ran to the fact that his father would buy whiskey over underwear for his children. He turned his mind to Amy as Keenan drove. A sigh from him brought a glare from his father.

"What?" Keenan snapped.

"Nothin'. You mind if I sleep on the drive in?"

"No skin off my nose so long as you remember how to git here later."

"I don't think I can forget the way." Alain closed his eyes and pretended to sleep, a knot forming in his stomach.

Alain made the rounds at the farmer's market and listened as Keenan negotiated contracts. The boy scowled. *They're cheatin' Pa. They know he's already shit-faced.* He focused on the faces of the men he felt were being dishonest. *For damned sho, I'll remember yo faces when I do have to do business with you.*

By mid-afternoon, business was concluded, and they got into the old pickup. Keenan drove away and turned the direction that led away from the road back to Possum Holler.

"Where're we goin'?" Alain asked.

"To have some fun." He looked at his son and chuckled. "Could be 'bout time you had a womern."

"Ain't the womern I want."

Keenan roared with laughter. "You got eyes for Amy Dent. That ain't gonna happen. Lucille'll kill ya."

Pulling into Jacqui's Gentleman's club, Keenan gave Alain a hard shove against the passenger side door. "Suit yoself, but this is the only time I'm gonna offer to buy you some."

"You have a wife at home."

"Don't matter a hill o' beans to me." Keenan got out. "You comin'?"

"No. I think I'll wait here."

Hours later as Alain's stomach complained of emptiness, Keenan staggered out the door of the whorehouse.

Alain held his hand out when Keenan got to the truck. "Give me the keys."

Keenan grunted but handed his son the key to the truck. "You best git me home fast. I didn't git what I wanted. Shirley best be ready. If she ain't I know who will be." He gave a sinister laugh.

Alain said nothing, but clutched the steering wheel with a grip that made his knuckles turn white. He drove in silence as Keenan snored.

Pulling into their yard right at midnight, Shirley came out of the house in her white flannel nightgown with a shawl wrapped around her. The late night wind whipped the garment, causing it to cling to her body.

Before Alain cut the engine, Keenan jumped from the truck and stumbled toward his wife. "I knew you'd be waitin' for me." He grabbed her and planted a rough, sloppy kiss on her, hiking her gown and pushing her toward the plank porch.

"No!" Shirley yelled, shoving against his shoulders. They toppled to the ground where she continued to kick and struggle against his advances.

Alain screamed in sheer exasperation, but Keenan seemed oblivious that the boy was even present. Alain put the truck in first and slung gravel as he headed out the long, curved driveway.

A couple of miles away, Tal Jones slept soundly until he heard pounding on his door. He groaned and rolled out of bed. Gator stared down from the loft as Tal lit a single candle.

Tal opened the door to see Alain bouncing up and down. "What's wrong?" Tal demanded. "I don't see any bruises."

"Come quick!" Alain said trying to control the tears that threatened.

"What's he done to Shirley?" Tal asked, his heart sinking. Without waiting for an answer, he threw on jeans and a plain white t-shirt and his boots with no socks. "Gator, I'll be back," he hollered up the ladder to the loft.

Tal got in the truck with Alain. The boy burned rubber as he headed home.

They skidded to a stop. Tal took in the on-going struggle.

Shirley had managed to put the porch rail between her and Keenan, but her gown was ripped from the arm and fluttered too much like a flag of surrender in the wind. Keenan reached over the railing and jerked the woman to the ground.

Tal sprang from the truck and used his former training as a football player to tackle Keenan with a shoulder to his gut. Straddling the larger man, Tal came around with a right cross that knocked Keenan's head into the hard, packed dirt. "I told you I would kill you if you hit one of them!" Tal bellowed. He put his hands around Keenan's neck and squeezed.

Several of the other children began to come outside as the loud sounds woke them. Alain shooed them back inside.

Shirley clutched Tal's arm. "Stop, Tal. Don't kill him. He didn't hit me."

"No! He was just going to rape you—again!"

"Please?" Shirley's voice rang with terror. "They'll lock you up. What would we all do then?"

Tal pushed with all his might as he stood, leaving Keenan lying in the dirt. He clenched his fists and brought his right hand to his mouth. He turned to Shirley. "Leave the bastard! You and the kids can camp in tents at my place if nothing else."

Keenan's groan before he rolled over and vomited brought their attention back to him. Shirley's emerald orbs looked with pleading at Tal. "Help me get him inside."

Tal walked away and ran a hand through his still thick dark hair. "Fine."

With Alain's help, they wrangled the drunk man to bed where he passed out.

As Tal walked out of the house, he placed his hand gently on her neck. "Shirley…" He sighed. "I don't know if I can stop the next time." He kissed her forehead, and Alain drove him back to his house.

Tal got home and made sure Gator had gone back to bed. He sat down at his table and opened his own bottle of whiskey. He poured a glass, something he had not done since the night Alain came to him with a broken arm. He held the glass to his lips. "Whew!" *Lord, this is too much. I love her so much. I would do anything for her.*

Tal stood and walked onto his porch where he emptied the entire bottle of booze onto the ground. He lifted his head, not believing his eyes.

Shirley made her eldest go to bed before she changed into a shift and sat on her porch for a long time, thinking. Finally she stood, took a piece of her ripped gown that still lay nearby, and cracked the door, leaving the cloth sticking out.

With great determination, she walked to Tal Jones's home. Coming up the rutted drive, Shirley saw him pouring out a bottle of whiskey.

Walking up the two steps, she pointed.

Tal shook his head. "I never want to be like Keenan."

"You ain't." She came to him and pushed his hair back from his temple with a gentle caress.

The same height as he was, she looked him directly in the eye. She took a breath. "You were right. He has always forced me. I hate him, Tal, but I cain't leave him. Still, is that all I'm to ever know—cruelty?" She blinked tears back. "I love you. Once...just once...I want to feel what it's like for a man to love me."

"Oh, Shirley," Tal choked. "Haven't you felt my love for you all these years?"

"That ain't what I mean." She looked at her feet.

Tal lifted her chin. "I would do anything for you." He kissed her deeply and passionately. She slipped her arms around his neck and returned the fire that finally exploded into flame.

Tal scooped her into his arms and carried her across the yard to his barn. "I can't take the chance that Gator could wake up," he whispered.

"I understand."

Tal laid her on the soft, sweet hay. For the next two hours, they made love, gently, yet full of passion.

Close to dawn, Tal drove Shirley home. He chuckled. "I see you put another sign on the door."

"Yeah."

Both got out of the truck and closed the doors as quietly as possible. Tal held her close and kissed her once more before he drove away.

Shirley watched as Tal's truck rounded the bend out of sight. The rain started in a gentle mist. With upturned face, hands out from her sides, Shirley spun around in the falling rain. Faster and faster she whirled until she became dizzy. She stopped, brought her hands to her mouth, and flung her arms skyward. Real laughter bubbled from within her.

She started in the house.

Alain watched his mother and Tal discreetly from the window. "Oh, Ma. Pa will kill you," he sighed.

As Shirley put her foot on the porch, her son ran back to bed and pretended to sleep.

Breakfast was strangely quiet at the Richter home. Keenan dragged to the table. He glowered at his wife. "Outside! All of you!" he bellowed at the children. Alain was already headed out to get to town for the school bus.

Once the door closed behind all the children, Alain leaned his ear against the door.

Keenan growled, "Tal Jones came here last night when that little bastard went to get him."

"He sho did," Shirley said with more defiance than Alain had ever heard in her voice.

"He tried to kill me. What did he do after that?"

"You listen to me, Keenan Richter. You have raped me for the last time. No, you have *touched* me for the last time. I ain't yo whore. Tal helped me put you to bed and then he went home. If you lay a finger on me, next time I won't stop him from killin' you."

She went about clearing the table. Keenan sat speechless. Alain jumped on his bicycle and barely made the bus.

The next time Tal came to check on the Richter family, Keenan literally snarled at him and went to his barn. Tal quirked an eyebrow at Shirley who just smiled. He carried in a large container of cracklings.

At the door he whispered to Shirley, "If we are together again—like that—I have condoms. We can't take a chance. I love you too much."

Shirley scowled but kept quiet.

Tal left with a wave to the children.

A couple more weeks went by before Gator handed Tal an envelope with just his name on the outside. Gator shrugged in answer to Tal's unasked question. "Alain said his ma sent it."

Tal opened and read a short note written in an almost childlike hand:

Tal,

I'm pregnant. This one is yours. It's okay to let Keenan believe it happened that night and he don't remember. He was too drunk. I love you too. Yeah, if we ever do again after this baby, use them things you got.

Promise me one thing. If anything does happen to me, take care of my babies. Until you, they were my only joy.

Shirley

Tal buried his face in the letter and cried.

Gator knew what it said without reading it, just as he was sure Alain did.

Tal looked up and toward the Richter home. "I promise," he said.

8

Forbidden Love

Ina Campbell often took it upon herself to hunt and fish while Tipper was in school. The first time she had come upon Shirley Richter sitting alone on a boulder in the woods, she had been shocked. They talked for a long time, and Ina realized quickly that Shirly was in a bad situation. Keenan Richter was an evil man in Ina's eyes, worse than Nathaniel Campbell had ever been. Nathaniel had been a womanizer, but he had never laid a hand on Ina. That day when she had stumbled upon Shirley, Shirley was black and blue. Shirley almost fled when she had heard Ina's gasp. But placing a hand over her heart, Shirley had murmured, "Oh, Ina. You scared me to death." The two women had talked a while, and now they met frequently just to have a sisterhood of sorts—especially when Ina realized Shirley was in love with Tal Jones.

Ina reluctantly confided her love story with Ander Reardon, even the baby she had to give up for adoption. Shirley had mumbled, "I ain't doin' nothin' with Tal like that. He's jest my protector, and my kids' 'uncle.' He told 'em to call him Uncle Tal."

Ina had taken Shirley's hand. "I worry about you. Temptation will come knockin'. Sooner or later, you and Tal won't be able to resist."

Shirley's grass green eyes had brimmed with tears. "Ain't no man ever loved me, Ina."

For a long time, they just sat holding hands and feeling a connection few could understand.

Today, Ina brought sandwiches and tea to share since the woman had established the first day of each month as "girls' day out." Ina noticed that Shirely sat quietly knitting what looked like a pair of baby booties as she waited for Ina to arrive.

"Whatcha got there?" Ina asked.

Shirely gave her friend a radiant smile, but Ina's brow formed a deep vee. "Shirley, what's goin' on?"

"Tal loves me, Ina. And I love him."

"Okay? This is not news to me." Ina set down the basket. "What's changed?"

Shirley held up the knitting.

Ina put a hand to her mouth. "Oh, Shirley. You and Tal have made love," she whispered through her fingers. "And now, you're pregnant again. This one is Tal's, isn't it?"

Shirley nodded. "Keenan don't know about Tal, so don't worry. He thinks he was too drunk to remember comin' to me. That ain't a stretch 'cause he has been before."

"Still, my dear friend, be careful. Keenen is evil—what's that word Tipper learned in school—personified. Yeah. That's it. Keenan is evil personified."

"What does that mean?"

"Well, Tipper said it means givin' human traits to nonhuman things. It's like in the story they were reading where the animals talked."

Shirley nodded. "Yeah. Keenan is an animal. A mean, vicious, rabid grizzly bear."

"That's what scares me."

Shirley packed her knitting away. "Well, I'm just enjoyin' being loved. And this baby is proof of that love."

"I understand," Ina choked as she remembered having to give away the proof of her and Ander's love.

Shirley grabbed her friend's hand. "I'm sorry, Ina. I wudn't thinking about how that sounded. It ain't fair that people like my dear sweet"—she snorted—"cousin Lucille woulda made your life miserable. Ain't none of my babies ever had a godmother. I want you to be this one's godmother. Promised me you'll help Tal take care of it if something should happen to me."

"Shirely! That's dark thinkin'."

"No, it ain't." Shirley shook her head. "It's smart. Promise me."

"I promise. I'll help the best I can with all of 'em."

"Good. That's settled. Let's eat."

Ina slowly unpacked the food. She sighed. "Shirley, why is it that we both had to have a forbidden love?"

"I don't know. But jest remember that we have both been truly loved by wonderful men. And I love you."

Ina smiled. "I love you too, Shirley."

Shirley leaned forward and kissed Ina full on the mouth. "Now"—she giggled—"*that* would definitely be forbidden."

Ina couldn't help but laugh as she served Shirley a plate.

8

Scrappers

When Mac, Tipper, and Gator were in first grade, Ander Reardon, Ina Campbell, and Talmage Jones had been called to the school because the boys had been in a fight. Leo Tomlin had accompanied the parents because they asked. Leo and Ina Campbell had been to the school once for the talent show. Not long after Ander's death, when all four boys had actually gone to class, Leo, Ina, and Tal had been summoned to the school again for the boys' scuffling with some city children. Not one of the boys was unscathed, but their knuckles looked worse than any other part of their bodies, black eyes included. For a time the fighting seemed to have stopped.

Early on this spring morning before the sun had topped the mountain ridge, Gator and Alain pedaled fast to be greeted by a cloud of dust. Both boys let their bikes fall hard in front of Leo Tomlin's door and ran waving at the bus driver, who chuckled at their rushing.

"Oh, come on!" Mac Reardon said, disgust pouring from his tone. "They were half a minute late. Stop."

"Yeah," Tipper Campbell reiterated his best friend's sentiment.

"Please," Amy Dent begged. "Please."

When the girl looked as if she would cry, the bus driver stopped and opened the door to both Gator's and Alain's surprise. Normally the driver would have left them standing in the dust.

Gator plopped onto a seat and Amy stood to let Alain sit by the window then sat back beside him. "How'd y'all get him to stop?" he asked.

"Maybe he had a kind moment." Tipper shrugged.

Alain snorted a laugh.

As the bus continued its route, several city kids got on. One boy kicked Gator's foot. "Go sit with your friends. You don't get a seat to yourself."

"And you do, Truman?" Alain snapped.

"Yeah, I do, unless Amy wants to sit with me."

"No!" she shook her head and scooted closer to Alain. "Sit by me, Gator. Let the jerk have the seat. Nobody wants to sit with him anyway."

Gator scrunched onto the seat with Amy and Alain. Mac mumbled under his breath from the seat behind them, "Asshole."

"Mac, hush. You'll get in trouble," Tipper warned.

Truman laughed. "Reardon won't do nothin'. He's too much of a pussy."

Mac glared at the older boy, but Tipper elbowed his friend in the ribs.

The students settled back for the rest of the ride to the different schools. The first stop was the elementary before the middle school, and then the high school. The bus slowed, turning into the drop-off lane for the elementary school. Gator stood and started forward to get off.

Truman hollered, "Yeah, let the retards off at the elementary school."

"Shut up," Amy snapped as she stood to let Alain off.

The bus driver braked hard. Amy fell into Truman's lap. He clamped both hands over her developing breasts, squeezing hard, and asked, "You got any ripe apples, baby? You ain't a retard. Why you hang out with these losers?"

"Get your hands off me!" Amy screamed.

The next thing anyone knew, Alain Richter punched Truman in the nose. "Get your hands off my girl," Alain growled.

Blood already dripping from his nose, Truman roughly pushed Amy to the floor of the bus and came up with an uppercut to Alain's jaw.

"No, you don't!" yelled Tipper, coming over the seat to grab Truman in a head lock.

"Stop!" Mac bellowed, grabbing at Tipper to keep him from getting involved.

Gator turned around to a fist in the face from one of Truman's friends. Barely flinching, Gator came back with a jab he'd learned from his father.

The boy in front of Truman's seat hit Alain in the head with a book. Then, a girl threw her hairbrush at him and caught him in the face.

Within minutes, the seats, except for the smaller children who crawled under the seats, had emptied. Alain, Gator, Tipper, Mac, and Amy punched, pulled hair, and bit even as the city children did the same.

In the pandemonium, the bus driver tried to get into the middle of the fray. He wrapped his arms around Alain but received a back fist to the cheek. The principal and several teachers from the elementary school, Ms. Butler included, boarded the bus to help break up the fight. All parties were dragged off the bus so the children not involved could get off. Then the brawlers were transported to the central office. Daneen Butler shook her head and walked away.

Leo had not been summoned to the school in five years. As far as he knew, neither had the other parents unless it had been by letter since the church was one of only five buildings with a phone. Even then, Ina would have asked him to take her because she could not drive. When the church phone rang, he nearly jumped out of his skin. He had an instant foreboding.

"Possum Holler Community Church," he answered.

"Dr. Tomlin, this is Mrs. Seavers, the assistant superintendent with the county school system. I need you to come to the district office immediately."

"Has something happened to Mac?"

"Yes and no. He's been in a fight."

"Oh," groaned Leo.

"Can you, please, bring Mrs. Campbell, Mr. Jones, and Mr. Richter?"

"All the boys?"

"Yes, and Amy Dent. Her mother is en route."

"Wonderful." The sarcasm was not lost on the woman speaking with the preacher. "I'll be there as soon as I can."

Leo drove first to the Richter place. Keenan guffawed when he heard. "Maybe they'll kick his ass out."

"Mr. Richter, the boy needs an education," Leo argued.

"Didn't help me much. Still got the fuckin' farm."

Leo's back stiffened. Keenan said, "Tell Tal to handle it. I ain't goin' to town for this." Keenan stomped to the barn.

The minister sat behind his steering wheel a moment, deep in thought. A light tap on the window startled him. Shirley Richter stared at him in wide-eyed fear. He lowered the window.

"Is Alain all right?" she asked.

"I don't know. He apparently had a fight at school."

She nodded. "I bet them city boys were makin' fun of 'em again."

"You're his mother. Get in."

"Cain't, Preacher Tomlin." She looked toward the barn. "He'd be furious. Git Tal. Tell Alain to do what Tal says. Tal promised to help my kids." She hurried back inside.

Taking a deep breath at the plight of the Richter family, Leo cranked the car and drove to the Jones's farm. He found Tal replacing a fence post.

Tal looked up with a worried expression. "Leo?"

"Hey. The school district called. Gator's been in another fight. We have to go to the district office this time, though. It must've happened on the bus. Even Amy's involved."

"Shit." Tal looked up. "Sorry."

"Keenan won't go. You'll have to help Alain."

"I promised I would." He looked at his hands. "I'll clean up fast and meet you there. You goin' to get Ina?"

"I promised I would," the preacher replied with the same tone Tal had used. The two men nodded understanding.

Ina Campbell hung the last piece of laundry on the line as Leo drove up. She asked, "Somethin' wrong?"

"I'm afraid so. Tipper's been in another fight. We have to go."

She wagged her head before she hung the washtub on a nail and laid her apron across the porch rail. "Do I look okay?"

She wore a pair of blue jeans and a blue plaid flannel shirt. "You're fine, Ina."

She got a big straw bag from inside. Stopping near the car, she broke a keen hickory switch and placed it in the bag. Leo laughed. Ina had given up on a strap, but a switch didn't take much strength. He knew one flick of that switch would get Tipper's attention.

Tal's truck drove by as Leo and Ina turned to go through town to the main road. Lucille Dent was just getting into her car. Leo laughed out loud.

"What?" asked Ina.

He pointed. "'En route.' Amy's involved this time. The lady on the phone said Lucille was on her way."

"She had to git all dolled up. I bet she ain't even told Royce."

He glanced at Ina and could not help noticing she was ten times prettier than Lucille even without a hint of makeup. When the woman beside him put on a little rouge and lipstick, she was a beauty queen.

Leo's thoughts wandered. He knew Ina was related to Grandma Newton, and he saw the family resemblance. He pictured in his mind a few old photographs he had seen at Miriam Newton's home—pictures of her six marriages. He realized that the old matriarch had been a beauty in her younger years as well. Good looks definitely ran in the Newton genes. He had never met June Jones, but May Reardon had been gorgeous, and she had inherited the ginger hair from Grandma Newton. Ander Reardon had been loved by two stunning women. He smiled at the thought as they drove on in silence.

All five children sat on a bench in front of the office of Mrs. Seavers, the assistant superintendent, when the parents arrived. All but Alain jumped up to tell their parents what had happened. Alain took a jagged breath of abandonment. Tal gave a shrill whistle and all quieted. The assistant superintendent stepped out. "Well, is this everyone?"

The parents introduced themselves, and the school official asked, "Where's Mr. Richter?"

"He couldn't get here," lied Tal. "I'm Alain's godfather. I have permission to deal with him."

Alain stared at the floor, and though he tried not to, tears slipped down his cheeks at the feeling of rejection. Tal touched his arm and gave him a reassuring nod.

"Come this way," the woman instructed. Parents and children followed to a conference room. Mrs. Seavers waved her hand. "Find a seat." She flipped open Alain's file and saw that Tal Jones was listed as the contact person for the child, not Keenan Richter. She felt a pang of compassion for the boy.

She sat down. Looking up from the file, she said, "You have a bunch of scrappers here. They caused a full-blown brawl on the bus. This usually results in suspension."

"They were fighting with one another?" asked Leo.

"Well, no."

"Well, where are the others?" demanded Tal.

As the woman started to speak, Lucille blurted, "I'm sure Amy is innocent."

The assistant superintendent slapped her hand on the table. "First, the other boys and girls are in a different room to make sure the fight stopped. Second, Amy is the catalyst here."

"The what?" whispered Ina to Leo.

He replied, "The reason for the fight."

"How?" demanded Lucille.

"Amy," said Mrs. Seavers, "why don't you tell us?"

Amy's big brown eyes looked around the group. "My friends were protecting me."

"How?"

The girl sighed. "A high school boy pulled me onto his lap when I stood up to let"—She looked nervous—"one of my friends off the bus." Alain had been sitting with her, and she knew her mother would not approve. "Truman, the boy, put his hands on my"—She patted the air above her breasts—"He said he wanted to see if I had ripe apples. Alain punched him. Truman pushed me on the floor and hit Alain back. Then, everybody started fighting." She folded her arms across her breasts as if making a shield.

"Did you hit somebody?" asked Lucille.

"Course I did," Amy snapped as if that question should never have been asked.

Lucille began to speak. Mrs. Seavers held up her hand. "She had every right, but the situation became pandemonium for the bus driver."

"What's that word?" Ina whispered to Leo.

"It got out of hand," he whispered back. He turned to the assistant superintendent. "What did our boys do and why?"

"I'll let them tell you. Mac, your dad is asking. You go first. Just know I expect better control from a straight-A student."

Mac's voice cracked as he spoke. "Amy told you what started it. That Truman boy from Centerville sexually assaulted her. Alain defended her, and all Truman's friends jumped Alain. He won't fight alone."

The school official took a deep breath. "Tipper?"

Tipper shrugged. "You heard. We stick together in Possum Holler. We're not morons and trash like the boys called us. They used words Ma would wash my mouth out with soap for using."

"I see. Gator?"

"I ain't got nothin' to add." He paused and took a thoughtful breath, his brow creasing in contemplation. "'Cept, those fellas pick on us all the time. We git our trays dumped on the floor in the cafeteria. They make fun of us 'cause we poor. They laugh at our clothes. They call us retards, me and Alain at least, cause we're behind. Now, they tryin' to molest our girls, and we the ones in trouble."

The woman assured, "They are too, Gator, I promise. It seems you have lots to say, actually. I'll look into your allegations. Alain, your turn."

Alain had been slouched down in a chair with his arms folded defensively. His left eye was almost swollen shut. He mumbled, "I ain't gonna let no sumbitch grab Amy's tits."

"Ahem." Tal cleared his throat. "Alain, there are several ladies here."

"Sorry." He sat up straight. "Truman wudn't bein' a gentleman." He pointed at the other boys. "We musketeers. Like the books says, 'All for one and one for all.' Amy's our one. It don't matter her ma don't like us. We ain't puttin' up with nobody treatin' her like that."

Amy mouthed, "Thank you."

The assistant superintendent looked down at the folders. "It's policy for fighting to get three days suspension."

"You cain't do that!" Alain blurted, jumping to his feet. "It might make me and Gator fail again. It might make us miss more'n twenty days."

"You should've thought about that and reported the incident to the bus driver rather than fight."

His voice shrill for a boy whose voice was changing, Alain argued, "He wudn't gonna do nothin'. He don't never do nothin' when they mess with us. He don't care 'bout us. He even leaves me and Gator runnin' up the road to catch the bus jest 'cause we might be a couple o' minutes late." He plopped back into the chair.

Mrs. Seavers said, "Alain, I appreciate your trying to be chivalrous. Amy's lucky to have friends like you. But you can't afford to be chivalrous right now." She looked around the table. "No more fights—any of you. If those hooligans do something else, let *me* know. I'll talk with the bus driver, but he's the only one we have who'll drive out that far. My daddy's from Possum Holler. I'll do something."

The woman signed five referral forms: three days' suspension for fighting. "Spring break is starting early for you. I'm counting today. I'll see you five the Tuesday after spring break."

"But..." Alain began.

"I'm sorry."

"Truman's gang too?" the boy asked full of defiance.

"Yes, and Truman gets a whole week for sexual harassment. That's the most I can give him unless Amy presses criminal charges."

"That's not happening," grunted Lucille.

Alain nodded. Mrs. Seavers handed the referrals to the parents. "Take these kids home."

She watched as the parents left with their children. Noticing Lucille dragging Amy away from the boys and muttering about her daughter associating with riffraff, the woman marched over before meeting with the other group. "Mrs. Dent."

"Yes?"

She lowered her voice. "How dare you? Those boys sacrificed for Amy. They're not riffraff. Scrappers? Yes. So is your daughter. But they're all good kids." She looked over her shoulder. "Some are in a real bad situation. Rather than badmouthing them, thank them." She walked away.

Lucille narrowed her eyes to slits, took a deep breath, and walked briskly to the others from Possum Holler. "Thank you for trying to help Amy. Good day." Then, she dragged the girl away, Amy looking back, mortified and crying.

Tal Jones rubbed his left arm. "Let's get the boys home before they have another fight in the parking lot, and I pull that ungrateful woman's head off."

At the door, Ina dropped her switch in the trash and tousled Tipper's hair. Leo patted Mac's shoulder. Tal hugged Gator and put his arm around Alain's neck. He whispered, "You in love with her?"

The boy shrugged.

10
Rafting

From spring break the year the scrappers were suspended, the boys began building a clubhouse on the bank of the creek at the bottom of their waterfall, a good five miles north of the Richter home. Once they had a habitable structure built, they stuffed flour sacks with pine straw, making a bed for each of them, covering the makeshift mattresses with old blankets or quilts. Then, they stocked the clubhouse with nonperishable food and slept there many nights, Alain, alone, more often than any of the others. When he felt the need to be even more secluded, he ventured behind the falls to his secret sanctuary.

Once school got out, the boys began a raft with plans to float from the waterfall to their fishing hole on Alain's fourteenth birthday. The other three would be thirteen by then, and they were attempting to duplicate the exploits of Tom Sawyer and Huckleberry Finn.

The boys felled pine saplings and lashed them together with rope supplied by Amy Dent who asked no questions. Two days before Alain's birthday, the four boys met at the clubhouse, bringing edible supplies for their special place, including Tipper's moonshine and Alain's cider. They put the finishing touches on the house. As they worked in nothing but their underwear, for the heat was oppressive, Gator dragged Alain to the side.

"What are the bruises on yo back?" he demanded.

"Sh." Alain waved his hands. "I don't want them to know."

"Yo pa do that?"

"Duh! Whatcha think?"

"Alain, you need to tell my pa."

"No! He'll kill my pa. I don't want yo pa to go to jail. Pa's been good. He was mad 'cause I took his ax without askin'. It was dull when he went to use it. It's my fault that I forgot to sharpen it when Polly was born."

"It don't make it right to leave bruises. Damn it, Alain!"

"At least he's been good lately, and he ain't hittin' nobody else. I can take it, and I'm 'bout as big as him. I'm fixin' to start hittin' back. Don't you dare tell Tal. My ma couldn't live without him. If they ask, I fell off a ladder."

"Fine," hissed Gator.

"Come on. Let's finish this so's we can camp out tomorra night and go raftin' the next day."

"Is everything all right?" asked Mac when Gator and Alain rejoined him and Tipper.

"Yeah," Alain answered. "Y'all ready to hit the water?"

"I'm hot enough," said Mac. "Let's take a break and cool off."

The boys gave the vessel a trial run a few yards down and it sailed fine. Then they jumped in to cool off before they headed home for the night.

The next day the boys showed up with more food and drink. "This is gonna be fun," laughed Gator. "What y'all got? My pa said we needed some real food, so I brought ham and boiled eggs."

"That'll make a good dinner," said Tipper. "Ma sent biscuits and sugar cookies."

"Are they hot?" asked Alain.

Tipper rolled his eyes. "Not hardly."

"I love Miss Ina's sugar cookies," Alain countered. "Mac, what's in the huge bag?"

"I've got cans of root beer that Papa got," said Mac, "and franks, buns, mayonnaise, ketchup, and mustard packets, and marshmallows. Oh, and four coat hangers for roasting the wieners and marshmallows. Papa said to build a fire at sundown and roast 'em for supper."

Alain laughed. "We're gonna get fat tonight and sink the raft. I've got a peck of fresh blueberries and a bottle of muscadine wine besides some o' my cider."

"Naw, we won't gain that much weight," said Tipper, "Hey, let's name the raft and use a bottle of moonshine to christen it."

"What'll we call it?" asked Gator.

"A ship's a girl," said Mac. "What'll we name *her*?"

Alain said, "There's only one girl that's been a part of us."

Mac scowled while Tipper grinned. Gator asked, "*The Amy*? Naw!"

"Why not *The Queen Amy*?" asked Alain. He laughed. "It would infuriate Lucille."

Mac dug through the hardware supplies he had brought weeks before. "Ha!" he exulted. "White paint. Let's paint it across the bottom in big letters. If it'll make Lucille mad, I'm all for it."

"We ain't got brushes," said Gator.

"We got fingers." Mac wiggled his fingers in the air. "Let's do it now so it has plenty of time to dry. We'll christen her before we take off in the morning."

They painted " *THE QUEEN AMY!* " in big bold letters and surveyed their handiwork.

"We need to make sho Amy sees it," said Alain, resting the backs of his hands on his hips with the palms facing out.

"Why?" snapped Mac.

"If she don't know, how's Lucille gonna know?"

Mac huffed, "Well, we can't drag the raft back up stream, so it'll be sittin' at the swimmin' hole. She'll go swimming eventually."

"I guess," sighed Alain. "But how will she know we did it?"

"She's smart enough to figure it out. Who else would do it?"

"Mac's right," said Gator. "Nobody else would know about Amy being the queen."

"Okay, you make sense." Alain gave up the debate.

After they left the raft to dry and ate some of the food around noon, they hiked above the waterfall for the first time.

They came out on a wide meadow where the stream meandered lazily for miles.

"This is beautiful," breathed Alain, taking in the lush green dotted with a prism of wildflowers. "Are we still in Possum Holler?"

"I don't know," said Mac in as much awe of the picture as Alain.

"I wanna live here one day," confessed Alain. "The stream, the mountains, and freedom all combined."

Pointing, Tipper said, "When I make you rich one day, you can build a great big house out here. Build it big enough so we can each have a room for when we come to visit." He grinned.

"I will."

"Dream big," said Mac. "I'm gonna be a doctor, and Tipper's gonna be an entrepreneur who's gonna make you rich too. Gator, what about you?"

"One day, I'm gonna own the slaughterhouse and turn it into a full processing plant. People in Possum Holler can have jobs not in a mine."

"That's good," agreed Mac. "Alain, if Tipper's gonna make you rich, what are you gonna do?"

Wistfully, Alain replied, "I'm gonna be free."

The four got back to camp and roasted the hotdogs and marshmallows. They drank the muscadine wine and got silly, but they decided to save the cider and moonshine for another day.

The boys got up early the next morning and ate boiled eggs that they had floated in one of their socks in the cool water, blueberries, and biscuits. They stored their nonperishable foods in a box in their clubhouse and stripped to their underwear, stuffing their clothes in a plastic trash bag to keep them dry.

"I don't know about you, Tipper," Mac said when they had stripped to their underwear.

"What?"

"You're sort of burnt already."

"I got lotion. It ain't that bad, but that's why I work in the shade. Let's get goin' before the sun gets too high. The fishin' hole is shady."

The boys made sure to wedge the clubhouse door shut. Then they christened *The Queen Amy!* with a bottle of moonshine and shoved off.

The beginning of the voyage was smooth. Half a mile downstream, they hit a few rapids and had to hold on tightly, but nobody fell off although they were soaked by the turbulent water.

An hour downstream, they drifted into the deep part of their swimming and fishing hole. They paddled to shore using their hands and pulled the raft into a little stand of saplings. The boys celebrated a successful voyage with excited whoops.

"That was fun!" declared Gator. "We should do it again."

"We'd have to figure out how to get the raft back up stream or build another one," said Mac, the pragmatist.

"Well, we'll think of somethin'. Let's swim for now and then catch some fish to cook. I'm starving. Rafting is hard work," said Alain.

Alain hung his threadbare briefs on a limb to dry and plunged back into the water. The other boys laughed with mirth and did the same. Mac jumped in last as he hung out their damp clothes from the trash bag to dry first.

As the boys dunked one another and pranked and splashed, their frivolity was suddenly interrupted by a female voice. "Are the fish bitin'?"

The boys treaded water and looked at Amy as she sat on the bank with her sketch pad and colored pencils. She wore a yellow and white striped bathing suit with a pair of cutoff jeans over it.

"We ain't fishin'. We swimmin'," said Alain with his brow furrowed. "How would we know if the fish are bitin'?"

"Well," said Amy with a grin and batting her eyelashes, "I thought with four little worms swimmin' around, the fish might be bitin'."

"Little worms!" Alain shouted. "Girl, whatcha got here is four big snakes, and I think you want all four of 'em to bite you."

"Alain Richter! You're disgusting! But you're right. There aren't four little worms. There are three little worms"—She held up her thumb and index finger to barely show a millimeter—"and one teeny, tiny maggot."

"Maggot! You wanna see this maggot?" Alain hoisted himself out of the water. Amy screamed and ran behind a tree. Alain followed her and pinned her escape with one arm on either side of her. "Like what you see?" he asked softly so the others could not hear although they were laughing uncontrollably as they, too, got out and flopped on the grassy bank like fish out of water.

"Okay, so, you're not a maggot." Amy glanced down. "Or even a worm. Please, put some clothes on." She looked up at the tree leaves and bit her lip. The sun flickered through the leaves casting alternating shadows and sparkling.

"Why? We're skinny dippin'. You comin' in, or would you rather stay here?"

"You want me to take my clothes off?" She wiggled to try to escape, but Alain pressed closer to her.

"You plannin' on swimmin' in yo clothes? Jest think: You can go home and tell yo ma you swum naked with four boys. You can give the old battle ax a heart attack."

"I'm wearin' a swimsuit." She tilted her head to the side so that her long brown ponytail fell over her shoulder.

"So?"

"Will y'all turn around while I get in?"

"Why?"

"Alain, I don't want all of y'all seein' me naked."

"What about me? It's only fair."

Gator yelled, "What y'all doin' back there?"

"None o' yo business," Alain yelled back.

Amy blushed crimson. "Alain, they'll think we doin' something."

He gave a one-shoulder shrug. "So?"

With a scowl of jealousy, Tipper echoed, "Yeah, what *are* y'all doin'?"

"Amy's apologizin'," laughed Alain. "Tell 'em."

Amy felt the burn of the blush on her face. She hollered, "I'm sorry. Alain ain't a worm. I'm sure y'all ain't either."

"Need proof?" yelled Tipper.

"That's okay," said Amy. "I'm gonna swim with y'all, but y'all gotta turn around while I get in."

"We'll let you see if you let us see," teased Mac.

Tipper hit Mac. "You don't even like her."

"Oh, she's okay. It's her momma that I really don't like. Besides, I need to study anatomy."

Tipper hit Mac again, and Gator laughed at them.

Amy said to Alain, "Are you gonna move?"

"Do you want me to?"

Amy looked down again and smirked. "Tell all of them to stand up so I can peek around the tree."

"Only if we git to watch you git in."

"Okay, you can peek, but then you gotta turn around."

"Actually, I'd like to stay right here."

"Uh, no."

"Come on. Admit it. You like what you see."

Amy looked down again. "Okay. I like what I see. Now, I wanna see the others so I can compare."

"You're bad," laughed Alain.

"I can be worse."

"How?"

"Can I touch?"

Alain grinned. "Yeah. Go ahead."

Amy touched Alain and he groaned as his body reacted. Amy squealed as Alain's penis moved.

He moaned again. "Do I get to touch?" asked Alain.

"No."

"Not fair."

"You'll get over it."

Alain got his face very close to Amy's. "One day, Amy Dent, I'm gonna kiss you."

"One day, Alain Richter, I'll kiss you back, but for now, get out there with everybody else."

Alain laughed. "Chicken." He leaned his forehead against hers and took several steadying breaths until he felt his erection subside. Then he joined the other three boys.

"Okay," Alain said, still feeling his pulse pounding in his groin. "Stand up and strike a pose so Amy can see you."

"What?" said Tipper.

"It's the deal I made. She sees us, and we see her, but only for a second. Then, we gotta turn around."

The boys struck their pose, and Amy peeked around the tree. She shrieked, and the boys laughed. Amy hollered, "That was the silliest thing I ever saw."

"Your turn!" the boys chorused.

"Worms?" Tipper asked.

"No worms. Normal guys, I guess." Amy hung her clothes over a bush. "I only just turned thirteen," she said. "Don't expect a model for a dirty magazine." Amy stepped out.

"Whoa!" said Alain and Tipper together.

"Now, turn around!" Amy ordered.

The boys turned around until they heard a splash. Then they went back in. After a while, Amy said, "I'm gettin' out. Turn around."

The boys turned around, and Amy went behind her tree to get dressed. By the time she came out, the boys had put their pants on.

"Darn it!" Amy laughed. "I thought I'd paint y'all."

"You still can," said Alain. "Jest not naked."

"We did somethin' for you. You wanna see?" asked Tipper.

"Yeah."

The boys showed Amy their raft.

"That's so sweet," said Amy, a small catch in her voice. "I know. Turn it on its side and stand behind it. I'll draw y'all behind *my* raft."

"We're kinda starvin'," objected Mac.

"It won't take long to sketch you. I can do the color later while y'all are catchin' fish."

The boys turned the raft so the name could be read and stood behind it. Amy sketched quickly and added shadows and color while the boys caught a dozen fish with nightcrawlers that were easy to find beneath the moist leaves and rich soil. They cleaned the bass and bream and roasted them over an open fire.

As the fish roasted, Alain peered over Amy's shoulder. "Nice. It looks like us. You're talented. How'd you sneak off?"

"Momma went to Wilmington. She said she wouldn't be back until tonight. You?"

"I told Pa what I was doin' for my birthday."

"Alain, I saw your bruises. He hadn't hit you for a long time. What happened?"

"I used his ax without askin' and dulled it. I guess I should be happy he didn't use the ax on me."

"Did you tell Mr. Jones?"

"No. I don't want him to go to jail. He would kill Pa." Alain sighed.

"What's wrong?"

"Nothin'."

"You can trust me."

"I know, but it's not my secret to tell."

Amy spoke even lower. "Is it your ma and Mr. Jones? I think he loves her."

"Don't let that git back to my pa."

"I bet Grandma Newton has some poison you could slip him."

"Amy!"

She shrugged and dipped her mouth into a pout. "Alain, he's gonna kill you one day. I couldn't lose you."

"Do you care about me?"

"A lot."

Alain grinned broadly. "Then, this has been the best birthday ever."

"*Today's* your birthday?"

"Yep. That's why we went raftin'."

"Happy birthday, Alain."

"Fish is ready," called Gator.

As they ate, Alain discreetly rubbed his hand along Amy's leg. She jumped. He whispered, "Do you shave your legs like city girls?"

"Yes."

"I like the way it feels. Just to let you know, I've looked at a few dirty magazines, and I've been to Festers to sell my cider. I seen some naked women. You're prettier."

"Thanks. I don't have big boobs."

Alain sniggered and leaned closer. "More than a mouthful is too much."

"Alain!" Amy could feel her face burn, and it was not from the fire.

"You're perfect. Just right for your body. Don't go gettin' fake boobs when you git older."

"I promise."

Tipper sat on the other side of Amy. Alain sighed, "I have competition."

Amy laughed and Tipper scowled. When they finished eating, they doused the fire and headed home in the twilight. Tipper, Gator, and Alain headed away from town while Amy and Mac walked into town. The boys agreed to meet the next day at the waterfall to get their bikes.

Mac teased Amy on the way home. "Well, Amy, which one of our hearts do you plan to break?"

"None. Y'all are all my friends, but Momma wants me to like you because you're"—She mocked Lucille—"'the only one with any potential.' But don't worry. We would never work. One of us would end up dead. Gator's nice. He's funny. He always knows how to laugh. I like Gator, but he's just a friend. Alain's so sweet. I could fall for him, but Momma would have a fit. She thinks the Richters are trash. Maybe Keenan, but not Alain. Then, there's Tipper. Tipper is scrumptious."

"Scrumptious?" Mac cackled. "Do you plan to eat him?"

"You know what I mean. I adore Tipper. Once again, though, Momma hates him, and I don't know why. Tipper has never hurt anybody. The only thing he does is make moonshine. So, Mac, I don't know. Maybe it's none of y'all. I know Momma would be happy if I left here." Amy shrugged.

"Are you gonna tell your momma about today?"

"No, unless she makes me really mad. Today was nice. I enjoyed being with my friends. It's not my fault all my friends are boys. Momma won't let me do anything with the other girls in Possum Holler because none of them go to school, although I used to play with Fay Richter when we would both sneak off. Remember that day when Momma and Keenan both showed up?"

Mac nodded.

"That's the last time I got to play with Fay except at Hog Rendering or Harvest Fest." Amy sighed. "Not even Alain's sisters and brothers go to school. How and why does Alain? Why don't the others?"

"Their pa won't let 'em. Alain goes because my pa started taking him. Amy, Alain had bruises all over him. Didn't you notice?"

"Yes. His story is he fell off a ladder."

"He lied. His pa did it."

"Did he tell you that?"

"No. He doesn't want us to know, but it's not the first time I've seen him beat up—Remember his broken arm?"

Amy shuddered. "It's awful. It was because he dulled the ax. He told me. Maybe that's why my momma doesn't like the Richters."

"Maybe, but that doesn't explain Tipper."

"No, that's a real mystery. Well, thanks for walking me home." Amy snickered. "Momma's home and looking out the window. She thinks I don't see her."

"How about a pretend kiss?"

"Okay. Just pretend?"

"A real kiss that means nothing. Then, when you spring the one you really want on her, she'll have a stroke."

She put her hand over her heart. "Kiss me, Mac!"

Mac gave Amy a friendly kiss. "Good luck. Which one do you want?"

"Honestly?"

"Yes."

"Alain."

"Lucille will have a stroke."

11

Bloodbath

Amy loitered along the road as she waited for Alain to ride by on his bike. Although his question sounded suspicious, Alain grinned from ear to ear. "Whatcha doin' way out here?" he asked when he finally pedaled by.

"I wanted to see you."

"Really?"

"Yeah." Amy handed him a box.

"What's this?"

"A gift for the baby. Will you take it to your ma?"

"Sure. That was sweet. Does your ma know where you are?"

"No. I was scared to go all the way to the house too."

"It's prob'ly good you didn't. Pa ain't friendly. How'd you git up here?"

"My bike." Amy pointed.

"Nice bike. Is it motorized?"

"Yeah. It's a mo-ped. It doesn't go very fast. Only about thirty miles an hour."

"When you gonna git a car?"

"I don't drive yet. Daddy says when I get old enough for a car. he will help me find a good used car. Momma says it'll be new."

Alain snickered. "I bet your ma wins that argument."

They laughed. "You think I'm spoiled?" asked Amy.

"A little, but you're still sweet."

"It's easier to spoil an only child."

Both teenagers jerked their heads up as they heard several screams come from the Richter home hidden from their view just around the bend. Anxiously, Alain said, "Go home, Amy."

"What's wrong?"

"I don't know, but you're not safe here. Please, go home as fast as you can. I gotta git to the house."

"Alain, don't let him hit you." Amy squeezed the boy's hand before she hopped on her motor-scooter and headed home. She was worried sick, and tears stung her eyes as she drove.

Alain flung his bike down as he saw Fay, carrying the baby, fly out the door with her blouse ripped, showing her breasts without a bra. "Fay!" he called.

"Run, baby! Get away from this bastard!" Shirley hollered from the door.

Keenan jerked Shirley back inside. Alain grabbed Fay by the shoulders. "What happened?" he demanded.

Fay could hardly talk she trembled so hard. "Talk to me Fay," Alain encouraged. "Did that son-of-a-bitch rape you?"

"It's n-n-not the first time," stammered Fay, "but Ma caught him. She said she's gonna castrate him. She got the butcher knife."

"You get all the kids and hide in the barn. I'll take care of this. It's over. We ain't livin' in fear no more."

Alain kissed Fay on the head. "Fay, if I die, go to Uncle Tal, and tell Amy I love her."

"Alain, I'm scared."

"Me too. Now, go!" His voice hitched.

Fay rounded up her younger siblings while Alain burst through the front door in time to see Keenan punch Shirley in the face even as she shouted, "Git outa my house and don't you never come back!"

"No more!" Alain bellowed as he flew into Keenan with all the pent-up rage erupting. He and his father fought like two grown men. Keenan was still bigger and stronger than Alain, but Alain was younger and more agile. They fought fiercely; however, after a time, Keenan pinned the boy to the floor and pummeled him across the face.

All of a sudden, Shirley, who had begun to bleed profusely from having delivered a baby only two weeks earlier and looked as if she had been used as a punching bag, jumped on Keenan's back with her arm around his throat and plunged the butcher knife into his groin. "Get off him!" she screamed like a banshee. "I told you what I'd do if I ever caught you with Fay!"

Keenan flung Shirley off him with a bear-like growl. She hit the wall.

For a moment, Alain lay on the floor, dazed, and Shirley could not catch her breath. Keenan kicked Shirley hard in the stomach. "You stupid whore! You ain't nothin' to me, but a whore to gimme some young'uns. Fay's a good one, much better'n you! She does what I like." A malicious grin spread across his face. "Maybe it's time to see if Gloria and Glenda can be as good as Fay. You cain't throw me outa my own house. It's time for you to join the other four, and you can take yo whore spawn with you."

Keenan strode to the fireplace and got his double barrel shotgun off the hooks above the mantle. As Shirley struggled to cover Alain, Keenan shot her in the chest.

"No! Ma!" Alain shrieked in fury. He staggered to his feet as Keenan pointed the shotgun at him. Not caring if he died, oblivious to the searing heat from the freshly fired shotgun Alain grabbed the barrel of the shotgun and forced it back toward his father.

Alain snarled through clenched teeth, "I want you to know before you go to Hell that you sired me, and you were wrong about Tal Jones. He's been in love with Ma for years, and Polly is *his*! Now, die, you son-of-a-bitch!" Alain pressed his finger on top of Keenan's and pulled the trigger. The boy was drenched in blood.

After the two blasts, the silence became even more frightening. Alain dropped to his knees and crawled to Shirley. "No, Ma, please?" Alain sobbed as he held his mother close to him. "Why didn't you run away? I told you he would kill you one day. I don't know what to do."

For what seemed ages, Alain sat on the floor holding Shirley to him. Darkness fell before Fay looked in with a lantern. She let out a blood-curdling scream.

"Go back, Fay," Alain said quietly.

"Alain, are you alive?"

"Yeah."

"What happened? We only heard two shots."

"He killed her."

"The gun's in his hands. Did he kill hisself?"

"No, I killed him, and I ain't sorry."

"Alain, *he's* holdin' the gun."

"What do I do, Fay? He was gonna shoot me. Then, he woulda come for y'all. He said it was time for Gloria and Glenda to be like you." His thoughts ran to his visit to the cemetery with Grandma Newton years before. He shivered, realizing that Keenan was just like Coleman Richter—*He would have killed his whole family, most likely.*

Fay started inside. "No!" called Alain, lifting one hand in a stop motion. "Don't come in. Don't git no blood on you. You ain't seen nothin'. You been in the barn with the others. I'm so scared, Fay. I'm a murderer."

"No, you ain't, Alain! You a hero. You saved us."

"What do I do now?"

"Uncle Tal."

"Yeah. Yeah. You stay in the barn 'til I git back with him. Oh, Fay. He's gonna be broke again."

"He's all we got. We can do this, Alain. Hurry. Polly's hungry."

"Okay." Alain finally laid Shirley's body on the floor. "It was awful. He called her a whore. She threatened to kill him 'cause of you. She tried."

"Alain, go."

"Go to the barn, Fay. Give Polly some cow milk. I'll be back."

As Tal and Gator Jones slept, they were awakened by pounding. Tal lit a lantern, and Gator descended the loft ladder. Tal grabbed his shotgun before he opened the door.

"Pa?" Gator asked wide-eyed. "Who are you gonna shoot?"

"Just in case." Tal called, "Who is it?"

"Uncle Tal, it's Alain. Please open the door. I didn't know where else to go."

Muttering, "I'll kill the son-of-a-bitch if he's hit that child," Tal opened the door. The young man who had celebrated his fourteenth birthday so happily one week earlier by rafting with his friends and having an intimate moment with the girl of his dreams trembled, covered in blood in the Joneses' doorway.

"What the hell happened?" screamed Tal, pulling Alain inside and examining him as the boy began to cry. It was apparent Alain had received some savage blows, but nothing to have coated him in blood. Tal sprinted into his bedroom. "Where's Keenan?" he demanded as he dressed rapidly.

"You ain't gotta kill him. He's already dead."

With one arm still out of his shirt, Tal took Alain by the shoulders. "What happened? Whose blood is this?"

"He shot her. Then…then…"

Tal tried to stay calm as pictures he could not bear raced across his mind. *Alain's in shock. I have to take care of the boy, Shirley's boy.* Gator helped his father slip his arm into his shirt. Tal jerked the quilt off his own bed and wrapped it around the terrified child. "Sit down, Alain," he requested in a strained voice. "Gator, make some hot tea. Put in a shot of moonshine and be quick about it."

Alain sank into a ladder-back chair at the table. "Alain, talk to me. You're safe," Tal continued to coax.

For quite a while Alain sat at the table and stared at his bloody hands. Gator set the spiked tea in front of him. "Drink," Tal ordered gently.

Tal stroked Alain's hair as the boy gagged on the tea. "Talk to me now," asked Tal. "Who did your pa shoot?"

"Ma," Alain replied as tears came afresh. "She's dead too."

"No!" Tal choked. "Please, no. Why? Did he find out? Whose blood is on you?"

"Hers. His. Both." Alain shook his head. "I don't know."

"Where are your brothers and sisters?"

"I made 'em stay in the barn. I didn't want 'em to see."

Shaking, Tal said, "Alain, please tell me what happened?"

"Amy was waitin' for me at the end of the drive to our house. She brought Polly a gift. I don't know what I did with it."

"It's okay. We'll find it. What happened?"

"We heard screamin', and I made her go home."

"You did the right thing."

"When I got closer to the house, I heard Ma screamin', 'Get out! Run, baby!' Alain almost could not talk for crying. "Pa raped Fay."

"Drink again," said Tal as he shed his own tears. The cup shook violently as Alain raised it to his lips. He gagged on another swallow of tea. "Go on," encouraged Tal. He felt Gator's arm around his shoulders. He reached up to take his son's hand.

"I told Fay to gather the kids and hide in the barn. I could hear Pa hollerin' at Ma. I went inside. He hit her. I couldn't take no more. I jest flew into him. He sho hit me a bunch o' times, but I fought back this time."

"Good for you," grunted Tal.

Alain continued his story through gasps. "Ma jumped on his back with the butcher knife. She tried to cut his dick off and hit his leg. I ain't never seen her like that. She tried to make him leave. She caught him with Fay. She screamed, 'I told you what I do if I ever caught you with Fay.'"

Alain jumped and spilled the tea. Gator grabbed the dishtowel and mopped up the liquid. "Sorry," muttered Alain.

"No big deal," said Tal, his voice tremulous. "Finish the story."

The boy nodded mechanically. "I tried to git to Ma after he threw her into the wall and kicked her. I couldn't breathe. I think my ribs are broke." He wrapped his arm around his middle.

"She struggled to git up. She was bleedin' from havin' the baby. He told her it was time for her to join his other four wives. He grabbed the shotgun and shot her."

"Oh, my God," groaned Tal. "Go on. We're listening."

"Then, he pointed it at me. I knew he was gonna kill me and go after the others. It was in his eyes." He gazed past Tal with deep V in his brow as if in a faraway place. "Did you know that Pa's pa killed his whole family except Pa? Grandma Newton told me. She showed me the graves. Do you think it runs in the family?"

Tal stoked Alain's hair. "No, it's not hereditary. Tell me the rest about Keenan."

Nodding, Alain went on. "He told her he was gonna kill *me*. I grabbed the gun. We struggled. I shoved the barrel toward him. I told him Polly is yours." He finally made eye contact with Tal. "I made his hand pull the trigger. I killed him. I murdered my pa." Alain began to sob, and his whole body shook.

"No, you didn't!" snapped Tal. "He killed himself." He jumped to his feet and paced. "You listen to me. Do whatever I tell you. First, we're goin' to your place."

"No!"

"Alain, I'll take care of it, but you have to go with me." Tal shuddered with grief and rage. "Trust me."

"Yes, sir. I'm so scared," said Alain.

"I know you are." Tal hugged Alain close. "I'd do anything for Shirley. I wish I had killed the bastard myself. I should have shot him the night he came looking for you. I begged her to leave him."

"What about me, Pa? What do you want me to do?" asked Gator.

"Stay here."

"But Alain needs me."

"Gator! I don't want you to see it. I'll take care of Alain. I promise."

"What's gonna happen to us kids?" asked Alain.

"One step at a time. Let's go. Gator, start a fire."

"In the middle of the summer?"

"Start the damned fire!"

"Yes, sir. Pa, I'm so sorry about Miss Shirley."

"Me too." Tal's shoulders shook with silent sobs as he led Alain out the door.

Tal and Alain drove into the Richter yard. They saw the barn door crack. "Come on," said Tal gently.

The sweet smell of hay and the soft lowing of the jersey were incongruent with thoughts flying through the man's mind.

Alain still had the quilt wrapped around him as he and Tal entered the barn. Everyone was hiding. "Kids," Tal ordered but in a soft voice. "Y'all come out. It's Tal. I'm here with Alain. We need to talk."

Slowly, the children emerged. Tal took Fay's face in his hands. She looked so much like her mother that his tears flowed unabated. "You'll be okay. I'll always be here for you. I think y'all know I loved Shirley. I'll do everything in my power for you children.

"Everybody, listen to me. Y'all don't know what happened. Y'all were hiding in the barn because you were scared with all the hollering. Do you understand?" asked Tal, urgency tingeing his voice.

The children nodded. Calvin stuttered, "I-i-it's t-t-true. W-w-we d-d-don't know."

"Good," said Tal. "Cal, relax." He patted the boy's shoulder. "You're safe now. He hurt you a lot, too, didn't he, because of your stutter?"

Calvin nodded. "Nobody will ever hurt you again," Tal assured. He turned to Fay. He noticed she was wearing Robert Lee's shirt, and her brother was shirtless. He started to give the boy his shirt but realized his had blood on it.

"Robert Lee, if anyone asks, you were hot. That's why you don't have on a shirt. Fay, all you know is your ma sent you out when your pa hit you. Nobody else has to know he was touching you inappropriately. I'm so sorry. I didn't protect you enough. I didn't realize he was doing that. Tuck the shirt in so it looks like yours."

"It ain't yo fault," said Fay softly.

"Don't let it make you hate men," Tal said fearfully. "We're not all perverts."

"I know."

"Alain," Tal turned to the boy. "You don't know what happened either. Your pa was beating you. Then, he hit Fay. Your ma sent you out. You heard screaming and hollering and two shots. Was it just two?"

"Yes, sir."

"You went in and saw the bodies and came to get me. Do you understand?"

"Yes, sir."

"Everybody else stayed in the barn until I got here. I want you to stay here until I come back to get you. Understand?"

"Yes, sir," said Fay as the others nodded. "Uncle Tal, Polly's hungry. Alain said to give her some cow milk, but I didn't know how."

Tal nodded. "Milk the cow so all of you can have a snack. We'll figure something else later. Dip your finger in and let her suck it off." Tal took the baby who had cried herself to sleep and held her for a moment, and then he kissed her on the forehead. "Daddy's here. I'll take care of you." He looked at all the frightened faces staring at him. "All of you. Robert Lee, milk the cow."

"Yes, sir."

Tal handed Polly back to Fay and put his hand on Alain's shoulder. "We have to go inside."

Alain nodded but shivered.

Tal picked up the lantern on the front porch rail and lit it with the matches that were beside it.

Inside, Tal almost vomited and almost lost control of himself. He had to lean against the wall for several minutes before he stepped carefully around the bodies. He used one of Shirley's potholders to touch anything. He assured the gun in Keenan's hands looked as if he had aimed for himself. The shot had entered under his chin, so it looked self-inflicted. Tal placed it to indicate he had pulled the trigger without help.

Tal softly touched Shirley's hair, and a sob caught in his throat. "I love you so much. Why didn't you leave him? Why didn't I kill him years ago? Oh, baby, I'm so sorry."

"Uncle Tal." Alain's voice quivered when he spoke.

Tal shook his head. "It's Tal from now on. You're the head of your family now. Alain, get some clean clothes. Be careful not to get blood on them. Leave the quilt with me."

Alain came back with clean clothes. "Uncle, I mean, Tal, I ain't got but two pairs of jeans."

"It'll be all right. I'll get you some. Get in the truck." He doused the lantern and put it back on the railing.

Tal stopped at the barn. "Fay, I'm going to get the constable. Remember what I told you. I'll be back soon." He noticed Robert Lee's shirt was tucked into the old jeans the girl had on. It was good the boy had not grown a lot and was about the same size as his sister. Tal nodded his approval. "I'll be back."

Tal stopped by the creek. "Okay, Alain, take off those clothes and wrap them in the quilt. Jump in and wash off good. Then, put your clean clothes on."

While Alain bathed in the creek, Tal made sure his seats were clean and threw all the bloody clothes and quilt in the back. He leaned his hands on the tailgate. Suddenly, he punched the metal repeatedly and screamed over and over.

"Uncle Tal?" Alain called scrambling up the creek bank.

"Sorry." Tal leaned his hands on his knees and caught his breath in gasps. He heaved and finally vomited. Alain popped his hand over his mouth. "Sorry," Tal said again.

"You really loved my ma, didn't you?"

"Yes, Alain, I did. I *do*. Oh, God!" He held his arms out to the boy who fell into them. The two held onto each other for a few minutes. "We need to go," Tal finally whispered as if the forest animals could understand him. Alain slipped into his clean clothes, and they climbed silently into the truck.

Tal stopped at his house. "Stay here, Alain," he said. He took the bundle of bloody clothes in and threw them on the fire Gator had in the fireplace, along with what he was wearing and changed clothes.

"Pa?" Gator questioned.

"Gator, when Alain came, all he asked was for me to go with him. He didn't tell us anything. You got that?"

"Yes, sir. Is that why you're burnin' the clothes?"

"Yes."

"But, Pa, Alain didn't do nothin' wrong. He was defendin' hisself."

"We know that, but we don't want the authorities to ask questions."

"Okay." He pointed around the house. "I cleaned everything."

"You're a good boy. You going with us?"

"Yes, sir. Alain's my friend, and he needs me."

"I'm proud of you, Gator."

"Pa, I'm sorry about Miss Shirley."

"Gator, I really loved her. I won't ever fall in love again. I know how Ina feels now. It hurts too much, but I can't let it show. I won't have anybody talking bad about Shirley."

"You can cry with me, Pa."

"Thanks." Tal hugged Gator. "I love you. *Never* forget that. Let's go."

Driving into town, Tal asked, "What happened, Alain?"

"My pa was mad about somethin'. He hit Fay and me. Ma stood up to him for once and sent us out. We hid in the barn. They were hollerin' and screamin'. Then, there were two shots, and it got quiet. After a while, I had to go see. I looked in and saw 'em and came to git you."

"But I saw your bloody footprints. Did you go near the bodies?"

"Yes, sir. I had to be sure they were dead."

"You've got blisters on your hands. Is that from the gun barrel?"

"Oh." Alain looked at his hands. "No, sir. I grabbed the pot handle this morning at breakfast before I knew it was the one Ma had used."

"Good. Stick to that. How's your breathing?"

"It don't hurt so much. Maybe my ribs ain't broke. Maybe I was just so scared."

"You were in shock. We're all gonna be all right, Alain. We just have to stick together."

Alain nodded.

"Gator?"

Gator nodded.

12

True Lies

In town, Gator said, "Pa, maybe we should git Preacher Tomlin."

"Good idea. I'll get him first."

Tal knocked on Leo Tomlin's door. Knowing it was never good news when he was awakened in the middle of the night, Leo asked anxiously, "Tal, has something happened to Gator?"

"No, Leo." Tal started to cry.

"Tal, step inside."

Tal took several deep breaths. "No, I need Preacher Tomlin. I've got Alain Richter in the truck. Apparently, Keenan went crazy and killed Shirley and himself. Alain's got bruises all over him. Keenan's always beat the kid. I thought his ribs might be broken, but maybe just bruised because he's finally breathing. He was in shock when he came to the house."

"You've been to the Richter place?"

"Yes, I went back with Alain." Tal nodded. "All the other kids are in the barn. They're scared to death. I came for the constable, but they need you."

"Tal, I can't take them in."

"They can't go to a home, and nobody will take all fourteen kids."

"I don't know." Leo covered his mouth in thought.

"I'll take 'em."

"Tal?"

"They can stay at their own place, but I'll check on 'em every day. I gotta get Polly some formula."

"Tal, is there something you aren't saying?"

Tal took a deep breath. "I need my friend, Leo, now. I don't need Preacher Tomlin. I need Leo." He nodded. "I've loved

Shirley for years. We didn't act on it until recently. Polly is my daughter."

"Tal! Good God!" Leo ran his hands through his hair and turned around in a full circle. "Don't let Lucille know she was right."

"I know it was wrong, but I loved Shirley so much. I tried to get her to leave that animal, but she was afraid for her children, especially Alain."

"Did Keenan find out?"

"Maybe. I don't know."

"Oh, Lord, Tal. You could claim her, but *all* the others?"

"They have to stay together."

Leo put a hand on Tal's neck and leaned his forehead against the other man's. "It might work. I'll help all I can. Nobody will hear about you and Shirley from me. Let's get Constable Hill. Is Gator with Alain?"

"Yeah."

Leo hollered up the stairs. "Mac!"

Groggily, Mac said, "Yes, sir?" and came down the stairs.

"Go out to Mr. Jones's truck and stay with Gator and Alain while I go with Mr. Jones to get Constable Hill."

"What happened, Papa?"

"Oh, Mac, it's bad. Alain's father killed Mrs. Richter, then himself. Your friend needs you."

"Yes, sir."

"Put on some clothes quickly. Tal, let me change." He rushed to put on day clothes.

Mac went to Alain while Leo and Tal walked to the constable's house. Leo asked as they walked, "What happened to your hand?"

Tal realized his hand was severely bruised. "I punched the tailgate."

"You sure you didn't punch Keenan?"

"No, Leo, I didn't kill the bastard. I wish I had."

"Try to keep it out of Hill's sight. He might be suspicious."

"Okay."

Leo knocked on the constable's door. Norman Hill jerked the door open. "What's happened?" he asked.

Leo said, "Murder-suicide at the Richter place."

"Alain do something?"

"No!" shouted Tal. "Why would you assume Alain did something other than be Keenan's punching bag, which you never did anything about?"

Leo laid a calming hand on Tal's shoulder. "Tal."

Hill said, "Well, Lucille Dent says…"

Tal roared, "I don't give a damn what that woman says. If she ever said a nice thing about anybody, I'd drop dead of a heart attack on the spot." He rubbed his left shoulder.

"Calm down, Tal," said Leo.

"Who then?" asked the constable.

Huffing, Tal said, "Keenan shot Shirley, then himself."

"You already been out there?"

"Yeah. Alain came to get me. I went out there to see. I was hoping he was wrong. Then, we came here."

"I see. What did the boy tell you?"

"Ask him yourself. That's what you get paid to do."

"Tal, calm," said Leo, rubbing Tal's back.

"It's hard to be calm after seeing that."

Norman saw Tal's hand. "Just how upset are you, Tal?"

"What?"

"How'd you hurt your hand?"

Leo huffed and rolled his eyes.

"I punched the tailgate of my truck after I saw the carnage. I knew something awful would eventually happen out there. I feel like I failed those kids."

"And Shirley?"

"And Shirley, damn it! The bastard beat her. Now, he's killed her, just like two of his other wives, I'm sure. Nobody around here cared enough to investigate."

"I'll go talk to Alain," said the constable. The man threw on his clothes and stomped out. He glared at Tal.

"I ain't exactly a big city cop, you know. I ain't got training or equipment," he said. "And Keenan had alibis for both those times. Maybe folks lied out of fear or stupidity—I don't know. But there wudn't no proof to do anything to that monster."

"Sorry," said Tal. "I know you have limited resources. I'm just upset."

"Understandable. Let me talk to the boy."

The men walked back to Tal's truck where the boys waited. Brusquely, the constable demanded, "Alain, what happened?"

"Norman, that's a child you're addressing," Leo reminded the constable.

"Alain?" Hill said in a softer tone.

"I don't know." Alain shook his head in confusion. "Pa was mad. He hit Fay, and I stepped in. He hit me a bunch of times. Ma jumped on his back and yelled for us to git outa the house. I got all the kids, and we hid in the barn. They yelled and screamed for a while. Then, there were two shots. It got quiet. I waited a long time to hear something else. I was scared." Alain could not help but cry. "I went inside. They were dead."

"Did you touch anything?"

"I don't remember. I walked to 'em to be sure, so I mighta checked for a pulse on Ma. Pa's head's 'bout gone, so there wudn't no doubt 'bout him. Then, I run all the way to Mr. Jones's 'cause he's our friend." Alain cried harder.

"I told you the rest," snapped Tal.

Norman Hill nodded. "Fuck! Sorry, Preacher Tomlin. I gotta go out there and call the coroner and, I guess, Children's Welfare Services."

"No!" said Tal, Leo, and Alain simultaneously.

Firmly Tal added, "I've got the kids."

Hill argued, "Tal, there's fourteen of 'em."

"I know that. I'll work it out. You can't separate them."

"What's gonna become of fourteen kids? Alain's the oldest, and there's a baby."

"We'll work the farm and orchards," said Alain.

"What about school?" asked the constable.

"I'm the only one that's ever went. I guess I've come to an end. I gotta be a man now."

"Alain, no," said Leo.

"I ain't got a choice, Preacher Tomlin. We'll be okay. Jest don't send us to a children's home. Uncle Tal will check on us. We're only a couple of miles up the road. Please, Preacher Tomlin? We gotta be a fam'ly." The boy's voice broke.

Leo nodded. His heart ached for this child who was somewhere between being a boy and a man. "We'll work it out. Norman, no welfare."

"Whatever you say, Preacher Tomlin."

"Excuse me a minute," said Tal. "I gotta wake Royce and get Polly some formula."

Hill asked, "Preacher Tomlin, can I use your phone to call the coroner since I'm right here by your house?"

"Of course. It's on the wall in the kitchen. I'll be here with the kids."

Hill went to make his call.

While Tal talked to Royce Dent and got him to open the store so he could get the baby some formula, Amy watched from her window. She knew something was terribly wrong. Amy peeked around her door to make sure Lucille was not about. Royce held Tal up while he packed cold cuts, bread, and sodas so the other children could have something to eat that night.

"Tal, this is horrible. What else can I do?"

"Tonight, I don't know. We'll have a major clean-up tomorrow."

"Where are the children going to sleep tonight?"

"God! The barn, I suppose."

"Let me send some blankets. Be patient while I pack it up for you. Oh, and don't tell Lucille."

Amy, in her nightgown, dashed out the door to Tal's truck. "Alain!" she shrieked. "What happened? Are you all...oh, my God!" She stopped babbling when she saw the bruises on Alain. The boy's eye was swollen shut, and his lip was still caked with blood even after washing.

"I'm okay," Alain assured her.

Amy demanded furiously, "Mr. Hill, are you gonna put Alain's father in jail?"

"No, Amy," said Alain.

"Why not?" she huffed. "He needs to go to jail."

"He cain't."

"Why?"

"He's in Hell."

"What?"

"He shot my ma and then himself. They're dead."

"Oh, Alain!" She popped her hand over her mouth.

"What do you know about it, Amy?" asked Constable Hill.

"Nothing, except I heard screaming when I road by there on my motor-scooter today."

"Did you hear gunshots?"

"No, I rode by pretty fast because the screaming scared me." Amy stared at Alain. She knew there was more to the story than he could tell her with the constable there.

"What were you doing way out there?"

"Drawing. I do that a lot."

Tal walked up with the boxes of food as Royce brought the blankets and some diapers for the baby. "Amy?" said Royce.

"Daddy?" Amy replied in the same questioning tone.

Royce indicated with a nod for her to go back to the house. "Don't wake your momma," he warned sternly. "What she doesn't know won't hurt her."

"Yes, sir. I'll check on you tomorrow, Alain." Amy went inside, followed closely by her father.

Tal drove back to the Richter place, followed by Hill and Leo Tomlin. First the constable went into the barn and questioned the other children. They apparently knew less than

Alain. He asked candidly, "Fay, why are you wearing a man's shirt, apparently Robert Lee's. Where's yours?"

Fay picked up the torn blouse from behind some hay and handed it to the constable. He asked, "Did Keenan do something really bad, and that's what the fight was about?"

Fay nodded. "But I run out and hid like Ma said. Alain only defended me before Pa hit him, and Ma made us leave. She got the butcher knife after Pa."

"I see. Are you all right?"

"Yes, sir."

"Do I need to take you to a doctor?"

"No! They'll come out here. They'll make us go to a children's home. Please, no?"

Hill exchanged looks with both Leo and Tal. He heaved a great, heavy sigh. "All right, sweetheart. You feed your family while I go inside." Tal left the food with Fay for her to take care of her siblings and followed the constable.

"Stay outside, Tal. Just shine the lanterns in the doorway for me. You too, Preacher Tomlin. I need some light."

Constable Hill shined as much light as he could on the scene and took several pictures with a Polaroid camera. The coroner arrived to take the bodies and his own pictures of the incident. He had to make a preliminary ruling as to cause of death.

Tal went back to the barn and settled the children as the two officials worked. "Mr. Dent sent these blankets," he explained. "Just sleep out here tonight. We'll clean up tomorrow."

"Will you stay?" asked Alain.

"Yes, Gator and I will be here all night."

"Thank you."

Leo put an arm around Alain. "Do you want Mac and me to stay?"

"Would you?"

"Yes, of course."

While the responsible adults settled the children for the night, Constable Hill talked with the coroner. "This is a bloodbath."

"Yeah, gruesome. But it does look like murder-suicide."

"I still think Alain was involved."

The county coroner asked, "Is that the oldest boy?"

"Yeah."

"I got a good look at him. If he killed the bastard who put the bruises on him, good for him. That little girl, the oldest one, has been molested. Maybe she killed him. If so, good for her. If you want me to, I'll check the boy for gunshot residue, but there is no doubt who killed the woman. I see the knife wound in the old goat's leg. He might have bled out without medical care, which this community doesn't have. I don't think he could have gotten himself to Wilmington. Nonetheless, there was a real struggle out here. That man, Jones, might have even been involved. There's too much blood on him to just have walked in here. I saw blood on the boy too. I think he washed it off. Yet, I also see a monster who beat his wife and kids. Look at the woman. Hill, if that boy killed this jackass, he did the world a favor. I still say it was murder-suicide, plain and simple."

Norman Hill looked down at Keenan Richter's body and then toward Shirley's. He kicked the dead man in the buttocks. "I've always wanted to kick his ass." Even he choked back tears at the thought of what might have happened. Being just a couple of years younger than Keenan, he well remember the other murder-suicide at the Richter home. He sent up a silent prayer on behalf of the present generation to be spared such torment and violence. "You're absolutely right." The constable nodded decisively. "This was no doubt a murder-suicide. We're lucky we aren't carting off sixteen bodies. This bloodbath is enough."

13

Girl Talk

The next day Tal came back to town and the general store to order clothes for the Richter children. "Royce, they don't have any to speak of. Keenan never took care of these kids like a father should."

"Tal," Royce spoke in hushed tones, "rumor says you spent a lot of time out there."

"I did. I started the first time Alain came to my place with a broken arm. I was trying to keep the kids safe."

"And Shirley?"

Tal didn't answer but began to gather cleaning supplies. Lucille came in.

"Tal, what are the cleaning supplies for?" Lucille asked, placing a jar of pickled pigs' feet on the counter.

"Stop fishing, Lucille. I'm helping the Richter kids clean up after last night."

"That was such a shame."

"I see your big crocodile tears. Damn you! Shirley was your cousin."

Amy came in wearing a plain, white t-shirt and a pair of cut-off blue jeans with holes in them. "I'm going with you, Mr. Jones," she declared.

"I don't want you near those Richters!" snapped Lucille.

"Lucille!" Tal raised his voice. "Those *Richters* are fourteen orphans now under my care. If you were any kind of Christian, you'd be going."

"I never!"

"I can believe that, but you must have at least once. You had Amy."

"Uh!"

"Lucille," said Royce, "shut up. Amy's going. You go find something to do."

Lucille stomped out. Tal went to the counter. "How much, Royce?"

"No charge, and I've got the clothes covered. I can't go, but I can do this. Amy can go. Keep her straight."

"Thanks, Daddy." Amy smiled.

Tal said, "Wear something you don't mind throwing away."

"I have it on."

"Okay."

Royce said, "Tal, the clothes will be here in about a week. Should I deliver them?"

"To my place."

"Will do."

Tal, Gator, Amy, Leo, Mac, Ina, Tipper, and Grandma Newton arrived to help clean the blood from the Richter home. While the women washed each stitch of cloth in the house, the men scrubbed every surface with bleach, being sure to open all windows and doors. As they worked, Fester Munro drove up. Pure rage emanated from his expression. "I'm here to help take care o' my grandchildren," he growled. "Constable Hill tells me the plan is for 'em to stay here and work the farm and orchards. If the welfare tries to git involved, Tal, you can call on me for backup. I'll be comin' in at least once a week."

Tal nodded at the older man. "Appreciate it."

"Me too," Alain mumbled.

"'Bout time you stepped up," Grandma Newton said. She huffed and snapped her hands to her hips. "Alain, how y'all sleep?"

"Whatcha mean?"

"Boys and girls?"

"Oh. That big sheet y'all washed separates our areas."

"Like two big rooms?"

"Yes, ma'am."

"You take your ma and pa's room. You the man of the house now." She ran her hand back and forth in a line. "Build a wall at least to separate boys and girls. Y'all need more privacy."

"Yes, ma'am."

"How y'all feedin' the baby?"

"Tal got formula."

"Okay." The old matriarch put a hand on the boy's shoulder. "You ain't quite grown, Alain Richter. I'll do anything I can to help. You jest come to me."

"Yes, ma'am."

"What about school?"

"I'm done."

"No, no."

"Yes, ma'am. I gotta be."

"Don't throw yo future away."

"I ain't. It's jest on hold."

"I guess I understand." She rubbed the boy's back. "You're a good boy. Never doubt it."

"Yes, ma'am."

"Let's git busy and finish cleanin'."

Amy went with Fay to gather eggs. She gazed at Fay questioningly. "Fay, are you okay?"

"No, Amy, I won't never be okay."

"Why? What did he do?"

Fay began to cry. Amy put her arms around the childhood playmate. "Talk to me."

"Please, don't tell nobody."

"I promise."

"He used me like his wife."

"Do you mean sex?"

"Yeah."

"Oh, Fay!" Amy stroked the other girl's long dark hair. "How long?"

"The first time was the day we went swimmin'. Do you remember?"

"Yeah." She reached into the nest and deposited an egg in her basket.

"Alain tried to save me. Alain has always tried to save me."

"Alain's a good man."

"He *is* a man now. He's gotta be. He needs a good womern."

"Fay, he's fourteen."

"He's old enough."

Amy paused in gathering eggs. "Did you have someone in mind?"

"You."

"I'm only thirteen like you. Do you have your eye on someone?"

"Gator, but now he won't want me. I been ruined."

"No, you haven't. You've been hurt. Maybe if Gator knew the whole truth, it wouldn't matter. Maybe he would rescue you like a musketeer."

"Amy, I ain't no damsel in distress." The hen clucked and pecked Fay's hand. She pushed the fat bird off. "The only musketeer I ever knew was my brother."

"Gator's a sweetheart."

"Like his pa."

"Whatcha mean?"

"Never mind."

"Did Mr. Jones love your ma?" Amy pulled her hand quickly from beneath another fussy fowl.

"Yeah, and she loved him."

"Is that what the fight was about?"

"No. She caught him with me. At least this time, she stopped him. Thank God I ain't never got pregnant."

Amy put her hands on her hips. "You should go to school now."

"I don't think so. I read, you know, and do math. Alain taught me, and I taught the others."

"I wish Alain wouldn't drop out. I only get to see him on the bus. Momma, well, you know how she is."

"Mean," said Fay, depositing an egg in the basket.

"Yeah."

"Do you like Alain?"

"Yeah."

"Show him."

"I brought him something special."

"That'll make him feel better. He's got a lot on him."

"So do you."

"I'll be okay...eventually."

Amy and Fay held hands as they walked back to the house with a basketful of eggs.

Grandma Newton and Ina Campbell prepared a meal for the Richter children and hung clean curtains and put clean sheets on the beds, tying the sheets over the ends of the army cots. With the house clean, the friends prepared to leave. Amy came to Alain and took his hand. She whispered, "I have something for you. It's in Mr. Jones's truck."

"What?"

"Come out with me while everybody's fixin' the beds. They won't miss us for a minute."

Alain went to the truck with Amy where she retrieved the painting of the boys and the raft. She had matted and framed it. "That was your birthday, wasn't it?"

"Yeah."

"Happy birthday. Hang it on your wall."

Alain blinked hard not to cry in front of Amy. "Thank you," he said huskily. "That was the happiest day of my life."

"Why?"

"My friends. I was so free. You."

"Me?"

"Yeah. I like to watch you draw. I can tell that's when you're happy."

"Yes, it is. I thought it was because I touched you." She nibbled her index finger.

Alain smiled. "That was nice too."

"Are you gonna be all right?"

"I gotta be." Alain bit his lip.

"Alain, it's all right to cry," Amy said softly.

Alain broke down. Amy hugged him and let him sob on her shoulder as she stroked his hair that hung below his shoulders. She whispered in his ear, "One day, Alain Richter, I'm gonna kiss you."

Alain choked through his tears, "One day, Amy Dent, I'll kiss you back."

Alain's three friends began to look for him before they left. When they saw him with Amy, Tipper scowled. Mac whispered, "He needs her right now."

"I know," said Tipper grudgingly. "I still don't like it."

Leo murmured, "Never let a woman come between you and your friends. Tipper, Alain just lost both parents. Who needs a hug more right now?"

"Preacher Tomlin, I know, but I'm still jealous. I'll get over it."

"I'm sure you will."

Amy lightly brushed her lips against Alain's cheek. "I gotta go."

"Thank you, Amy, for everything."

As all the people left, Fay walked outside with Alain and put her arm around his waist. He put his arm around her shoulders. "You okay?" she asked.

"Yeah." Alain showed her the picture. "See what Amy drew for me."

"I like Amy."

"Me too. Did y'all have a good girl talk?"

"Yeah. Are you gonna court her?"

Alain laughed bitterly. "Can you picture Lucille's face?"
"Not really."
"I'll see, Fay. I'll see."

14

Avoiding the Welfare

Once the coroner released the bodies of Keenan and Shirley Richter a month after their deaths, which had been ruled officially murder-suicide, Leo Tomlin performed a solemn funeral. There were few mourners, and Leo's words offered little comfort. The only people who attended the funeral besides the Richter children were Tal and Gator Jones, Ina and Tipper Campbell, MacKenzie Reardon, Royce and Amy Dent, Norman Hill, Grandma Newton, Fester Munro, and a woman that nobody knew.

Before the graves were dug, Alain spoke to Leo with a solemn request. "Preacher Tomlin, I don't want my pa buried beside my ma. Can we put him in the back with his fam'ly? I know that sounds weird, but I jest feel like it's an insult to my ma to have her murderer beside her." The boy rubbed his eyes to stem tears. "Besides, if you notice, his other four wives are buried behind June Jones. There ain't room for Ma beside them. I think Tal would appreciate Ma bein' next to him someday. Leave a space between Gator's ma and my ma for Tal."

The pastor scrutinized this boy before him. Obviously, Alain knew more about Tal and Shirley than he would say aloud. He beckoned Tal to join them and relayed Alain's request.

Tal nodded. "That suits me fine." Leo consented to the separation of burial sites.

Thus, Shirley was buried next to June Jones with a space between June and Shirley for Tal, and Keenan's remains joined his slaughtered family from decades earlier. Grandma Newton nodded her approval toward Alain. He felt some relief having her agreement.

Alain drove his father's truck into town with most of his siblings in the back. Fay, Debbie, and Polly rode in the cab with him.

After the funeral, Royce put a hand on Alain's shoulder. "You drivin' now?"

"I gotta, but I been drivin' a long time."

"Of course, you have. Do y'all need anything?"

"Not right now. Thank you, Mr. Dent."

Royce went on to the store where Lucille worked, having refused to attend the funeral. Amy stayed with Alain.

"So, you really aren't goin' back to school?" she asked.

"I cain't. I gotta take care of my fam'ly."

"How am I gonna see you? You gonna come into town?"

"You want me to?"

"Yeah."

"Your ma won't like it."

"We'll be sneaky."

"I promised Preacher Tomlin we'd be in church, so that will give us Sundays."

"And Momma will probably make a scene." Amy rolled her eyes.

"School starts next week." Alain put his hands in his pockets.

"Yeah." Amy looked at him expectantly.

"Be at the fishin' hole next Friday at sunset. I'll meet you there."

"Okay."

Alain looked up. "That strange womern is headed over here. Who is she?"

"I don't know. I better go. See you next Friday."

"Sunday." Alain gave her a wink.

"Alain Richter?" the woman asked as Amy ducked behind Alain's truck to listen.

"Yes, ma'am."

"I'm Carla Stokes with the county Children's Welfare Services. I've come to take you children into custody."

"You what?" Alain shouted, drawing attention to the situation.

"It's been reported that fourteen minors are living at your place without adult supervision. I've come to take you to the children's home in Wilmington."

"We ain't goin'," said Alain defiantly.

"Young man!"

"No ma'am! Uncle Tal!"

Tal came to Alain and the woman. "What's wrong, Alain?" Tal asked.

"This womern says she's come to take us. She's from the welfare."

"Ma'am, that's not necessary. I'm caring for my nieces and nephews."

"Mister?"

"Tal Jones."

"Mr. Jones, I'm Carla Stokes. We had a report that fourteen children were living at the Richter farm without an adult since their parents' tragic deaths."

"That's not true. The children are under my care. Who told you such a thing?"

"I'm not at liberty to tell you who filed the report."

"I can guess." Tal turned a scathing gaze toward the general store. "Lucille Dent is an evil, vindictive woman. Shirley Richter was her cousin, but she refuses to lift a finger to help these children. I'm taking care of them."

"Do you live with them?"

"I live two miles down the road, but I am with them every day."

"Are they in school?"

"We home-school. Miss Stokes, the county has never cared that these kids were not in school. Why now?"

"We never had a report before. I need to inspect the premises."

"No, ma'am, you don't." Tal folded his arms across his chest.

"Mr. Jones. Tal Jones? Talmage Jones, running back for the University of Florida?"

"The same."

"Well, that's where I went to school."

"Good to hear. Miss Stokes, you don't need to bother these kids. It wouldn't be safe for you to go to Richter Farms and Orchards. You're a woman alone in the hills of Appalachia. There are those who would do you harm."

"Is that a threat?"

"No, ma'am," he growled. "A word to the wise. Don't send a man out there either. He might be mistaken for a G-man. There are moonshiners in these hills who would shoot him on sight, and his body would never be found. You need to heed my words."

Leo joined the tête-á-tête. "Tal, is something wrong?"

"Preacher Tomlin, this is Carla Stokes with the county welfare office. It appears Lucille filed a report."

Leo took the woman's hand. "Miss Stokes, let me assure you that you have nothing to fear concerning these children. In addition to Tal, I'm checking on them, as are their grandparents." Leo motioned Miriam Newton and Fester Munro to join them.

"Carla Stokes, meet Miriam Newton, the children's great-great-grandmother and Fester Munro, their grandfather. As you can see, the children have family and friends caring for them. You have no reason to worry."

Carla Stokes scowled. "I don't believe a word of it, but I feel I'm fighting a losing battle."

"Miss Stokes, I'm a man of God. Do you think I'm lying to you?" Leo's eyebrows shot toward his hairline.

"The person who filed the report said they had no family."

Fester spit a line of tobacco near the woman's shoe. She jumped back. "Miss Stokes, Shirley was my daughter. And if you really care, you can call me Judge Munro. I'm a municipal judge."

"Miss Stokes," grunted Grandma Newton, "I assure you these kids have lots of family takin' care of 'em. I cain't believe a young woman like you would question the integrity of a man of the cloth like Dr. Leo Tomlin. You best be headin' to the city now."

"Mrs. Newton, what do you do?"

"That would be *Ms.* Newton. I own the slaughterhouse, and I'm on the city council. You have overstayed your welcome. Git! I said, 'Git'!" She shook her cane in the air. "Don't make me git my shotgun."

"You wouldn't!"

"I would."

Leo could not help but laugh when the social worker squealed her tires leaving. "Grandma Newton, I thought I was too damned young to be a preacher."

"You still a whippersnapper, but a damned good man, Leo Tomlin. I cain't believe some womern ain't snapped you up. Alain, you okay?"

"Yes, ma'am. Were you really gonna git your shotgun?"

"I don't bluff. If she comes back, I'll give her a buttload full of buckshot. Keep yours loaded, baby boy. Right now, I'm goin' to give another womern a load full of what I think of her. Lucille Dent, I'm a'comin'!" The old woman hobbled off, leaning on her cane.

Tal put his arm around Alain. "I told you I'd take care of you. Now, you see. We're all behind you."

"Thanks."

"There are two boxes of prepared food in your truck. Are y'all ready to go?"

"Yes, sir. You and Gator gonna stay and eat with us?"

"Of course, we are."

Alain looked at Fester. "Fester, are you really my grandpa?"

"I doubt it, Alain, but I could be. I lay with Beverly 'bout the time Shirley woulda been conceived. I don't usually have nights with my girls, but Bev, she was special. That's why I made Keenan marry Shirley, 'cause maybe she was *mine*. Miss Stokes don't need to know no diff'rent. She don't have to know I wudn't married to Bev. If she asks, I'm your grandpa, and proud to be so. And I'm still buyin' cider. That'll supplement y'all's income."

"Thank you, sir. You gonna come eat?"

"Am I invited?"

"Yes, Grandpa."

"Like Miriam said—Load the gun. Avoid the welfare. Keep your family together. Grandpa will be there in an hour." Fester laughed as he left the group.

Alain looked at Leo. "Preacher Tomlin, you did lie."

"I had never heard the whole story about Fester and your mother. Even now, as far as I know, Fester's your grandfather. Y'all have the same eyes. That's genetic proof. Grandma Newton is everybody's grandmother."

"Thank you jest the same."

"I'm here for you. Alain, I expect to see y'all in church."

"That won't be easy."

"Try."

"Yes, sir."

15

Romeo and Juliet

For the next year, Alain dragged his family to church. It was one way he could sneak a little time with Amy. Amy, Mac, and Tipper sailed along in ninth grade while Gator plodded through sixth grade again and brought his lessons home every night for Alain who made his younger siblings study around the table. Working together, the Richter children brought in a good harvest and got their produce to market with Tal Jones's help to make sure nobody tried to cheat Alain, although Alain still remembered and pointed out the officials that had manipulated his father. Every Friday, Alain and Amy met somewhere.

At Harvest Fest, Alain and Amy sneaked off on a hayride right under Lucille's nose. Farmer Maddox clicked the mules to a gallop before anyone else could get into the wagon.

"Buster Maddox," said Alain, "I didn't pay for a whole wagon."

"Oops! I thought it was full. Oh, well. Smooch with your girlfriend, Alain. I still remember Shirley puttin' Lucille in her place. Take advantage of the time."

Alain sank into the hay and pulled a blanket over him and Amy. "Am I your girlfriend, Alain?" asked Amy.

"I wish I was brave enough to ask your pa, but I'm scared of your ma."

Amy snuggled close to Alain and laid her head on his shoulder. He put his arm around her and inhaled. "You smell like rose petals."

"My bath soap is rose scented."

"I like it."

"You smell like the woods."

"Bad?"

"No, rugged."

"I don't have cologne."

"Hmm. Christmas is coming."

"Are you gonna buy me cologne?"

"I might."

"Amy, I don't got a lot of money."

"I don't need money, Alain." She ran her hand back and forth across the boy's chest in absent-minded caresses. "You take care of the little kids. Don't worry about me."

"I think about you all the time."

"Really? What do you think?"

"How pretty you are. How much I'd like you to touch me again."

"Alain!" Amy blushed.

"You asked."

"Do you think about touching me?"

"Yeah. Then, I see this big ugly witch choppin' off my hands with an ax."

"Alain Richter!" Amy took Alain's hand and placed it on her breast. "Like this?"

"Almost. Mm. They feel good." Alain ran his hand across Amy's breasts.

Amy sighed. "It does feel good."

"I think about touchin' your skin. I saw 'em. Remember?"

"I remember. So did your friends."

"Yeah. Well. I'd just as soon they not see them again."

"Jealous?"

"Only of Tipper."

"Alain!"

"Mac and Gator ain't interested in you."

"You think Tipper is?"

"I *know* Tipper is."

"I'm not on a hayride with Tipper."

"True." Alain eased his hand under Amy's sweater. "You're wearin' a bra."

"Yeah."

"That makes things harder."

"You do this often?"

"No." The boy could feel his own face burn.

"Hey, kids, we're back," warned Buster Maddox. "Jump over the side before I pull in. That way Lucille won't see you."

Alain and Amy jumped over the side and headed back to the dunking booth. "Amy," said Alain, "it's gittin' a bit cold for meetin' at the fishin' hole. Friday after school, meet me at the bridge over the big creek. I wanna show you somethin'."

"Okay. See you then."

Amy met Alain at the bridge. "Whatcha got to show me?" she asked.

Alain took her hand. "Come on. We gotta hike."

Alain led Amy upstream to the musketeer camp. "What's this?" asked Amy.

"Our clubhouse. We ain't been here since we went raftin'. It's sheltered. I thought we could meet here since it's gittin' colder."

"What about winter?"

"Would you come to the Reardon place? I could build a fire there."

"Yes, I'll come."

"Amy, I really like you."

"I like you, Alain. I always have."

"Why?" He cocked his head to the side. "I ain't good-lookin' like Tipper."

"Yes, you are. You have the most beautiful eyes." She ran her index finger along his eyebrow.

"You think so?"

"Uh-hum."

"You're jest plain beautiful."

"Do you want to see me again?"

"Oh!" The boy's eyes popped wide.

"You seem surprised."

"I am a little. Maybe we should slow down before we do something we'll regret."

"Like what?"

"Amy, I'm a man. I git man urges."

"Oh," she said, putting her hand to her mouth. "I ain't ready for that."

"I know. So, let's jest snuggle up like always. We ain't got the safety of Mr. Maddox."

"You respect me?"

"Course, I do. You're a real lady, Amy. A real queen. One day, Amy Dent, I'm gonna kiss you."

"One day, Alain Richter, I'll kiss you back."

Amy and Alain met at the clubhouse until it got too cold. Then, they moved to the old Reardon place. The Friday before Christmas, it snowed, but Amy still trudged to the Reardon place with a gift in her hand. Breathlessly, Alain popped in a little later. Amy had started a fire.

"Oh!" he gasped. "I wudn't sure you'd make it."

"I would've had to be snowbound not to come. Merry Christmas, Alain." She handed her gift to him.

"Oh. Thanks. I got you somethin'."

"I told you not to." She arched her eyebrow.

"I made it." Alain handed Amy a box without wrapping. "I didn't have no fancy paper."

"It doesn't matter. Open yours first."

"Okay." Inside was a bottle of Polo cologne. Alain sprayed a little on himself. "Mm. You like this?"

"It smelled real good," said Amy.

"I'll wear it every time I see you. Your turn."

Amy opened her package to find a trinket box made of black walnut with a rose carved on top. Alain said, "It's to hold your rose soap."

"It's beautiful, Alain." Amy blinked back tears.

"You ain't supposed to cry," said Alain frantically.

"I'm not crying. I'm happy. You made this for me." She clutched the gift to her chest. "It came from your heart. I'll cherish it always."

"Maybe I should put my heart inside it."

"Alain."

"Amy, I..."

"Don't say it. It'll jinx it."

The slamming of a car door scared both kids. The door swung open. "Good God!" exclaimed Tal, startled by their presence. "I didn't know who was in here. What are y'all doing?"

"Exchanging Christmas gifts so Momma won't know," said Amy honestly.

"You'll get in trouble sneaking around," said Tal.

"Mr. Jones, you know my momma would have a fit about me and Alain."

"Yeah. So, Alain, talk to Royce."

"You think I should?" asked Alain.

"Definitely. You two ain't done nothing, have you?"

"No, sir!" exclaimed Alain. "I ain't even kissed her."

"Okay." He held up a hand. "Calm down. Kissing's okay. Sorry I interrupted. I was heading to your place and saw the smoke."

"I need to get back," said Amy. "Merry Christmas, Alain. Merry Christmas, Mr. Jones."

"Merry Christmas, Amy," said Tal and nodded his head for Alain to follow the girl out. He whispered, "There's probably mistletoe in the trees."

Alain grabbed Amy's hand. "Merry Christmas, Amy." He looked up.

"What are you doing?"

"Looking for mistletoe."

Amy laughed. "One day, Alain Richter, I'm gonna kiss you."

"One day, Amy Dent, I'm gonna kiss you back."

Amy had left her motor scooter by the ancient oak. She hopped on and drifted away into the flurries that were coming down again.

Tal came outside. "I doused the fire."

"Obliged."

"How long have you two been meeting up?"

"Since school started back."

"Do you love her?" Tal placed a hand on the boy's shoulder.

"More than anything."

"Oh, Alain, that's trouble waiting to happen."

"Not if Miss Lucille would die."

Tal laughed. "Yeah, Lucille's a pain in the ass. Talk to Royce *soon*. If Lucille gets wind of your clandestine rendezvous, all hell will break loose. Be careful. I know how it feels to have to take stolen moments."

"You really did love my ma, didn't you?"

"Yes, I did. I tried to get her to divorce Keenan. I would have found a way to take care of all of y'all."

"You've been the only father I've ever known. One day, Amy will be mine. I'll never hit her. I'll love my children the way you do. I'll never hit one of 'em."

Tal moved his hand to Alain's neck. The boy was taller than he was. Still, he pulled Alain into fatherly arms. "You're a good boy, Alain. I wish you were mine. I love you."

Alain Richter fell apart in Tal Jones's embrace six months after his mother's murder. Tal let him cry. Tal cried with him.

Tal and Gator celebrated Christmas Day at the Richters' farm. They prepared a huge meal and had small gifts for every child, such as coloring books and crayons; puzzles; jacks; card games; a bingo game; pocketknives; embroidery thread, needles, and patterns; checkers; and candy canes and chocolate covered cherries for everyone. The Richter children had never had gifts to open on Christmas Day. They felt rich.

Fester put in an appearance with a new outfit and shoes for each child and gladly joined the festivities.

Ina Campbell and Grandma Newton had worked to either make a quilt or a knitted blanket for each child, and Leo Tomlin joined the gift-giving with New Testaments with for each child with his or her name printed on it. Tal delivered these along with his.

A car door's slamming startled all of them as they fellowshipped around the table. Tal picked up his shotgun from the mantle where he had laid it, and Alain got his off the hooks above the fireplace. Fay looked out the window.

"Who is it, Fay?" asked Tal.

"That womern from the welfare and a man."

Tal snorted. "Well, she didn't come alone. Open the door, Fay."

"I left my gun in the car," Fester growled. "Didn't think I'd need it on Christmas Day."

As Carla Stokes lifted her hand to knock, she was met by two double-barrel shotguns in her face. Tal snarled, "I told you not to come back. What did you expect to find?"

"Mr. Jones, I had to check on these children."

"On Christmas Day? Very unlikely. Are you in need of family on this day? As you can see, I'm with my family. We're celebrating our Savior's birth. Maybe we don't have fifty gifts per child, but everybody has a gift, and we have a bountiful table. This house is small and rather cramped, or I would love to invite you and your friend to dine with us. Under the circumstances though, seeing as how you're uninvited, get the hell away from here. Next time, I will shoot you for trespassing."

"Mr. Jones!"

Tal fired the first barrel over the woman's head. The man scurried for the car.

"Miss Stokes, do you know anything about shotguns?" Tal asked without changing his tone of voice.

"No."

"Let me explain. Shotguns are designed to take out a large target with many small pellets in a single shell. Even a novice almost can't miss. I am *not* a novice. That was one barrel. I have two. Each barrel contains a cartridge. Alain has two. Unfortunately, Fester left his in his vehicle. If I had not wanted to give a warning, I could have pulled the second trigger quickly, and I would have hit your scrambling friend. Alain is a hunter. He knows how to pull his triggers in fast succession so he can bring down a buck for food. Now, leave."

Carla Stokes stayed rooted to the porch. "Carla!" the man called from the car. "Don't be stupid. I told you hillbillies would be hostile."

Tal smirked. His next shot took out the rear driver's side window of the sedan in the yard. Tal leaned his gun against the door frame and took Alain's gun. "Miss Stokes, I don't miss unless I mean to." Tal pointed the gun directly at Carla Stokes's chest and let his eyes appear to rove. "That's a pretty large target."

Carla Stokes screamed and ran to the car. Tal shut the door. "Do y'all know any Christmas carols? Sing for the old bat."

In a beautiful soprano, Fay began, "Angels we have heard on high…"

Tal sat down at the table as she sang. "Alain, bring out the cider. I'll teach you how to make a Christmas delight using it called wassail."

Alain and Amy continued to meet every Friday, even sneaking into Grandma Newton's root cellar during the spring rains. As the weather improved, Amy took her art supplies out every afternoon so that Friday appeared no different.

Hog Rendering came and Amy and Alain took advantage of the crowd to dance with each other. Amy danced with Gator, Mac, and Tipper as well, but Lucille flew into a rage when Alain snagged Amy for a second dance. She jerked Amy away declaring, "Git home! You ain't dancing with that good-for-nothing trash again."

"Momma!" cried Amy. "Alain's a good person."

Lucille popped Amy on the mouth, and Tal had to restrain Alain to keep him from hitting Lucille. "Let it go." Tal prodded, "She'll cause trouble for you. I told you to talk to Royce."

"She's always around."

"So? Just knock on their door and tell Royce you need to speak to him in private. You're gonna lose the girl if you don't act soon."

Alain considered how to talk to Royce Dent and shared his plan with Amy as they met under the little creek bridge. First, Amy handed him a large box. "Happy birthday!" she chirped.

"You remembered it's my birthday?"

"Of course, I did. It's hard to forget what happened last year on this day. Open it."

She gave him a new pair of jeans and a Kelly-green, button-down shirt. "Nice," said Alain, "but green?"

"To show off your eyes. You have beautiful eyes. Lavender would have been even better."

"Thanks. Amy, I've decided to talk to your pa today. Will you let me court you?"

"Yes. It's taken you long enough."

Alain smiled and his eyes sparkled. "I promised to kiss you. Can I kiss you?"

"Yes."

Alain leaned in to kiss Amy just as Lucille shrieked, "No! You will not kiss her, and you will not court her!"

Lucille dragged Amy from under the bridge and began to whack her with a switch.

"Stop it!" yelled Alain. "Don't you hit her!"

"Listen to me, Alain Richter," Lucille spat venomously, pointing the switch at him. "If you so much as speak to Amy again, I'll call the welfare down on you. I'll make sure the state police come with Miss Stokes. You little varmints will be sent off to a home, maybe fourteen different homes if I have a say. Don't cross me, boy! I'm sure you're a killer, and God only knows what y'all do out there with your sisters. But you won't do it with Amy. Do I make myself clear?"

"Momma, stop!" Amy wailed. "I love him."

"No you don't. He's trash. You won't stay here and be pulled into this Godforsaken life. Now, git home." She jabbed the switch sharply in Alain's direction. "You git back to that farm and don't come back. You need to make a choice—Amy or your family. I'll make it for you, and it ain't Amy. When the state police come, Tal Jones will go to jail. Uncle Tal! He might be the daddy of some of y'all, but he ain't no uncle. If Fester is your grandpa, he runs an unlicensed honky-tonk. He'll go to jail too. Judge? Only because he's crooked. Miriam Newton is just an old busybody. They'll jest cart her off to an old folks' home. And I'm sure I can find something to pin on the hypocrite preacher we have."

"You're meaner than my pa," yelled Alain. "Look what happened to him."

"You threatening me, boy? I'll have you put in jail too. Then, you heathens will be sent off for sure."

Lucille turned to Amy. "I said for you to git home!"

"I'm sorry, Alain," Amy wept as Lucille forced her home with blows from a hickory switch.

"Amy!" Alain's voice echoed miserably. The sadness pierced Amy's heart.

In panic, Alain ran all the way home where he instantly armed himself and waited. He didn't know what else to do.

16
Brotherly Love

Fay Richter asked in almost as much panic as her brother, "Alain, what's wrong?"

Alain snatched the shotgun from the hooks and loaded both barrels. "Lucille Dent!"

"What'd she do this time?" The girl's voice sounded tired.

"She caught me and Amy. She said she's callin' the welfare and the state police."

"Go git Uncle Tal."

"No! She said she'd have him put in jail. Grandpa Fester too, and Grandma Newton in an old folks' home."

"Alain, Lucille might be mean and rich, but she ain't that powerful. What she say 'bout Preacher Tomlin?"

"That she'd find something to pin on him. She called him a hypocrite."

"Go git him anyway. He ain't scared of her."

"I cain't leave y'all."

"Alain, ain't nobody comin' out today. Even if'n they come, they gotta come from the city." Fay shook her head in disbelief. "You cain't let her git to you."

"Not the state police," he argued. "They could be right down the road. If they git a call on the radio in their car, they come. That Tench fella left here. Ain't he a sheriff or something? I seen him at Fester's a couple times."

"Alain, you gotta calm down." She slapped the dishtowel she had in her hand against her leg.

"I want you to git the kids inside."

"Whatcha gonna do? Lock us in forever?"

"I don't know, Fay. Y'all my responsibility. I gotta take care o' you." He rubbed the heel of his hand across his eyes to stop the tears that threatened to spill.

"What about Amy?"

Alain shook his head hard. "Amy? I guess I made my choice. I have to choose my fam'ly. Lucille's seen to that. I hate that womern. I hope she dies a slow agonizing death. She don't deserve to be shot. She needs to suffer."

"Alain, you scarin' me. I thought you were happy. You ain't been angry since Pa died."

Silent tears dripped down Alain's cheeks. "It couldn't last. It was a dream. I woke up." He wiped his face with an angry swipe.

"Give me the gun, Alain." She held out her hand. "Ain't nobody comin'. It's dark."

"You make supper. I ain't lettin' go o' this gun."

Fay fried the fish Calvin and Robert Lee had caught and cleaned earlier in the day. She made cornbread, boiled new potatoes, and sliced cucumbers and tomatoes. All during supper, Alain stared out the window. The younger children ate in silence, sensing their brother's fear. Fay brought a plate to Alain. "You gotta eat. Give me the gun. I'll keep watch."

Alain nodded. He ate while the other children bathed on the back porch. Male and female anatomical differences were perfectly clear to the Richter children. There was no privacy, even with the wall built at Grandma Newton's suggestion. It was no more than several sheets of plywood with white paint slapped on them.

After Alain ate, he took up his watchful post, and Fay cleaned the kitchen before she put everybody else to bed. She escaped to wash on the back porch.

When she returned, Alain still stood stiffly and stared into the darkness. Fay put her hand on Alain's shoulder. "Ain't nobody comin' tonight. It's almost midnight. Alain, let me take care o' you."

"How can you do that?"

"Give me the gun." Alain finally relinquished his vigil, and Fay returned the gun to its hooks. Alain sank into a chair at the table.

Fay walked behind him and massaged his shoulders. "You need to relax. Let me take care o' you. I'll make you forget."

He rubbed his hands across his face. At fifteen, he actually had evening stubble. "I cain't forget, Fay. There's too much to remember."

"Amy?"

"I love her, Fay." Alain sighed again. "Did she tell you when y'all talked what happened on my birthday last year?"

"No."

"She touched me."

"She touched you?"

"Without my clothes. She went skinny dipping with us. Oh, Fay, she's so beautiful."

"All o' y'all saw her naked?" She stepped back. "Who else did she touch?"

"Jest me. We only saw her for a second before she made us turn around, but I'll never forget how beautiful she was. Now, I've lost her."

Fay laid a hand on her brother's head. "Sh. Let me help."

"How?"

"Trust me, Alain. Come on." Fay took Alain's hand and led him to the bed Shirley and Keenan had used.

"Wahtcha doin?" asked Alain.

"Alain, you've always sacrificed for me. You took beatin's for me. I love you, Alain. This is the only way I know to show you."

"No, Fay. It ain't right."

"Do you love me?"

"Of course, I love you."

"Then, trust me. Let me take care o' you. We cain't count on nobody else without hurtin' 'em. Lay down. I'll take care o' you."

Alain lay back on the bed. Tears streamed down his face. "Don't cry," soothed Fay. "I'll take care o' you, always."

Alain felt Fay unzip his jeans. He felt her hands on him and closed his eyes and remembered Amy's touch. He breathed,

"Amy." Then, he felt himself inside Fay. The release was bittersweet.

Alain slept.

Fay shook Alain gently. "Time to git up."

Alain groaned, "Oh," and turned over. He drew himself into a ball and moaned, "I'm sick."

Alain vaulted from the bed and vomited over the side of the back porch. Fay followed him. "Alain, what's wrong?" She reached out to comfort him.

"Don't touch me! Oh, God!" Alain sobbed. "I'm as disgusting as Lucille said."

"No you ain't! You a wonderful man."

Alain screamed, "I'm your brother! Fay, what we done was wrong. It cain't never happen again."

"You don't love me no more."

"Fay, I will always love you, but not like that."

"Alain, you the only man I trust. Ain't nobody gonna want me after what Pa done. I ain't purty like Amy, but I won't never betray you. I know you won't never hurt me. You won't hit me, and you won't force me."

"Fay!" Alain screamed in exasperation, fisting his hands against his temples. "Don't you realize I did hurt you already? I love you, Fay, but that ain't brotherly love. That love'll send us to Hell. If the welfare finds out about that, they'll put me in jail."

"Why? I done it. They can put *me* in jail."

"No! I don't know what to do. That just cannot happen again."

"Didn't I please you?"

Alain banged his fists against his head. He was so frustrated with trying to explain. "Fay!" Alain ground his teeth. "That ain't the point."

"I don't mind if'n you call me Amy."

"Oh! Amy? She'll *never* be mine now. She'll hate me. Even if Lucille dies, I've lost Amy. How could I do that?"

"I won't tell nobody. I won't do it again, but if'n you want me, okay."

Fay went to the well and drew a bucket of water. Alain went back to bed. He curled into the fetal position and slept all day.

Many months passed. Alain stopped going into town. Tal and Gator picked up supplies for the children. The Richters even stopped coming to church. Leo drove to their place, but Alain would only talk to him in the yard.

School started back with Amy, Tipper, and Mac in high school and Gator in seventh grade. On the bus, Amy sat beside Gator. "Whatcha want?" asked Gator in a hostile growl.

"Did Alain send a message for me?"

"No. He's shut them off out there. All I know is that yo ma had somethin' to do with it. Alain, Robert Lee, and Calvin all carry shotguns now."

With quavering voice, Amy said, "Oh, Gator. Momma caught Alain and me together. She threatened to call the welfare lady and the law. She threatened to have your pa and Fester put in jail and Grandma Newton in an old folks' home, and even Preacher Tomlin."

"I'd like to see her try," huffed Gator. "When Pa or me goes out there, Alain talks to us. He takes supplies. Yeah, he lets the little kids see Pa, but they like hermits, though I guess you cain't be a hermit if there are fourteen of you. I'm scared for him, Amy. Did your ma call the welfare?"

"I don't know. She beat me. Daddy was furious and put his foot down, but he told me the next boy I step out with has to get his permission. Gator, he would've given Alain permission. Have I lost him? I miss him." Amy shed honest tears.

"You want me to talk to him?" Gator's tone softened.

"Please?"

"I'll try. He won't even let me see Fay. He says he's protectin' her."

"How?"

"I don't know." Gator folded his arms across his chest.

"You like Fay?"

"Yeah. She's purty."

"I told her somebody would like her."

"Why wouldn't they?"

"Her pa."

"What about him?"

"Don't you know, Gator? Don't you know what he did to her?"

"He beat her."

"Worse."

"I know he raped her, Amy." Gator hit the seat with his fist.

"Yes."

"It wudn't her fault."

"Maybe he felt guilty, and that's why Keenan killed himself."

Gator snorted.

"Gator, did Keenan shoot himself?"

"Looked like it."

"Did you see them, the bodies I mean?"

"No, pa wouldn't let me go with him and Alain. He said I didn't need to see it. He was right. The next day with all that blood was bad enough."

"The old goat deserved to die." Amy huffed in anger. "I just find it hard to believe he killed himself. He was too damned mean for that."

"That's what the authorities ruled."

"Oh, my God! Alain *did* kill him." She set her jaw and nodded defiantly. "It was self-defense though. It had to be because Alain's too sweet to kill anybody unless he had to."

"Keenan deserved to die. Pa woulda killed him if he had known about Fay."

"Your pa didn't kill him, did he?"

"No. It was a murder-suicide."

"Gator, which ones are your brothers and sisters?"

"What do you mean?"

"I know about your pa and Miss Shirley. I think it's romantic in a way. I'm glad somebody loved her. Don't worry. I won't tell Momma."

Gator relaxed a little beside Amy. "Only Polly, though Pa feels responsible for takin' care of the others. He made Miss Shirley a promise."

"So, they weren't lovers for at least five years?"

"Close, and real good friends, but not in that way."

"Gator, you know, your pa's a handsome man. Why doesn't he court Miss Ina?"

"Neither of them ever wants to be hurt that much again. That's what Pa says. I miss Alain. He's my friend."

"I miss him too, Gator. I love him."

Gator squeezed Amy's hand. "I'll talk to him."

She smiled and nodded with tears still on her cheeks.

Gator started driving Tal's truck on the back roads. As he drove into the Richter yard, Simon and Yvonne bounded out the door with Alain following holding Debbie's hand and carrying Polly on his hip.

"Uncle Tal!" Simon called.

Gator got out. "Not this time, peewee. It's Gator."

Gator picked up Simon and swung him around. Then he picked up Yvonne and did her the same. When Alain got close enough, Gator kissed Polly and took Debbie on his hip.

"We thought it was Tal," said Alain. "When'd'ya start drivin'?"

"Not long. Pa has two sows deliverin'."

"He's gotta take care o' business."

"Yeah, he's got midgets to help feed." Gator rubbed noses with Debbie.

"Yeah," said Alain in a strange voice.

"You okay?"

"Yeah. Did you jest come to visit?"

"Yeah. What's happened to our friendship?"

"I grew up."

"You grew bitter."

Alain shrugged. "I guess."

"Lucille Dent shouldn't cause you this much pain. Amy asks about you. She misses you. She loves you."

"No. She cain't. I had to choose. Gator, my fam'ly comes first. Soon enough, Amy won't even say my name." Alain almost started to cry. "No! I won't cry. Tell Amy I said Tipper's a better man."

"Why?"

"I'm trash, jest like Lucille said."

"Bullshit, Alain! You are not."

"Gator, please, don't bother me about Amy. If you love me like a brother, let it go."

"Okay." He released an exasperated breath. "I promised her I'd talk to you. I have."

"Tell her to go on with life." Alain called the children to him and took Debbie from Gator. The conversation was over.

The next day, Tipper fumed as he watched an exchange between Gator and Amy that looked intimate, but Gator was only hugging Amy after delivering Alain's message. After school that day, Amy sat beside Tipper on the bus.

"To what do I owe this honor?" asked Tipper.

"I'm not with Alain anymore."

"No? Gator?"

"No."

"Are you telling me you want to go out with me?"

"Momma hates you as much as she hates Alain, but if you want to try, I'm game."

"You sound mad."

"I am, but I'll get over it."

"When you stop being mad at Alain, talk to me again. I won't be a rebound." Tipper changed seats.

"What's up?" asked Mac as Tipper plopped beside him.

"She wants to get together."

"Thought you did."

"Not until she's over Alain."

"Good for you."

A little more time passed, and Gator delivered groceries to the Richters just before Thanksgiving. He was quite aware that Alain was at market since Tal had gone with him. He knocked. Fay cracked the door. "Gator, Alain ain't here right now."

"I know. Pa went to market with him. I came to see you."

"Why?"

"Well, Fay, I like you."

"Oh, I don't think so."

"Why? You turned out right purty. What happened with yo pa don't matter to me. I like you."

Fay snorted. "Why didn't you say so sooner?"

"I'm a little shy around girls, but I don't wanna wait too long. Um, do you think Alain would object?" Gator fidgeted. "You gonna talk through the door all day? If you scared for me to come in, you can come out."

"Oh, Gator. I didn't think no man would ever want me."

"You ain't give us much of a chaince."

"I'm sorry. You won't like me no more." Fay opened the door.

"Dear God!" exclaimed Gator. "You're..." He ran his hands up and down in the air parallel to her body.

"Don't be so shocked, Gator."

"Who?"

"Who do you think? Alain."

"No!" Gator twisted the ball cap in his hand in a vise grip. "That ain't Alain."

"No, he feels bad about it."

"Did he force you?"

"No, I forced him."

"For God's sake, why?" He slapped the cap against the porch rail. "Hadn't you been used enough?"

"He needed comfort after Lucille caught him and Amy. He made me say we won't never do it again."

"I should hope not!" He paced back and forth across the porch. "You really never realized I liked you?"

"No." She looked at the ground.

Alain drove up and slammed the truck door. "Gator, you got somethin' to say to me?" He stepped onto the porch.

Gator wheeled on Alain and belted him, knocking him off the porch into the dirt. "Why? Did you ever think I liked Fay?"

Alain rubbed his mouth and pushed up on an elbow. "You never said so. What's done is done. I cain't take it back, but it won't never happen again."

Gator started to cry. "Is this why you're hidin'?"

"Partly."

"Well, it gives new meaning to the term 'brotherly love.'" Gator stomped off toward Tal's truck, cramming the cap onto his head.

"Gator!" Alain called

"I'm mad, Alain." He stopped with his hand on the door handle. "Give me time. I don't wanna hit you again."

"You gonna tell Tal?"

"You bet." He jerked the door open. "You cain't hide her forever, and you cain't hide the baby."

"Gator, if the welfare finds out…"

"Maybe you shoulda thought with yo big head before now."

"It wudn't my idea."

"She told me. You coulda pushed her off o' you. She ain't that big."

"Gator, please?"

Gator gripped the side of the truck door. "I still love you, Alain. Remember that a friend loveth at all times. I jest need a little time to take it all in. At least take her to Grandma Newton to be sure she's okay."

"Gator, I'll love my baby."

"As its father or its uncle?"

"Gator, I don't know." He shook his head and looked at the ground.

"Think on that." Gator slung gravel as he peeled out.

Gator had never been so angry. For a short moment, he thought about turning around and going back to offer a solution. He could be the baby's father. "I cain't," he said to himself. "That's somethin' I jest cain't give. Alain has to make that choice. Is he a father or an uncle? Damn you! Brotherly love? I thought that's what we had, Alain. I feel like I been stabbed in the back. Now, I know how Julius Caesar musta felt when he looked at Marc Antony or how Jesus felt after Judas's kiss." Gator entered his home in tears.

"Gator?" Tal asked with concern. "What's wrong?" He lowered the chair he had leaned back on two legs.

"Pa, next time you go to the Richters' make Alain let you see Fay."

"Maybe you'd better prepare me."

"It looks like you're gonna be Granduncle Tal."

"What? Do you mean Alain and Fay?"

"Yes, sir, and I'm right angry."

"Did you go to ask to court her?"

"I had planned to."

"What was their excuse?"

"Lucille!" He plopped into a chair at the table. "Pa, I'm hurt. I love Alain like a brother, and this hurts."

Gator told Tal about his conversations with Amy, Fay, and Alain. Tal rubbed his head, his neck, and his shoulder.

"You okay, Pa?"

"Yeah, just real tired tonight, too tired to deal with this, but I'll be back."

Tal had a long talk with both Alain and Fay and left with the promise that it would not happen again. Alain drove into town with Fay the next day and went straight to Grandma Newton. Lucille spied out the window. "Lordy, mercy! Trash!" she growled and picked up the phone.

17

Line in the Sand

Miriam Newton examined Fay and pronounced, "Everything looks good, as good as a fourteen-year-old girl can. Who's the father?"

"I am," said Alain.

"Good Lord! What y'all doin' out there?"

"Don't blame Alain," said Fay. "It was my idea. I was tryin' to comfort Alain after Lucille."

"Babies, that don't make it right." The old matriarch shook her head slowly. "I know y'all feel alone, but y'all ain't. Lucille Dent is evil."

"Why?" asked Alain. "She's got money. Royce's a good man. Amy, well..." Alain let his thought die.

"I ain't sure, baby. Well, y'all cain't take it back. How you gonna raise this baby?"

"It's my child. I'll love it and take care of it."

"So, you gonna be its daddy?"

"I am."

"Okay."

"Grandma?" Alain said barely above a whisper.

"What, baby?"

"Am I trash?" Tears splashed down the boy's cheeks.

"Oh, baby, no." The old woman put a spotted hand on Alain's head. "You made a big mistake. Don't do it again."

"I don't plan to, but ain't nobody gonna ever want me."

"Have you let Amy go?"

"I ain't got a choice."

"I guess I understand. Don't hide out there though. I enjoy seein' you."

"Even now?"

"Even now." Grandma Newton patted both their cheeks.

A few days after Alain took Fay to town, Gator pedaled in to catch the bus. A strange car was parked in front of the general store, but it was too early for the store to be open. The sun had not even risen. Gator heard Amy scream, outraged, "Momma, how could you?"

Through the window, he saw Carla Stokes. "No, no, no," he muttered to himself. "I might be mad at Alain, but I cain't let this happen. I better not miss too many days because of this." Gator turned his bike around as Tipper drove into town.

"Where you goin'?" Tipper called.

"The welfare lady's here." He pointed toward the store.

"What?"

Gator did not answer. "Damn it!" Tipper muttered.

Tipper banged on Leo Tomlin's door. "Tipper you're a little early," greeted Leo.

"No, I'm not. I might be too late. The welfare lady's with Lucille."

"What?"

"Yes, sir." Tipper pointed out the car.

"Tipper, get to Alain's. Mac, run get Grandma Newton. I'll call Fester. He has a phone."

Tipper informed, "Gator's headed back."

"Give him a ride."

Grandma Newton held tightly to Mac's arm as she carried her shotgun in her other hand. "Get in the car, both of you," Leo urged.

Leo took Grandma Newton's shotgun and put it in the trunk along with his own.

"Papa?" Mac asked without more words.

"I will not let Lucille Dent destroy that little family."

"Papa, are they better off living like they do? Fay's pregnant with Alain's baby."

"I know. I can't answer you. I just know what I promised. Don't judge them, Mac. Love them."

The school bus pulled in. Amy screamed as Lucille dragged her toward the bus. "I'm not going!"

"Yes, you are." Lucille stopped. "Where is everybody?"

"Not going like me." Amy jerked her arm free and sprinted toward Richter Farms and Orchards.

Amy thought her lungs would burst as she ran in crisp late fall air. Tipper skidded to a stop as he came out of his driveway inches away from hitting the girl. "Get in," he said.

"Gator?" Amy was confused at seeing Gator in the truck with Tipper.

"Get in," said Tipper impatiently. Amy climbed in. "Can you shoot a gun?" he asked.

"What?"

"Can you shoot?"

"I've never tried."

"I've got a shotgun and a rifle at your feet. All you have to do is point and pull the trigger on the shotgun. You just about can't miss. I'll use the rifle." Tipper swung into Gator's house.

"Pa!" Gator shouted as he jumped out of Tipper's truck, climbing over Amy.

"What?" asked Tal, running outside.

"The welfare lady's here."

"You're joking."

"No, sir."

Tal pointed at Tipper. "Go!"

A minute after Tipper stopped, Tal and Gator pulled in. Both had shotguns. "Leo, Grandma," Tal acknowledged the others. "Alain?"

"We got three shotguns."

Fester wandered out. He handed a .38 to Mac. "I've got my shotgun. All you have to do is point and pull the trigger."

"Are we gonna kill the woman?" Mac asked in horror.

"Only if we have to," said Leo.

"Papa!"

"Mac, surely this firepower will scare her away permanently." Leo looked at Amy. "Mac, trade guns with Amy."

Fay came outside. "Go inside," Alain ordered.

"Amy's here," Fay argued.

"She's not pregnant."

Amy stared at Fay. She looked at Alain. Alain stared at the ground. Amy said softly, "Fester, show me what to do."

Fester put his hand on Amy's. "Point and pull the trigger." He leaned in close. "Don't hate him."

"I'll try, but I can't be his girl anymore."

With Alain and Tal at the center, the others made a line across the dirt drive. They drew the line in the sand. The welfare would not get across.

They waited.

Half an hour later, Carla Stokes, accompanied by one deputy sheriff, bumped up the rutted drive, a weak rim of sun at the back of the vehicles. They stopped as they saw the armed citizens. The deputy got out of his car. "Alain Richter?"

"Yes, sir?"

"This woman has orders to take you kids."

"It ain't happenin'."

Carla Stokes got out. "Young man, it has come to my attention one of the girls is pregnant."

"So?"

"Who's the father? Are you selling your sister?"

"I will shoot you," he answered through clenched teeth. "No. My sister ain't a whore."

Tal growled, "If it wasn't for Lucille, the girl wouldn't be pregnant."

"Mr. Jones, are you the father?"

"Hell no!"

"I am," said Alain. "There's not a damned thing you can do about it."

"Alain," said the deputy, "did you force her?"

"No."

"You sixteen?"

"No, fifteen."

The deputy spit a stream of tobacco juice. "You gonna shoot?"

"I don't want to, but my fam'ly stays right here all together."

"Fester, that you?" The deputy stood behind the open door of his cruiser.

"Yes, it is, Don."

"What you doin' here?"

"I done told Miss Stokes I'm the kids' grandfather."

The deputy looked at Miss Stokes. "Miss Stokes, where are you from?"

"Charleston."

"I suggest you go back there. This is hillbilly justice, hillbilly government. The folks up here ain't like you city folks."

"Do you condone this behavior?"

"They ain't no worse than the high and mighty Lucille Dent." The deputy looked at the line of humans. "Ain't you the little Dent girl?"

"I am," said Amy. "My mother caused this trouble. Everything was fine up here until she caught Alain with me. She refused to let us see each other. Apparently, Alain found inappropriate comfort." She glared at Alain. "Still, they stay here. You'll have to go through all of us to get to them."

The deputy blinked several times. "You in on this too, Preacher Tomlin?"

"I'm shepherding my flock. I gave my word to Alain."

"Grandma Newton, what's your story?"

"I'm their great-great-grandmother. This is my fam'ly too. You ain't takin' my fam'ly."

The deputy spit another stream of tobacco juice into the dirt. "Tal, that you?"

"You know it is."

"Is it true some of 'em belong to you?"

"It is."

Mac was the only one who looked surprised.

"I guess you're their daddy. Ain't taking kids from their daddy."

"Mr. Tench! You are a law enforcement officer. I have orders!" ranted Carla Stokes.

"Show me." He held out his hand.

Carla handed the order to the deputy. He nodded, looked at the crowd, and threw the document into the air. Every weapon fired at it.

"Nice paper shredder. No more orders, Miss Stokes."

"Mr. Tench!"

"Listen up." Tench spit another stream of tobacco juice right at the woman's feet, barely missing expensive black pumps. "Leave this place. Leave these people alone. If Lucille Dent calls again, don't take the call. Alain is the head of his family now. Like it or not, his call stands. That's the way it works for us hillbillies."

"Mr. Tench, I will report this."

"Won't nobody corroborate your story."

"I'll be…"

"Dead if you don't leave," Alain finished her statement.

Carla Stokes looked around. "How do I turn around?"

"You'll have to back up," said Alain.

"It's too far."

Alain pointed the shotgun. Carla Stokes jumped in her car and backed up. The sounds of her scraping and bumping several trees echoed as she fled.

Deputy Tench sighed and spit again. "She won't be back. Alain, don't break any laws. Be glad you yourself aren't legally of age to consent to sex. Don't diddle your sister. Be glad she got me and not somebody else, or all of you would be going to jail, and the minors, even Mac, Amy, Tipper, and Gator would be going into foster care. Any takers on how many trees I don't hit backing up?"

"No, sir. Jest go," said Alain.

Don Tench noiselessly backed almost a mile out.

All weapons lowered when Alain said, "Thank you. All of you." He gazed at Amy who shook her head.

The line in the sand went deeper for Alain. Fay had a baby boy that Alain named Matthew, but Alain kept to himself. The only people who felt truly welcome at Richter Farms and Orchards were Tal and Gator Jones and Tipper Campbell on occasion once he actually began to use Alain's fruit some time later. Alain would never tell Leo Tomlin not to visit, and the pastor did often over the years. Neither would the boy deny Miriam Newton visitation. Mac felt awkward, and Amy felt sick. She sealed that crack in her heart and refused to look at it. Tipper Campbell became her obsession, partly because she knew her mother hated him too, and he would take her away if she asked.

18

Farmers' Market

As Gator struggled through seventh grade, he became painfully aware he would not be able to graduate high school. He attempted to get into the Fast Track program that could have accelerated him to high school, but he was rejected due to his attendance record. Gator called it quits and learned the ins-and-outs of hog farming instead.

Tal took both Gator and Alain to the farmers' market. He taught them how to get the best price possible on their futures.

Farming was a speculative business. Pork futures were determined by the pound. The hog farmer entered into a contract to sell his hogs at a given rate at a date in the future. If actual market prices rose, the farmer lost money because he had contracted at a lower rate; however, if the actual prices fell, the farmer made money on that contract. The next contract would be modified to fit the market at that time.

For several years, Tal had made good profits on his futures. At least the weather did not impact hog futures much. On the other hand, produce, fruit, vegetables, and nuts, were greatly affected by the weather. Too much rain or too little rain or extreme temperatures affected crop yield tremendously. And both had to hope and pray no disease or pestilence attacked whatever they grew.

Whereas Gator had to learn to negotiate contracts for pork futures affected by the stock market, Alain had to learn to negotiate multiple contracts that could be affected by both the stock market and the weather. He had to consult almanacs and pray the forecasters were accurate.

Not only did Alain need to be a mathematician, but he also had to use scientific practices to get the best yield year after year in addition to thinking about the legalities of contracts. He still remembered the men who had cheated his father, and those men learned quickly that in Alain's case, the apple had fallen far from the tree and sprouted its own firm roots. Besides that, the negotiators knew Tal Jones kept his eyes and ears trained on the young man.

Tal stood back to watch both boys work. He decided only to intervene if they got into trouble.

Gator's youthful appearance made him a target. However, Gator was sharp. He countered and re-countered, negotiating wisely. The older man working with Gator asked, "What's your name again, boy?"

"Gator Jones."

"Tal's kid?"

"Yes, sir."

"How old are you now?"

"Sixteen."

"You look twelve, but Tal has taught you well."

"Yes, he has."

"Where is Tal?"

"Behind the partition watching everything."

"Of course, he is. He's grooming you. Ask for me every time you come in, Gator. I won't cheat you. Melvin Hawkins." The man extended his hand and Gator shook it. "Don't forget. Tal, you coming in? Gator's too young to sign."

"How old do I have to be to sign?" asked Gator.

"Eighteen."

"Alain's only seventeen."

"He's an emancipated minor. That means…"

"I know what it means. I'm smart."

"Yes, you are."

"Because Alain ain't got parents, he's considered an adult now that he's over sixteen."

"Yes."

"Is anybody trying to cheat him?"

"Tal would kill 'em. Your pa came with Alain two years in a row. He couldn't be emancipated until he was sixteen even without parents. Tal watched out for him, but Alain Richter is a genius. That boy's got smarts, real smarts. It's too bad he didn't get the education too. Just like you."

"I'll be fine, Mr. Hawkins."

"Somehow, I believe you. You are Tal Jones's kid. Oh, Gator, one thing that helps Alain is he can grow a full beard. He doesn't look seventeen. How often do you have to shave?"

Gator blushed. "Once a week."

"Enjoy it while you can."

Tal and Gator met Alain. "Tal," said Alain, "you didn't look over my shoulder."

"No, you can handle yourself."

"Will you look at the contracts?"

"Sure." Tal reviewed the paperwork.

Alain said to Gator, "This always gives me a headache."

Tal handed the paperwork back. "Why so low on the nuts?"

"Rain, too much."

"Umm."

"That was as high as I could git 'em."

"Well, maybe you made up for it with the melons."

"I hope. I'd really like to sell my cider."

"It's good. You will in time."

"I'm gonna try."

"Good for you. What do you boys say to supper in a restaurant?"

"I promised to bring pizzas back," said Alain

"We'll get 'em before we leave."

"What kind of restaurant?" asked Alain.

"Not Jacqui's place."

"Just food, huh?"

"Yes." Tal put his arm around Alain's neck and gave him a noogie, but he had to pull him down to do it. Alain was six inches taller than Tal. At six-two, Alain was thin at only one-sixty. He had grown a full beard which was a shade lighter than his shoulder-blade-length, caramel-brown hair, which he wore pulled into a ponytail at the nape of his neck most of the time. His vivid jade-green eyes still sparkled with mischief.

Gator looked like a little boy in comparison. He still only needed to shave once a week, and he kept his light brown hair cut short. His soft hazel eyes exuded compassion. He weighed as much as Alain, but at five-nine, Gator was stocky and muscular. Gator looked a great deal like his father; whereas, Alain looked like his mother.

The three men decided to eat at a Chinese buffet. Neither of the two boys had ever eaten Chinese. Tal watched them eat and could not help but laugh. He was certain they tried every item on the buffet.

During the meal, Tal rubbed his left shoulder. "Something wrong, Pa?" asked Gator.

"No. I'm getting old. My joints are hurting. It might even be an old football injury. I took a few good hits."

"What was college like?" asked Alain around a bite of egg roll.

"Tough. I had a scholarship, so I had to keep my grades up. Classes were great because the professors challenged us to think."

"Why didn't you finish?"

"When I got hurt and couldn't play football, I didn't have a scholarship. Even a grant wasn't enough. I had a wife and a baby on the way. Corky was born shortly after we came back to Possum Holler. Like you, Alain, I gave up a dream for my family."

"Do you regret it?"

Tal put his hand on Gator's head. "Sometimes. Sometimes I wish I could give Gator more than a hog farm, but I wouldn't trade Gator for anything. I love my other boys, but Gator is my crowning achievement. He looks like me, but he's so much like June."

"Do you regret my ma?"

"No," said Tal with a decisive shake of his head. "I regret not taking her away. I love Polly." He twisted his mouth to the side. "I love all of Shirley's kids. I'm trying to show them."

"You do. You even show me."

"I love you too, Alain. I love all of you."

"Even Matthew?"

"Yeah. He's a sweetie."

"I love him."

"Show him. *Always* show him."

"Tal, is it wrong to regret making him?"

The older man took a long drain from the Coke he had. "That's a hard one. Cherish the child, but don't repeat the act."

"Yes, sir. I'm sorry I was so angry with you at first. I was feeling guilty."

"All is forgiven."

"I think Mac has a real problem with me. I know Amy does."

"I can't speak for them or even Gator."

"I'm over it," said Gator. "But I just can't be Fay's man. Can you understand that, Alain?"

"Yeah. You and Tipper seem to at least accept us even if Tipper is a little wary."

"I love you like a brother."

"I know. I wish I could rewind time."

Tal sighed. "You can't. You can only go forward. Y'all ready? We gotta get those pizzas. Gator, you drive. I'm kind of tired."

"Okay, Pa."

19

Another Loss

As time went by, Gator convinced Tipper and Mac to visit Alain with him. Mac was more reluctant than Tipper. Mac was mortified by the relationship between Alain and Fay. He gave in after Gator and Tipper shamed him into being honest about passing judgment.

They pulled into the Richter yard in Gator's truck. Alain came out to meet his friend and was surprised to see Tipper and Mac.

"Well, blow me down," said Alain. "Are y'all talkin' to me again?"

"Hey, Alain," said Tipper offering his hand.

"Tipper, you're taller'n me."

"You're skinnier."

"Yeah."

"How's everybody? The baby?"

"His name's Matthew. He's walkin' and talkin'. He's real smart. He ain't retarded." Alain set his jaw to defensive mode.

"I'm sure he's great," said Tipper.

"How's Amy?" The hurt still lingered in Alain's voice.

"Great."

"She still drawin'?"

"Yeah, she paints with all kinds of things now. She's taking art lessons."

"You courtin' her?"

"It ain't official. Lucille would have a stroke."

"Yeah, she don't like you neither."

"Lucille doesn't like anybody."

"Do you know anybody that likes her?"

"No."

Mac got out of the truck. "Mac," said Alain.

"Alain."

"You ain't comfortable with me."

"No."

"I made a mistake. Are you perfect?"

"No."

"Jest so's you know, it only happened that one time. It ain't like we share a bed. As a matter o' fact, Matthew sleeps with me now that he's stopped nursin'." Alain laughed. "Thing is, he ain't quite stopped wettin' the bed, but that's okay 'cause he's barely two."

"Good," said Mac, offering his hand. Alain took it.

"Y'all want some cider?"

"Yeah," said Mac.

The boys visited over cider. Alain laughed, "So, y'all are driving yourselves to school. That's good. Tipper, you still drivin' Ander's truck?"

"Yeah, I keep it up."

Alain nodded. "What about you, Mac?"

"I got a Grand Am. It's used, but in good shape. I used some of my savings to get it."

With a little head tic, Alain said, "My money's still in the bank. I'm savin' it to buy my meadow."

"Alain, you really gonna buy that land?" asked Tipper.

"One day." He nodded.

"When?" asked Gator.

"When I have the love o' my life to share it with."

Tipper inquired, "Who's that?"

"Never mind." Alain waved a hand to dismiss the conversation. "What's Amy drivin'?"

"A brand-new Malibu," said Mac. "She's too spoiled to be a hillbilly."

"Mr. Dent buy it?" Alain cocked an eyebrow.

"No, Lucille. Mr. Dent thought she should earn it. We heard him and Lucille arguing down the road." Mac took a swallow of cider.

"I bet," said Alain with a knowing smirk.

"Well," said Mac. "We need to head back."

Alain stood with his friends. "Come again."

"We won't get shot?" asked Tipper.

"No, we won't shoot you now that I know what you're drivin'." Alain grinned his mischievous smile.

Another year flew by. Robert Lee and Gloria and Calvin and Glenda coupled much to Alain's disappointment. He knew he could not forbid the actions. To drown his sorrow, he drank, but he did not hit anyone. None of them listened to him or Tal.

While Amy and Tipper and Mac and Susan Ames, a girl from Wilmington, went to prom, Gator Jones helped Tal bury Tal's prize hog, Spot, which had been born the same day as Gator. Gator chose a new hog for breeding and called him Patch.

Tal breathed deeply and rubbed his left arm. "Pa, you okay?" asked Gator.

"Tired. Aching. Sad over Spot. I think I'll take a nap."

"Okay, Pa. Take some aspirin. I'll get Patch settled, and I'll make supper.

"Fine."

Tal clapped Gator on the shoulder. "I'm proud of you, Gator. Don't desert Alain. Take care of your siblings."

"How am I supposed to do that? They ran off."

"Not really. I have letters. Read them. Corky"—Tal dipped his head side to side—"he'll be back someday. Polly—she is your little sister."

"Best I can, Pa," Gator promised. "You sound strange."

"Gator, I love the rest of the Richters too. I wish I really could be their pa, but they just don't listen to me. That's too much of Keenan's influence."

"Alain's just real scared. They don't listen to him neither."

"I know, but when I'm gone, don't forget them."

"Where you goin'?"

"Heaven. I know that." Tal laughed sadly. "Will I be with June or Shirley?"

"Pa, I don't think it matters. You'll be with Jesus. Let's hope that's a long time. You're only fifty. I need my pa."

"You're a good kid, Gator. I love you."

"I love you too, Pa. Take a nap."

"Yeah." Tal nodded and went to the house.

Gator transferred Patch. "You better be as good as your pa, just like me, huh? I'll be as good as my pa too. We'll do this together. You're a fine fellow like Wilbur. I'm glad you won't be pork."

Patch grunted and rumbled off to meet his females. Gator laughed at the hog's cockiness. He thought if hogs could smile, Patch was smiling.

Gator continued the chores that needed to be done. Finally, he settled the stock for the night and remembered he had promised to make supper. Gator was surprised he wasn't already smelling food because Tal did not like to eat late. Gator said to the hogs, "Pa's takin' a long nap. Supper's gonna be late."

No light showed from the house. As Gator entered, he stumbled over Tal lying in the middle of the floor.

"Pa!" Gator shouted.

Gator examined Tal and realized he was dead. Gator sobbed alone. He did not want to be alone. He was not ready to be a hog farmer.

After a while, Gator carried his father's body to the truck and drove into town to Preacher Tomlin. Leo opened the door in surprise. "Gator? Mac's not here; he's gone to prom."

"I didn't come for Mac. I need you. Pa's dead." Though the words were curt, Leo saw the young man trembled.

"Dead? How?"

"I don't know. He said he was tired, and his joints ached. He went to take a nap."

"Left arm?"

Gator backhanded tears from his face. "Yes, sir, a lot."

"Heart attack. This is why we need a doctor. Pain in the left arm is a symptom."

"I didn't know."

Leo held his arms out to the boy who was not quite a man. Gator slipped into another fatherly embrace. "I'm so sorry, Gator. Stay here tonight. I'm sure some of Mac's clothes will fit you. I'll get Grandma Newton and Norman Hill to prepare the body."

"Yes, sir, I'll stay, but I gotta go tell Alain first."

"Why?"

"You know why."

"You know?"

"Yes, sir. Polly is my sister, and now I gotta keep a promise to help take care of her."

"I'm here for you if you need me."

"I know that."

Constable Hill also served as undertaker in Possum Holler. One room off the jail was the funeral home. All services were held in the church. Leo and Gator took Tal's body to the small room. Grandma Newton came over to prepare Tal for burial.

The old woman held Gator close and let him cry some more. "You ain't alone, Gator," she assured. "I really *am* yo great-great-grandma. Come to me if you need me."

"Yes, ma'am. I gotta go tell Alain. I'm gonna stay the night with Mac."

"That's fine."

Gator knocked on Alain Richter's door after all of them had gone to bed. Alain answered with his shotgun.

"Go ahead and shoot," said Gator. "It would hurt less."

Alain lowered the gun. "Gator? What's wrong?"

"Can I come in?"

"Course, you can."

Gator stepped inside as Alain lit a lantern. "Gator, have you been cryin'?"

"Yeah. Alain." Gator started to cry.

"Gator!" Alain put an arm around his friend. "Tell me what's happened."

"It's Pa. He had a heart attack."

"Where is he?" Alain asked, not wanting to hear the answer.

"He's dead, Alain."

"No, not Tal." Alain did not hide his tears either. "I cain't lose Tal too. I cain't handle another loss, Gator. Please?"

Both boys wept. Finally, Gator choked, "I'm all alone, Alain."

"No, Gator, you won't never be alone. You always got us."

"Yeah, I know that. You gonna bring ever'body for the funeral?

"Yeah. Damn Lucille."

"Preacher Tomlin won't let her cause trouble."

"I guess. It's jest that Robert Lee and Cal, you know. We done the wrong thing."

"I know. Lucille won't even come. Amy probably will."

"Yeah, Amy would." Alain pulled a bottle of moonshine from behind some preserves and poured both boys a shot in a mason jar. They drank together.

"Alain, Tipper asked to court Amy officially," Gator informed his friend. "Prom was tonight."

"Tipper'll be good to her. I can let Tipper love her, but I cain't quit. It's jest one more loss. Gator, will I ever git to be happy?"

"I don't know. I better go. Preacher Tomlin wants me to stay with them tonight."

"See. You ain't alone. You got friends."

"You my best one."

"Still?"

"Yeah, Alain. You practically my brother."

"I hope I don't never lose you."

"Only by death."

"Jest like Tal. Don't you die on me."

The next day, Gator's friends all came to show support for him. Mac, Tipper, Alain, Robert Lee, Calvin, and Royce Dent served as pallbearers as they laid Tal to rest in a simple pine coffin next to June and, unbeknown to most, next to Shirley Richter.

Lucille Dent actually attended the funeral but could not keep her eyes off the Richter family. After the funeral, Lucille hurried back to the store. Royce and Amy stayed a bit to offer Gator their condolences.

In passing, Amy's hand brushed Alain's. She jerked it away quickly.

"Sorry," Alain muttered. "Am I that disgustin' to you?"

Amy hissed, "How could you? Are they all yours?"

"No. Only Matthew."

"So, you're all doin' it?"

"I cain't speak for them. I only done it that one time."

"With your sister!"

"I cain't take it back, Amy."

"No, you can't."

"So, you cain't forgive me?"

"Alain, that's askin' a lot. If it had been anybody but your sister, I would have scratched her eyes out."

"I'm so sorry."

"We can't go backward."

Alain put his hands in his pockets to be sure not to touch Amy. "No. So, it's Tipper, huh?"

"Yes, it's Tipper."

"How's Lucille takin' that?"

"She threw a fit."

"Why? Tipper's a good man, not like me."

"Alain, you're not a bad man." She reached toward him but pulled her hand back quickly.

"Jest not good enough for you."

"I never said that."

"Amy, could you really accept Matthew?"

Amy sighed. "Could you accept it if it was me?"

"Yes."

"No hesitation?"

"No."

"I'm not you."

"I know. Good luck with Tipper."

Alain walked away. Anyone who saw him crying assumed he felt Tal's loss deeply, and he did. However, the loss he felt worse was Amy. He had held a small hope that she could love him. That was gone. Alain Richter did not think he could handle another loss.

20

Please Come Back

A week after Talmage Jones was laid to rest between the two women he had loved, a new Honda Civic drove through town. Lucille Dent flew out the door to see who was driving the strange car. Her effort was futile because the person drove straight through without stopping to ask directions. Whoever was driving knew where to go.

Gator stood from the new litter of piglets as he heard a car coming into the yard, but he did not recognize the vehicle. He doubted his senses when a man who could have been Tal Jones in full-dress uniform got out. For a moment, Gator stared before, in a fit of anger and tears, he barreled toward the man who merely engulfed him and took the punches to his body that Gator threw.

"Hush, Gator," the man said gently.

"Why'd you come?" Gator choked. "You're too late. He's dead. Where are the others?"

"They won't come, Gator."

"Not even to tell Pa good-bye?"

"I'm sorry." Captain Corky Jones hugged his baby brother and let him cry some more.

Anger spent, Gator asked, "Why'd you come?"

"To tell Pa good-bye. To see you. What are you planning to do?"

"It's my farm now. I'm gonna be the best damned hog farmer ever."

"Leave, Gator. Come with me."

"No. This is my home. I'm gonna put Possum Holler on the map."

"How do you plan to do that?" He leaned against his car with his arms across his chest.

"One day I'm gonna own the slaughterhouse and make it into a packing plant. Mac…"

"Mac?"

"MacKenzie Reardon, Uncle Ander's son, your cousin."

"Oh, yes." Corky nodded.

"Mac is gonna be a doctor and come back here. Tipper…"

"Campbell?"

"Yeah. He's gonna be an entrepreneur."

"In what?"

"He's gonna bottle his moonshine and sell it to city folk one day."

"He's a moonshiner?" He pushed himself up from the car.

"Yep."

"What else?"

"Alain is gonna make Richter Farms and Orchards a household name."

Corky nodded, his lips puckered. "And this affects you how?"

"We're musketeers. We're a team."

"Real heroes. I don't believe any of it. You dropped out of school. Pa wrote me."

"Yeah. Pa told me y'all write. That's how I had the addresses to send you a note. He said you got married and have three kids. Why didn't you bring 'em?"

"I will *never* bring them to Possum Holler. The others won't even come back for Pa's funeral."

"It was last week. You sorta missed it."

Corky cocked an eyebrow. "Short of putting Pa in the slaughterhouse cooling locker, how could I have gotten here before the rest of Possum Holler would have left for the stench?"

"Asshole."

Corky chuckled. "I came as soon as I got your letter. Gator, you're a kid."

"I'm an adult. I jest turned eighteen. I'll be fine."

"Gator, I want you to come with me."

"I belong here. I hope you'll keep writin', so I'll know you're okay, but I belong here, Corky. Pa left me a legacy." He looked around. "I know you cain't see it, but it's here."

"He changed, didn't he?"

"A lot. Pa was a good man with a big heart."

"He wrote me about Shirley Richter. Do I have a sister?"

"Yeah, but that ain't common knowledge around here."

"Did Pa kill Keenan Richter?"

"No."

"So, it really was a murder-suicide?"

"Yep."

"Gator, I wish you'd come with me."

"Nope."

"You're as stubborn as Pa."

"Yep."

Corky chortled. "I'll write." He opened his car door.

"You ain't even gonna stay one night?"

"Am I wanted?"

"Yeah." Gator pushed the door shut. "Stay a few days with me. Hell, Corky! At least go to church with me and give Lucille Dent somethin' to gossip about."

"Is she still a busybody?"

"Oh, yeah."

"All right. Take me to visit my other sibling."

Corky Jones visited Richter Farms and Orchards. He was appalled by the situation.

"Wow!" said Alain. "You a real officer."

"I am. I got a college degree."

"Still too good to come back to Possum Holler though."

"I guess you could look at it like that."

"Mac says he's comin' back."

"You believe him?"

Alain shook his head. "I wouldn't if I left."

"So, you understand me, then."

"Yeah, Corky, I do, but I won't leave. I won't leave Gator."

"I guess you're a better brother than I am."

"A friend forever."

"I'm glad Gator has you." Corky looked around. "But you have to put a stop to this."

"Yeah, I know."

Corky could hear the frustration in Alain's voice, but when he left, the situation was unchanged.

Sunday at church, Corky was the center of attention. He talked to Leo. "Preacher Tomlin, sorry I left before I got to know you. I've read a lot about you. Pa held you in high esteem."

"And I him. Tal was a good man. I miss him."

"I'll be leaving after church. I just want to make sure Gator's okay. He refuses to leave with me."

"He'd like you to come back."

"Not happening."

"I understand."

"Do you really think Mac will come back?"

"I do. He's committed to it."

Corky chuckled. "I guess the stubbornness must be a Newton trait."

"Must be. Grandma Newton is as stubborn as they come." The preacher tucked his Bible under his arm.

"Will you keep an eye on Gator?" Corky asked.

"Always."

"Then, I leave him in good hands."

Corky enjoyed the church service and fellowship. It was one change in Possum Holler that he liked. Nonetheless, he was ready to leave. He surveyed his baby brother again.

"I can't believe you're all grown up. Take care. I'll write." Corky and Gator embraced.

As Corky drove away, Gator called, "Corky!"

The car stopped. Corky got out and hugged his brother again. "Please come back," Gator sobbed.

"Maybe one day after you put Possum Holler on the map."

"I'll hold you to it."

"Okay. I love you, Gator. I always have."

"I've hated you sometimes."

"I know. I guess you had good reason."

"I love you, Corky."

"'Bye."

"'Bye."

It seemed time took wings as summer sped toward autumn. Mac packed his Grand Am to head to Marshall University. Along with Leo, Tipper and Ina Campbell, Amy Dent, and Grandma Newton came to see him off. Each one brought him gifts.

"I won't be gone forever," assured Mac.

"Ten or twelve years is a long time!" yelled Alain as he and Gator roared into town just to say farewell.

"Look what the cat dragged up," laughed Mac.

"We had to see you off too," said Gator.

"I'm glad you came," assured Mac.

"You really comin' back?" asked Alain.

"Yes, I am."

"I wouldn't," said Alain.

"Me either," said Gator.

"You had a chance to leave, Gator," Mac reminded him.

"I belong here."

"So do I. I *will* be back."

"You gotta come back," said Alain. "It's gonna take all of us to put Possum Holler on the map."

"You're right. We'll change Possum Holler."

Alain sighed. "At least you will."

"So will you."

"Think I'm still good enough?"

"It doesn't really matter what I think. It's what you think that counts."

"I think you gotta come back. Please come back."

"I will."

Mac hugged Gator and Alain, one under each arm. "I'll see y'all in about ten years. I'll be Dr. Reardon."

Alain whispered once more, "Please come back."

21

Broken Heart

The pounding on Alain Richter's door terrified him. He got the shotgun off its hooks and cautiously opened the door. Lucille Dent screamed at him, "This is your fault!"

"What did I do?"

"Amy! Amy's pregnant, and it's all because of you."

"I ain't never touched Amy."

"God! She's just like you."

"What are you talkin' about, you crazy old bat?" Alain pointed the shotgun at Lucille. "Git off my property. You are *insane*."

"I could kill you."

"I'm gonna kill *you*. Now, git!"

Alain fired over Lucille's head. She screamed, fled to her car, and sped away.

The pounding on Gator Jones's door terrified him. He got the shotgun off its hooks, but put it back as Alain yelled, "Gator, open up!"

Gator yanked the door open. "What's with you comin' here in the middle of the night?"

"That wicked witch come to our place. I shot at her."

"Who?"

"Lucille Dent!"

"What did she want?"

"She was rantin' and carryin' on nonsense 'bout me gettin' Amy pregnant. I ain't never touched Amy like that."

"Alain! *You* kinda rantin' right now."

"Gator, what if she calls…"

"Stop." He held up a hand. "She cain't do nothin'. You a grown man who can have custody of his younger siblings whether she likes it or not."

"That don't mean she won't try."

"We'll find out what's goin' on tomorra."

"I'm panickin' *now*." His voice rose an octave.

Gator snapped his fingers. "I got it. We'll go now."

"Where?"

"Grandma Newton."

The pounding on Grandma Newton's door terrified her. She got her shotgun off its hooks. The old lady grumbled about being woke up because nobody was due to deliver. She jerked the door open. "What do you two fools want?" she demanded.

Alain stammered, "Grandma Newton, you told me to come to you if I needed help."

"Alain, you ain't havin' another baby, are you?"

"No, ma'am, but…"

"But what?"

"Mrs. Dent come out to our place rantin' 'bout it bein' my fault Amy's pregnant. I don't know what she's talkin' about."

"That wicked, wicked womern," growled Grandma Newton. "Ina, come here, please?"

Ina Campbell came into the room in her nightgown. "What's wrong, Grandma?"

"Lucille Dent's done gone to blamin' Alain."

"What?" Ina looked sympathetically at Alain. "Y'all come in and sit down."

Gator and Alain sat down in the early-twentieth-century furniture, and Ina explained as Grandma Newton replaced her shotgun. "Lucille's whacky. Yes, Amy is expectin'. Her and Tipper done got the cart before the horse. They got married this afternoon. Lucille's mad as the devil, but it ain't yo fault, Alain."

She patted the young man's hand. "Amy and Tipper brought it on theirselves. Course, Lucille 'bout drove the girl away."

As if in a trance, Alain said, "So, Tipper and Amy are married and expectin'. Why's that crazy womern blamin' me?"

"She hates Tipper more'n she hates you because she hates me because she thinks I took her man." Ina dipped her head back and forth from shoulder to shoulder as she spoke.

"No, you didn't; jest like Tipper didn't take my girl."

"But you feel that way a little bit, don't you, honey?"

"Maybe, but Lucille made sure Amy wudn't my girl. Then, I made things worse. Amy was free, and she won't ever love me again." Alain swallowed hard to keep from crying. "Tipper'll be good to her."

Ina squeezed Alain's hand. "Lucille has hurt a lot o' folks, most o' all herself."

"I guess," said Alain. "I'm afraid she'll call the welfare again."

"Come with me," commanded Grandma Newton.

"Where?"

"To put that womern in her place once and for all."

The pounding on the Dent's door terrified Royce. He got his shotgun off its hooks after the events of the day and opened with a look of consternation. Seeing Grandma Newton, Alain, and Gator, he wearily asked, "What's Lucille done now?" then lowered the shotgun.

"Git that womern in here," commanded Grandma Newton.

"She cried herself to sleep."

"Wake her up, so I can give her a reason to cry."

Royce put his gun back in place and dragged Lucille out of bed. "Oh, what do you want?" she wailed when she saw who had come.

"Listen to me, Lucille Munro Dent," said Grandma Newton forcefully, shaking her cane at the other woman. "Alain Richter ain't to blame for Amy and Tipper. They made their own choices although you mighta shoved a little, no, *a lot.* You sho 'nuff shoved Amy away from Alain. That's squarely on you 'cause you think you better'n ever'body else in Possum Holler. Yo pa was Fester Munro's half-brother, so you ain't got no room to talk. This poor man you hoodwinked into marriage done saved yo ass from prob'ly bein' one o' Fester's girls after yo folks died. You a selfish, spoiled bitch."

Lucille started to speak.

Grandma Newton put a finger in Lucille's chest. "Shut up. I ain't done with what I gotta say. From now on, *YOU... WILL...LEAVE...ALAIN...AND...HIS...FAM'LY...A...LONE!*

"He's got enough to deal with without you addin' to his misery. Do you understand me? Now, you can speak."

"Yeah!" Lucille snapped.

"Don't be sassy with me! I'll pop you upside yo face. You apologize to him. You actin' like a child yoself."

"I will not apologize."

"Yes, you will," said Royce. "I can't believe you blamed Alain. You made sure he was out of Amy's life. If you want to blame somebody, blame yourself. Now, apologize."

Sulkily, Lucille said, "I apologize. It wasn't your fault. Good night." She stomped out and could be heard bellowing.

"Alain, I sincerely apologize," said Royce, rubbing his head as if it would explode from the pain inside. "She won't bother you anymore. I'll see to it."

"Thank you, Mr. Dent. Believe me when I tell you I would never hurt Amy." Alain dropped his voice. "I love her."

Royce Dent felt as overwhelmed as Alain. "I believe you, Alain. Go on with your life. You'll find love."

"If you say so. Good night."

The boys escorted Grandma Newton home. She made them stay the night and fed them breakfast before they went home.

Late the next afternoon when Fay started to make supper, her eye caught the empty hooks over the fireplace where Alain's gun usually hung.

"Alain?" Fay called into the room where Alain slept. He was not there. Fay climbed into the tree house. Alain was not there. Fay screamed in panic, "Robert Lee! Calvin!"

The two boys came from the field at the sound of their sister's screams.

"What's wrong?" they demanded.

"Where's Alain?"

"Don't know," answered Robert Lee.

"What's wrong, Fay?" asked Calvin.

"His shotgun's gone."

Calvin shrugged. "Maybe he went huntin'."

"No, he's gone crazy with grief over Amy. I'm scared he's hurt hisself. Take me to Gator's."

"Why?" asked Robert Lee.

"Maybe he went there."

"The truck's here," argued Calvin.

"Maybe he walked."

"It ain't likely he's at Gator's," said Robert Lee. "Maybe he went up to the waterfall."

"To that old clubhouse o' theirs?"

"Yeah, Fay. He was always happy there. It's a happy place for him."

"Okay. I'm goin' up there."

Robert Lee said, "Why?"

"'Cause he ain't *happy* right now." She huffed in exasperation.

"I'll go with you," offered Calvin.

"No, y'all take care o' ever'body else. I'll see to Alain. If he ain't there, then we'll hafta look."

Fay hiked up to the waterfall. Alain was not on the bank. She noticed that the clubhouse door was ajar. Anxiously, she opened the door.

Alain held the shotgun under his chin, and his hands trembled.

In alarm, Fay shrieked, "Alain! Whatcha doin'?"

Alain breathed, "Go away. Jest let me die. I cain't do it no more, Fay. My heart is broken. I jest cain't do it no more."

"You coward!"

"What?" Alain lowered the gun.

"You gonna take the easy way out? You gonna jest leave all of us? I didn't think you were that selfish."

Alain glared at Fay. "I ain't a coward."

"And yo life ain't over." She popped her hands to her hips, arms akimbo. "You'll git over Amy Dent."

"Fay, go home. Leave me alone."

"You gonna shoot yoself?"

"No."

Her tone much softer she asked, "Swear?"

"I ain't gonna kill myself. I'm too much of a coward."

"I didn't mean that."

"Fay, please leave."

"Why?"

"I don't wanna hurt you."

"You talkin' nonsense."

Alain threw the gun down. "Fay, I'm angry and hurt. I wanna hurt somebody, but I don't wanna be like Pa. You the closest person to me right now. I don't wanna hurt you."

"Alain."

"Damn it, Fay!" Alain stood and clenched his fists. "If you don't get outa here, I'm gonna throw you down on this bed and fuck you. Is that what you want?"

"You gonna what?" Her voice shrilled and echoed.

"Damn! You are ignorant!"

"That was mean. I know what it means. I jest cain't believe you said it to me." Fay turned to leave.

Alain grabbed Fay's wrist. "I'm sorry. I need you, Fay."

"You said never again."

"I need you."

"No. You said never again."

"Please?"

"I ain't a whore, Alain."

"No, you ain't. You my comfort."

"You said it ain't right."

"It ain't, but I don't care. I need you."

As the stars twinkled overhead, Fay came out of the clubhouse to see Alain staring at the water. She put her hand on his shoulder. He gently squeezed her hand.

"You ain't screamin' or cussin' or vomitin'," Fay noted.

"I'm so sorry." He backhanded tears from his face. "I broke my promise to you."

"I forgive you."

"I was wrong, Fay. How could I do that to you? You're sweet and loving, and you deserve a man who will love you. I'm so sorry. I swear to God, that was the last time."

"Alain, what if there's another baby?"

"Then there is."

"Is your heart still broke?"

Alain laughed sadly. "Yeah, Fay, it is, but it ain't your fault."

"I didn't comfort you?"

"No. I was wrong. I jest made things worse. That ain't your fault neither." He threw a rock into the water and watched the ripple as it slowly came to the bank.

"Am I ignorant, Alain?"

"I'm sorry I said that too. You're precious. I'm gonna make sure none o' y'all are ignorant."

"You always have."

"Forgive me for what I did?"

"Yes. You wouldn't have forced me."

"You sure?" He tilted his head to the side. "I *did* force you. I manipulated you. I coerced you. It's jest as bad as physically forcing you."

"You ain't evil."

"I feel evil."

"No more, right?"

"No more."

"Then, let's go home."

"Yeah."

Alain wedged the door on the clubhouse shut after he got his gun. He took Fay's hand and kissed it. "I love you, Fay. It jest cain't be like that."

"I know. And I love you. Alain, what's the cure for a broken heart?"

"There ain't one."

22

Brothel

A couple of months after Amy and Tipper Campbell had a baby girl they named Betsy, Alain and Fay Richter had a baby girl they called Mary. Gator visited Alain and brought a rattle for the baby.

"You don't hate me?" Alain asked.

"No. Why did you choose Matthew and Mary?"

"Promise not to laugh?"

"Yeah."

"Matthew means 'gift of God.' He's my gift. I love him very much. I want him to always know I treasure him even if others think he's a curse, punishment for my sin."

"I understand. I think it's sweet; mushy, but sweet. You *should* love him. Pa always said that. Why Mary?"

"She's a bittersweet blessing. Mary means 'sea of bitterness.' I will never touch Fay again. *I swear it*. Mary was born of my bitterness, but I will love her. That's the sweetness."

"Alain, you don't sound like a hillbilly when you talk about them. You sound old and educated."

"I can read, Gator." He crossed his arms across his chest. "That's how I know the meaning of their names. I get books at the county library. I'm gonna teach my kids and my siblings. I promised Fay I would make sure none of us were ignorant. We ain't stupid or retarded. I might not be a teacher, but I can teach everybody out here to read and do arithmetic."

"Yes, you can. Pa would be proud of that."

"It's sort of Tal's idea. Remember when he told that welfare lady we home-schooled?"

"Yeah."

"That's what I'm gonna do. You can order books in the mail. I've been reading about it."

"Pa would truly be proud of you."

"You can do it too. You can teach yourself. You're welcome to any books we get."

"Thanks."

Alain did teach his family, and three hours a day were devoted to lessons around the table. He spent time every day with Matthew and Mary.

On his twenty-first birthday, Alain decided to give Matthew his first fishing lesson. They hiked to the fishing hole, cane poles in hand, with Matthew having periodic piggyback rides. As they approached through the woods, Alain heard laughter.

Matthew slid off Alain's back. "Somebody's here, Papa," he said.

"Stay here. Sh."

Alain peered through the trees to see Tipper stretched full length, propped on one elbow, one knee in the air, completely naked as Amy painted him.

"Tipper, be still," Amy chided.

"The grass is itchy," Tipper complained.

"Just cooperate. I'll pay you back. How many condoms did you bring?"

"Two."

"Hold your position long enough for me to get this down, and we'll use one."

"Keep talking like that, and my position will change drastically of its own accord."

"Hush! You're bad."

"I thought I was good. You don't complain."

"Tipper Campbell, be quiet. I'm done. Come see."

Tipper walked behind Amy. "Oh. Don't *ever* show that to anybody. Do I really look like that?"

"You're better in person, every inch of you."

Tipper ran his hands up Amy's legs, lifting the sundress she wore. "Where did you leave those little panties?"

"Somewhere by the stream. I'll find 'em later. Mm. Oh."

Alain whirled around to see Matthew watching the scene with big, wide, innocent green eyes. He reached up for his father to pick him up, which Alain did. The little boy put one hand on each of the man's cheeks. "Don't cry, Papa. I love you."

"I love you too," Alain choked.

Alain closed his eyes and remembered Amy's touch seven years before and how warm her body had felt next to his on a private hayride. For a moment he let himself imagine he was in Tipper's place.

Matthew whispered, "Papa, let's fish another day."

"You're right. Sorry."

"Why are you so sad?"

"Women."

"Momma's nice."

"Yes, she is."

"Papa, do you like Mrs. Campbell?"

"Mrs. Campbell." He gusted a breath. "I used to. Seeing her makes me sad, so let's go home. Let's go make me a birthday cake."

"With candles?"

"Twenty-one."

"Okay. Just don't cry."

Alain kissed the little boy on the forehead. "I'll try."

Gator welcomed the knock on his door as he started to make supper for one. Eating alone depressed him. Gator opened the door. "Alain, I ain't goin' to Fester's with you. Once was enough."

"Happy birthday to me!" laughed Alain. "I ain't goin' to Fester's neither. I've got Robert Lee and Calvin in the truck. I'm twenty-one today. I want you to celebrate with me."

"Have you already been drinkin'? Yo eyes are bloodshot."

"Can I come in a minute?"

"Sure. You got somethin' on yo mind?" He opened the door wide.

Alain stepped inside. "I seen somethin' today that got me real upset. Don't you laugh. I been cryin'."

"Why?"

"I seen Tipper and Amy together. She was paintin' him naked."

"Amy was naked?"

"Not at first. She was paintin' Tipper without his clothes on. Then, they, well, you know." Alain did a rolling hand motion. "I thought I was past it, but it hurt, Gator."

"You gotta git over that womern."

"I know. That's why we goin' to the city. Come with me. You the only real friend I got."

"Oh, okay. Make me feel guilty, why don't you? Happy birthday. I won't fix me any supper."

"We'll eat in the city. Let's go."

The four young men packed into the truck and drove to Wilmington. They stopped in front of a big, fancy house across the railroad tracks on the far side of town. The house was ablaze with lights, and music wafted from the open windows. There were no other houses nearby, and cars lined the street. A neon sign above the door flashed the name of the place, "Jacqui's Gentlemen's Club."

"What kind of place is this?" asked Gator.

"You can read," laughed Alain. "It's a gentlemen's club."

"Ain't that jest a fancy name for a whorehouse?"

"Let's go find out." He clapped Gator on the shoulder. "I ain't been to Jacqui's since she changed locations."

A gigantic man stopped the four at the door. "I.D.," he demanded. "You gotta be eighteen to enter." He pointed at Gator. "You might be fifteen."

"I'm twenty," contradicted Gator.

Gator looked much younger than his age. He kept his chestnut hair cut short and still only had to shave once a week. He was short and stout, but muscular. Compared to the Richter boys, he looked young. All of them were tall and lean with caramel brown hair. Robert Lee and Calvin had their father's light golden-brown eyes while Alain's were cat-green. In addition, all three had full beards. Alain's was even long and shaggy, much like a member of ZZ Top.

"Humph!" grunted the man as he checked driver's licenses. "You really are." He handed Alain a golden ticket. "Happy birthday. Your birthday entitles you to a free lap dance. Have fun."

The house was divided into several sections. The first room was a restaurant where appetizing dishes were served. There were no waiters, only topless waitresses.

Two rooms on either side of the dining area were bars with stages and two cages. Women danced nude inside the cages, and every half hour a woman performed a striptease on stage.

The four Possum Hollerites took a table in the bar on the left. A topless waitress wearing only a thong came to their table. "I'm Candy. What can I get you fellas?"

Alain held up his golden ticket. "Happy birthday," said Candy in a sugary tone. "I'll let Tori know. You want drinks while you wait?"

"What's good?" asked Alain.

"For the birthday boy, I recommend a sloe screw."

"With you?"

"That's not my job. If you're looking for more intimate entertainment, you need to go to the parlor, through there." Candy pointed out a set of French doors. "You gotta buy a drink though. That's my job. Tori will be able to dance for you in about ten minutes unless you would like to visit the parlor first. I'm supposed to make sure you're all twenty-one to have drinks, but I'm going to assume you are, so what'll you have?"

Alain winked at Candy. "Bring a round of your recommendation."

"Comin' right up."

"Whoa!" whispered Gator as their waitress walked away. "They at least look better'n Fester's girls."

Alain gloated, "I hear they git regular checkups too. No diseases."

"Is this place legal?"

"If you know how to grease some palms." He placed his hands flat on the table and leaned back in the chair. "Jacqui's been around a while."

Candy brought the drinks. "You gonna run a tab or move to the back?"

"We'll take our drinks to the parlor, but we'll be back," Alain promised as he slid the money for the drinks and a tip for Candy's service under the strap of her thong and let his fingers trail down her thigh. "You sure I cain't interest you into goin' to the back with me?" Candy giggled and walked on.

"Let's go to the parlor, gents," Alain suggested. "Gator, you ready to become a man?"

"I *am* a man, Alain." There was no levity in Gator's statement.

"Course, you are."

The four men entered the parlor where women in sexy lingerie lounged and walked everywhere. From time to time a woman would go upstairs with a man.

"'Welcome to my parlor,' said the spider to the fly,'" Gator said under his breath.

"Good pickin's," mumbled Robert Lee.

"Uh-huh," agreed Calvin, pointing to a set of twins.

"Let's socialize," said Alain.

The four men moved in different directions. Gator was ready to run out the door until he saw a young woman with sandy-blonde hair wearing a baby-blue teddy and sitting alone on the seat of the bay window. He could not take his eyes off her.

Alain caught his brothers' eyes and indicated Gator who crossed the room to where the young woman sat. They all felt triumphant at having found a woman for Gator as they continued their prowl.

Alain found a tall, slender brunette with brown eyes. She wore a scarlet bustier. "Hello," he said.

The woman looked at him with a little disgust. Alain truly looked as if he could be a member of the band ZZ Top with his chestnut hair long and in a ponytail and his caramel beard long and frizzled. Still, his green eyes danced.

"Hello," the woman said.

"Jest tell me your name is Amy."

"My name is…"

Alain held out a twenty. "Off the books if your name is Amy. I'm Alain."

"Good evening, Alain. I'm Amy."

Alain stuffed the twenty into her cleavage and pulled out a hundred. "Twice the going rate, right?"

"Yep."

He stuffed the one crisp bill into her cleavage and pulled out another twenty.

"What's that for?" she asked.

"I want it rough."

"How rough?"

"I'm not gonna hit you, but I don't want to be gentle. I'm right mad at you, Amy. You hurt me. You broke my heart, and I'd like a little payback. I wanna bend you over a table and take you from behind like a dog fuckin' a bitch in heat. To hell with the foreplay."

"Double it."

Alain pulled out another twenty and stuffed the forty into the woman's cleavage.

"Let's go, Alain."

"Lead the way, Amy."

The door had barely closed before "Amy" could be heard making very crude guttural sounds as Alain relieved all his frustration.

Sometime later, Alain, Robert Lee, and Calvin were back in the bar. Gator plopped into a fourth chair.

"Where you been?" asked Alain.

"Meetin' a purty womern."

"Ho! Ho!" laughed Alain. "Do tell."

"Alain, are you still a musketeer?"

"Depends."

"A damsel in distress needs yo help."

"You better explain," insisted Alain. "Am I gonna go to jail? I don't like jail."

"You won't know nothin'. I jest need a distraction. You might git thrown out though."

Alain held up his ticket. "I ain't got my birthday present yet. Maybe, I'll need to inspect it." Alain grinned. "If'n anybody messes with me, my brothers have my back. How 'bout you?"

"Ain't I always?"

Alain leaned in close. "Are you sneakin' a girl out?"

"The less you know, the better."

"The little girl in the blue teddy?"

"What?"

"The one that looks like Miss Ina?"

"What?"

"I seen her. Yeah, she needs to git out. She don't belong here."

Alain sat back as a woman with breasts too big for her frame came up. She wore a see-through robe trimmed in feathers and nothing else. "Whose birthday is it?" she asked.

Alain held up his golden ticket and grinned. The woman straddled Alain, and the music started. She began to writhe and grind on his lap. Alain smirked as he winked at Gator. Alain calmly grabbed the woman's crotch and slid his fingers inside her.

She screamed and slapped Alain. "Stop that! I'm not a hooker. I don't get paid for that."

Alain purposely slurred his words. "Who you tryin' to fool, me or yoshelf? You jesht ash much a whore ash any o' them women upshtairs."

"Oh! You disgusting hillbilly." The woman hit Alain again.

"Bitch!" Alain yelled and grabbed her wrist.

The woman screamed shrilly. Jimmy Joe, the bouncer and bull from the door, ran into the bar as Alain tried to kiss the woman. Jacqueline, the owner, followed closely on Jimmy Joe's heels.

Gator saw a blue lightning streak out of the corner of his eye. Jimmy Joe barely turned his head toward the door before he got Alain in a bear hug and dragged him away from the woman. Alain struggled.

"Whoa! Whoa!" shouted Gator. "Alain, stop. Look at me." Gator took Alain's face in his hands. "That ain't her job. You in the wrong room."

"He's in the wrong house!" shrieked Jacqueline.

"I'm sorry, Ms. Fields," said Gator. "It's his birthday, and he's jest real drunk. Let us take him home."

Jacqueline looked at Gator. "You a Richter? You Sherry's little friend."

Gator grinned. "Sherry was real good to me. You woulda thought it was *my* birthday, not Alain's."

"Take the lug home. He ain't usually this bad. I assume he's very drunk. Still, don't come back for a long time."

"Yes, ma'am. Robert Lee, you drunk?"

"Naw."

"You drive."

Robert Lee fished the keys from Alain's pocket. Calvin and Gator draped one of Alain's arms over their shoulders and escorted him out of Jacqui's Gentlemen's Club.

The Richter boys could hardly contain their delight. At the truck, Gator offered to sit in the back because the cab was too crowded.

Alain whispered, "Is her name Sherry?"

"Yeah. Sherry Fields."

"Holy shit! Jacqui's daughter is runnin' away with you?"

"I'm rescuin' a damsel in distress."

"I hope you don't get yoself killed. You're a good one, Gator. That's what I should've done to Amy. That purty girl don't belong in a brothel."

23

Hunter

The next morning, Jacqueline Fields raged through her establishment. "Where is that girl?" she screamed.

Jimmy Joe came down the stairs. "Jacqui, all her clothes are gone."

"She ran away?"

"Looks like it. I don't think if somebody forced her to leave, they woulda waited for her to pack," Jimmy Joe said, rolling his eyes.

Jacqui scowled at him. "With whom?"

"I didn't see her leave, Jacqui. She musta snuck out when I was breakin' up that Richter mess. That was the only time I wudn't at the door except I took a piss once."

Jacqui shook her head. "I can't believe she would've left with them. She wouldn't have trusted them. They would've scared her." She held up a hand. "Wait. That other boy that was with them. She liked him. Did you check his I.D.?"

"Of course, I did."

"Where do those hillbillies live? It would've been on there."

"Jacqui, I checked their age, not names or addresses. Alain Richter has visited your establishment often, but I have no idea where they live." He pointed skyward. "Up in the hills somewhere. I'm not going after those Richter boys. I wanna stay alive."

"I have a hunter if I need one," Jacqui snarled.

Jacqui rounded up all the girls, rousting them from their sleep. She grilled them about the Richters. The tall brunette said, "I was with Alain last night. He's the one with the long beard, right?"

Jacqui nodded. "Yes, Blanche, it was his birthday. He assaulted Tori during his lap dance."

Blanche snorted and continued, "He was real angry. He wanted to call me Amy and wanted to forgo foreplay."

Another woman piped up. "Alain Richter is a sweetheart. I've serviced him a few times. He has always been gentle as a lamb. As a matter of fact, that young man is quite talented in the lovemaking department."

Blanche stared at the slightly older woman. "I didn't say it wudn't good, Delilah, but he was angry with Amy."

"Oh, my God!" shouted Jacqui. "Stop fighting over Alain Richter. If you wanna fuck him off the clock, that's your prerogative, but if he's here, he pays. Back to the matter at hand. Blanche, did he give you a last name of this Amy?"

"No, just Amy."

"His woman?"

"I think she broke his heart."

"What about the others?"

"Which ones were they?" asked Delilah.

A blonde said, "You know the two that looked like twins, Robert Lee and Calvin."

Jacqui indicated for her to continue. "That's all I know. Violet and Pansy took 'em. They said they wanted flowers, and they wanted to be together. Violet and Pansy are twins too."

Jacqui stared at the twins who were no more than fifteen. "Well?"

"They didn't tell us where they lived," said Pansy. "We thought they were twins like us, and that's why they wanted us. Rob and Cal is all we know."

"What aren't you telling me?" asked Jacqui. She shook a chastising finger. "I can tell you're hiding something."

Violet barely whispered, "They flipped us."

"Did you charge twice?" asked Jacqui.

"No."

"Your sacrifice. You will give me the other half as soon as we leave this room. Those Richters must be damned good the way y'all treat 'em." Jacqui turned to Jimmy Joe. "Get Bilbo on it. I want her found and brought home. For this, I'll let you break her, maybe Bilbo. He'd like that. That boy said she was good to him. I bet he lied because he got sweet on her."

"Jacqui," said Jimmy Joe. "Maybe you should let her go."

"I paid good money for her!"

"She was a baby. She's cost you more than she'll make for you."

"Because she was puny and stubborn like all damned hillbillies. You've always babied her. Did you help her escape?"

"If I had done that, I would've gone with her, you bitch."

Jacqui glowered at Jimmy Joe whose scars from Jacqui's domination were visible. "Just find her, and I don't care who gets hurt in the process."

Bilbo Jenkins, Jacqui's hitman, got his assignment. Jimmy Joe warned, "You better not come back without her. Jacqui's pissed."

"She's got three other little girls."

"I think she's crazy, but I won't cross her ever again." Jimmy Joe pointed to the scar across his cheek. "There are others from before you were employed. She'd have you kill me, and you'd do it."

"I've done some nasty things for Jacqui to be sure."

Jimmy Joe was a huge man at six and a half feet, and three hundred pounds; however, he had proven no match for Jacqui's goons. Of course, he had not been much more than a child of the streets himself when Jacqui took him in, no older than Alain Richter had been when he lost his parents. His light brown hair and blue eyes indicated some Viking heritage, but he was a gentle soul and conflicted about Sherry. He loved the child.

Bilbo Jenkins was not as big, but big enough at six-two, two hundred pounds. He was the antithesis of Jimmy with his black hair and eyes that showed no emotion or compassion. He was hard and cold and calculating. Bilbo had more than one body notched on his gun belt. He was a misanthrope; he cared very little for mankind.

Bilbo left Jimmy Joe and began his research. He liked to know his target, but in this case, he was unsure exactly who to target. The only name he had was Alain Richter.

What little information he could find on the Richter Clan made even a seasoned killer wary. He read and re-read the account of the murder-suicide at the Richter home. *That boy killed his old man. I don't care what the ruling was. Alain Richter is a badass. I'll have to be careful with him. Now to find my way there.*

A couple of nights after Sherry ran away with Gator, there was pounding on Alain's door. Alain held a finger up to all his siblings and the children before he took the shotgun off its rack. He stood to the side as Robert Lee opened the door. Alain stepped up with the shotgun aimed.

"Who are you, and what do you want?" Alain demanded of the man in a suit.

"My name is Bilbo Jenkins. Ms. Fields would like her daughter returned to her."

"Who the hell is Ms. Fields?"

"Jacqui."

"She's got a young'un?" Alain feigned surprise.

"Sherry Fields disappeared the night you and your brothers came to Jacqui's establishment. Jacqui wants her back."

"Mister, ain't nobody here but my fam'ly. You best be movin' on. Hillbillies don't trust strange men in suits. Might think you're a G-man. You might git shot."

"Mr. Richter, may I, please, speak with your three brothers who came with you?"

"No. It ain't none o' yo business."

"Alain?" said Fay from the shadows.

"Fay, shut up."

"Mister," said Fay, "you the law?"

"No, just Ms. Fields's messenger."

"Fay!" Alain snarled. "Shut up!"

"What's this to do with us, Alain?"

"Not a damned thing. Now, shut up."

"Is this man lookin' for Gator?"

Alain signaled to Robert Lee who dragged Fay out the back door with his hand over her mouth.

"Mr. Richter," said Bilbo, "is Sherry Fields with this Gator?"

"Damned if I know."

"Mr. Richter, does Gator know Sherry's a child?"

"Does Ms. Fields? Was she workin'? Surely not, if she's a child. Mr. Jenkins, I'm right sorry somebody kidnapped little Miss Fields, but nobody in Possum Holler kidnapped nobody. Has Ms. Fields received a ransom note? Which girl was she?"

"I don't know. No, there's been no note."

"Then, maybe the young'un didn't git kidnapped. Maybe she run off. Maybe she didn't wanna be a whore." He put the barrel of the gun into Bilbo's chest. "Now, git off my property before I shoot you." He slammed the door in the interloper's face.

Bilbo Jenkins realized he had met his match. He went back to his car and sat for a few moments in thought. *Whoa! He would shoot me. Damn it, Jacqui. I'm charging double for this pain in the ass.*

Once the gravel crunching indicated the city slicker was gone, Alain yelled, "Fay Richter!"

Fay came in. Alain glowered at her. "Fay, if somethin' happens to Gator because of yo mouth, you're gonna think Pa's back. I will wring yo neck. When I tell you to shut up, I have reason." He pointed. "That man is a hired killer. Now, I'm gonna have to go to Gator and warn him. What if he follows me? We could both end up dead."

Emotionally, Fay stammered, "I-I-I didn't know, Alain. I was tryin' to keep you safe."

"I don't need yo help," Alain lamented.

"Is that girl with Gator?"

"Yep."

"By choice?"

"Yep."

"I'm sorry."

"I know you didn't mean no harm. Next time, let me handle it."

"I think you scared him."

"Not enough. I'm worried. If he found us, he can find Gator. Gator ain't as mean as me."

"If you think he'll follow you, don't go nowhere. If you don't run out, he'll think he was wrong."

"She could have a point," said Robert Lee.

"Maybe," agreed Alain, stroking his long beard in thought. "But I'm gonna go tomorrow. I'll take some produce, so it looks like a delivery."

"Okay. Alain, I'm sorry," Fay said again.

"I know, Fay. Maybe, it'll be okay."

Bilbo had wasted two days searching legal documents to find the Richters; they had been a dead end. He had waited for hours for Alain to lead him to Gator. He wondered if he was on the wrong track.

After getting very little sleep, Bilbo tried a different approach on the heart of Possum Holler. *How many "Gators" can there possibly be?*

He drove into Possum Holler in a regal Pontiac Bonneville and was dressed in a double-breasted suit. Several residents eyed him curiously. He watched a number of women talking, most likely about him. The women stood on the steps of Dent's General Store. He took in the small hamlet. *Backwoods.*

He noted the one church, white clapboard. The house next to it was neatly kept and of the same general design. *Must be the place where the preacher lives.*

He saw that the power lines strung in town stopped abruptly just before the bridge over a small creek. All the homes in the area were simple wood structure, not a brick building to be seen. The largest house by far sat at the end of the only real road, and it was packed gravel rather than pavement. A little farther around a corner sat the only business he could make out—a slaughterhouse. Besides that, Dent's appeared to be the only other place people might work. *Most must work in the mines outside of town.* He nodded to himself. *Makes sense.*

Climbing out of his car, Bilbo walked to the women. He was not an unattractive man with a trim, firm body and slick gelled black hair and dark fathomless eyes. He flashed a charming smile at the group a females. "Ladies, good morning. I'm Bilbo Jenkins. I'm from Wilmington. I'm looking for a young man named Gator. I don't know his last name."

"Is he in some kind of trouble?" asked Lucille.

"No. He accidently picked up something that belongs to a friend of mine. She sent me to retrieve it, but we don't know his last name or where he lives."

"Jones," said Lucille. "He's a good boy. He's never been in any trouble. He lives by himself way out, Jones Hog Farm."

"Thank you so much. How do I get there?"

"You go straight on out this road 'til it forks." She pointed back the way Bilbo had come. "Take the right fork. You'll pass the old Reardon place on your left, but it's far off the road. The next turn on the left will be the Jones place. If you keep goin', you'll get to the Richter place." She shook her head. "You don't wanna go there."

"Thank you, ma'am."

As Bilbo drove the way Lucille had instructed, he thought, *you are so right. I don't want to go to the Richter place again.*

Alain Richter jerked his head up from gathering the butterbeans he intended to take to Gator so he could warn him about Bilbo. "Why would there be shots at Gator's. That was two diff'rent guns," he said out loud. "The first one was a handgun. That second was a shotgun."

Alain glared at Fay. "He found Gator"

Before anyone could stop him, Alain bounded into the pickup and slung dirt and gravel as he left. Another shotgun blast resounded as Alain turned into the Joneses' drive. Seconds after Gator fired a deadly blast into Bilbo Jenkins, Alain screeched to a stop. "Gator! What happened? I heard shots."

"He's dead," stammered Gator. "I shot him. Alain, there's a dead man in a fancy suit laying in my yard. What do I do?"

24
Reciprocating Aid

"**Stay** calm, Gator. Did he come lookin' for Sherry? He showed up at our place last night. I was comin' over with butterbeans to make it look like I was bringin' 'em to you jest in case he was watchin'. I didn't wanna look suspicious. Sorry I was so slow."

Alain looked at the terrified girl standing there. *Lord! She looks like Miss Ina.* Alain said, "Sherry, ever'thing's okay. Are you hurt? I'm Gator's friend, Alain Richter."

"Hey," said Sherry in shock. "This ain't how I wanted to meet you. Yeah, he was lookin' for me. He was tryin' to make me go back. I done shot him inside. I guess I kindly missed. He said I shot him."

"Good girl. Even a few pellets slowed him down." said Alain. "You ain't gotta go back. We'll see to it." He turned back to his friend. "Feed him to yo hogs, Gator."

"No! I don't want none o' him on my property."

"Then, we gotta feed him to the gators. Gators don't leave no evidence. They eat bones and all."

"How you know that?"

"I read, Gator."

"What do I do?"

"First, Sherry, git a couple o' changes o' clothes. You goin' to our clubhouse. There's food there. You'll be okay for a couple o' days. I promise they won't never come lookin' for you again."

Sherry blinked her big blue eyes at Alain. "How, Alain? How can you be sure?"

"Trust me. You too, Gator."

"Okay," said Gator.

"Relax. Breathe," said Alain. "I owe you for my pa."

"I ain't keepin' score," said Gator.

"Me neither," assured Alain, "but do you remember what Tal said about us bein' friends through all kinds of things?"

"Yeah."

"This is one of those things. Sherry, git yo clothes."

Sherry ran into the house.

"Put the shotgun up," Alain said to Gator

Gator took the firearm inside and came out with Sherry. "Come on, both o' you. Leave the vermin where it is," said Alain. He looked at the sky. "It's gonna rain soon. All the blood'll be gone."

The three of them got into Alain's truck. Alain drove as close to the waterfall as he could. Then, they hiked up. Alain showed Sherry the food. He encouraged her, "You'll be okay for a few days. There's food, water, and a place to sleep. The clubhouse is solid. If it rains, you'll be protected. It's warm, so you won't need a fire."

"What if you don't come back?" Sherry asked fearfully.

"That won't happen, but *if*, go to my place just up the road from Gator's and get Robert Lee, my brother, to take you to Grandma Newton. Tell her *everything*. She won't let nobody hurt you; she'll help. But give us a whole week. Okay? We got a long drive."

Sherry nodded.

Alain nudged Gator. "Hurry up."

Sherry flung her arms around Gator. "Thank you. I love you forever."

"I'll be back, Sherry. We can trust Alain. Sherry, I love you. I really love you."

"I love you too, really."

Gator kissed Sherry the way a man kisses a woman for he feared he would never return.

"Come on, Gator," urged Alain.

Gator and Alain got back to Gator's farm. Alain asked, "Do you have an old blanket?"

"Yeah."

"Git it."

The two men wrapped the body in the blanket and deposited it in the trunk of Bilbo's own car.

"Gator, you gotta relax," said Alain. "It's fixin' to rain. That'll wash all the blood away. We goin' to Florida. They got lots o' gators." Alain looked at the body. "You got butcher saws?"

"Yeah."

"Bring 'em and some aprons and gloves if you got 'em."

Gator put several saws, some that looked like hack saws and others that could have been small wood saws, along with his chain saw, in the trunk. He threw in two aprons with bibs and two pairs of rubber gloves he used around the farm. Alain clapped Gator on the shoulder. "I'll drive. You too wound up."

As they drove to Florida, Gator told Alain Sherry's story. She was Jacqueline Fields's adopted daughter. Her mother had been an unwed hillbilly. Jacqui had paid all the bills for the woman to get the baby, just as she had for several women to get baby girls to fill her stable of prostitutes. Sherry had refused to turn her first trick, and the john had hit her, which made Jacqui mad. However, when Gator had met Sherry, Jacqui thought the perfect customer had propositioned the newbie hooker. Sherry and Gator had eloped. Fester married them. Alain looked as much in shock over the story as Gator did over killing a man. A million secrets swirled through Alain's head.

Seventeen hours later, Gator and Alain turned onto a dirt road in Miami-Dade County, Florida. It led to an area of everglades. Alain parked. "Okay, Gator," assured Alain. "You didn't murder nobody. This fool come on yo property and tried to take yo womern. You defended her. That's it. Yeah, he looks fancy, but he ain't nothin' more'n one o' Jacqui's goons. Don't you know, Gator, she's a part o' organized crime? What she done to Sherry's real ma was illegal. She stole that baby. That ignorant hillbilly didn't know no better. Now, help me feed the gators."

Alain and Gator laid the body on the blanket in front of the headlights. Alain revved the chainsaw.

"I'm gonna be sick," said Gator.

"No, you ain't," said Alain sternly. "I need yo help."

Still, Gator vomited into the bog. Alain laid the chainsaw aside. Then the two men stripped the body, throwing the bloody clothes back into the trunk. Alain handed Gator one of the aprons and donned one himself. "We gotta use the butcher saws. Chainsaw might get stuck." The two men cut the body into pieces and fed the Florida alligators. Butchering the dead man wasn't much harder than cutting up pigs, cutting in the joints and making almost bite-sized pieces for the huge reptiles to eat. Dividing the torso proved the hardest and provided the most need to be covered with the aprons.

They watched as the creatures devoured the body parts. Satisfied, Alain said, "They won't never find a part o' him."

"What about the car?" asked Gator.

"That's what a blow torch is for. I'll take care of it. I can use these parts."

Alain pulled off the gloves and apron, tossing them in the trunk. Gator followed his example. Alan stopped his friend near the car door. "You look good. I don't see blood on you. You'll be okay, Gator."

Alain and Gator drove into Wilmington. "You gotta do it, Gator; it's gotta come from you," Alain said encouragingly. "You brave enough to do this for Sherry."

The two men broke the lock on the door to Jacqui's Gentlemen's Club as the occupants slept. They cracked doors until they found Jacqueline Fields. A door down the hall barely parted and closed quickly. Alain looked around, wary, as he thought he heard a squeak.

Gator popped his hand over Jacqui's mouth. "Shut up and listen," he whispered. "You won't never see Bilbo again. Anybody else comes lookin' for Sherry, they gonna end up the same. Then, I'm comin' for you. Do you understand? Jest nod."

Jacqueline nodded. "Leave Sherry alone, or you're gonna meet Bilbo in Hell real soon," Gator reiterated. "You best remember hillbillies don't like outsiders. Nod if you understand."

Jacqueline nodded.

Gator added, "If I ever come in this room again, it'll be to kill you. Don't make me do it."

In the car, Alain said, "You done good. Damn! I believed you."

Gator said, "That's not the scary part. *I* believed me."

Alain nodded. "Good. That's jest like a gator. They won't mess with you unless you mess with them, but if they bite, you'll know you've been bit. If you have to come back, I'll help you."

"Thanks."

Alain pulled the Bonneville behind his barn. "Oh," he sighed. "It's a shame to destroy this baby."

"Wish I could give it to you," said Gator.

Alain shrugged. "Cain't be helped." Alain fired up the acetylene torch, and with the help of his brothers, the Bonneville was in pieces within a couple of hours. The parts found their way to a junkyard, and the metal found its way into a number of stills.

Fay walked outside and looked forlornly at Gator. She had desired him once. "I'm sorry, Gator," she said contritely.

"It's okay," Gator said.

"How can I make it better though?" asked Fay.

"Be my wife's friend."

"Yo wife? Y'all married?"

"Yeah. Fester married us."

"Bring her over to meet all of us."

"I will, Fay."

Alain changed clothes and rolled the ones he had worn into a bundle. He and Gator walked back to Gator's place. The rain had washed away the blood from the yard. "Change clothes and go git yo bride," Alain encouraged. "I'm gonna burn the blanket and our clothes and put in a new window and lock." He took a deep breath. "I gotta go to town. I hope I don't see Lucille. When you git back, Sherry can hang her new curtains over a new glass window."

"How can I ever thank you?"

"Be my friend."

"Always. I love you like a brother."

Alain smiled, then, laughed. "You ain't a Richter."

"I ain't?"

"Nope. Maybe we Joneses. At least one of us really is. Tal was more like a pa to me than my own. Yeah, Gator, you my brother. I love you too."

Gator and Alain embraced.

Alain laughed. "Go bring yo bride home and git some sleep. You look awful."

"You looked in a mirror lately?" Gator grinned.

"I'm fixin' the window and burnin' the stuff. Then, I'm goin' home and sleepin' for two days. Bring Sherry over to meet ever'body."

Gator left to get Sherry. Alain drove to Dent's General Store.

The second Alain entered the store, Lucille retreated to the back. Royce shook his head. "Alain, what can I do for you? You haven't been in for a long time."

Alain pointed toward the back. "I won't be coming often." He handed Royce measurements. "I need you to cut me a piece of glass to fit a window. The kids broke one."

"Not a problem."

While Royce cut glass, Alain got a new door lock and caulking to seal the window. Royce came out with the glass pane. "What else can I get for you?"

Alain laid his other items on the counter. He added a package of bologna and sliced cheese and a loaf of sliced bread.

"Unusual purchase."

"With the broken glass, we didn't have time to cook. We'll have some bologna and cheese sandwiches for supper."

"You need some mayonnaise and mustard to make 'em taste good."

Alain grabbed a small container of each. "Thank you, Mr. Dent."

Alain paid for his purchase and went back to Gator's place.

Lucille came out after he left. "What'd he want?"

"He's got rambunctious kids. They broke a window, and he's replacing it. Not that it's any of your business," replied Royce. "You were downright rude to a customer. Don't do it again."

Alain got to the Jones farm. He burned the blanket and clothes and replaced the window and the door lock. He made half a dozen bologna and cheese sandwiches and covered them with a dishtowel. He made two for himself and ate them as he drove home.

Gator brought Sherry into a safe house and a simple meal, courtesy of a man he loved like a brother. Alain got home to a thousand questions.

He held up a hand to silence all his siblings. "Let's just say I was reciprocating aid. Gator's safe. None of you will discuss any of this with anyone."

25

Pastoral Visit

Gator took Sherry to the Richter place the next day to meet the whole family. She felt as if she actually belonged with these people. No one judged her or questioned her.

He brought his new wife to church the following Sunday after being the focus of speculation for having missed one Sunday. Naturally, Sherry was the topic of conversation. Gator looked around hoping that Alain had decided to come to church. Of course, that hope was dashed quickly. Alain did not bring his family into town anymore as a way to shield them from gossip and ridicule.

Once everyone had greeted Sherry perfunctorily after she made a profession of faith, Lucille made a point of trying to get to know her better at the potluck dinner on the grounds that was the weekly ritual for the congregation of Possum Holler Community Church.

"Congratulations," said Lucille with sticky sweetness.

"Thank you." Sherry smiled winsomely.

"You look so young."

"I'm sixteen."

"What do your parents think of Gator?"

"I ain't got none."

"Oh. I thought, perhaps, Mr. Jenkins came on behalf of your family."

"You mean the man with the black hair?"

"Yes."

"No, ma'am. We sorta got our papers mixed up at the judge. It's straightened out now."

"Hm. So, he wasn't a business acquaintance of Gator's?"

"No, although his woman is sorta in livestock."

"What kind?"

"Heifers."

Gator almost choked on one of Ina's stuffed eggs as he overheard Sherry's comment. He rescued his bride. "I'm stealin' her away, Mrs. Dent."

"Of course."

"I'd like her to meet some other people." Gator steered Sherry toward the Campbell family. "I'd like you to git to know some of the people I actually care about," he whispered. He chuckled in Sherry's ear. "Heifers? You have a great sense of humor. Let me introduce you to the bane of Lucille's existence."

Gator approached Tipper, Amy, and Ina. "Tipper, Amy, Miss Ina, I want y'all to git to know my Sherry."

It was Ina's turn to choke as she stared at a reflection of herself.

With a smile, Tipper said, "It's nice to see someone has finally snagged Gator. Welcome to Possum Holler."

"Thank you. Have you and Gator been friends as long as him and Alain. Ain't you one of his musketeer friends?"

"Yep. He told you about that?"

"Yes. I think it's nice. I ain't got many friends."

"You do now," said Amy sweetly. "I see you met my momma."

"Who?"

"Lucille," grunted Tipper.

"That's your momma?" asked Sherry, her voice squeaking in shock. "How'd you turn out sweet when she's an old heifer?"

Tipper cackled. Amy scowled at him. "She is," said Tipper defensively. "Sherry's only met her once and can tell. Trust me, Sherry, Amy's good temperament must come from Royce."

"The man that owns the store?" asked Sherry.

"Yes," said Amy.

"He's nice."

"Yes, Daddy is," agreed Amy. "So, what do you like best about Possum Holler?"

"Gator."

"Naturally. Least?"

"It's too dark, I ain't got runnin' water, and I hear strange sounds. But Gator just puts his arms around me, and I feel safe."

Ina finally found her voice. "Well, we're mighty glad to have you. Gator, you bring her to the house often, you hear?"

Gator nodded. "Yes, ma'am. Thank you, Miss Ina."

"Matter o' fact, y'all come for supper on Wednesday."

"We will. Thank you."

Gator moved on and introduced Grandma Newton who looked from Sherry to Ina and back. "How old did you say you are?"

"Sixteen."

"Where are yo folks?"

"Dead. I was raised in a home with a lot of other girls."

"How'd y'all meet?"

Gator took over. "Sherry was workin' in a place I ate in Wilmington. I saw her, and it was love at first sight."

"How romantic. Did you carry her over the threshold?"

"Yes, ma'am."

"Well, darlin', you part o' my fam'ly now. If'n you need anything like womern advice, jest ask. I've satisfied six husbands."

"Thank you." Sherry blushed.

When they got home, Sherry said simply, "I liked church and almost ever'body I met, 'cept Lucille. She ain't nice. She's just a nosy old heifer."

Gator laughed. "No, she's not real nice."

"Gator, why don't Alain go to church?"

"He don't think people like him."

"Why? He's nice."

"He's a good man. He jest made a couple o' mistakes."

"What kind?"

Gator hesitated. Finally, he said, "Young'uns with his sister."

"Oh. Why? Fay?"

"Yes, Fay."

Sherry folded her arms across her chest. "Gator, did you want Fay?"

"Once. A long time ago. Why do you ask?"

"She looked sad."

"Don't worry about that. Now, I got you. I cain't explain Alain and Fay. I know Alain took comfort with her after Lucille broke him and Amy up."

"Tipper's wife?" Sherry sat at the dining table.

"Yeah, but Lucille likes Tipper less than she did Alain. I don't know why. Alain and Fay don't do it no more, but the rest of 'em seem to have coupled up too. Not the young ones yet, but they will. That would kill my pa."

"Why?"

Gator sighed. "Polly belongs to my pa. Him and Miss Shirley fell in love. Keenan Richter was a mean son-of-a-bitch. He used to beat all of 'em, but Alain worst."

"Nobody knows about Polly?"

"Very few, 'specially, Lucille. Preacher Tomlin knows and Fester. I think Tipper knows. I know Amy knows 'cause I told her. We jest don't talk about it. That's the best way to keep a secret in Possum Holler."

"It's a good thing Lucille don't know." She rubbed her hand over the threadbare tablecloth.

"Yeah. Alain would never have been with Fay if Lucille had left him and Amy alone."

"Does Alain still love Amy?"

"Yeah, and it's killin' him."

"Gator, does Lucille like anybody?"

"No."

Sherry sniggered. "Don't nobody like her neither."

"I guess not."

The next day, Leo paid a visit to the Jones farm. He came to discuss baptizing Sherry the next week since she had made a profession of faith.

Sherry said, "I didn't go to church in the city."

"I gathered that. Sherry, exactly where were you working when Gator met you?"

Gator and Sherry exchanged glances. Leo patted Sherry's hand. "You know, what you tell me is held in confidence."

"What's that mean?"

"I can't tell other people."

"I was workin' in a brothel."

"I see."

"No, you don't. I hadn't never been with a man, and I didn't want to. Gator rescued me. Gator's the only man I'll ever have."

Leo cocked an eyebrow at Gator. Gator quickly said, "I didn't do nothin' with no womern there. I went with Alain for his birthday. I'm sure he wanted me to git with a womern because I hadn't ever…"

"Oh," said Leo.

"Well," said Gator, "Preacher Tomlin, I think God let me go jest so I could meet Sherry."

"Maybe. Well, about next Sunday. We'll meet at the fishing hole. Sherry, I have a robe you can wear in the water, but you'll need to bring a change of clothes."

"Yes, sir."

"You aren't afraid to go under the water, are you?"

"No. I don't think you'll let me drown."

Leo chuckled. "No, of course not. I'll have a handkerchief in my hand, and I'll put that over your mouth and nose. My other hand will be behind your back. I'll say, 'As an outward sign to the world that Sherry has buried her old life.' I'll bend you backward and dunk you under the water for a couple of seconds while I say, 'and has been raised to new life in Christ Jesus, I baptize you in the name of the Father and of the Son and of the Holy Spirit.' I'll bring you up. It'll take five seconds underwater. Any questions?"

"When do I change clothes and where?"

"We always rig a sheet for cover. I'll help you back on the bank, and you'll change. So will I. I'll be wet too." He laughed lightly. "Tipper'll get the congregation to sing while we change. I'll preach, and it'll be just like it was last week, but outside."

"Okay."

"If you'd like, Gator can be with you while you change."

Leo noticed the furtive glance again. "Hm," grunted Leo. "Have you two consummated your marriage?"

"Not yet," said Gator softly.

"What does consummate mean?" asked Sherry.

Leo raised an eyebrow again. He could not believe a girl that had been in a brothel did not know that word. And she sounded just like Ina the day they had been called to the school for the boys' fighting.

"Sex, Sherry," Gator said even more softly.

"I see," said Leo. "Are you actually married?"

"Yes, of course. I have our marriage license." Gator felt flushed.

"I'm still scared, and Gator's bein' patient," said Sherry matter-of-factly.

"I believe you. Don't worry about the physical part. It sometimes takes a little time. There's no rush."

Leo stood to go. He looked around. "I like the yellow paint. It's cheerful."

"Thank you," said Sherry.

"I'll see y'all Sunday. Gator, may I speak to you outside?"

"Yes, sir."

Outside, Gator hastened to ask, "Did I do something wrong?"

"No. I wanna ask about Alain."

"What about him?"

"How is he?"

Gator sighed. "I wish he could git over Amy."

"Still hurt?"

"I thought he was better. Then…"

"What happened?"

"He seen Tipper and Amy together, intimately together. That's why we went to the city."

"Oh, I see. Why does he think so little of himself?"

Gator shrugged. "Fay?"

"Guilt?"

"I guess

"I'm going to see him."

"He might pull out the shotgun."

"Not on me. He hasn't so far every time I've gone. He might not listen, but he won't shoot me. He's getting a pastoral visit today, though."

"Good luck."

"Say a prayer."

In his new burgundy Chrysler Le Baron, the first car he had bought since coming to Possum Holler fifteen years earlier, Leo Tomlin pulled into the Richter yard. Fay peeked out the window as the family finished lessons.

"Who is it?" asked Alain.

"Preacher Tomlin. He got a new car."

Alain sighed. "His other one was fallin' apart."

Alain walked outside and greeted Leo. "Preacher Tomlin."

"Alain, you look good." Leo extended his hand, greeting Alain as an adult.

Alain shook his hand. "Nice car."

"They said it would cost more to fix the other one than it was worth."

"It was real old, but I bet I could've fixed it."

"I'll remember that if I have problems with this one."

"Any time. Is this a social call, or have you brought bad news?"

"A pastoral visit."

"We ain't been to church in a long time. People don't cotton to us. We're riffraff."

"Not my words or my opinion."

"You one o' the few."

"Still friends with Gator?"

Alain grinned. "Always. His new wife is a real spitfire."

"A city girl."

"Sherry's a good lady. I like her. She's been here and don't treat us like vermin."

Leo nodded. "She is really sweet. I hear you're sort of responsible for their meeting."

Alain shrugged. "I'm glad somethin' good came from that trip."

"Sherry's decided to join the church. We'll have a creek-side service Sunday. Why don't y'all come?"

"Preacher Tomlin, I cain't see Lucille Dent nor Amy no more."

"What about Tipper?"

"He's okay. I ain't got no hard feelings toward Tipper. Still, Amy looks at me like I'm a bug. She's lost all regard for me; rightly so, I reckon. We don't live like y'all."

"Alain, God's love is unconditional."

"I don't know 'bout that. I'm real sure I'm goin' to Hell."

"Why? Because of Fay?"

"I deserve it, Preacher Tomlin, more'n you know."

Preacher Tomlin disappeared, and Leo Tomlin put his hands on the young man's neck. "Alain Richter, we *all* deserve it. We all sin. When I look at you, I still see a sweet boy who needs a father's love. I want you to feel the Heavenly Father's love, the love that sacrificed his Son so we can live. Thank God I'm not Keenan. That man was a fool. I'm not Tal Jones, though he was a friend. I am Leo Tomlin. I will always be here for you in whatever capacity you seek me. I love you, Alain Richter."

"That's good to know." Alain smiled sadly. "You already know I won't shoot you if you come to visit, pastoral or otherwise. Glad you showed me your new car, though. I'll think on what you said."

"Then, I'll come more often, just as your friend. You come to me anytime you need me."

26
Brawl

Alain did sneak into the back of the crowd on the banks of the creek, but he disappeared as soon as the service was over. He only cared that Gator and Sherry knew he had come to support Sherry's decision. He still did not come into town for regular church services although he pondered the sermon taken from Psalm 1:

> *¹Blessed is the man that walketh not in the counsel of the ungodly, nor standeth in the way of sinners, nor sitteth in the seat of the scornful. ²But his delight is in the law of the LORD; and in his law doth he meditate day and night. ³And he shall be like a tree planted by the rivers of water, that bringeth forth his fruit in his season; his leaf also shall not wither; and whatsoever he doeth shall prosper. ⁴The ungodly are not so: but are like the chaff which the wind driveth away. ⁵Therefore the ungodly shall not stand in the judgment, nor sinners in the congregation of the righteous. ⁶For the LORD knoweth the way of the righteous: but the way of the ungodly shall perish.*

Alain wondered if he could be a tree planted by the rivers of water or if he was innately chaff to be driven away by the wind. He had so many thoughts that he began to write them down.

Over the passing years, Alain Richter's farming practices produced excellent crops, and he manufactured larger quantities of cider to sell. Alain found a market for his cider in several states, just as Tipper had for his moonshine.

Alain, Robert Lee, and Calvin clunked into the parking lot of one of the bars that bought Richter's Hard Apple Cider near Richmond, Virginia. Robert Lee growled, "Alain, we gotta git a new truck."

"Yeah," Alain agreed reluctantly. "Nothin' lasts forever. We'll shop tomorrow. Let's deliver and have some fun tonight."

The Richter boys unloaded a hundred bottles of cider to the back door of the bar before they went to the front entrance to have a good time.

Two florescent lights hung far apart and half a dozen neon lights displaying various alcoholic beverage logos offered the only light in the place.

The clientele was far from classy. There were no doctors and lawyers in the mix. As a matter of fact, the men leaned to the rougher side: bikers, construction workers, and manual laborers. The women tended to be somewhat older, peroxide-blondes with too much makeup. More than half of the patrons smoked. The bar did not enforce a smoke-free environment. The jukebox blared a mixture of country and southern rock.

The Richters sat at the bar beside a man with dark hair and eyes who was about as tall as Alain but heavier. The man's square jaw sagged. "Cryin' in your beer?" Alain asked.

"Yeah," grunted the man.

The bartender asked, "What's your poison, gents?"

Alain looked at his brothers. "Bud?" Robert Lee and Calvin nodded. "Budweiser, and another for our friend."

Alain offered his hand. "Alain Richter. My brothers, Robert Lee and Calvin."

"Clarence Dayton."

"What's got you down?"

"Had a fight with my wife."

"Ah, true love." Alain laughed sardonically.

"Woman troubles for you too?" asked Clarence.

"Nope. Ain't got one."

"That's the trouble," said Clarence as the beers came. "Can't live with 'em; can't live without 'em. Bad thing is, she was right. I gotta go home and tell her."

"Well, have another beer first."

"Thanks."

"Any of these women available jest for a good time?"

"Lots. See if you can find a real blonde or one without fake boobs."

Alain laughed at Clarence's sarcasm. "Okay. I'm on the prowl. Nice to meet you, Clarence."

Half an hour later, Alain sat in a corner with two women, one a tall bleached-blonde with large breasts, obviously implants; the other, a petite brunette with a slight frame. Both women wore halter tops and tight jeans. The blonde had tribal tattoos around both upper arms and numerous body piercings. The brunette had a butterfly tattooed above her left breast, most of it visible in the halter top.

Alain slid his hand up the blonde's thigh and looked the brunette over. "Which one of you would like to take me home?" Alain asked.

The brunette dropped her eyes coyly while the blonde laughed seductively. "What about both of us?" she asked. "Has a country boy like you ever had a threesome?"

"Well," said Alain agreeably, "that could be interesting. Who's place?"

"Mine," said the brunette as she looked up through long, lacy lashes.

Alain leaned over and planted a wet kiss on the brunette. "Lead the way."

As the trio headed for the door, out of the blue a man who dwarfed Tipper Campbell, who was six foot four, in leathers and chains sucker punched Alain, sending him flying into Clarence Dayton.

"What the hell?" yelled Clarence as beer splashed all over him.

The bull of a man bellowed, "Get your hands off my girl!"

The petite brunette said defiantly, "We broke up, Tank. I'm not your girl."

"You know you'll be back. You always come back."

"Don't you see I found a new man?"

"A stinking hillbilly?"

Recovered from the sucker punch, Alain put his shoulder into his assailant's mid-section. Within two minutes, it was evident the Richter boys were battling the rest of the bar.

"Ugh!" Clarence groaned and downed another beer. "Unfair odds!" He joined the fray with his back to Calvin Richter. "Need a hand?"

"We *are* outnumbered."

"I don't think that would stop you."

"Nope, so, thanks."

A few minutes later, police swarmed the place and began to haul the brawlers to jail, including the blonde and the brunette.

At the jail, the arresting officer said, "You better put these four together and away from the others. Call Dayton's wife. Don't book."

"What about the other three?"

"It was self-defense," declared Clarence Dayton. "Alain got jumped. His brothers just had his back, but they were outnumbered. There were a dozen Jackals and some of their bitches."

"Clarence, why were you brawling? Do you wanna lose your job?"

"I was off duty."

"Off duty?" said Alain as he and his brothers were locked in a holding cell with Clarence Dayton.

"Yeah. Highway patrol."

"No shit?"

"Yeah, I'm a cop."

Alain laughed. "Thanks."

"Where y'all from?"

"Nowhere."

"Do tell."

"Possum Holler, West Virginia."

It was Clarence's turn to exclaim, "No shit?"

Dismayed, Alain said, "You heard of it?"

"Yeah. Met an interesting bootlegger from there. Tipper Campbell. You know him?"

"Yeah. We were friends."

"Were?"

"I don't know what we are now."

"He had a kid."

"Yep."

"Hm." Clarence rubbed his bruised chin. "That's the woman trouble. Alain, don't ever let a woman come between you and your friend."

"I'll try to remember that."

An hour later, an attractive tall, thin, natural blonde with blue-green eyes tapped her foot and crossed her arms outside the cell. Clarence leaned his head against the bars.

"Sorry," he said. "I was wrong."

The woman sighed. "You got a black eye."

"My friends were outnumbered."

"You could have whipped out the badge and stopped the whole thing."

"Off duty. Besides, Alain got sucker punched by a Jackal. He deserved some payback."

The woman kissed Clarence through the bars and looked around him. "Y'all need an ice pack too. Who's Alain?"

"Me, ma'am. Sorry about Clarence. He's a good man. These are my brothers, Robert Lee and Calvin Richter."

"I'm Patsy. Which Jackal did you take on?"

"Didn't git a name, ma'am, but I bet it's Goliath. He was huge."

The woman laughed. "Petite brunette girlfriend?"

"Apparently."

"Tank."

Alain nodded. "Yeah. The girl did call him that."

"The last time I got my husband out of jail was because of him. He was being physical with the girlfriend who is too stupid to leave and stay gone. Clarence intervened while off duty. Well, I'm taking Clarence home. Y'all need to call somebody. You'll have a two-hundred-fifty-dollar fine. Pay it and go home."

"Give Tipper my best. I'll see y'all around." Clarence left with his wife.

The Richters slept the night in jail, battered and bruised after their brawl.

27

Jailhouse Blues

Alain woke up the next morning to see the bull Jackal and the petite brunette leaving all armed up. He laughed, "She always goes back."

Calvin woke up to Alain's laughter. "Alain, who we gonna call?"

"Don't know."

Robert Lee groaned, "Two-fifty might not be a lot to some folks, but there's three of us. My jaw hurts. Why were we fightin'?"

"One of the Jackals' bitches. I was leavin' with his woman." Alain laughed. "I jest saw 'em leave together. She said they were broke up."

"Guess they made up," Calvin sighed. "Clarence sho did."

Alain laughed again. "Can you believe he was a highway patrolman? He's the one that pulled Tipper over." Alain grunted. "I'm sore too. Damn! That was a good fight."

Robert Lee agreed. "Yeah, but I was headed for some other kind o' fun."

"She prob'ly belonged to one of them too," said Alain with a cynical smirk on his face.

Calvin laughed. "All of 'em were part of the Jackals."

Alain laughed harder. "I guess we were destined to sing the jailhouse blues."

Robert Lee laughed too. "It's not the first time. Won't be the last, I'm sure. I'm surprised we got outa Jacqui's place that time."

"That was Gator," said Alain.

"He got the girl too," laughed Robert Lee.

"Lucky dog," laughed Alain.

Robert Lee suddenly belted out, "'Warden threw a party at the county jail.'"

Alain and Calvin joined in song of "Jailhouse Rock" and added a few dance steps and body gyrations.

A policeman came up. "Y'all still drunk?"

"Wudn't never drunk." Alain laughed harder. "Officer, don't you recognize the jailhouse blues when you hear 'em?"

"Don't y'all wanna call somebody?"

"Ain't got nobody," Alain answered.

"Nobody?"

"Ain't nobody we know got a phone."

Stretching his eyes wide with an incredulous stare, the officer said again, "Nobody?"

"Well, our grandpa has one, but he wouldn't like the idea of authorities associating him with us—for his own protection," Robert Lee stated.

"Alain," said Calvin, "Preacher Tomlin's got a phone."

The cop started laughing. "You gonna call your preacher, but not your granpa?"

Alain stopped laughing. "Yeah, I am. It's long distance though."

"You better call collect then."

"Give me a phone," said Alain.

"Come on," the policeman said as he opened the cell. "You gotta use the phone up front."

Leo Tomlin answered the phone, "Possum Holler Community Church."

A computerized voice said, "This call is coming from a detention center. The cost will be one dollar per minute. Will you accept the charges from?" The computer stopped talking.

Alain Richter said, "Alain."

"Alain? Yes, of course." Leo furrowed his brow.

"Your party is on the line." The computer disconnected with a beep.

"Preacher Tomlin?"

"Yes. Alain, where are you?"

"Richmond, Virginia."

"Why?"

"We're sorta in jail."

"I got that from the little computer voice. What did you do?"

"We got in a fight."

"Were you drunk?"

"No, sir. Hadn't got that far. We were in a bar. I was leavin' with a couple of ladies."

"Prostitutes?"

"No, but one of 'em, her man come in and took exception. He sucker punched me. Course, a fight broke out. They put us all in jail."

"Who's with you?"

"Robert Lee and Calvin."

"How much?"

"Jest a second." Alain turned to the officer. "How much to git out? Mrs. Dayton said two-fifty."

"Yep. Each."

"Preacher Tomlin, it's two hundred fifty each. We gotta enough on us for one."

"Let me speak to the officer."

"Yes, sir." Alain handed the phone to the officer. "He wants to talk to you."

"Yes, sir?" asked the officer, taking the receiver.

"Can they bond out on a credit card?"

"No, sir. It's not a bond. It's a fine. Cash, money order, or cashier's check."

"Oh."

"I know some places take 'em."

"I would have thought Richmond."

"We're not exactly Richmond. Little town called Blue Bird Spring."

"Oh. Okay. Tell Alain to sit tight. I can't get there before tomorrow. You will feed them?"

"Sure. They fought some Jackals. We'll feed 'em some good food."

"Jackals?"

"Motorcycle gang. Rough set."

"May I talk to him again?"

"It's your dime." The officer handed Alain the phone.

"Yes, sir?" Alain said.

"Sit tight. I'll be there tomorrow."

"Obliged."

The officer escorted Alain back to the cell. "Sorry about the accommodations."

"You ain't got a real jail?"

"No. We ship real criminals to the county lockup. You're not criminals."

"Glad you think so."

"I'll be back in an hour. I'll bring food and some pillows and blankets."

An hour later, the man returned with a basket of sandwiches, fruit, chips, and juice. He slid the door open and passed the goods to the prisoners. "Officer, what's yo name?" asked Alain.

"Dwayne Pritchard."

"Where'd you git the food, Officer Pritchard?"

"Wife."

Alain laughed. "Well, you got more cells than we do."

"We got four. Three on this side for men and one on the other for women."

"Two."

"Where you from?"

"Possum Holler, West Virginia."

"Long way from home. Exactly where *is* home?"

"More than fifty miles from Wilmington, up in the mountains, hidden from the world."

"And your preacher's coming to get you out?"

"Yeah." Alain took a swig of juice from the thermos the officer handed him.

Officer Pritchard leaned against the open cell door. "I never met a preacher like that."

"He held a shotgun on a welfare womern with me once too. He's a good man."

"What denomination?"

"Never asked. We only got one church. They dunk."

"That rules out Catholic, Episcopal, Methodist, Lutheran, and Presbyterian that I know."

"Baptist I guess."

"Southern, Missionary, Hardshell?"

Alain snickered. "Damned if I know."

"Maybe nondenominational. They're real popular these days. Y'all speak in tongues?"

"Not that I know, though we don't go often. So, maybe if the Spirit leads. They do clappin' and shout 'Amen' sometimes and hold their hands up in the air."

"Thought you didn't go."

"Well, we ain't been for a long time."

"Y'all ain't snake handlers?"

"No." Alain shook his head and laughed. "Grandma Newton might take on a snake. Leo Tomlin's smarter than that."

Officer Pritchard laughed.

"How many cops you got?" asked Alain.

"Eight. We trade off shifts, two at a time."

"More than two came to the bar."

"Yeah. Got a call at home. It happens now and then, especially when the Jackals roll in."

"How often they come?" Alain asked around a mouthful of peanut-butter-and-jelly sandwich.

"Every couple of months. They stay a few days and go on."

"The women?"

"Oh, that's why they come back. A few of the women live here."

"The little brunette?"

"Lysette Strong. Trouble with a capital T."

Alain rubbed his jaw. "Yeah, I'm feelin' it."

"Can you eat?"

"It ain't broke."

"Then, eat. I gotta make rounds. My partner's down the hall. Officer Jeff Boykin. Just holler." He slid the door closed.

Later before shift change, Officer Pritchard brought fried chicken, biscuits, fried okra, and apple turnovers with a jug of tea.

"Wife again?" asked Alain.

"Yeah."

"Tell her I might stay in jail. She's a good cook."

"Yeah," agreed Calvin. "She got a sister?"

"Yes, but she's fifteen."

"I'll wait."

The night passed without event although the floor was hard, and Robert Lee grumbled about not even a washtub to bathe.

Alain chortled. "At least the toilet flushes." The stainless-steel toilet sat against the outside wall under a barred window.

Next morning, Officer Pritchard brought a pan of scrambled eggs, bacon, and toast with a thermos of coffee. "Rise and shine," he joked.

Alain laughed. "I never had breakfast in bed."

Dwayne Pritchard chortled. "Breakfast is good. Bed? Ouch!"

"It could be worse. You did bring us pillows and blankets, but we beginning to smell worse than my friend, Gator's, hogs."

The cop could not stop chuckling with these men around. "Yeah. Calvin, I told my sister-in-law what you said."

"What'd she say?"

"You must be crazy."

"Figures."

"Trish is a sweetheart. She's disabled."

"How?"

"Hit and run when she was twelve. She's in a wheelchair."

"Oh. Will she ever walk again?"

"We don't know. Her back's not broken."

"What then?"

"She can move her legs, but she can't stand."

"Maybe she'll git better."

"Maybe."

Calvin ambled to the door. "Is she purty?"

"Yeah, real cute. She's about five-foot-four"—He held his hand palm down and parallel with the floor to show height—"blue eyes, and real curly brown hair."

"Well, tell her when she walks into Possum Holler, I'll marry her." Calvin sounded absolutely serious. "Handicaps can be overcome. I used to stutter real bad."

Pritchard hooted. "I'll do that. Remember what you said. One day, when Trish Jolson walks into Possum Holler, you have to marry her." Pritchard laughed all the way down the hall.

Near lunch time, Officer Pritchard swung the door to the cell open. "Time to go."

"Preacher Tomlin here?" asked Alain.

"Waiting up front. All paid up. Come back to visit; just don't get in a fight."

Leo looked the three young men over. He informed them. "Fay is a nervous wreck. She's worried about her jailbirds." He held up a paper sack. "She sent all of you a change of clothes. Her exact words were, 'A bet they stink to High Heaven.'"

"Thank you, Preacher Tomlin, for thinkin' to tell her what happened."

"Alain, be glad you were in another Podunk town. Brawling could have gotten thirty days. I considered letting you sit here."

"How long did you consider it?"

"About ten minutes," Leo grunted.

"'Preciate it. We'll pay you back."

"Yep. You will."

"We gotta git the truck."

"Where to?"

Alain told Leo where to find the bar when they climbed into the Chrysler.

"No!" exclaimed Alain when he saw the truck as they pulled into the bar's parking lot. It was stripped.

"Oh, boy!" Leo echoed Alain's sentiment.

"Now, Preacher Tomlin, that ain't right," lamented Alain.

"No, Alain, it's not."

"Please go back to the jailhouse."

"You gonna file a report?"

"Yeah, and then, I gotta git to Wilmington and a car lot."

"Have a salvage company tow the truck for scrap. You might get five hundred. We'll stop tonight, and I'll take you tomorrow."

"Our debt to you is addin' up fast."

"No charge for this part because it's not your fault."

Alain filed a report with Dwayne Pritchard. "Man, I'm sorry," said Dwayne. "I should've brought it here. I'm pretty sure who did it."

"Do what you can," said Alain. "You can call Preacher Tomlin. We ain't worried about gittin' the parts back. Just lock some Jackals in a real doghouse."

The men stayed in a hotel off the interstate and drove into Wilmington the next afternoon. All the men greatly appreciated the shower in the hotel, and their admiration for a thoughtful sister grew when they put on clean clothes. They visited a Ford dealership once in the city and looked at several trucks. Alain sighed. "We could really use at least two, maybe three."

The salesman's eyes widened. "Let's do a credit check."

"I ain't got credit cards, but I do have money in the bank. I own Richter Farms and Orchards."

"Let's run the report. I have to do that. Which three did you have in mind?"

"The white, the dark blue, and the wine F350 crew cabs with the eight-foot beds."

The salesman ran Alain's credit report. "Mr. Richter, you have no personal credit history."

"I told you that. I wanna do this as a business purchase. I can write it off on my taxes then."

"Let's go that route." The man did some more work on the computer. "Yes, I believe we can do this. I can go sixty months and get your payments to fifteen-sixty-seven. Doing this as a fleet purchase, I can knock off another thirty—fifteen-thirty-seven."

"What's the interest rate?"

"Four and a half, really good since you have no credit history."

Alain turned to Leo. "Preacher Tomlin, is that good?"

"Actually, yes, unless he can get you zero percent finance."

"I don't think so," said the man shaking his head.

"Try," said Leo.

"A co-signer?"

"Run my credit."

"Sir?"

"What if I co-sign?"

"No, Preacher Tomlin," objected Alain.

"Why? You're gonna make your payments, aren't you?"

"Yes, sir, but farmin' is speculative."

"I'll take a chance on you."

"I already owe you." Alain stroked his shaggy beard.

"What did I tell you about always being here for you? Would you accept *Tal's* help?"

"He was like my pa."

Leo crossed his arms over his chest. "Is it because I'm a minister?"

"Oh, I guess. You'll hold me real accountable."

"I will."

"I need the trucks."

"I know you do." Leo rested a hand on Alain's shoulder. "Let me help."

Alain sighed. "Okay."

Leo turned to the salesman. "So, Mr. Dawes, how does it look?"

"Zero percent, sixty months, payment fourteen-seventy-five. I threw in no taxes because you're a minister."

"It's not for the church."

"Want me to put the taxes back on?"

"No, we'll take it."

In the new trucks, the Richter boys came home. They were no longer singing the jailhouse blues.

28
Artistry

"Nice," Gator said with a measure of covetousness when Alain drove into his yard in the new wine pickup.

"Didn't have any choice."

"Why? What happened?"

Leaning against the shiny new paint with both hands resting gently on the hood and his feet crossed over each other, Alain related his jailhouse experience.

"Sounds like some bad people," Gator concluded.

"Yeah. The old thing was about gone, but we had to have wheels."

"Well, you got some nice wheels." Gator walked all the way around the truck. "Did you use the money we been savin'?"

"I couldn't touch that without you too. I would never do that to you anyway."

"Might come a time we have to cash in."

"I suppose, but let's save it 'til then or 'til we git our rigs."

"Your little secret account?"

"Nope. It's still there too," Alain replied with a deliberate, slow head shake and deep scowl.

"You didn't use either? How'd you git 'em? Stop being so secretive."

Alain laughed. "Preacher Tomlin is a shrewd businessman. Don't let him fool you."

"Preacher Tomlin?"

"Yeah, Gator, we talk. I don't shoot him."

Gator nodded his approval. "Good."

"Well, how's it feel to be a pa?" Alain changed the subject abruptly.

"Jest fine."

"You chose a weird name."

"Fox?"

"Yeah."

"I'm Gator."

"You weird," teased Alain.

Gator pretended to punch him and laughed with him. "Seriously," said Alain. "Why?"

"A fox is clever. He's real clever. And, um, Sherry's expectin' again. So is Amy. Amy knows hers is a girl."

"That's good. Is that city fellow still sellin' Amy's paintings?"

"Yeah. She's makin' good money."

"She should." Alain nodded with a closed-lip smile. "She's an artist."

"You sound more content."

"I met some interestin' people in jail."

"Really?"

"Yeah. It made me think."

"What did you think?"

"I want Amy to be happy."

"Okay."

Sherry came out with the baby. "Hey, Alain."

"Sherry."

"Nice new truck."

"Necessity." He held his arms out to hold the baby and Sherry passed Fox to him.

"I heard y'all talkin' 'bout Amy."

"Nothin' bad," assured Alain.

"No. You should see her paintings. I seen a bunch of 'em. They real good. That Roscoe wants to git her a show in a big city."

"You meet him?"

"One time." Sherry cocked an eyebrow. "Now, *he's* right weird."

"How?"

"I don't know. He said I look like Tipper."

"You do."

"I noticed that. It wudn't that so much as the way *he* looks at *Tipper*."

Alain laughed. "Whatcha mean?"

"I ain't been around him much, and I don't really want to; but I seen him watchin' Tipper's every move like you men used to watch Jacqui's girls."

"You mean you think he likes Tipper and not Amy?" Alain hooted with laughter. "Does Tipper know?"

"I don't think so. Tipper don't like him though."

"I should visit Tipper."

"Alain!" scolded Gator.

"What? Yeah, you're right. I'd jest git upset, but I would like to see Amy's paintings. I ain't watched her work lately."

Sherry volunteered, "I could git her to show you some."

"That's sweet, Sherry, but Amy don't wanna be around me."

Feeling melancholy, Alain hiked to the waterfall, intending to spend a day behind the falls or in his meadow. He stumbled out of the forest, having tangled in the wild blackberry vines.

The scream as he sprawled into the clearing startled him as much as his sudden appearance startled the person who screamed.

"What are you doing here?" demanded Amy as she jumped up.

A little irritated, Alain growled like a little boy, "It's my clubhouse."

Suddenly, Amy laughed. "Alain, have you been drinking?"

"No. Not today." Alain stood and dusted himself off. "I got tangled in the briars."

"What are you doing up here?"

"Walkin' to clear my head. I end up here sometimes. It's a place where I was happy. I didn't know you were here."

"I decided to paint the waterfall."

"Can I see?"

Amy looked around uncomfortably.

"I won't bite you," Alain said sullenly. He heaved a sigh.

Ashamed of her hesitation, Amy said, "I know that. Sure. Come look."

Alain looked over Amy's shoulder. "It's beautiful, Amy. You have real artistry."

"Do you really like it?"

"I do."

"I've got a show coming up in Philadelphia."

"You think you oughta go?" Alain asked skeptically.

"Why not?"

"Amy, you're pregnant, very pregnant."

"Momma's going with us."

"Oh."

"Alain." The moment of silence before he spoke again screamed of pain and resentment.

"She'll prob'ly try to git you to divorce Tipper while you're there."

"That's not happening."

"Do you love him?"

"Tipper?"

Alain hollered, "I sure as hell hope you don't love Roscoe!"

"No!"

Alain gagged at the very thought of what Sherry had told him. "Yes, of course, Tipper. Do you love him?"

Amy looked at the ground. She felt as if Alain's gaze burned through her soul. "Yeah, Alain, I do."

He nodded. "Tipper's a good man. I'm glad it's him if anybody."

"Alain."

"I'm okay, Amy."

"Are you? Why did you sleep with Fay?"

"I don't know. I wish…"

Amy put a hand on Alain's bearded face. "We can't go backward."

"No." He pressed her hand harder to his face and squeezed it before she dropped it to her side. "You have a real future. Take the world by storm, Amy. You deserve it."

"You deserve good things too."

"Do I?"

"Yes!"

Alain laughed sadly. "There's only one good thing I want, and I cain't have it."

"What's that?"

"Never mind, Amy."

Getting the gist of Alain's statement, Amy asked, "You wanna see some other paintings?"

"You have them with you?"

"In the trunk of my car. If you help me load this stuff, I'll show you."

Alain helped Amy load her supplies, and she pulled out a portfolio. Alain looked at each one until he got to one of a hog. He laughed. He actually laughed, a deep-belly, happy laugh. "Oh, Amy! Don't sell this one."

"Why?"

"Give it to Gator. Who will appreciate Wilbur more'n Gator?"

Amy giggled. "Oh!" She caught her side.

"You okay?"

"Yeah. The baby just kicked real hard." Amy took Alain's hand and laid it on her abdomen.

Alain smiled. "Wow! You sure it's a girl?"

"That's what the sonogram said."

"Kicks like a football player."

"Maybe she'll be a dancer."

"Who knows?"

Amy picked up the charcoal of Wilbur. "You're right. I'm gonna stop by Gator's and give this to him."

"You better git goin'. It's gittin' dark."

"Yeah. I leave tomorrow."

"Good luck." Alain started through the woods.

"Alain?" Amy called.

"Yeah?"

"I could drop you. It's getting dark."

Alain hesitated. "I won't bite," said Amy with a genuine smile on her face.

Alain nodded. "Yeah. Okay. 'Preciate it."

Amy dropped Alain at his door. Alain placed a small kiss on Amy's cheek. "Knock 'em dead in the big city."

"Thanks."

Amy drove off. Fay came outside. "Alain, who was that?"

"Artistry."

"What?"

"Nothin'." Alain started into the house.

"Was that Amy?"

"Oh! Fay, I gotta go."

"Where?"

"You don't wanna know. Jest not here."

Alain drove to Jacqui's Gentlemen's Club and found a tall brunette named Blanche.

29

Killin' Time

Alain spent more and more time alone in his secret cave. He began to write in a notebook. He wrote the history of Possum Holler. He wrote anecdotal incidents. He wrote his feelings. He wrote poems. He wrote stories and changed the people's names. He hid his writings in a plastic storage container in his secret cave.

When Alain came in one evening, Fay asked, "Where you been? Have you been with some womern?"

Alain laughed. "No, Fay. I jest needed time alone."

"Are you drinkin'?"

"Sometimes."

"Why?" She snapped her hands to her hips.

"It helps me sleep. I don't dream. I don't hurt."

"Do you need…?"

"No! Please, never suggest it again."

Fay clenched her fists and glared at Alain. "I wudn't gonna say that."

"I'm sorry. What?"

"Do you need to talk?"

"No. I need to think. I need to kill time."

"'Til when?"

"I don't know, Fay. I jest want a life."

She relaxed her hands to her sides. "So do I, Alain."

"I'm sorry. I'm a selfish ass. Y'all must hurt as much as me." Alain kissed Fay's forehead.

"How do you kill time, Alain?"

"Promise not to laugh?"

"I ain't never laughed at you." She dipped her head to the side and puckered her lips.

"I write."

"What you write?"

"Stories. Poems."

"Read it to me."

"No, not yet."

"I bet it's good."

Alain laughed bitterly. "When I git famous, I'll dedicate a book to Ms. Butler."

"If you ever wanna share some of it with me, I'll listen."

"I'll remember that. How do you kill time?"

"I been embroiderin' pillowcases and linens. They real good, Alain. You think you could take me to the fair and let me sell 'em?"

"Show me."

Fay showed her needle point to Alain. He handled them carefully. "They are good, Fay," said Alain in awe. "Your scenes in thread are as beautiful as Amy's paintings."

"Do you think folks'll buy 'em?"

"I do. I bet city folk would even order special things."

"Will you take me to the fair?"

"Yeah. They always have craft judging on Friday night. We'll all go as a family."

"You sure?"

"Yes. Nobody at the fair will know anything about our relationships. We'll have some fun. To Hell with Lucille Dent! If we wanna go into town, we'll go."

"Good for you!" She dropped her head to stare at the floor. "Alain, you need to know Sherry told me Lucille's real sick and done somethin' to upset Amy."

"Amy is Tipper's problem."

"Okay."

"Thanks for tellin' me. Maybe the old bat'll die."

"That's cold, Alain."

He shrugged. "I guess."

Fay laughed. "Maybe you gittin' over Amy. I'm glad. I want you to be happy, Alain."

"I know you do. I'm tryin'."

Fay got excited over the prospect of going to the fair. "Do we have the right clothes to wear to the fair?"

"Yes. Just wear some jeans and a sweater and bring a jacket. It gets cold after dark."

"It's a good thing we got three trucks now."

"Yes, it is." Alain laughed at her enthusiasm.

"Oh, my goodness! Supper's late."

"It don't matter."

She started to add wood to the wood-burning stove and stopped with a small log in her hand. "Alain, I ain't never been to the fair."

Alain could not help but appreciate his sister's childlike eagerness. He knew in his heart this was the right thing to do.

At the fair, Alain caught up with Gator at the livestock arena. "Well," said Gator, "you livin'?"

"I brought the whole family."

"Good for you!"

A shadow crossed Alain's face. "What?" asked Gator.

"What did Lucille do to Amy? Fay said Sherry told her Lucille had upset Amy real bad."

"I don't rightly know. Sherry ain't with me. She's with Amy. Sherry thought Amy might need her. Lucille died today."

"Oh." He scanned the lights of the midway and listened to the joyful sounds. "Gator, I cain't pretend I feel loss or sadness for Lucille."

"I suppose not. Will you come in for the funeral tomorra?"

"Whew! I'll come for Amy and Mr. Dent, not to mourn Lucille."

Alain did not tell his family about Lucille until they got home because he wanted them to have a good time at the fair. Fay never seemed so happy as when she made her very own five hundred dollars from the sale of her handiwork. The children loved the lights and sounds and smells and tastes. For that evening, Alain Richter killed time with joy.

Lucille Dent's funeral was well attended. Alain watched Amy. He did not see sadness in her face, but rage. It was the same emotion he had felt for Keenan. The darkness in her eyes frightened him. Yet, he dared not speak to Tipper about it. He briefly offered Royce his condolences, and Royce told him that Lucille had suffered from pancreatic cancer. Alain felt a twinge of guilt for having wished years before that Lucille would suffer a painful death. He knew that cancer of any kind would be torturous.

On a dreary afternoon following Lucille's funeral, Alain hiked through the woods. He came into the clearing by the fishing hole to a sight that froze his blood.

"What the hell are you doing?" Alain roared. He sprang across the dirt path and seized Amy under her arms, ripping the noose she had thrown over a limb from her grasp. "Are you crazy?"

Amy screamed and dug her nails into Alain's face. "Leave me alone! Just let me die!"

"Amy!" Alain held her wrists and pulled her hands firmly from him. "You're not the only one that would die. You're having another baby! You're not a murderer!"

"It doesn't matter, Alain!" Amy dissolved in tears. "I just wanna die." She collapsed into his arms.

He stroked her hair. "No, you don't. What happened? What did your ma do to you? Talk to me."

"No. I can't. It would kill Tipper."

"I won't tell him."

Amy shook her head. Alain pushed her hair from her face and asked gently, "What were you doing?"

"Killing time."

"Amy, it cain't be that bad."

Tipper's voice called, "Amy?"

Amy grabbed Alain's flannel shirt at the neck. The expression in her eyes looked like a wild animal. "Don't tell him you saw me. Please?"

"Stay alive."

"You ask so much."

"Please? For me?"

"Don't tell him you saw me." Amy ran off, away from Tipper's voice. Alain picked up the noose.

"Amy?" Tipper called again as he crashed through the thicket.

Tipper bellowed, "What the hell are you doing?"

Alain looked down at the rope. Of course, Tipper did not understand the picture. "Give me that damned rope," Tipper demanded, snatching the rope from Alain. "It's not enough that my wife's gone crazy. Now, I find my friend trying to hang himself. What were you doing?"

Alain closed his eyes and whispered, "Killin' time."

30

Beauty Lost

Tipper dragged Alain to his truck. "You fool!" he yelled.

Calmly Alain replied, "I'm okay, Tipper."

"You're trying to kill yourself. That's not okay."

"I'm not. I won't. I swear."

"Why should I believe you?"

"I'm okay now."

"I'm taking you home. I'll get Fay to tie you up with that rope."

Alain laughed. "It's good you actually care."

"Of course, I do."

Alain laid the rope on the seat between him and Tipper. "I don't need this. You keep it. I got Matthew and Mary. I won't leave them."

Tipper looked at Alain. "What were you doing?"

"Nothin'. I found the rope."

"Did you see Amy?"

"Have you lost her?"

Tipper shook his head. "She's been acting strange."

"If I see her, I'll tell her you're lookin' for her."

"Sorry I jumped to conclusions."

"At least I know you still my friend."

"Always, Alain."

Alain slid out of the truck once Tipper parked at the Richter home. "Thanks for the ride. I ain't crazy, Tipper. Find Amy. She's more important than me."

Tipper left to find Amy, and Alain went inside. Fay asked, "Was that Tipper Campbell?"

"Yep. Fay, Amy's gone crazy. She was fixin' to hang herself when I found her."

"I'm sorry, Alain."

"I don't know what to think or do."

"Thought you said she was Tipper's problem."

"I cain't imagine not ever bein' able to see her again."

"She's Tipper's wife."

"I said see her. Jest to see her keeps me goin'. If she died, I'd go crazy, Fay. That would be so much beauty lost."

"*That's* crazy."

"Maybe."

"Alain, don't be crazy."

"Oh, I'll try."

Fay smiled. "I got you somethin'. I got Robert Lee to take me to town to the store now that Lucille's gone. Royce is a nice man."

"Royce?"

"Yeah, Royce. I got you this." Fay handed Alain a stack of notebooks and pens.

"What for?" asked Alain.

"Writin'. Write somethin' for me."

Alain laughed. "I'm not crazy, sis. I'm fine."

She patted his arm.

Alain disappeared to his cave. For quite some time he stared at a blank page. "Yeah, Fay, you deserve somethin'. As screwed up as you are in the head, you still deserve somethin'."

For two days, nobody seemed to know where Alain Richter was. Fay walked to the Campbell home. "Fay?" said Amy who answered the door.

"Yeah. I'm lookin' for Alain."

"He's not here."

"Where's Tipper?"

"Working at the mine."

"Miss Ina?"

"Out back."

"You crazy?"

"What?"

With a hand on her hip and a scowl on her face, Fay said, "Alain told me; now, he's missin'."

"I don't know where he is, Fay. Come in."

Fay entered the Campbell home and looked around. She had never been inside. One open room with a sofa and two chairs along with a dining table covered in a plaid tablecloth and surrounded by six ladder-back chairs connected to the kitchen with a pump at the sink and a propane tank for the stove. Three doors showed down a small hallway. Though small, the place was spotless and inviting.

"I know you don't think much o' me no more, but I love Alain," said Fay, getting straight to the point. "He's the only person that ever took care o' me against Pa. I'm scared, Amy. I ain't meanin' I love Alain like a man. He's my brother and my best friend. He thinks the world would be empty without you, but it's him. Without him, the world would be empty." Fay brushed tears from her cheeks.

"Fay, I agree. Alain has a beautiful soul. He always has. Did you check the clubhouse?"

"Yeah. Robert Lee went there."

"I don't know."

Tipper came in smudged with coal dust. "Fay?"

Amy said, "She's looking for Alain."

"How long has he been gone?" Tipper asked.

"Two days,"

"Oh, my God!" He ran his hand through his long curly blond hair. "He said he was fine."

"Whatcha talkin' 'bout?" Fay quirked an eyebrow.

Tipper explained, "I caught him with a rope, a noose."

"No, you didn't." Fay glowered at Amy. "I gotta go 'fore I say somethin' wrong, 'fore I make Alain mad at me."

"I know a place to check," said Tipper. "I'll come by and tell you. You want a ride?"

"Yeah, thanks." Fay looked back at Amy.

Amy said, "He'll be fine. I know it."

Tipper took Fay home and drove to the clubhouse. He hiked over the ridge to the place where Alain had seen the meadow. There was no sign of Alain. Tipper left.

Through the curtain of water, Alain saw Tipper. "Damn!" he thought. "They're lookin' for me. Fay's gonna hit me with a rollin' pin."

Tipper knocked on the Richter door. Fay jerked the door open. "No?"

Tipper shook his head. "No."

"He ain't been to Grandpa Fester's. Gator ain't seen him. Preacher Tomlin ain't seen him. Tipper, I'm scared."

"Fay, is his gun here?"

"Yeah. He ain't gonna hurt hisself, Tipper."

"You sure?"

"Yeah." She rubbed the back of her neck. "I won't say no more."

"If he's not back by tomorrow, we'll get some search parties."

"'Preciate it."

Fay sat at the table and waited. The guttering candles flickered as they melted to nothing. One by one they went out until only one faintly sputtered as it slowly died. The opening door startled Fay awake. She jumped from the chair. "Oh, you!" Fay pounded Alain until he grabbed her wrists.

"Settle down," he commanded softly.

"Where you been? I thought you were dead. Gator and Tipper were lookin'."

"I'm fine." Alain produced a piece of paper from the notebook he was using. "Read. I'm going to bed. Good night."

Fay unfolded the paper and read:

Born to Be My Friend

My sister
    Born to be my friend;
Facund, fair, faithful, fallible,
    Familial, fanciful, fantastic,
Feeling, feisty, felicitous, feminine,
    Fervent, fierce, fine,
First-rate, flexible, fond, forgivable,
    Forgiving, forthright, frantic,
Fresh, frightening, funny, fussy.

My friend
    Born as my sister;
Acute, adaptable, affirming, afraid,
    Aidant, altruistic, amiable,
Amusing, anchored, anticipatory,
    appreciated, Apt, ardent, artful, Askant,
assertive, astute, attentive,
    Attractive, authentic, averring, avowing.

My sister—my friend;
    Yacking, yapping, yawping, yielding.

My friend—my sister:
F-A-Y.

Fay went to the bedroom door. "Alain, you asleep?"
"Almost."
She sniffled. "You went away to do this?"
"I had to think."
"I don't know what most of these words mean."
"They all describe you. Use the dictionary."
"Pick three."
"Faithful, astute, yacking. You talk too much. Good night."

Tipper knocked on the Richter door early the next day with Gator by his side. Alain answered.

"Where the hell have you been?" demanded Tipper, and Gator nodded agreement.

"I needed time to think."

"About what?"

Alain smiled. "That's really none o' yo business."

"Well, you're welcome. We've been looking all over for you."

"Much obliged. I'm fine. Tipper, you got yo own problems. They worse'n mine."

"You might be right."

"I'm grateful y'all cared enough to look for me. I wudn't in no danger. Next time, I'll tell Fay before I leave. She already beat me black and blue."

Tipper laughed. "I don't see any bruises."

Alain laughed. "She didn't hit that hard, but it was her intent."

"Don't scare us like that again."

Alain held up his right hand. "I swear."

A little more than a year passed before Alain hiked through the woods again. This time he ended up near Tipper's still where he grabbed a man by the scruff of the neck and demanded, "Who the hell are you?"

The man spun around. "Don't shoot me."

"I ain't armed." Alain viewed the man in fancy clothes. "You that weasel DuBlane, the one that sells Amy's art? Whatcha doin' skulkin' 'round Tipper's still? You watchin' Amy?"

"No."

Alain grinned malevolently. "That's right. You watchin' Tipper. You one o' them that likes men."

"My sexual preference is none of your business."

"Nope, yo choice, but I wonder how Tipper would like it. I seen him in a few scraps. He'd rip yo head off."

"Tipper's hit me."

"I heard 'bout that. Wudn't no secrets when Lucille was alive. DuBlane, which you like better—lookin' at Tipper or linin' yo pockets by sellin' Amy's work?"

"You got a name, mister?"

"Richter."

"First name?"

"Got one o' them too, but I ain't tellin' you. What I *am* tellin' you is git the hell outa here!"

"Relax. Yeah, I was looking at Tipper, a last look since I won't be coming back."

"Good riddance! Now, git!"

Alain went home without much thought of Roscoe DuBlane after watching him scurry off like a cockroach when light comes on. However, he did wonder what Tipper would do if he knew Roscoe had been watching him. Alain shivered. "That wouldn't be a purty sight," he said to himself. "I seen enough blood."

Tipper pounded on Alain's door. Alain opened. "Tipper?"

"She's gone."

"What?"

"She left with Roscoe DuBlane."

"Amy?"

"Yeah. She just up and left."

"That don't make sense." Alain's face contorted in confusion.

"You're telling me."

"No, Tipper, DuBlane likes men. I seen him watchin' you night before last. I chased him off. Oh, Lord!"

"What?"

"He said a last look, and he wouldn't be comin' back. Damn! I thought he was quittin' as Amy's agent. I thought it was a good thing. I'm sorry. If I had known, I woulda snapped his neck like I thought about doin'."

Tipper laughed bitterly. "Looks like she left both of us."

"Tipper, I don't know what to say."

"Ain't nothin' to say." Tipper turned to leave.

"Where you goin'?"

"Just out. Virginia. Jail. I don't care."

"Tipper, think about your girls."

"Amy didn't. She left, Alain." Tipper started to cry. "She left us, all of us. Lucille won after all."

Tipper floored the GTO as he left Alain's yard. Alain stared after him; he knew Tipper's pain and felt his own afresh. He leaned against the door facing. "Amy, why? I don't think I can bear not seeing you."

Alain called over his shoulder, "Fay, I'm goin' out. Don't send a search party. I'll be back."

In his special place, Alain opened a bottle of moonshine before he found his pen and paper and wrote:

Beauty Lost

Beauty lost:
   O, fair maiden who left these hills,
Did you really count the cost
   Or consider the pain on us you did instill?
O, fair maiden, you to describe:
   Absorbing, adamant, addlepated,
Admirable, adored, adventurous,
   Afire, aggravating, alluring,
Ambiguous, ambitious, angry,
   Agonizing, antithetical, appealing,
Arousing, artistic, ascendant, aspiring.

Beauty lost:
   O, fair maiden who left these hills,
Did you think who would hurt the most,
   Yourself, by far, with pain to fill?
O, fair maiden, you to measure:
   Mad, magical, magnificent,
Manic, manipulative, mannered,

Masterful, matchless, mellow,
Mindful, mischievous, mistrustful,
  Modern, morbid, morose,
Motivated, muliebral, museful, mysterious.

Beauty lost:
  O, fair maiden who left these hills,
Did you contemplate leaving my soul afrost
  Or understand the other spirit you would
  kill?
O, fair maiden, you to present:
  Yare, yearning, yummy.

Beauty lost:
  O, fair maiden who left these hills,
Did you ponder without you I would aside be
tossed
  Or care that you would reduce me to nil?
O, fair maiden, your name I call.
  Amy! Amy! Amy!

Beauty lost.

As Tipper Campbell drank himself to a stupor in his backyard, Alain Richter succumbed to drunken slumber in his sanctuary. The name both men called was Amy.

31

Silver Thread and Golden Needles

Hog Rendering came and Alain took his family to town for the first time since he was fourteen. Many people whispered and commented about the Richter family, but Gator chatted with his friend. Alain said, "They're all lookin' at us, Gator."

"Don't let it bother you."

"I ain't worried about me, but if they say anything to hurt my kids, that's different."

Tipper came over. "Alain." The two men shook hands and did a half-hug with a clap on the shoulder.

"Hey, Tipper. You okay?"

"No. You?"

"Yeah. I'm tryin'."

Royce Dent came over to speak. "Good to see you."

Alain and Royce shook hands. "Thank you, Mr. Dent. You okay?"

"No. I can't understand why Amy ran off and deserted her family."

"I don't understand that either." Alain put a hand on Tipper's shoulder. "You gonna call a dance?"

"No. I can't. I just can't."

"I understand."

"Buster Matlock is gonna do it. You gonna dance?"

"Who with?"

"Fay."

Alain arched an eyebrow. "Add fuel to the fire?"

"Who cares?" Tipper snapped.

"I do."

Leo Tomlin came over with a petite strawberry-blonde. "Alain! Good to see you." They shook hands and Leo gave the young man a full embrace.

"Thank you."

"I'd like y'all to meet somebody. This is her first Hog Rendering, and she hasn't run away. As a matter of fact, we just got in last night from Chicago. Gentlemen, Miss Sunny Bankston. She's here to help me set up a school."

"A real school?" asked Tipper.

"Yep. We'll meet in the Sunday school rooms to begin."

Tipper extended his hand. "Tipper Campbell. Enroll my daughter, Betsy, today. She'll be fourth grade."

"A pleasure," said Sunny shaking hands.

"Gator Jones," said Gator, shaking hands. "You can enroll my son, Fox. If we'd had a school when I was a kid, I woulda graduated. This is wonderful!"

"I hope your enthusiasm is contagious," said Sunny with a cheerful smile.

"My young'uns will be there ever' day."

"How many do you have?"

"Five: Fox, Rooster, Lily, Rabbit, and Buck."

Cocking her head to one side, she asked, "One girl?"

Gator nodded. "Lily, but Fox is the only one school age."

"Your wife must be amazing. I'd like to meet her."

"Will you come for supper? Sherry's a good cook."

"I'd love to. When?"

After a second's thought, Gator replied, "Wednesday would be good."

"I'll get directions and be there." Sunny turned her gaze to the man with startling eyes hidden in a mass of hair. "And you are?"

"Alain Richter, ma'am." Sunny shook his hand and felt the calluses.

"Do you have children?"

"Yes, ma'am, but they won't be there."

"Why?" She took a step back.

"They wouldn't fit in."

Sunny furrowed her brow. "Of course, they would."

"No, ma'am. You don't understand."

"Enlighten me."

Leo tensed, and Sunny noticed. Alain smiled, showing teeth that needed dental care. "Ma'am, they're inbred. The other kids would treat 'em bad." Alain pointed out a little group of kids. "Those are mine and my brothers' and sisters'. Do you see a single child other than Gator's and Tipper's even speakin' to 'em? But I guess you wouldn't know the children yet. That purty little girl talkin' to my Matthew is Betsy Campbell. A few of the little ones belong to Gator. People 'round here shun us."

"I wouldn't treat your children badly," Sunny said with a slow, deliberate head shake.

"I don't doubt *you*, ma'am. You seem right kind, but I won't expose them to the hurt. Sorry, ma'am."

Buster Matlock began to call the dancers to the floor. Alain looked around. "Maybe we should go."

Sunny scowled deeply. "You don't dance?"

"I dance, but nobody will dance with me. I told you: People shun us. The people you see talkin' to me are all that do, except Grandma Newton, and she does what she damned well pleases."

"Change that," Sunny challenged.

"How, ma'am? I am what I am."

"Dance with the new schoolmarm."

"You a spitfire!" Alain laughed. "Miss Bankston, I drink too—heavily."

"Are you drunk?"

"Not yet, ma'am, but I was considerin' it. Tipper makes good moonshine."

Sunny gawked at Tipper. "You make moonshine?"

"Yes, ma'am."

Sunny glanced at Gator. "You?"

Gator shrugged. "I make babies. I'm a hog farmcr."

"I own the store," said Royce. "But my daughter was Tipper's wife."

"Was?"

"I'm divorced," said Tipper. "Well, I signed the papers. I assume I'm single again. I ain't heard back."

"Where is she?"

"Don't know. Ran off."

Alain said, "Tipper, you dance with Miss Bankston."

"Nope. Don't feel like dancin' yet."

"Well," Sunny said, "being rejected by two men in five minutes makes me want to go home."

Alain shrugged. "I'll dance with you, but then the townspeople won't talk to you, and they won't want you teachin' their kids."

"Leo?" Sunny turned to her boss.

"Are you asking me to dance?"

"I'm asking what to do."

"Hmm. You two are fools. Come on, Sunny."

While Leo and Sunny danced, Alain said, "That womern's dangerous."

"Pretty," said Tipper. "You shoulda danced with her."

"I was protectin' her."

"You get in with the schoolmarm, and you could regain respect."

"At what cost?"

Tipper huffed, "Alain, you're free to choose your own path."

"I don't want it with her. She is purty. You free now."

"No, I'm still hurting too much."

"I understand." He stroked his long beard. "I wonder what folks would do if I sang."

"Try it and see."

"You sing great, Alain," said Gator, offering encouragement.

"I thought of a song. It kinda fits our situation, Tipper."

"Sing," Gator encouraged.

"What if they throw stones?"

Tipper laughed. "We'll have to get our swords. All for one and one for all. We're musketeers. I'll sing with you. Let's go."

"It's a sad song."

Tipper rubbed the back of his neck. "I don't feel happy. Sad works."

Alain and Tipper hit the packing-crate stage. "Guitars," Alain said.

Seeing Alain Richter on stage silenced the entire crowd. Tipper and Alain began to strum, Tipper picking up Alain's lead. Alain's raspy voice added a tone of melancholy to an already sad, sad song as he changed a few words to make it appropriate to be sung by a man rather than a woman.

The resonance of the man's voice and the depth of the words touched Sunny's heart as she listened.

Leo listened intently and saw the sorrow on the faces of two young men he loved. His heart felt its own pain as he considered the woman he'd left behind to come to Possum Holler.

Royce Dent cast a longing glance across the way to where Fay Richter stood. Lucille had long ago ripped his heart apart. Could it ever be mended?

Alain's haunting voice finished the song.

Sunny thought that her own heart after losing a love she had never expressed and after having been shot by an angry parent could not be mended by silver thread and golden needles, but whatever had torn that man's heart from his chest could never even be mended with super glue or a welding wand. Sunny found herself brushing away a stray tear.

After Alain and Tipper finished the song, the crowd murmured. Sunny heard a few derogatory remarks: "He should have considered a broken heart when he diddled his sister...I wonder how many of the kids belong to him...How could those girls allow themselves to be used like that...Lucille was right; they're thrash...Did you know some of the youngest ones belongs to Tal Jones...Joneses ain't much better...I wonder if the kids are retarded..."

Sunny had to be sure none of the Richter children were within hearing distance. The children were innocent, and apparently Alain Richter loved those children. She saw none of them, but she did see a pretty young woman with eyes just like Alain's blinking back tears.

Sunny put her hand on the woman's shoulder. "Are you all right?"

"No. Those people are mean. Alain ain't never hurt them. He's a good man. They won't let him forget."

"Who are you?"

"Fay Richter."

"Sister?"

"Yes. You?"

"Sunny Bankston. I came to help set up a school."

"Good. Can you teach compassion?"

"I can teach tolerance, and I will."

"I hope."

Sunny looked back at the stage. "Was he right? Would people talk about me if I danced with him?"

"Prob'ly. Tipper don't care. He'll tell 'em where to stick it."

"Are you the mother of Alain's children?"

"Yes."

"What those people said hurt you."

"It ain't the first time. Won't be the last."

"It was cruel," Sunny maintained as she felt irritation creep into her chest.

"You seem real sweet, but you better grow a thick skin."

Alain looked into the crowd and saw Fay and Sunny talking. Momentarily, he wondered if Sunny Bankston might have silver thread and golden needles, but when he closed his eyes, he could only see Amy. *Yes, Sunny Bankston is here to mend a broken heart, but not mine. Tipper's? Maybe. Gator's the happiest person I know. Perhaps the heart she came to mend is her own.*

"We goin' on home," he said to Tipper.

He rounded up his family and they headed out. He sang as he drove home with a bottle of moonshine for when he stopped.

"For this night alone I'll drown my sorrows in the warm glow of moonshine...Still, silver thread and golden needles cannot mend this heart of mine."

32

There's no Place Like Home

Sunny Bankston visited the Richter farm with Leo. She tried again to convince Alain to allow the children to attend school, to no avail. When Gator came a few weeks later with another woman, Alain stared in disbelief. "Miss Langston?" he asked, stunned.

"Same person, new name. I'm Lauren Tomlin."

"You the one Preacher Tomlin married?"

"I am."

"What you doin' here?"

"I came to see you, and I want a hug."

Alain hugged the teacher who had fought for him. "Mrs. Tomlin. Wow! You know a million rumors are floatin' around."

"What do you want to know?"

"Y'all have a child?"

"Yes, from before Leo came here. He never knew until a few weeks ago. Her name is Jessica; she's twenty-two, and she'll be coming here in a couple of years to be Mac's nurse."

Still not believing his eyes or ears, Alain shook his head. "I'm surprised he ain't been tarred and feathered."

"Maybe things are changing in Possum Holler."

"Not for me."

"Why?"

"I'm jest a nasty little hillbilly that won't never amount to nothin'."

"Bull! Ms. Butler was a bitch. Don't let her be right. I still think you're my precious boy who will help put Possum Holler on the map."

"You always did believe in me."

"I still do. I want to talk about your children."

"You must be disappointed."

"You messed up. We all do, but it can be forgiven."

Alain laughed bitterly. "You talkin' about Jesus?"

"Yes."

"I'll think on it."

"Will you think about sending the kids to school?"

"They ain't retarded, and they ain't ignorant. Still, people won't treat 'em right." He folded his arms over his chest in a tight shield.

"How do you know?"

"I heard what they said at Hog Rendering. They made Fay cry. Mrs. Tomlin, I been teachin' 'em."

"How?"

"Home-school. I git books and study packets."

"You do it?"

Alain nodded.

"Of course, you do. Alain, if you change your mind, I'll be teaching."

"I'll keep that in mind."

"One more hug?"

Alain wrapped his arms around Lauren Tomlin. She could feel the man shake with silent tears. She whispered so that not even Gator could hear, "I'm not disappointed. God is not finished with you yet. I love you. You were always my favorite." The two released each other. "Now, if I could just see Amy; I've seen everyone else."

"She left. She broke my and Tipper's heart."

"Yours?"

"I've always loved her."

"Oh, Alain, is that why?"

"Mostly, yes, ma'am."

"I'm always here for you. Always."

"Thank you. I'm glad you're here."

"Let me be here for your children."

"I'll think on it."

Lauren kissed Alain on the cheek. "Think hard."

Alain could not believe Lauren Langston Tomlin was there. Her presence almost persuaded him to send the children to school. However, his fear of their being subjected to cruel ridicule was stronger than Lauren's presence.

Not long after Lauren's visit, Alain had another surprise with Tipper. Dr. MacKenzie Reardon greeted him.

"What you doin' here?" asked Alain.

"That's some greeting. I came to see you."

"You don't wanna see me, Dr. Mac."

"I'm still Mac."

"No, you're different."

"Maybe you're different. If you don't even wanna try, I'm gone." Mac got back in Tipper's truck.

Tipper looked hard at Alain. "You know, you gotta make some effort."

"Like I did at Hog Renderin'?"

"What do you mean?"

"Lucille might be gone, but there are still some gossipin' biddies. They made Fay cry. I won't subject my fam'ly to that. Miss Bankston seems nice. Lord knows! Havin' Miss Langston, I mean Mrs. Tomlin, tempts me to send the kids to school. Then, to hear the cruel things"—He shook his head—"I won't do it!"

Tipper spread his hands as if he did not understand.

"Did you know, Tipper, we done raped half a dozen girls in Possum Holler? I got kids I didn't know I had. Least, the Silsbee girl claims so.

"Now, I sinned with Fay. I visited Fester's and Jacqui's Gentlemen's Club, but I ain't *never* raped nobody. I never touched the Silsbee girl—none of us did. I'm sure they don't want nobody knowin' they've done the same thing we've done. So? Blame us. Damn it, Tipper!" He stomped his foot like a petulant child. "I tried. There's no place like home. We're safe here."

Alain leaned in the truck window. "Dr. Mac, that's a compliment. I'm proud of you. I much appreciate the thought for you comin' out here. You really comin' back here?"

"Yes. There's no place like home, like you said," Mac replied still miffed.

"You a better man than I am. We'll see you when you come to stay."

Mac gave a curt nod. "Yeah."

Tipper looked back at Alain. He *had* tried.

Alain took a deep breath. "Have you heard from Amy?"

"I got the final divorce papers."

"I'm sorry you're single again. It hurts, don't it?"

"Yeah."

"I guess that's why I stay out here. I git real tired of salt in the wounds."

"Fight back."

"I'm tired."

Tipper put a hand on Alain's shoulder. "Me too."

They clasped hands and performed a shoulder bump. Alain mumbled, "Take Mac home."

Time sped forward. Lauren had a child named Rushton with Leo in their middle years. Before anyone realized it, two years had passed. Dr. MacKenzie Reardon, with his wife, Felicia, and their son, Chambry, came home.

Early on the first Monday in June, Fay walked onto the porch where Alan sat. "Wahtcha thinkin' about?" she asked.

"I'm goin' to Hog Renderin'."

"Why? Gator'll git you our pork."

"Mac's home."

"So?"

"I'd like to see him."

"You jest gonna git hurt."

"Maybe. I ain't askin' nobody else to go."

"Good. Y'all jest sleep all night in jail anyway."

"Fay, maybe it's time to fight back."

"Alain, y'all ain't criminals. We ain't whores. We ain't retarded." She ground her teeth. "I don't wanna hear it."

"Well, suit yoself. I'm goin' today."

"I'll see you tomorra."

Alain chuckled. "Yeah, you will." He kissed Fay on top of the head. "'Bye, now."

In the midst of the chaotic fun, Lauren Tomlin spotted Alain. She made her way to him. "You alone?"

"Yes, ma'am. Fay wouldn't come 'cause the last time she came, folks made her cry. The only nice person to her 'sides the folks that ain't changed toward us was Miss Bankston."

"That's awful."

"Yeah. I actually sang with Tipper—well, I sang; he played."

"Sing today."

"No, ma'am." He shook his head.

"Have you been drinking?"

"A little."

"Alain."

"Don't worry." He held up his hand in a stop motion. "Ev'rybody's drinkin'."

"I know."

"They'll be dancin' soon."

"It's fun. You should be my partner." She took his hand.

"Thank you for the invitation, but I think I'll pass. I only came to see Mac, but I don't think he wants to see me."

"He's singing with Tipper."

"Jest like old times."

"Oh! Shoot!"

"Somethin' wrong?"

"No. Rush is just too far from one of us. He's too little to be that far away from a parent. I gotta go be a momma."

"You're a good momma."

Lauren kissed Alain's cheek and went to snag her son.

Alain hung at the back of the crowd. He swayed a bit; he knew he had had too much to drink. He was headed home when a pretty blonde-haired, blue-eyed woman ran smack into him as she rushed to an errand of her own.

"Sorry," they said simultaneously.

"Pardon me, ma'am," said Alain.

"No harm done. I was in a hurry."

Alain had never seen this woman. *Of course!* Alain asked through slurred words, "You Mac'sh wife?"

"Yes, I'm Felicia."

"I ain't shurprished he didn't introdushe you to me. I'm a disgrashe, but it'sh nishe to meet you. I'm Alain Richter."

"Oh!"

Alain chuckled. "Oh ish right. I can tell from your expression that Mac mushta told you shomethin' about me"— He wagged his head—"and it wudn't good."

"He said you used to be friends."

"Ushed to be." Alain nodded. "I guessh that meansh we ain't no more."

"I don't know. I'm sorry I bumped you. I was rushing to get my flute. I'm gonna play."

"Don't let me keep you."

Felicia started on but turned back. "Be sure to listen. I'm sort of a disgrace too." Felicia went to the house to get her flute.

Alain watched after her. "City girlsh are purty," he said to himself. "Yeah, Mac, keep her from me. I might hurt her." Alain snorted and took up a place discreetly hidden from the general crowd, but a place where he could see the stage and be seen. He wanted Felicia to know he had accepted her invitation to listen to her play.

Sunny Bankston with her violin and Felicia Reardon with her flute joined Mac and Tipper on stage. The quartet did a rendition of "Amazing Grace." Alain thought the flute sounded like a bird. As he watched Felicia, he said, "A captive bird."

Then, Felicia started to sing. "She's flat," Alain laughed to himself, but he listened to the words.

Felicia's voice was deep for such a beautiful woman, but oddly pleasant, even flat. Alain listened and caught her eye. Felicia scratched out the melody

The words hit hard on Alain's heart and caused him to think.

The melody and the depth of thought caused a lump to form in his throat. He wanted to leave, but the song mesmerized him.

"Free?" Alain muttered. "When will I be free?"

With a nod of his head to this new woman whom he felt would impact Possum Holler for years to come, Alain disappeared to contemplate how long he could exist and not feel free. He had to ask himself how many roads he had walked. When would he be a man? The waterfall was calling him—the place there was no one to consider but himself.

A few days later, Tipper came to see Alain. "Tipper?"

"I saw you at Hog Rendering, but you left."

"That song Felicia Reardon sang, haunted me."

"Felicia is haunting."

"Mac got himself a fine lady."

"I agree. She's got a friend that might be able to market my moonshine legit."

"For real?"

"Yeah. I want to get that fruit going like we talked about once. This could be it, Alain." Tipper clapped his friend on the shoulder. "Time to get rich."

"Git whatcha need."

"I'll pay you for it."

"I know. We agreed, ten percent off the going rate."

"When I get a distillery, I want you to brew your cider."

"It's a deal, Tipper."

"You'll have to come to town."

"I'll work it out."

Tipper presented a list. "I need some apples, pears, blackberries, watermelons, peaches—a couple of pecks to brew some samples to send the city, the big city, New York."

"We loadin' some now. Git whatcha need before we go to market. Jest remember that these are early apples and pears. They won't be the sweetest."

Walking toward where the trucks were being loaded, Tipper asked, "You helpin' Mac build the clinic?"

"Tipper, he don't want me around."

"You're too sensitive."

Alain cracked up. "Not popular opinion. Most think I'm a brute."

"They don't know you."

"Thanks. I'll prob'ly go in and help after I git this fruit to market."

"I can't help much either. It's dark by the time I get in since we're sinking a new shaft."

Tipper took the fruit he came for. Alain went in a few times and helped with the building. He stayed to himself, did what was needed, and did not bother other people.

After weeks of hard work, Mac received a shipment of supplies and installed the equipment. As Mac dedicated the clinic, Alain saw another new woman.

Alain stood beside Lauren Tomlin as the people began to go home. "Who's that?" he asked.

"Well, hello. It's good to see you. That's Jessica."

"Your daughter?"

"Yes. Come and meet her." Lauren dragged Alain with her. "Jess! I want you to meet Alain Richter."

"Hello, ma'am." Alain dipped his head.

"Ah! Momma's other baby. She's talked a lot about you and Gator."

"Good I hope."

"Of course."

"You here to stay?"

"Oh, yes! There's no place like home."

"Possum Holler's home?" He stretched his eyes wide.

Vigorous head nodding accompanied, "It is when you've been dealing with tsetse flies and terrorists for two years."

"Tsetse flies are in Africa."

"That's where I've been. I am so glad to be here."

"Well, welcome."

Tipper walked up. "Jessica."

"Yes, Tipper?" Jessica walked off with Tipper.

Alain chuckled. "What's funny?" asked Lauren.

"I think Tipper has a new womern."

"You think?"

"Yes, ma'am."

"You're not interested?"

Alain chortled. "Mrs. Tomlin, I will *never* like the same womern as Tipper Campbell again."

Lauren rubbed Alain's arm. "I guess he saw her first. You'll find somebody."

"You keep believin' that for me."

"Have you thought any more about school?"

Alain folded his arms across his chest. "You don't give up."

"Nope."

"Well, I'm still thinkin'. You'll have some seniors this year."

"Yep."

"Matthew ain't quite that old. I'll think on it some more."

"All right. I'm going home."

"Me too. Ain't no place like it. Night, Mrs. Tomlin."

33

Bachelorhood

Alain did watch the school closely. He watched all the people that he desperately wanted to be friends with. Feeling even more unwanted, he drank more.

Alain watched as Tipper's bachelorhood ceased. Tipper and Jessica were obviously happy. He was becoming an entrepreneur, and he did business with Alain, which padded the Richters' income.

Alain left for Wilmington early on October 31st. He bought new clothes for all the children in Wilmington and ran into Jessica Langston and Lauren Tomlin. "Well, hello!" Lauren greeted warmly.

"Mrs. Tomlin. Miss Langston. What y'all doin'?"

"Jess is shopping for Tipper's girls."

"I hear congratulations are in order. Tipper's a lucky man."

"Thank you, Mr. Richter," said Jessica. "I see you're shopping too."

"Kids grow fast."

"Yes, they do."

"I'm done, though. I'm about to head back." The cart he had was loaded.

"I have a wedding dress to find."

"You set a date?"

"Valentine's Day."

"Good. If I ever git married, I wanna git married in August."

"Why's that?" Jessica asked in genuine curiosity.

"Well"—He stroked his beard—"January has New Year's; February has Valentine's; March has St. Patrick's Day and sometimes Easter, but that's usually April, which also has April Fool's Day, and I guess I'm the biggest fool of all to believe I'll ever git married."

"Now, that's foolish," Lauren said with a grin.

Alain smiled and shook his head. "May has Mother's Day and Memorial Day; June has Father's Day and my birthday. July has Independence Day. September has Labor Day, and October has Halloween. This'll be your first Harvest Fest tonight. We don't usually go."

"Why?"

Alain wagged his head slowly for emphasis. "People are cruel, and I won't have my kids hurt. Anyway, then, November has Thanksgiving, and December has Christmas. The only month left without a holiday to celebrate is August."

Jessica laughed. "That's romantic. Why hasn't some woman snagged you?"

"I never wanted but one. I gotta go. See you, ladies."

Alain left the two women and made a stop at Jacqui's Gentlemen's Club to see a tall brunette. Jessica looked at her mother. "Momma, that man is so broken. What woman did he love?"

"Amy."

"Tipper's Amy?"

"The same."

"Now, that's truly sad."

As Alain turned onto the narrow dirt road into Possum Holler in his Ford F350, he was almost sideswiped by a silver Volvo as it streaked to the highway. He swerved to miss the car and grazed a tree as the car fishtailed and had its back passenger side tire drop into the inadequate drainage ditch.

"What the hell?" exclaimed Alain. He got out of the truck and crossed the road to the other vehicle. The blonde curly head of the hysterical female driver was bent over the steering wheel.

Alain tapped the window. Felicia Reardon raised her head and turned red eyes and a tear-stained face to Alain. Reluctantly, she let the window down.

"You okay?" asked Alain.

"No! Do I look okay?" she snapped.

"You look upset, but are you hurt?" Alain asked patiently.

Felicia shook her head. "No, I just need to get out of here."

"The ditch or Possum Holler?"

She glared at the man. "Alain Richter, right?"

"Felicia, right?" his tone matched her cool, icy tenor perfectly.

"Yeah. I gotta get out of the ditch so I can get out of Possum Holler."

"And go where?"

"New York."

"You leavin' Mac?"

Felicia shrieked and pounded the steering wheel with the heels of her hands. "I'm leaving Possum Holler! Mac's part of Possum Holler. Are you gonna help me?"

"Felicia, you were drivin' like a fox with its tail on fire. What's wrong?"

She looked at her hands and wiped them on her sweater as if they were dirty. "All that blood, and Mac made me help with surgery. I don't belong here. I'm a horrible person." She laughed hysterically. "Tipper almost died, and I'm worried about helping with surgery."

"Tipper?"

"It's my fault. I introduced him to Ron."

"What happened to Tipper?" The look on Alain's face showed panic.

"Lacerated femoral artery. Mac fixed it."

When Felicia looked at Alain, she looked lost. "I'm a disgrace, like I told you."

"How? 'Cause you cain't handle blood?"

"No. It's worse. I'll die if I stay in Possum Holler. Mac'll be better off without me."

"Where's your boy?"

"With Mac. Mac'll be better for him too."

"You talkin' crazy. You jest upset. Let me git you outa the ditch so you can git home." Alain opened the car door.

"Yes. Home. To Ron."

"Ron?"

Felicia nodded. "Alain, what did you do that was so bad except make kids with your sister? You're so nice."

"I ain't nice."

"Yes, you are. You couldn't have done anything so awful."

"I loved Amy."

"Tipper's ex?"

"Yep." He rolled his lips together.

"When she was married to Tipper?"

Alain shrugged. "Since I was a boy. Always."

"Did you sleep with her?"

Alain shook his head hard. "No, her ma broke us up before she went to Tipper."

"I slept with Ron."

Alain scowled. *Why is this woman telling me her secrets?* "While you were married to Mac?"

Felicia nodded. Alain asked, "Is the kid Mac's?"

She shrugged.

He sighed. "You love Mac?"

"Love isn't enough."

"You love Ron?"

Felicia nodded.

Alain shook his head in disbelief of what he was hearing. "I guess I ain't the only one screwed up in the head," he said matter-of-factly. "You wanna know what else I've done?"

Blonde curls bobbed as she nodded.

Alain asked, "You ain't afraid of me?"

She shook her head.

"What if I tell you I killed a man?"

"Did you?" She stared at him with wide eyes that were curious, but not frightened.

"Yeah. My pa."

"I heard it was suicide."

Alain snorted. "I ain't sorry. He was gonna kill me."

"Then, it wasn't murder. I heard you raped women."

Alain looked over the top of the car. "No. I ain't never."

"Anything else?"

"I helped a friend dispose of a body."

"Tipper?"

"Naa. Tipper's a lover, not a killer, but he can fight."

Felicia started to cry again. "I made Tipper get a hard-on. He's Mac's best friend. I didn't mean to."

"How'd you do that?"

"I was teaching him to salsa."

Alain took a deep breath. "Felicia, are you okay? Why are you tellin' me these things?"

"We're disgraces, remember?"

"I reckon. Whatcha gonna do when I git you outa the ditch?"

"I'm going to New York."

"Mac know?"

"I left him a letter. I'm not deserting Chambry. I'm just going where I belong. I'm getting a divorce."

"Bachelorhood's a bitch."

"No, that's me."

Alain gave Felicia a sympathetic look. "No. You a good lady. We coulda been friends. Hop out. Let me see if I can rock it out. The ditch ain't deep."

"You gonna tell Mac?" She got out of the car.

Alain thought as he got behind Felicia's steering wheel. "No."

"Why?"

"The song you sang. You cain't exist long, like you said, before you crumble. You like the white dove. Sooner or later, you gotta rest. I been watchin' you. You might be leavin', but you'll be back."

"Alain, why didn't you graduate? You aren't shallow or stupid."

"Missed too many days; then, when Ma and Pa died, I had to be a man, though I often wonder if anybody else sees me that way, like the song said. I don't know how many roads I gotta walk."

"I think you're a nice man. I wish we could've been friends." Felicia smiled sadly.

Alain pointed to the other side of the road. "Go stand by my truck. This might sling mud."

After several attempts, he had the Volvo back on the road. Felicia looked up at the tall, thin man. "How can I pay you?"

"Don't be silly, womern. One day, you'll do me a good turn."

"Thank you."

"You welcome. Slow down. Ron'll be waitin'."

"You don't hate me?"

"No. I don't know you well, but it seems we a lot alike."

"Watch out for Mac."

Alain sighed. "If he ever decides to be a friend again. Mac'll survive. Go now." He rapped the roof of the car.

Driving through town, Alain realized his detour at Jacqui's place had allowed Jessica to get home. He watched for a minute while the residents of Possum Holler set up for Harvest Fest. He watched Mac burst into Leo's home. *Ah, he knows she's gone. Sorry, Mac.* Alain laughed sarcastically. *Might be good you ain't got a sister tonight. Bachelorhood. It's a bitch.*

Alain delivered the new clothes to the Richter children and took comfort in the love of his family.

34

Pomp and Circumstance

A few weeks after Felicia left Possum Holler, Fay found Alain attending a cow about to deliver a calf. The Richters kept a few dairy cows and occasionally bred one. A bull they would sell, but they needed another dairy cow since one had recently died. Fay was frantic because it was well after dark.

"Fay, what's wrong?" he asked, harried.

"Matthew ain't come home. I don't know where he went."

"The boy's sixteen, Fay."

"So? It ain't like he's courtin'."

"What do you want me to do?"

"Find him."

Alain left the cow with Calvin and took Fay from the barn. "Where do you want me to look?"

Fay huffed. "He's sixteen. Maybe he went to Fester's for, you know."

"I don't think so. If he ain't home in two hours, I'll go. Did he take a truck?"

"Yeah. What if he wrecked?"

"Fay, stop worrying."

Fay trudged back to the house, and Alain began to fret. Matthew had never done something like this. Before the two hours were up, Matthew came home. Alain waited on the porch.

"Hey, Papa," the boy said cheerfully.

"I hate to bring you down from whatever cloud you walkin' on, but you're in trouble. Your mother is frantic. Where have you been?"

"Um." He shuffled his feet and put his hands in the back pockets of his jeans.

Alain stopped rocking in the rocking chair. "Fester's?"

"No, sir! I been to church."

"Church? It ain't Sunday."

"Sort of church. They had this thing just for teenagers. I went."

"Church?" Alain asked again.

"You seem surprised."

"How'd the kids treat you?"

"Nobody was mean."

"Friendly?"

"Betsy was."

"Betsy? Betsy Campbell?" The pitch of Alain's voice rose a bit, and he leaned forward in the rocker to spit tobacco juice.

"Yes, sir."

"Is she the reason you went?"

"Yes, sir."

"She's too young for a beau," Alain said decisively, flopping back in the chair.

"Why?"

"Matthew! Please, tell me you didn't do nothin' with Betsy Campbell?"

"We ate hotdogs together."

"Does Tipper know?"

"Nurse Jess knows."

"They ain't married."

"They're gonna be. I didn't do nothin' wrong, Papa. I didn't even hold her hand."

Alain shook his head as if trying to clean water from his ears. "You seriously interested in Betsy Campbell?"

"I like her. She's nice. She's smart. Papa, I've been thinkin'."

"'Bout what?"

"I'd like to go to school."

"Oh." Alain stood from the old rocking chair where he had been sitting for over an hour and put both hands on the wooden porch rail.

"It ain't you or the home-schoolin'. I'd like to meet people."

"People who'd treat you bad?"

"They might, but I got a thick skin."

Alain stared at the ground. "It hurts, Matthew. It hurts real bad."

"Miss Bankston seems real nice. She looks puny, but the kids don't get much past her. She'd make sure they acted right."

"I don't know."

"Papa, I know what I am." Matthew continued to plead his case. "I'm a product of incest. I have to live with that no matter what people say."

"But you could leave here, keep it a secret."

"Are you sorry I was born?"

"I regret what I did. I ain't sorry to have you. I love you."

"I love you too, Papa. I ain't runnin' away. I can face this head-on. You should too. You should tell the judgmental assholes to kiss your ass."

"Matthew Richter! Your momma's got soap for that mouth."

"That's what I think. Will you think about school if just for me? I'd like a diploma." Matthew came up the steps to the porch.

"I'll think on it. I just don't want you hurt. Next time you go off without tellin' anybody, I'm gonna whoop you."

"How many times have you spanked me?"

"Three, and every lick broke my heart even if you did deserve it."

"You gonna appease Momma?"

"Nope. You're gonna tell her you went to see a girl, but you ain't ready to reveal details yet."

"She'll nag me."

"Yep."

"Can I go to other youth things?"

Alain gave one nod. "If you tell me where you're goin'."

"Yes, sir."

Matthew Richter began to attend the weekly youth meetings.

In February, Gator visited Alain and told him to keep his family home. There was an epidemic of the flu in Possum Holler.

"Mac send you?" Alain asked Gator.

"Yeah. He's got a lot o' sick folks. He asked me to check on y'all and tell you to stay outa town."

"Don't go in much anyway."

"True, but some folks have died."

Alain's brow creased. "Who?"

"All the Peacocks but Abner and Zeke."

"Thank Mac for his concern. Let me know when it's past."

"If anybody gits sick, take 'em to Mac. Lose the pride."

"If we git sick, I will."

"Promise?"

"Yeah, Gator." He nodded with slow deliberation. "I promise."

Gator turned to leave. "Gator?" Alain called.

"Yeah?"

"You like the school?"

"Yes. Miss Bankston is remarkable. Fox and Rooster are doin' real good. Why?"

"Matthew wants to go."

"Let him. He needs to be around other kids."

"What if they treat him bad?"

"Alain, you cain't protect 'em forever. Do you want 'em to do the same thing y'all done?"

"No. Gator, I tried to keep the last ones from doin' it."

"But you failed."

Alain nodded forlornly. "Yeah. Polly's pregnant."

"Shit! Who? Simon?"

"Yeah."

"Damn it! I even talked to him."

"Sorry."

"It ain't yo fault, but Pa would be so hurt. That's another reason to let Matthew go to school—girls." Gator huffed.

"That's another concern."

"He don't like boys?"

"No, Betsy."

"Campbell?

"Yeah."

"Tipper would kill him unless it was done proper."

"I know. I'll think on all of it."

Gator's next visit brought Alain news of yet another loss, Grandma Newton, who apparently died of a stroke associated with her raging fever that accompanied a new strain of influenza.

Matthew continued to attend church youth functions. Eventually, more of the children talked to him. By the time Possum Holler School held its first prom, Betty Jo Maddox asked Matthew to be her date.

Matthew burst through the door in excitement. "Papa!"

"What?" asked Alain.

"Please let me go?"

"Go where?"

"To prom. Betty Jo Maddox asked me. Please? Miss Bankston says the boys just have to wear suits. Please, Papa?"

Alain scowled. "Ain't you gotta be in the school?"

"I don't guess. Miss Bankston told 'em nobody under ninth grade. Papa, my studies are higher than that. Betty Jo's my age."

"I thought you liked Betsy."

"I do, but she's too young for prom."

Alain gave the boy a quick nod. Matthew threw his arms around his father, and Alain held him close. "When is it?"

"The first Saturday in April."

"We'll go to Wilmington this Saturday to git you a suit."

"Preacher Tomlin's gonna rent a limousine and pick the couples up. I'll have to go to Betty Jo's house. She said she's gonna have a pink dress. I gotta get her a corsage." The boy's words bubbled out.

Alain laughed at his son's excitement. "We'll take care of it."

"Thank you, Papa."

On Saturday, Alain and Matthew drove to Wilmington. They went to Jacqui's Gentlemen's Club.

"Papa, what is this place?" asked Matthew.

"You ain't comin' in."

Matthew looked scornful, his face puckering from brow to lips. "Papa?"

"It's a whorehouse, but I got a friend here that knows about suits."

"A woman?"

"Yes."

"A whore?"

"Yes, but you will not say that to her. She calls herself Blanche. You will be polite. I ain't here for sex."

"Have you been?"

"Yes. Always with Blanche."

"I'll be polite."

Alain went inside. A big man greeted him. "We ain't open yet."

"I know that, Jimmy Joe."

"Alain Richter?"

"Yep."

"It's been a while."

"Yep. Is Blanche here?"

"Sleepin'."

"I need a womern's advice."

"Not lookin' to get laid?"

"Nope. I got my son with me. He needs a suit for prom. I ain't got a clue. I'll pay her for her time."

"I'll see if she's willing."

"Obliged."

A little later, Blanche Proctor, tall and brunette, came downstairs wearing jeans and a red turtleneck sweater. "Alain! Where have you been?" she greeted the man with a hug.

"Tryin' to live a more decent life."

"You rascal! Your son? How old is he?"

"Jest turned seventeen. A girl asked him to prom. He needs a suit, and I ain't got a clue. I thought you could help. I'll pay you for your time."

"No. This is friend to friend. He doesn't need a tux?"

"No, they ain't wearin' tuxes, jest suits."

"At y'all's new school?"

"Yeah."

"Well, introduce me. Is he as handsome as you?"

Alain considered the question. "I reckon he looks jest about like me at that age. Not quite as skinny."

Alain took Blanche to the truck. "Blanche, this is my son, Matthew. Matthew, my friend, Blanche."

"Hello, Matthew. Blanche Proctor." She extended her hand and the boy shook it.

"Miss Proctor."

"Alain wants me to help you pick out a suit. You okay with that?"

"I reckon. You're Papa's friend."

"I am. I've known Alain over ten years now."

"You're mighty pretty for a…"

Alain shot Matthew a look, and he stopped talking.

Blanche laughed. "For a whore?"

Matthew said nothing.

"It's all right, Matthew. Do you have a suggestion for another job?"

"I don't know you."

"Well, let's get you a suit, and you can get to know me."

By the afternoon, Matthew Richter had a new blue double-breasted suit with a pale green button-down oxford shirt and an emerald-and-rose-striped silk tie and black wing-tip shoes with navy dress socks.

"You're handsome," said Blanche. "Your girlfriend is lucky."

"She's not my girlfriend, just a friend."

"Okay. Do you have a girlfriend?"

"The girl I like is too young to have a boyfriend. I'll have to wait for her."

"How old is she?"

"She's fixin' to be twelve, but she's real smart."

"Twelve? Like Sherry was?"

Alain cleared his throat. "Sherry?" asked Matthew. "Sherry Jones?"

"I don't know any Sherry Jones," said Blanche.

"Uncle Gator's wife is Sherry."

"Oh. Coincidence. You need a haircut while you're here, maybe a manicure. Yucky nails won't fly with this suit."

Matthew glanced at Alain. Alain nodded.

Blanche took them to the cosmetology school where they gave Matthew the works. Alain asked how long the school had been there and learned it had been around for a long time. He figured it had to be the place where Ina Campbell had obtained her barber's license many years before.

After the haircut and manicure, Blanche help Matthew order a corsage for Alain to pick up the next Friday. Then, Alain bought a late lunch for Matthew and Blanche before returning her to Jacqui's place.

"Miss Blanche," said Matthew.

"Yes, Matthew?"

"Thank you. You're real good at helping people pick out clothes, and you're pretty. I've read about women called personal shoppers. They usually help old folks who can't get around much. You'd be good at it."

Blanche looked at the building in front of her and back at the young man. "Thank you, Matthew. Monday I'll go to the employment agency. Maybe I can escape like Sherry. Alain." She gave the man a knowing look.

"Blanche."

As they drove Matthew said, "I liked her."

"She's not..." Alain let his thought trail.

"Who, Papa? Whom do you love?"

"Amy."

"Betsy's momma?"

"Yeah. Since grade school."

"Wow! Why did she marry Tipper?"

"Her ma was the bitch from Hell."

"Papa!"

"She hated me and broke us up. She hated Tipper too."

"Did she break them up?"

"Yep. Somehow."

"Jeez! Miss Blanche does kind of look a little like Mrs. Campbell did, at least what I remember. Is that why you saw her?"

"Yep."

They were quiet for a while. Finally, Alain said, "Matthew, when Betsy's older, talk to Tipper. I'm all right with it."

"Thanks, Papa."

Leo Tomlin picked Betty Jo Maddox and her date up in the limousine. Annie Mae Maddox and Beau Matlock shared the ride. Annie Mae gaped at her cousin's date. "You look good, Matthew."

"Thanks."

"Why don't you come to school?" asked Beau.

"Papa is scared people will mistreat us."

"Oh, because…"

"Because we're inbred. I know what I am."

"Does it make you mad?" asked Beau

"Sometimes."

"People say your pa's bad," ventured Annie Mae.

"Not true. He's a good man. He loves me. I've never doubted that."

"How many of 'em are your brothers and sisters?" Annie Mae continued to pry.

"Just Mary."

"So, Alain ain't everybody's daddy?" asked Beau.

"No."

Betty Jo glared at her cousin when Annie Mae said, "Some folks say they, um, rape women."

"Not true."

"I believe it after talking to you."

"Thanks."

Beau added his thoughts. "Lots of folks say inbred people are retarded. You're not retarded."

"No, I'm not, although I've studied that it can have that effect, as well as lots of other things, like hemophilia."

"What?" Beau knitted his brows together.

"Free bleeding, you know, when people get cut, they bleed to death. It's called the royal disease because of the inbreeding that took place in the royal families of Europe."

"You sound smarter than anybody I know," laughed Beau. "How did you learn?"

"Home-school."

"I guess that's good, but you could still come to school with us," encouraged Annie Mae.

"I'm trying to convince Papa."

"Good luck. My pa says one thing your pa is, is stubborn," said Beau.

Matthew laughed. "Now, that part is *true*."

When Matthew got out of the car, Leo put his hand on the boy's shoulder. "I overheard your conversation. You're a good kid. Alain should be proud."

Matthew smiled. "Thank you, Preacher Tomlin."

"Go have fun."

During the prom, Tipper danced with Jessica, and Mac danced with Sunny. Mac and Tipper were providing live music, but Sunny played some CDs to give them a break. While they danced, the students watched; none more closely than Matthew Richter. After the adults danced, Sunny stopped at the punch table where Matthew stood. She looked at the boy. "Who are you?" she asked. "You're not one of my students."

"No, ma'am. I'm Matthew Richter."

"Oh, I see. You've grown a foot since I saw you at my first Hog Rendering."

"Betty Jo invited me."

"I'm sure it's fine. Your father approved?"

Matthew nodded. "He gave his permission."

"Well, good. Are you having fun?"

"Yes, ma'am. What kind of dancing was that?" He pointed to the dance floor.

"Salsa, well Latin. That one was called a Cha Cha Cha."

"Papa would frown at it."

"Oops."

"Do they dance like that in the big city?"

"Yes."

"It looked like…"

Sunny blushed. "I shouldn't have danced that kind of dance here. I apologize."

"Beau said you and Dr. Reardon are a couple."

"No, we're friends."

"Okay." The boy sipped the punch.

"Are you going to come to school?"

"I'm trying to convince Papa. I don't know."

"I'd like to have you."

"Thank you."

Betty Jo waltzed up. "Are you gonna dance with me?"

"Yeah, sure. Excuse me, Miss Bankston."

Mac stood beside Sunny. "What a pleasant child," she mused.

"Normal?"

"Yeah."

"Alain Richter's kid."

"He seemed normal. He was very polite. I couldn't gauge how educated, but I liked him."

"I never said Alain was stupid. I just, um, disagree with his choices."

Alain was waiting on the porch when Leo dropped Matthew at home. The two men exchanged waves. The rain from earlier in the evening had stopped.

"Well?" asked Alain.

"I had fun. Miss Bankston is awesome."

"Awesome?"

"You should see her dance, not square dancing."

"What kind?"

"She called it salsa, Latin dancing. She danced with Dr. Reardon, and Nurse Jess danced with Tipper. It was rather…" He bit his lip.

"What, Matthew?"

"Suggestive."

"Sex?"

"Yeah. Like." Matthew hesitated trying to find the right words. "Well, parts of it looked like they were having sex with their clothes on, and they shook every inch of their bodies."

"Two questions: One—What do you know about having sex; two—You wanna go to school to learn that?"

"I have never had sex, Papa, but I've seen pictures." Matthew fidgeted. "I went to Fester's one night and just looked."

"Watched?"

Matthew nodded.

"Oh! We need to talk."

"Yes, sir. There's a lot more to learn at school though. Miss Bankston apologized. She said Dr. Reardon's just a friend."

"And their relationship would be important to me because?"

"You're single. She's single. She's pretty."

"No." Alain started inside.

"Amy's gone, Papa."

"She's too educated for me. She's nice, but, no."

"Okay. Papa, I wanna go to the graduation. Don't say no. The Matlocks and Maddoxes have been nice to me. Annie Mae and Beau are graduating."

Alain sighed. "If we go, all us men go."

"Okay."

When graduation day came, Alain kept his word to Matthew. They attended; all the Richter men attended. After the ceremony, Alain allowed the boy to join in the celebration. They all drank.

As the party wound down, Sunny noticed the constable rounding up all the Richter men, including Matthew.

After Sunny turned on a movie to watch at home, she felt compelled to go to the jail. The Richters had done nothing more than anyone else, less than some.

Sunny barged into the small two-cell jail. "Constable Hill, I'd like to talk to you."

"What's wrong, Miss Bankston?"

"Why are these men in jail?"

"They're Richters."

"First of all, one of them is a boy. Second, they didn't do anything. They are less drunk than half the town. Did you arrest them just because their last name is *Richter*? Is that fair?"

"They've been known to do crazy things when they're drunk."

"No. They've been *accused*. Do you have any proof?"

Alain came to the cell door. "Miss Bankston, this is how we're treated."

"Well, it's wrong."

"You're feisty, aren't you?"

"Yes." She nodded with vigor, causing her auburn hair to swirl around her face. "Constable, let them out. Let them go home."

"I don't know."

Sunny snapped her hands to her hips. "What's the charge?"

"Miss Bankston," Alain said gently, "don't worry about it."

"Oh!" Sunny stomped her foot. "Not fair! I'm getting Leo."

"No, no," the constable grunted and held up a hand. "Alain, you sober enough to drive?"

"No, but Matthew is."

"Okay. I'll let you out, but go straight home."

"Norman, this is why we don't come to town."

Sunny walked out the door with Matthew. "Matthew, I'm sorry."

"You didn't do it, but it didn't help my arguments."

"Don't give up. It could mean your graduation."

"Yes, ma'am. I know. Graduation. I can taste it. I can hear 'Pomp and Circumstance.' I want it."

"Matthew," Alain called, "come on. You gotta drive."

"Thank you, Miss Bankston."

Alain lingered a minute. "Miss Bankston, much obliged."

"It was wrong."

"Still, you came and fought for us. I appreciate that."

"You're welcome. Please, don't let this keep you from letting the kids come to school."

"I ain't convinced comin' is best."

"Matthew wants it so badly. Don't let him get too far behind."

Alain grunted, "He ain't. Thanks, again. Night."

Sunny stood still wondering what she had said wrong as she watched the Richters out of sight.

35

Skeletons in the Closet

Alain sat on the plank porch of his home very deep in thought on his thirty-second birthday.

"What's on yo mind?" Fay asked from the doorway.

"Sunny Bankston."

"Alain, she ain't interested in you."

"She's a nice lady, but, now, she's gone to New York with Mac."

"Her, Jessica, and Mac went with Tipper."

"Tipper and Jessica are engaged."

"Alain, she ain't in New York with Mac like *that*. Even if she was, it wouldn't be yo business 'cause she ain't yo womern."

"Could she be?"

"No."

"Why? Ain't I as good as Mac?"

"No," said Fay with a jerky nod of her head.

"What?" asked Alain, shocked by Fay's comment.

"It ain't a matter o' bein' good as. It's bein' matched. Y'all don't match."

"Who do I match?"

"Nobody."

"Thanks. I appreciate that." Alain walked to his truck.

"Where you goin'?"

"Out. I'll be back."

"You goin' to a damned whorehouse?"

"No, I'm goin' to a place that fits me. Nobody else will be there."

Fay released a long sigh. "Alain, I didn't mean it like that. Ain't nobody good enough for *you*."

"Thanks, Fay," he said, realizing what she meant was not an insult.

"I worry 'bout you when you off alone."

"Why?"

"You used to take the gun."

"I ain't considered suicide for a long time."

"So, you did think about it after that time I found you?" She cocked her head to the side.

"Yeah, but no more. I ain't that selfish. I'll be back, Fay."

"Okay."

As Alain approached his sanctuary at the waterfall, he was shocked to see Gator. "Gator?" he said walking up the slope.

"Hey. Whatcha doin' here?"

"Escapin'." Alain hooked his thumbs in the back pockets of his jeans.

"Me too."

"What's wrong?"

"I jest need to think." Gator ran a hand across his balding head.

"Wanna talk?"

Gator sighed. "You the only one that knows Sherry's real age. Well, not quite, Mrs. Tomlin knows, and now Tipper. Of course, Grandma Newton knew."

"Okay."

"Tipper's doing some DNA tests."

"Why?" asked Alain as he sat beside his friend on the creek bank.

"Miss Ina and Uncle Ander had a child, a girl given up for adoption."

"Uh-huh?"

"You don't sound too surprised."

"Gator, they look alike."

"Jacqui lied to her. She said she was rich, and her husband was in France."

"And this happened when?" Alain leaned back on his elbows on the soft grass.

"Remember when she went to barber school?"

"Yep. So, Preacher Tomlin knows?"

"He knows ever'thing in Possum Holler."

Rolling on to one side with his head resting on his hand, Alain asked, "Does he know why Amy left?"

"No. That's one thing he don't know. And he don't know about Bilbo. He might feel the need to report it, but, umm, I told Mrs. Tomlin."

"I ain't never told him about Pa neither. I ain't told nobody but you and Tal." He bit the inside of his cheek. *And Felicia.*

Gator chuckled. "Seems like Possum Holler's got lots o' skeletons in the closet. Even Preacher Tomlin had some skeletons, mighty purty skeletons.

"Maybe that's why he don't judge too harsh," mused Alain, sitting up, slipping off his shoes, and dangling his feet in the water.

"Maybe. Grandma Newton knew all. I bet she knew why Amy left. Too bad she passed with the flu epidemic."

"Yeah, I miss her." He let out a sad puff of air. "But you got the slaughterhouse and can turn it into a processing plant now. Your dream's comin' true."

"I suppose. I gotta hear back from all my brothers. Corky wants to keep his share, but be a silent and absent partner."

"Gator, what kind o' skeleton you think Sunny Bankston brought to Possum Holler?"

"Don't know. I know she was shot in Chicago, and Mac saved her life."

"Shot? Why?"

"I heard she had to report some daddy beatin' his kid, and he got real mad. He killed two people before the police shot him. He shot Miss Bankston and lots more."

"Damn! She seems so sweet."

"She didn't do nothin' wrong," defended Gator.

"Welfare take the kid?"

"No, his ma took him and disappeared."

"Okay, well, yeah, I can see that. I wish my ma had run off with Tal and took us."

"Me too."

"So, Gator, who all do we know with skeletons in the closet?"

"Me and you."

"Yeah. Sherry, Ina, and Preacher Tomlin. I think Mac." Alain leaned back again flat on his back and let the current wash over his feet.

"Why?"

"Felicia left him."

"Yeah. Why?"

"She didn't belong in Possum Holler, at least not permanent."

"How you know?" Gator lay back with his hands under his head.

"I seen her leavin'. She run off the road, and I got her outa the ditch. We talked."

"She got skeletons?"

"Oh, yeah." Alain nodded.

"Like?"

"Ain't mine to tell."

"You got secrets from me?"

"Naa. If you think, you'll know Felicia's skeleton."

"Ron?"

Alain nodded.

Gator surmised, "He ain't a bad sort."

"No? I ain't met him."

"He Chambry's pa?"

"Don't know."

"Felicia tell you?"

"She don't know."

"You think Mac knows?"

"Yep. He won't care. He loves the boy. That's one thing we got in common. We love our kids no matter how they were born."

"Hmm," sighed Gator. "I bet he done one o' them DNA tests."

"Me too, but he won't never tell. He should know he has a sister." Alain turned his head to look at his friend. "Y'all gonna tell him?"

"Eventually. Miss Ina and Sherry have to decide." Gator sat up and skipped a stone on the creek. "Why'd you ask about Miss Bankston."

"I don't know. She's nice and purty."

"Alain, you over Amy? You want Sunny Bankston?"

"I'm lonesome. You think she'd give me the time o' day, or is she with Mac?"

"Hmm." Gator rubbed his chin in thought. "She don't know she's with Mac. No"—He held up a finger—"Truth is, Mac don't know he's with *her*. You serious 'bout makin' a play for her?"

"I was thinkin' on it."

"You a glutton for punishment?"

"So? You like Fay. I ain't good enough for her." Alain sat up.

"That ain't it. Some folks jest ain't meant to be."

"I guess I ain't meant to be with nobody."

Gator gave him a half-frown and put one hand on his hip. "What would you do if Amy came home?"

Alain thought and sighed. "I'd be on her like morning dew on rose petals."

"Then, you don't need to think 'bout other women."

"She ain't comin' home."

"You never know. Now, that's a skeleton I'd like to know about."

"Me too, Gator. Me too."

36

Touching Sunshine

Alain watched Sunny and felt greatly disturbed about the time she spent with Mac, and then, Gator. Alain's interpretation of the situation was misconstrued. He could not believe a woman he held in such high regard had fallen from grace. Worse, he wondered what had come over Gator Jones. Mac, he understood.

Then, movie night started when Ron Norton, now married to Felicia, donated computers and other electronic equipment to the school. Matthew wheedled until Alain gave in and took everyone to movie night. When the Richter family got home after the third week of movies, Polly realized she had left the baby's blanket behind. Alain returned to get it and found it near where the truck had been parked. He saw Mac walk Sunny home as he did every Friday. However, this time Mac went inside. "No," moaned Alain. "Not you too."

Alain leaned against the truck for over an hour. He never saw Mac come out Sunny's door even after her lights went out. Alain felt as if his last illusion had finally been shattered.

"Damn you!" he muttered as he drove home. He left the blanket and retreated to his sanctuary where he stayed all weekend.

Alain drank and wrote the entire weekend. He had to get his feelings out. Although in his heart he knew Sunny Bankston was not for him, Alain felt betrayed. He allowed the hurt to flow as he wrote:

Touching Sunshine

I thought to touch Sunshine,
Perchance, to make her mine.

I thought the star shone bright,
Flooding with a brilliant light.
Why is it so suddenly dim
By a man's selfish whim?

I thought to touch Sunshine,
Perchance, to make her mine.

I thought the gloom might shatter,
That, perhaps, I, indeed, did matter.
How could I have been so wrong,
Once again to quell my heart song?

I thought to touch Sunshine,
Perchance, to make her mine.

I thought it was a voice of reason,
Singing triumphantly in season.

Why is the tune so quickly stemmed
By an act once condemned?

I thought to touch Sunshine,
Perchance, to make her mine.

I thought she was a vision,
A woman with real mission.
How could I not understand
That I could never be her man?

I thought to touch Sunshine,
Perchance, to make her mine.

By Monday evening, every pain, every wound, every hurt, every doubt Alain had experienced was poured onto paper. Still, he felt no better than a slug crawling upon the ground.

With a blood alcohol level that would have put most men into a coma, he drove into Possum Holler. He had to hear from Sunny's lips that she was not sleeping with MacKenzie Reardon and Gator Jones on the side.

Seeing Gator leave Sunny with a gentle touch made Alain's drunken brain fume. "No! No! No!" he growled. "She cain't be a whore. Not Sunshine! No!"

Alain staggered to the steps as Sunny locked the school, having finished a tutoring session with Gator who wanted to take his high-school equivalency. Alain slipped his hands around Sunny and groped her breasts as he slurred in her ear, "Teacher, teach me them thingsh you been teachin' Mac and Gator. Ain't I ash good ash them?"

Sunny's scream pierced the darkness, and MacKenzie Reardon leveled Alain Richter. "Get your filthy hands off her!"

Each word was accentuated with a blow. Alain did not fight back. He thought, *Good. He's mad enough to kill me. I'm sorry, Fay. I promised I wouldn't kill myself. I'll just let Mac do it. Oh, God, I wanna die.*

The sound of Sunny's sobbing penetrated his drunken thoughts. They changed. *I'm sorry. I didn't mean to hurt you. I'm sorry.*

After a time, many voices whirled around him. Tipper Campbell hauled Mac off Alain. "Mac! Settle down! You're gonna kill him!"

"Yes, I am! He's a low-life son-of-a-bitch! He's an inbred moronic drunkard! He makes a good argument for abortion!"

"MacKenzie Reardon!" Leo Tomlin scolded as he ran up in his pajamas. "You don't mean that."

"Yes, I do! If he ever touches Sunny again, I swear to God, I will kill him."

Constable Hill jerked Alain up. "Miss Bankston, what happened?"

Sunny sobbed, "He raped me, Mac."

Alain caught the words and instinctively defended himself. "I didn't rape that womern!"

"Obviously," snorted the constable. "You didn't have time. Miss Bankston, please, tell me what happened?"

Mac finally calmed Sunny as he held her close. Through gasped, she said, "He groped me and insinuated I was having sex with Mac and Gator."

"You fool!" Mac yelled. "Why would you think that?"

"I sheen you go in and not come out. She holesh up with Gator ever Monday night. Sunshine cain't be a whore. Jusht cain't be." Alain almost could not stand with help.

"You idiot!" Mac growled. "Sunny has been tutoring Gator so he can take his high-school equivalency. She has never done anything immoral with me. I left through the back door, but you should *all* know I am courting Sunny."

Constable Hill asked, "Miss Bankston, what do you want me to do with Alain?"

"Lock him up and let him sleep it off, but make sure he understands not to touch me again, or Mac will kill him. Mac, take me home."

"I knew Shunshine wudn't a whore," Alain said sluggishly. "Not Shunshine. I thought to touch Shunshine, perchanshe, to make her mine. Nope. She'sh Mac'sh. I ain't good enough."

Mac carried Sunny home, and Leo helped the constable drag Alain to a cot in the jail. "Alain," said Leo.

Alain could not focus. "Shorry. I'm shorry. I ain't no good, Preacher Tomlin. I shoulda let Pa shoot me. I wanna die." Alain started to cry.

Leo stroked Alain's hair. All he could see was a little green-eyed boy with bruises all over him and his arm in a cast. Leo flipped Alain's feet onto the bed and guided his body down. "Go to sleep. I won't let you die, Alain. Sleep now. I'll talk to you tomorrow when you're sober."

"Okay. I don't wanna dream about Shunshine. Leasht she ain't a whore."

"No, she's not."

"Mac love her?"

"I think so."

"That'sh good." As Alain drifted to sleep he mumbled, "I thought to touch Shunshine, perchanshe, to make her mine."

Leo looked at the constable. "Why would he think Sunny might be interested in him?"

"Maybe because she demanded his release at graduation."

"What?"

"Yep, and I let 'em all go."

"He's so lonely."

"He's trash. Mac's right."

"No. He's precious. Lauren's right. I'll get him tomorrow. Good night."

"You think he'll change? He's a Richter."

Fisting his hands, Leo wanted to hit the constable. "He's a lost lamb. Yeah, he'll change. Once he's touching 'Sonshine,' he'll change."

Leo left. Alain snored.

37

Repentance

Tipper Campbell went to MacKenzie Reardon's home and put Chambry and Abner and Zeke Peacock, who had come to live with Mac after the flu epidemic claimed their family, to bed.

"Uncle Tipper, where's Daddy?" asked Chambry.

"Taking care of Miss Bankston. She's had a rough night. He's being a doctor right now."

"You sure? He likes her, you know."

"I know. Now, off to bed. I have an errand to run, but I'll come back."

After Tipper got the boys to bed and checked on Sunny, he went to the jail. "Tipper?" Constable Hill asked.

"Hey. Let me in to talk to Alain."

"Why'd he come to town?"

"He's lost."

"He's trash."

Tipper glared at the man. "He's my friend. Let me in. I'll take care of him. I'll probably take him to my place."

"I don't get y'all. First, Preacher Tomlin. Now, you. Who's next?"

"Put money on Gator."

The constable handed Tipper the key. "You know where it hangs."

"Night."

Tipper went into Alain's cell. "Wake up," he commanded as he shook Alain.

"Go 'way," moaned Alain.

"Nope. Wake up."

Alain rolled over and whined, "Whatcha want, Tipper?"

"What were you thinking? Why did you attack Sunny?"

"I thought to touch Sunshine, perchance, to make her mine." Alain turned his back to Tipper.

"Nope!" Tipper jerked him back over. "We're talking."

Alain huffed. "I wanted some lovin'. I ain't had lovin' in a long time. She's so nice."

"So, you wanted to force yourself on her?"

"I didn't rape her!" Alain sat up.

"I know, but she *was* raped and tonight brought it all back to her. She is nice and sweet and innocent and totally in love with Mac."

"Yeah, well, he ain't nice no more."

"He was mad because you touched the woman he loves."

"I shouldn't've done that. I'm sorry. I'm purty damned drunk."

"Why?"

"It don't hurt so much when I'm drunk."

"What hurts so much, Alain? I know it's more than Fay or Amy."

Alain started to cry. "He shot her, Tipper. He hit her all the time 'til Tal came. He forced himself on her, and then, Fay. Ma caught him with Fay. She sent Fay runnin'. He was hittin' her. I jumped on him. He hit me, and Ma jumped on him and tried to castrate him. He kicked her. Then, he just shot her. Her blood went all over me." Alain wiped his hands down his body as if trying to wipe off the blood.

Tipper could hardly believe what he was hearing. "Alain, I never knew you actually saw it. I thought you came in after."

Alain shook his head. "He pointed the gun at me. I grabbed the barrel. I made sure it went off in his damned face. I wudn't gonna let him hurt any of us again. I killed my pa, Tipper. I'm goin' to Hell, so I might as well sin a lot. I'm a murderer."

"Oh, Alain." Tipper laid a hand on Alain's leg. "It was self-defense, justifiable at the least. No court would ever convict you."

"I lay with my sister. I visited whores. I helped Gator dispose of a body. I coveted your wife. I helped Felicia leave Mac. Now, I hurt Sunny."

"She'll live. How did you help Felicia?" Tipper sat beside Alain on the cot.

"She ran off in the ditch, and I helped her get out. She told me she was leavin', and I didn't stop her."

"It was for the best. Alain, do you still love Amy?"

"I'll love Amy until the day I die."

Tipper cried with his friend. "Alain, you need to repent."

"Jesus?"

"Yes."

"I don't wanna go to Hell, Tipper."

"Pray for forgiveness. I'll pray with you."

"I don't need Preacher Tomlin?"

"No, just you and Jesus. Then, you can talk to Preacher Tomlin and join the church."

"Okay."

Tipper sat beside Alain and held his hands. The prayer Alain said was so simple and childlike and heartfelt that Tipper cried harder. "Dear, God, I'm sorry for all I've done. I know you sent Jesus to die for me. Please forgive me and come into my heart. Thank You. In Jesus's Name, Amen."

Afterward, Alain smiled. "I need to sleep."

"Yeah. I'll see you tomorrow."

As Alain fell back to sleep, Gator came in.

"Is he okay, Tipper?"

"Now he is."

"What?"

"He finally actually gave his heart to Jesus."

"While he was drunk?" Gator's eyebrows merged into his receding hairline.

"It was real. You wanna tell me about the body you two disposed of?"

"It was that man that came after Sherry. I shot him."

"That wasn't murder either. You were protecting my sister. When Jess and I get back, I think there's a lot of confessions that need to take place." Tipper draped his arm over Gator's shoulder.

"Yeah. You sure Alain's okay?"

"Yeah. He just needs to sleep."

The next morning, Leo, Tipper, and Gator went to get Alain out of jail. "You look awful," said Leo. "Lauren says to come have breakfast."

"I'd love to. I need to talk to you." Alain looked at the three men and laughed, still a little sadly. "I see Mac ain't with y'all. I really messed that up, but at least it forced his hand with Sunny; so, something good came out of it, more than one good thing."

Tipper grinned. "I'm going to work. Come on, Gator. I told you it was real."

"Did you come last night too?" asked Alain.

"Yep, but Tipper beat me."

"Naa. You've always been there without question."

Alain walked to Leo's house and had breakfast. "What did you want to talk about?" asked Leo as they sat at the table.

"Repentance."

"Please, go on." Leo leaned back in his chair.

"Tipper came to see me last night. We talked. I prayed. Now, I want to be baptized and join the church. I want you to come and talk to the rest of my family."

"Wow!"

"Yes!" exclaimed Lauren from the sink where she washed the breakfast dishes.

"You must've been prayin', Mrs. Tomlin."

"Every day, darling."

"I'm glad."

Leo examined Alain's face. The hard lines were gone. "Of course, I'll go with you. Is there anything you'd like to tell me?"

"Okay. I killed Pa."

"I knew that."

"How?"

"Too much blood on you even if you did try to wash it off, but did you pull the trigger?"

"Yes. I made sure the gun was turned on him."

Lauren listened quietly as Alain continued. "He was gonna kill me and the others."

Leo shook his head with his lips in a firm line. "Not murder then, but you've felt guilty all this time?"

"Yes, sir. Do you need to report it?"

"No. The coroner's ruling stands."

"Preacher Tomlin, did you know that Pa's pa killed his whole family except my pa survived?"

"No. That was before my time."

Alain nodded. "Grandma Newton told me and showed me the graves at the back of the cemetery. I was scared I might inherit that evilness" He rubbed the back of his neck. "But, you know, I think it's because they never knew Jesus."

"You're probably right." Leo pushed his coffee cup away from him. "What else do you feel compelled to tell me?"

"Some things are not mine to tell."

"Okay. I have secrets for friends. I can understand."

Alain raised an eyebrow. "It's no secret what I did with Fay, but it was only Fay. Matthew and Mary are mine."

"Okay. The others have to answer for themselves. Alain, is it only Polly that belongs to Tal?"

"You knew?"

"I knew. Tal confessed to me."

"Yes, sir. Just her."

Leo leaned forward and laced his fingers together on top of the table. "Any of the rumors true?"

"No. In that respect, we've been scapegoats. I coveted Amy, but I never acted on it. Yes, I've visited prostitutes, and I've been drunk far too many times. What I did last night was stupid."

"Not the end part."

"No." Alain truly smiled. "I feel as if a weight has been lifted from me."

"I'm sure you do."

"You ready to go to my place?"

"When you are."

Alain finished the coffee he had. "Fay might kill me. I've been gone since Friday night. She worries. She's afraid I'll commit suicide." Alain chuckled. "Boy! She's gonna be surprised!"

Leo followed Alain home. The entire family turned out to meet them. Fay was not the only one showing signs of severe anxiety.

"Alain?" Fay asked dubiously when he bounced from the truck.

"I'm fine. No, I'm wonderful! Everybody, go sit around the table. I got somethin' to say, and I want y'all to listen to me and Preacher Tomlin."

All eyes were on Alain. "Papa?" asked Matthew. "Are you all right?"

"Yes." Alain smiled, and his whole face lit up. "Last night I asked Jesus into my heart. We read our Bible out here; that's one thing Ma taught us, and I know some of y'all have felt touched. Now, I know it's real. We, as a family, will be goin' to church. I know some of y'all already wanted to. A lot of things are about to change out here."

The Richter clan found places to sit before Alain laid down the new house rules. "First, there will be no more layin' with one another. It's *wrong*. I ain't sorry I have Matthew and Mary, but the way they were conceived was wrong. It won't happen again with any of you." Alain made eye contact with every person in his family.

"Second, the kids are goin' to school startin' Monday. We need to tie up loose ends. Preacher Tomlin, we've been home-schooling. I ain't neglected education."

"That's good to hear. Lauren told me."

"Third," Alain continued, "the boozin' stops. We'll have a drink to celebrate now and then, but we ain't drunkards.

"Fourth, I'm goin into partnership with Tipper to brew cider. I want to build my own home. I love all of you, but I gotta be free."

Alain looked around at the faces. "Last, no more whores, men."

There was a little murmuring. Alain continued. "I can't repent for you. Each one of you has to do that. I can't force you. That's between you and God."

Alain turned to Leo. "Preacher Tomlin, Matthew already prayed at youth group. He told me. I was okay with him goin' to church if he wanted to. So, now I guess I'll turn ever'body over to you. Anybody else that wants to pray can do so. Me and Matthew," Alain held an arm out for his son who slipped under it. "We'd like to be baptized and join the church."

"Matthew, is this your decision?" Leo asked.

"Yes, sir."

"Very well. Anyone else?"

For most of the day, Leo talked to various members of the Richter family. Fay fed him at noon, and talks continued. By the time Leo got home for supper, everybody except the children under eight had made a profession of faith. Leo was so anxious to see the expressions on the faces of his congregation Sunday that he felt as if he was seated on a porcupine.

38

A New Man

Tipper's wedding to Jessica Langston went off without a hitch on Saturday. Mac scowled slightly when he saw Alain Richter make a short appearance, barely long enough to congratulate Tipper and Jessica and call a few dances at Tipper's request.

The next morning the most astonished face in the congregation belonged to MacKenzie Reardon as he steered his family and friends, including Felicia and Ron who were in town for the wedding, as far from the Richter family as he could. The entire family sat on the back three rows on the right.

Alain caught Felicia's eye and gave her a true smile. She smiled back.

After Leo preached on forgiving one's brother, the Richter family came forward to make their professions of faith public. Leo and Alain talked for a while before Leo announced, "Be seated. Alain Richter has something he would like to say to the congregation. Alain." Leo indicated his spot.

Alain stood beside Leo and spoke. "The first thing I gotta do is to apologize to Miss Bankston for the other night. I'm real sorry. I ask your forgiveness." Alain made eye contact with Sunny and turned to Gator.

"Gator, I was a fool for ever thinkin' you would do somethin' with another womern. I know better'n anybody how much you love Sherry. I been with you from the beginning. I'm sorry." Alain looked his best friend squarely in the eye. Gator nodded. The forgiveness between the two self-proclaimed brothers was instant.

Alain found Mac's eye. "Mac, you still done wrong." Mac widened his eyes at Alain's audacity. "You made Miss Bankston look bad, and that was wrong; but I should've known she was a better womern than that."

Alain's gaze swept the congregation. "I ask forgiveness from all of y'all. I have been harborin' some real anger and resentment toward most o' y'all. Some o' y'all really hurt me over the years. Because of that, we been livin' in our own little world. I was tryin' to keep my fam'ly from experiencin' the cruelty I've felt. Some of y'all have said some real hurtful things. I confess we been doin' some things that were illegal and immoral. That's all stoppin'. We won't be drinkin' heavy or takin' our kin to use as our wives no more." He made slashing motions with his hand. "What's done is done; so, I'm askin' y'all to forgive us and accept us for who we are without judgin' or bein' cruel, especially to the children. They don't deserve your harshness. Know this: we're gonna be new people.

"I wanna tell y'all that contrary to rumor, we ain't murderers or rapists, and we ain't got no kids other than the ones you see here." Robert Lee fidgeted a little and Alain cut him a look.

Alain took time to let his words sink in. The silence told him that he was being heard. He continued. "Miss Bankston, come tomorra, all these kids five and older will be in school. You put 'em where they need to be. You teach 'em." Alain turned toward Lauren. "Mrs. Tomlin, I commit 'em to your safe keeping. You promised."

Lauren nodded her assurance to this young man she loved.

Turning back to Sunny, Alain continued. "Miss Bankston, I know you've been teachin' Gator. All of us grownups want to be in your adult education. We ain't stupid, we ain't morons, and we ain't retarded, unlike what Dr. Mac thinks."

Alain glared at Mac. His green eyes flashed. He was visibly still struggling with his anger when it came to Mac. He took a breath. "Preacher Tomlin is one man I respect. He ain't never judged me, and we've talked many times over the years. He stood by my side during the worst possible times. Him and Mrs. Tomlin talked to me about Jesus more'n once. I jest hadn't come to the place to admit I was a sinner that *could* be forgiven. I thought I had done way too much wrong to be forgiven. I didn't understand it wudn't my goodness that could save me. That belongs to Jesus.

"Gator is another I respect." He looked again at his friend, and his eyes misted. "He has always been my friend. And Tipper. Tipper Campbell straightened me out, but without judgin'.

"Y'all best git used to seein' us 'cause we gonna be right back there on them three pews ever Sunday from now on."

Alain exhaled sharply. Letting go of his pride was taking a great deal of effort. "I want y'all to remember that we're farmers. We ain't got no runnin' water or electricity, but we gonna be clean and groomed." Looking at Alain, anyone could see he meant it. His thin, six-foot-two frame was clad in a hunter-green corduroy shirt and jeans. His caramel brown hair and beard were clean, if long and shaggy. He had his almost waist-length hair held securely in a ponytail gathered at the nape of his neck.

"There's a dozen other fam'lies like us that ain't got the things we need to be as good as the rest o' y'all, and another half a dozen that jest have water, but no electricity. They didn't even pave the road all the way out to us when Ron Norton paid to have it done last spring, but that ain't gonna stop us from gettin' here.

"Last, 'cause it's a little bit of a grudge I gotta git off'n my heart. Preacher Tomlin jest preached on forgivin' your brother. MacKenzie Reardon'—He glowered at Mac and set his jaw—"I ain't vermin. I ain't no good reason to kill an unborn baby. What you said really hurt." Alain's voice broke. "We were friends; we were musketeers." He swiped tears from his cheeks. "You said you come back to Possum Holler to help people, and I guess you have. Still, you best be rememberin' you might be jest like me if'n Preacher Tomlin ain't took you in when Ander died. Yo old homestead ain't but two miles closer in than my place. You done told yo ex-wife that we *used to be* friends. You told her that long before I done *anything* to Miss Bankston. You didn't even introduce her to me, but I met her when she was dealin' with some guilt of her own 'cause she told me she was a disgrace like me. It ain't so. She's a fine lady that was jest confused 'bout where she should be. I ain't useless neither." He gripped the pulpit with both hands, his knuckles turning white. "Who do you think grows the fruit Tipper uses? Now, he pays us, and our crops have been good. We always worked even if we wudn't livin' right. Tipper and Gator ain't never turned their backs on me." He stopped and swallowed hard to keep from crying. "Mac, I miss you."

Alain had to turn away to compose himself. He felt Leo's hand on his back. After a moment, he continued. "I guess I'd like to conclude by thankin' Tipper, but he ain't here. He's on his honeymoon with a fine womern who's gonna make him real happy. Mac, you got another chance with a fine womern if'n you jest open yo eyes. Don't make it look like she's yo whore. That's jest wrong. Don't go out her back door no more. If you love her, marry her."

Alain turned to Leo. "I guess I'm done, Preacher Tomlin. I mighta said too much."

Gator muttered to Sherry. "Wow! Sounded like Grandma Newton."

"Sho 'nuff. I bet she's listenin'."

Leo looked over the congregation and saw many tear-stained faces. Alain's sermon had been more powerful than his. Leo made eye contact with Mac who dropped his head from Leo's penetrating gaze. Leo said, "The Richters will be at the front of the church after the service. Welcome them to the fold. Next Sunday, we'll have a creek-bank service if it's not too cold. This entire family wishes to be baptized. Let's dismiss by repeating 'The Lord's Prayer.' Take to heart what you're saying."

After the service the congregation extended a welcome to the Richters. Felicia started forward. Ron put a hand on her shoulder. "Honey, we're not members of this church."

"So? I want to talk to him. You coming?"

"Yeah. Okay."

Alain looked amused when Felicia, Ron, and their twins came by. "Felicia," he acknowledged. "Purty babies."

"Thank you, Alain."

Ron looked confused. Felicia said, "Alain, I don't think you ever met Ron."

"It's a pleasure." Alain extended his hand. Ron shook it.

"So?" said Felicia. "I'm a fine lady?"

"You are. Ron's a lucky man."

"Yes, I am," agreed Ron. "Alain, you want water and electricity and roads, right?"

"It'd be right nice."

"Let me see what I can do."

Felicia tiptoed to kiss Alain's cheek. "I met Jesus too," she whispered. "I guess we're not disgraces anymore."

Alain smiled. "Guess not."

Mac went forward once the crowd thinned. He looked Alain in the eye. "I'm sorry. The things I said were cruel. I miss you too."

The two men embraced and talked a while longer so Mac could be sure no one was gossiping about Sunny.

"Finally, Sunny approached Alain. "Mr. Richter."

"I really reckon you better use our first names if you wanna git the right one. There's a bunch o' Mr. Richters standin' here."

Sunny laughed. "That's a good idea, but if I do, then, I'm Sunny. Please, introduce everyone. Although I've been to your place several times, I've never met everybody. I know Fay and, of course, Matthew." She patted the boy's arm.

Alain nodded. "I'll go down the line. Meet Robert Lee, Calvin, Gloria, Glenda, Joel, Arlene, Aaron, and Oscar." Alain paused. "The last four are Simon, Yvonne, Debbie, and Polly's the youngest."

Sunny actually looked at the youngest. It was observable she did not share the same two gene pools as the others. As a matter of fact, Polly looked a lot like Gator Jones. "Good to meet all of you. The children?"

"We have four boys, Matthew, of course, Mark, Luke and John."

"The Gospels?"

"The truth," Alain said seriously.

"Go on."

"The eight girls are Mary, Suzy, Nettie, Zelma, Robin, Stormie, Autumn, and Summer."

"The last three are weather like me." Sunny laughed. "And there's Robin. My brother is River, and my two sisters are Star and Skye."

"Hippie parents?"

"Actually, yes."

"What do we do for school?"

"Can you have everyone at the school by seven?"

"Yes, ma'am."

"I'll need to test everyone. How old is Matthew?"

"Seventeen. He's the oldest."

"It might be good for him to go into adult education."

"No. I want him to get a diploma. He wants a diploma."

Sunny realized quickly that Alain Richter might have changed spiritually, but he was stubborn and would not be pushed around. He might not be the actual father of all the children, but he was the patriarch of the family. Sunny hesitated. "I'm just concerned he'll be behind."

"He ain't. If anything, he's ahead."

"How?"

"Sunny, I ain't stupid or ignorant. I know I need to speak better, but I ain't neglected education. I been home-schoolin'."

"What curriculum?"

"*Life Pac* for most things. *Saxon* math."

"*Saxon*?" she asked, knowing it to be a rigorous curriculum. "What level is Matthew?"

"Calculus."

"No way!"

"You seem surprised."

"I am," she admitted. "I'm not being judgmental." She raised one hand. "I'm impressed. Fine. I'll test him. What about the adults?"

"We can all read and do arithmetic."

"Are you as good as Gator?"

"Better."

She quirked an eyebrow at his cockiness on the subject. He smirked and matched her look of doubtfulness with a look of absolute assurance.

"Will you come Monday night so I can test you, only you? I'll have another class beginning in January for everyone else and Miss Ina and Sherry."

"I'll be there."

39

New and Improved

Alain showed up promptly Monday evening. Sunny had no doubt Gator was ready for the high-school equivalency test and scheduled him for January. After testing the Richter children and all of them placing exactly on developmental target or advanced, Sunny was certain Alain would amaze her. Lauren Tomlin had once told her Alain Richter was an undiscovered genius. Rather than testing him to see what he needed to know, Sunny allowed him to take practice tests.

Sunny sent Gator home and talked to Alain privately. "Alain, you're amazing. It would be a waste of time for you to take the class. I'm scheduling you for January with Gator. However, I want you to come and work on your speech and learn technology."

"Yes, ma'am."

"I read the essay you wrote. Your writing and grammar are perfect when you put it in print."

Alain blushed behind his beard. "I write."

"How so?"

"My feelings and thoughts. Lots of poems."

"I'd like to read some."

"Ain't nobody but Fay ever read any."

"Why?"

"What if it ain't good?" He took a sharp intake of air and held his breath.

"Take a chance. Let me read some."

Alain let out the breath he had been holding. "One of 'em is about you."

"Flattering?"

"You might be insulted."

"I'm a big girl. How many poems?"

Alain shrugged. "Maybe a hundred."

"Good Lord! Bring them next week."

"Yes, ma'am."

When Alain came the next Monday, he stacked several spiral notebooks and three binders on Sunny's desk. "That's everything."

"What?" Sunny asked in dismay.

"Memories and anecdotes are in the spiral notebooks. Poems are in the binders. I had a hell of a time gettin' Fay's poem back from her."

"You wrote one just for her?"

"Yeah. I had to promise you wouldn't lose it. Can you copy it down?"

"You can type it."

"How?"

"That is the first thing you'll learn on the computer—keyboarding. You can type your own material for practice."

"Slave driver."

"That's me!" Sunny quipped. "For your diction, you're going to read aloud to me. Let's get started."

"When you read, your poem's on top. I figured I'd get it over with."

Sunny laughed. She showed Alain how to place his fingers on the computer keyboard, gave him a chart with diagrams and instructions, and left him to practice.

Sunny delved in and read "Touching Sunshine." She was flattered he had considered her with such high esteem. As Alain practiced, Sunny laughed. Sunny cried. She heard, "Damn it!"

"What's wrong?" she called.

"My fingers don't cooperate. Sunny, can I listen to music while I type?"

"Of course, but why?"

"To feel rhythm. Even while we pick produce, I play music."

"Good idea." Sunny took several CDs to Alain. "You might try Mozart. It's very mathematical."

Sunny looked curiously at Alain. "Did you bathe before you came?"

"Of course. I stink to high heaven after workin' in the fields."

She puckered her lips. "That shirt brings out your eyes, but I bet you have a face hiding under all that hair. Come on."

Alain followed. "What we doin'?"

"I'm taking your picture."

"How come?"

"Alain, your writing is outstanding. My brother works for a publisher."

"You want my stuff in a book?"

"I do, and you're gonna type it. You'll need a picture. You can use the desktop publishing program and create two books, one poetry and one prose. We'll call the prose *Hillbilly Hijinks* and the poetry *Hillbilly Valleys and Peaks*."

"What if nobody likes it?"

"Take a chance. Here." Sunny positioned him against his truck and took several shots with her digital camera. "Now, back to work."

Music helped Alain concentrate, and by the time Harvest Fest came, he was stopping by the school every day to type. Harvest Fest showed another new face to the Richter family as they contributed to the festivities. Alain and Tipper instituted a cider sipping contest, which Mac and Sunny won.

The following Monday, Gator returned to class for one more practice test run. Alain left a little early to help Matthew with his science fair project after Gator invited the family to his home for supper on Thursday, leaving Gator to lecture Mac about his intentions toward Sunny. Then he asked Mac and Sunny to come for supper on Thursday as well. The evening ended with Mac and Sunny engaged.

On Thursday, all of Sherry's and Gator's friends learned the truth about Ina, Gator, and Sherry. The whole complexion of Possum Holler tolerance was changing, which was a good thing since Sunny planned a huge wedding, and her entire family came to Possum Holler. Mac asked Alain to be one of his groomsmen, and Alain stopped by Sunny's house to meet her family. When Eudora Bankston, Sunny's mother, saw Alain, she screamed and hid behind her husband.

Sunny was disgusted with her mother's behavior. "Mom! Cut it out! Alain's not going to grind you into sausage."

Outside, Alain said, "Sunny, I don't mean to be rude, but your ma's a loon."

"I know."

"Me and Gator…"

"Ahem!"

"Gator and I talked one time about skeletons in people's closets in Possum Holler. We wondered what yours was. Now, I know."

Sunny laughed. "Mom used to use drugs. She's a little flaky."

"I won't judge her for the drugs. I've smoked weed."

"Hers was a whole lot harder than weed. Did you do anything else?"

"Tipper's moonshine was as hard as I ever tried. The weed's milder than the moonshine."

"You said 'smoked.' Past tense?"

Alain sighed. "Sunny, would a joint chill your ma?"

"Probably."

"I got it covered." Alain went to his truck and retrieved what looked like a pack of Marlboros. He went back in the house. Eudora stiffened.

"Mrs. Bankston," Alain said, "care to take a walk with me? I promise not to hurt you."

Reluctantly, Eudora walked with Alain. When she returned, she was relaxed. Sunny looked at Alain with wide, questioning eyes. He winked.

Sunny dragged her brother, River, to the school where she opened a file on her computer. "Read," she said.

River read for a while. "Sunny, are these yours?"

"No. Alain Richter."

"They're great."

"Can you get them published?"

"Upload them to me."

"He's not quite finished typing."

"When he's done, upload the files. I'll talk to my boss."

Ron and Felicia Norton arrived with wedding clothes. Last-minute alterations were necessary. Felicia was Sunny's matron of honor, and she was ready to strangle Eudora Bankston.

Wednesday night, Alain, Tipper, and Gator, kidnapped Mac. They spent the night in the musketeer clubhouse. They drank a little and roasted hotdogs as they had on their rafting excursion so many years before.

Saturday, Felicia made sure everyone was ready for the wedding. She walked up and stroked Alain's beard that hung to his chest.

"I ain't shavin', Felicia," he declared.

"You'd look younger and better."

"You think?"

"I do."

He stroked his own chin. "I've had it a long time."

"Well, I guess it defines you."

Alain scowled. "What you mean is people see it and automatically think bad things."

"I'm afraid so." Felicia shrugged and tried to look innocent.

"Yeah. Sunny's ma saw me and screamed."

"In that case, keep it."

Alain laughed. "After the wedding, I'll let you shave it."

"Come to Mac's Monday. I'll have Miss Ina, the barber, there."

"Hair, too, huh?"

"Alain, I'll make you new and improved."

"Okay. I'm new inside, so, I guess, I should be new outside."

The wedding ended with Alain catching the damning garter; Mattie Boone, a new teacher at the school, catching the bouquet; and Tipper beginning to play matchmaker again.

Monday morning, Alain kept his appointment with Felicia. Ina Campbell stroked Alain's beard and lifted his heavy hair. "You sure 'bout this, Alain?" she asked.

"Yes, ma'am. Felicia promised to make me a new and improved man."

"Very well." Ina began to snip.

As Ina dusted Alain off, Felicia gasped, "Oh, my God!"

"What?" asked Alain.

"You're a good-looking man, Alain."

Alain smiled.

"Stop!" ordered Felicia, holding up her hand. "New problem."

"My teeth," said Alain. "They're awful."

"How do Mac and Tipper have such good teeth?"

"Dentist."

Felicia got a phonebook. "Three hours," Alain heard her say.

"What are you doing?" Alain demanded.

"We're headed to the city. Let's go."

"You driving?"

"I am."

"Stay out of the ditch."

Felicia laughed. "I will."

Felicia and Alain chatted like old friends on the drive. Finally, in the dentist's chair as Felicia watched, Alain squirmed.

Dr. Cuzak frowned. "Mrs. Norton, do you expect me to do everything today?"

"Can you?"

"I can, but the man won't be able to eat for a week."

"Can he eat soup, mashed potatoes, ice cream?"

"Yeah, but…"

"Felicia," said Alain, "it's my mouth and my stomach."

"Alain, the only flaw you have is your teeth. Damn! If your teeth were fixed, you'd look better than Tipper."

Alain raised an eyebrow. "Doc, what do you need to do?"

"Well, your bite is fine. Your teeth are straight. You have seven cavities, two in the front. Those two need to be capped. I need to clean your teeth first."

"But can you do it?"

"Yes."

"Lots of pain?"

"Lots."

Alain looked at Felicia. "Better than Tipper?" he asked with great skepticism.

Felicia nodded. "I think so."

Alain laughed. "Good enough for you to teach me to salsa?"

Felicia popped Alain's arm. "Only if you don't have the same reaction Tipper had."

"Better than Tipper?"

Felicia nodded again.

"Yeah," said Alain, getting as comfortable as he could in the dentist's chair. "I'm that vain. Do it, Doc. Just knock me out."

When they left at twilight, Alain laid his head back on the seat. "I cain't feel my fashe," he mumbled.

Felicia patted his leg. "You will. You got the prescription for Oxycontin?"

"Yeah."

"Let's fill it. You'll need it."

"Felicia, you think I've traveled enough roadsh to be a man?"

"I think you're a fine man. Never doubt that, Alain."

"Would you deshign a houshe for me?"

"Yes. It'll cost you."

"When you leaving?"

"When Mac and Sunny get back."

Alain touched both sides of his face. "Am I shwollen?"

"Not much yet, but you will be." Felicia rubbed his shoulder.

"Will you go shomewhere with me in the morning?"

"People are gonna start talking."

"Let 'em. I wanna show you the property I bought where I want my houshe."

"You bought some property?"

"Yeah."

"Got a lady?"

"No."

"Why not?"

"I cain't shtop loving Amy."

"I met her in New York. She's beautiful."

"You have any idea why she left?"

"No. She *is* a gifted artist." Felicia shrugged. "Maybe she just needed to make her fame and fortune."

Alain sighed. Felicia filled his prescription, and they headed home after Alain swallowed a pill, dribbling water down his chin. He slept most of the way back to Possum Holler.

The next morning, Felicia went with Alain to above the waterfall where he pointed out his meadow. "What a spectacular place!" said Felicia.

"Yeah. You see that rise?"

"Yeah."

"That's where I want the house."

"You said I'd come back here. Ron loves it here. You know he wants to build a subdivision out your way. Ron wants a house for us there. Oh, we'll live in New York but visit here often."

"You don't mind?"

"No. I'm with Ron. That's where I've always belonged. It doesn't matter where we live so long as we're together."

Alain tried to smile. "That hurts."

"When I come back at spring break, I won't recognize you."

"Nope. I'll have my high-school equivalency, and Sunny says I can take college courses on the computer."

"You really are a new man, aren't you?"

"New and improved."

Felicia nodded. "Just like Possum Holler."

40

A Surprise Visitor

The day after New Year's, Felicia called Tipper to New York in a panic. The nudes Amy had painted of him were on display and for sale; by the time Tipper got to New York, the paintings had sold.

Tipper had a long, serious discussion with his ex-wife. "Amy, it's time to tell me why you left, why you stopped loving me."

"I had to."

"Why? What did I do?"

"Nothing. Your only fault was being Nathaniel Campbell's son."

"That doesn't make sense." Tipper held Jessica's hand as he talked to Amy because he felt his current wife might keep him from killing his ex-wife.

Reluctantly, Amy confessed, "Momma told me that Royce is not my father. Nathaniel was my father."

Tipper's face blanched. "And you believed her as much as she hated me?"

Amy spread her hands as if begging Tipper to understand. "Not at first. I didn't want to, but when Laurie was born, I had some DNA tests done. She told the truth. It was better for you to hate me than yourself." Amy started to cry. "I wish I had never known. How could I fall in love with my brother? I'm just like Alain."

After a great deal of discussion and many secrets being revealed, including the fact that Sherry Jones was Ina and Ander's child, Jessica and Tipper brought the girls to New York for a few days and left Amy considering a return to Possum Holler.

Alain visited Tipper. "What happened?"

"Oh, Amy showed the nudes."

His green eyes popping fire, Alain asked, "Did you hurt her?"

"No. They've been sold to a European."

"You made peace?"

"You could say that." Tipper nodded with deliberation. "She might come home."

Alain said nothing for a while. Finally, he said, "Tipper, I'd appreciate you not trying to match Mrs. Boone and me. We don't fit."

Tipper asked, "Alain, do you want Amy to come home?"

"Would you object if I did?"

"No. If she's what you want, go for it."

"She's what I've always wanted."

"What if she doesn't come back?"

"I could visit New York."

Tipper laughed. "You would hate the city. You would be so out of place."

"Why? Am I too much of a hillbilly?"

"I know you. You're too grounded to be happy in a big city."

Alain cocked his head to the side. "Felicia would help me."

"You two got chummy."

"We're friends."

"Go. I'll give you her address."

"I've got her address and phone number." Alain flashed a smart-aleck grin. Then, he frowned. "I'd have to fly though."

It was Tipper's turn to grin. "Yeah, or you could take a bus."

"You think she'll come home?"

Tipper nodded. "Yeah, eventually. She misses the girls and Royce."

Alain backpaddled for a second because he had to admit he was afraid to fly. "I can't make plans 'til after the high-school equivalency test anyway."

Tipper snickered. "Scared to fly?"

"Yeah."

Tipper chortled. Alain got defensive. "I wouldn't have an entourage like you did. You were scared shitless, but Jess held your hand."

Tipper became serious. "If you decide you want to go to New York, I'll fly with you."

"Really?"

Tipper nodded. "Yes."

The next Saturday, Gator Jones and Alain Richter took their high-school equivalency test. While Alain was in Wilmington, Sunny Reardon uploaded both books to her brother.

The test finished, Alain suggested a visit to Jacqui's place. "You can't be serious!" Gator objected.

"I'd like to see Blanche to see if she recognizes me."

"Why?"

"We're friends."

"Just talk?"

"Yeah. Believe it or not, Gator, that's what we mostly did."

"Not always, though?"

"No, not *always*."

They drove by Jacqui's Gentlemen's Club. "Whoa!" both exclaimed as they saw crime scene tape around the establishment.

"I don't think they're open, Alain," observed Gator.

"No shit, Sherlock! What gave you a clue?"

"Smartass!"

"Better than a dumbass!" Alain laughed. "Sorry. I wonder what happened. I hope Blanche is okay. She's a good person, Gator."

"Is she the one that looked kind of like Amy?"

"Yeah."

"You want her to come home, don't you?"

"Amy?"

Gator nodded.

"Yes, I do," said Alain.

"Well, I'll pray about it for you, but I think this little surprise visit was a bust."

"Yeah. I wonder what happened."

"Maybe they finally put the evil bitch in jail," Gator suggested. "You know Tipper's lawyer was having her investigated."

"She must've done something worse than running a whorehouse or tricking women into giving up their little girls."

"Maybe she found a new Bilbo and got caught."

Both men well remembered that Jacqui would have gladly left Gator dead and forced Sherry into a life of prostitution. Alain proposed, "Let's ask."

"Who?"

"Library. We can use a computer. We can search old newspapers. Surely, the *Wilmington Witness* has something about it."

Some research showed Jacqueline Fields had been charged with multiple felonies under R.I.C.O., including kidnapping, prostitution, and conspiracy to commit murder. It appeared her faithful watchdog had turned rabid. Jimmy Joe Tillman was scheduled to testify, but they could not find a single photo of the witness.

"He's going into hiding," surmised Alain.

"Hiding?" asked Gator.

"Yeah. Witness protection. The government will give him a new identity and a new home."

"Where nobody knows him?"

"Yeah, so he'll be safe."

"No friends? No family? That would be lonely."

"I suppose. There was a time I would've liked to've vanished."

"Not now?"

"No." Alain shook his head decisively. "Tipper says Amy's coming home."

"When?"

"Don't know. I hope soon."

"Alain, don't build up hope."

"Gator, do you think she'll like the new me?"

"She liked the old you."

"Not enough to defy Lucille."

"You were children." Gator put his hand on his friend's shoulder.

"Yeah? Have I ever been a child, Gator?"

"Yes, even if it was hard."

"I can't believe Amy really ran off with that Roscoe person."

"Why?"

The two men walked back to the car. As they drove off Alain said, "I'm certain he liked men, especially Tipper."

Gator's eyebrows almost reached his receding hairline. "You think Tipper?"

Alain laughed so hard he had to put his foot on the brake. "Hell no! I didn't say it went both ways. Roscoe, I guess, went both ways."

"Yuck!"

Alain guffawed. After catching his breath he said, "If Tipper thinks I'd have a hard time in a big city, what would he say about *you*?"

Back in Possum Holler, Gator gleefully told Sherry the news about Jacqui. Then, he and Alain watched for the test results. Sunny told Alain what she had done with his books, causing him to stress and wait.

Sunny continued adult education classes for the rest of the Richter clan along with Ina and Sherry. It was quite apparent to Sunny that Alain had worked with his family. They would be ready for testing in June. Ina and Sherry would need to wait until September, at least. Ina's greatest need was math; her language skills were ready. Sherry needed work in all areas.

Sunny greatly admired what Alain had done for his family in the way of education.

In early March, both Alain and Gator received their test scores and certificates. Alain's packet included a letter.

Dear Mr. Richter:

It is said there is a first for everything. You are a first. I have been in education for fifty years, and you are the first person I have encountered who scored perfectly in all areas.

I will personally be visiting Possum Holler School on March 12th to award you with a plaque to honor your achievement and to offer my personal congratulations.

I look forward to meeting a man who refused to give up. Until then, I am

Sincerely yours,
Dr. Marvin Spalding
State Superintendent of Education

Alain showed the letter immediately to Sunny.

"Alain! Congratulations!" Sunny squealed.

"I thought you might want to get the school all ready. You have a week."

"He didn't say what time."

"Sorry."

"Well, we'll be ready all day."

Alain fretted a little. "It's the day after Miss Ina's birthday party."

"Yeah. That'll be fine."

"What should I wear?"

"A suit. Do you have one?"

"No."

"Get one. With your coloring, get something in dark brown, a cream-colored shirt, and a green silk tie."

"You think Mac would go shopping with me?"

"I'll make him. I'm so proud of you." Sunny hugged Alain.

"Thanks."

Mac went shopping the next day with Alain to help him pick out a suit. They passed a candy-apple-red Volkswagen Beetle on their way out. Neither of them recognized the female driver who had tightly curled shoulder-length brown hair.

"Who's that?" wondered Alain.

"No clue," Mac responded as he drove. "Lot's of strange people coming into Possum Holler these days. She was pretty though."

"Mac, you have a wife."

"Just because I'm on a diet doesn't mean I can't read the menu. I can still appreciate beauty, and that woman was pretty."

"Yeah, she was," Alain agreed. "Did you catch the license plate?"

"Nope."

"Me neither."

While the two old friends shopped for a good suit for Alain, the woman they passed stopped and asked directions. Then, she drove to Richter Farms and Orchards.

The woman, in her early twenties, got out of the car and walked with a slight limp to the front door. She knocked with self-assurance.

Fay opened the door. "Yes? May I help you?"

"Hi. I'm looking for Calvin Richter. My name is Trish Jolson, and he has a promise to keep."

"He's in the field."

"Oh. Do you mind if I wait?"

"What kind of promise?" asked Fay.

The young woman's blue eyes danced with mischief. "He promised to marry me if I walked into Possum Holler. Well, I actually walked to his door. Does that count?"

Fay was completely befuddled. "Oh, you have to wait, and I have to hear this. Please, come in. Coffee?"

Alain came home to utter chaos in his home and a red Volkswagen parked in his yard. When he walked in, he shouted over the din, "Whoa! What is going on?"

The noise ceased immediately. Alain saw the young woman from the morning sitting at the dining table with Calvin. She smiled radiantly at Alain. "Good evening," said Alain. "I'm Alain Richter, and it seems your presence has caused some kind of disturbance in my home."

"Not for long," said Calvin.

Alain held up a finger. "Cal, I believe the lady has a tongue."

"Yes, I have a tongue, and I have messages to deliver. My brother-in-law sends his regards."

"Your brother-in-law?"

"Dwayne Pritchard. I'm Trish Jolson. I've come to accept a marriage proposal."

"Oh, my God!" Alain exclaimed. "This is some surprise visit!"

"Alain," said Calvin, "I gave my word."

"Are you insane? You don't even know this woman."

Calvin shrugged. "I'll have a lifetime to get to know her."

Alain shook his head. "Preacher Tomlin won't go for this."

Calvin grinned. "I can ask."

"Did you forget to tell me something?" asked Alain.

"Sort of. You're not the only one who can write. Trish and I have been writing since we spent the night in jail in Virginia."

"Letters?"

"Yeah." Calvin nodded.

"You're serious," said Alain, flabbergasted.

"I am."

Calvin and Trish were married on Saturday.

The night of Ina Campbell's birthday party was brisk and clear, and the celebration at Tipper's huge new house in town boasted many friends. As the party progressed, a car with a U-Haul trailer attached snaked into Possum Holler.

The driver stopped in front of the house, a mansion by Possum Holler standards, that blazed with lights and activity. Amy Dent stepped from the car. *Wow! I'd say Tipper made it to Easy Street. What am I doing here? Oh! They're celebrating Miss Ina's birthday. Do I dare go in? I don't have a gift. Yes, I do, if they let me stay.*

Amy walked up the steps to the door. *Here I go.* She rang the bell and laughed, "A bell, not a knocker."

Tipper was contorted in a game of Twister with the children, so when a tall, thin, clean-shaven man with styled caramel-brown hair, vivid emerald eyes, and a smile that would dazzle any photographer answered the door, Amy blinked in confusion. "Is this Tipper Campbell's residence?"

At five-six, Amy looked up at the man. Her chocolate eyes were still confused. Her dark brown hair was shorter than his. "Yes," he answered.

The man flashed a alluring, expensive smile again. "You really don't recognize me?"

"Alain?" she barely whispered.

"Yes, ma'am."

"Oh, my! You look good. What happened to you?"

"Felicia Norton."

"Mac's ex?"

"Yes. I'm her pet project—haircut, shave, dentist. I like your hair short. It shows your neck and makes you look taller. Tipper said you'd be coming home, just not when. You coming in?"

"You just asked."

"Sorry." He stood back and held the door open.

"You sure it's okay? It's Miss Ina's birthday, isn't it?"

"Yes. Everybody's here, including your father. Come on. Tipper explained that you've been ill."

"You sound different."

"Educated?"

"Yes."

"Sunny's influence. I just passed my high-school equivalency test. I'm getting an award tomorrow."

"How nice."

"Come on in." Alain held the door wide. "If anyone's mean to you, I'll take care of it."

"Are you gonna be my musketeer?"

"If you need me to be." He offered Amy his arm and escorted her inside. He announced, "Look who's come home."

The Campbell girls greeted their mother. Then, she met the people she did not know and could not believe Lauren Langston was married to Leo Tomlin. Amy ran back to her car to get the gift she had thought of before she hugged Ina.

"Welcome, home, darling," said Ina. "I missed you."

"Happy birthday. I have something for you." Amy handed Ina the portrait of Tipper she had done in fourth grade. "It's the first painting I ever did of Tipper. I thought you would like it."

"Thank you. It's perfect."

The party continued, and Amy watched, still a little uncertain of being back. Alain handed her a glass. "My cider." He smiled again. "I'm brewing at Tipper's Bottling. He promised to make me rich too, remember?"

"How could I forget?"

"Well, I'm getting there. I'm much better off than I was."

"You'll have to tell me all about it."

"I'd love to. Will you come to the ceremony tomorrow?"

"Yes. What kind of award?"

"I'm not sure." He shrugged. "The state superintendent of education is giving me something because I scored perfectly on every section of the test. Gator's miffed because he missed something in the writing section. I'm a writer."

"A writer?"

He nodded and smiled again. "Yeah. Sunny's trying to help me get published, poetry and some anecdotal stories."

"Wow! Are you sure you're Alain Richter?"

"The real me. Maybe I was hiding all those years ago because I was so scared. The real me paid a surprise visit one day and decided to stay. I hope you stay."

"I want to."

"Then, don't let anything stop you. May I walk you home, fair maiden?"

"Yes, kind sir."

Rather than be surprised, Sunny Reardon had called Marvin Spalding to get a time. So, at ten in the morning the students of Possum Holler School, along with many community members gathered for an assembly.

Dr. Spalding arrived with a woman who had sworn never to return to Possum Holler. However, having married Marvin Spalding, Daneen Butler Spalding was compelled to accompany her husband. They toured the school first and were impressed with the day-to-day functioning and the test scores.

The assembly proved enlightening. On a dais with Dr. Spalding, sat his wife, Dr. Leo Tomlin, Sunny Bankston Reardon, Mayor Royce Dent, and Alain Richter. Alain's former teacher eyed him ruefully before the program began. She finally took a deep breath and approached the man. "Alain."

"Mrs. Spalding."

"You proved me wrong."

"How so?"

"You are obviously much more competent than I gave you credit for. I owe you an apology."

Alain stepped back. "Accepted. I suppose I owe you one."

"No. I was a bitch."

Alain laughed. "And now?"

"Wiser and more tolerant. I'm glad you proved me wrong, you *and* Gator. Even Tipper. I suppose Lauren was right. You and your friends are about to put Possum Holler on the map."

"I want my kids to have more than I did."

"I wish I had seen your potential."

"You did. You just didn't want to admit it." Alain smiled.

"You turned out okay, Alain Richter."

He leaned close to the woman's ear. "I have on underwear."

Daneen Butler Spalding laughed out loud. "You're still a scamp, but a likeable rascal."

The program progressed with Alain receiving a great deal of praise and a plaque. Alain stood behind the podium. He looked at the assembly and held up his plaque as he spoke:

I didn't do this alone. Mrs. Reardon pushed me and encouraged me. Gator Jones stood beside me. So, he missed some little something? He should receive a plaque, too, for having the courage to be first. My friends who never gave up on me deserve praise as well. Dr. MacKenzie Reardon, Tipper Campbell, Preacher Tomlin, Mrs. Tomlin, I owe you. Grandma Newton, I hope you're looking down here today. You were an inspiration to all of us.

Students, never give up. You have something here. Cherish it. Surprise the world. Surprise yourselves. We are not *'disgusting little hillbillies who will never amount to anything.' On the contrary, we are Possum Hollerites, and proud of it.*

As Alain finished his speech, he looked to see another surprise visitor at the back of the crowd. He made eye contact with Gator and tilted his head. Alain had secretly sent an overnight letter on Gator's behalf. Lt. Col. Corky Jones and his wife Letha stood at the back of the crowd. Gator made his way through the crowd. "What are you doing here?"

"Alain sent me a letter saying I should come to support you in receiving your high-school equivalency. He said a few other things that I won't repeat, but he was right. Gator, I'm proud of you. You deserve some recognition too. The best I can do is to introduce my family. This is my wife, Letha."

"I thought you were never gonna bring your family here." Gator turned to Letha. "It's nice to meet you." He motioned his family over and introduced all of them.

Alain came over. "Surprise, Gator! Corky, thanks for coming." The two men shook hands. "How long do you plan to stay?"

"A couple of days?" Corky looked at Gator for approval.

"I'd like that."

Alain's surprise visitor for Gator was a joy. He laughed and told Gator before he left that he would come back and retire to Possum Holler when it was on the map.

Gator visited Alain to thank him, saying, "Alain Richter, you're the best friend I could ever have."

Alain shook his head. "No, Gator that's you." He grinned. "Both our surprise visitors have had a change of heart about Possum Holler. Just wait until we actually appear on the map. But, you know, Gator, the best surprise of all for me was Amy."

"I don't think the surprises are over. Can you stand more?"

"If they're as good as the ones in the last few days? Absolutely."

41

Clarence Dayton

The first time Tipper Campbell was ever stopped during a bootleg run, a Virginia State Trooper, Clarence Dayton, stopped him. Somehow, a friendship developed. Tipper never delivered again to Virginia, but Clarence became an inspiration to Tipper who also inspired Clarence.

As a result, when Clarence retired, he came to Possum Holler to form a police force, initially of two with Norman Hill. However, there was more to Clarence than anyone, including Tipper Campbell, knew.

Clarence came for Tipper's wedding to Jessica and returned seven months later as the new head law enforcement officer of Possum Holler. The first thing Clarence did was to keep Constable Hill as an officer. Two officers were better than one even if there was little crime. His second act was a meeting with the city council. Those few people needed to know some truth about Mattie Boone, Tipper's failed match to Alain Richter.

She was not simply a widow with three children. She was, indeed, a widow, but her spouse had not died in Iraq. Her husband had been a crime boss in the Mafia. The federal government had placed her in witness protection. The main reason Clarence divulged the information was to protect the people of Possum Holler.

Clarence brought his family with him. As an author who was already published, Patsy Dayton developed a quick rapport with Alain Richter. She read his work and was impressed.

In addition to Clarence Dayton's arrival, John Mason, the owner of the coal mine, had come to stay. After the incident and averted disaster just before Tipper left the mining company, John had uncovered a great deal of dishonesty with the main office. In an attempt to salvage his integrity, he moved his small part of the company to Possum Holler. Almost upon arrival, he and Mattie Boone became involved.

Clarence suspected Mason of some involvement with the crime syndicate that had been a part of Mattie's life. He began an investigation into the man's background.

Tipper met with Clarence because he was certain Mason was quite honest. "I've known him for years, Clarence. I think he just wants a simple life. He has no idea who Mattie used to be. Let it stay that way."

"Well, I can't find anything on him. You could be right. Maybe his arrival is a coincidence."

"He hasn't denied wanting out of the big company's shady deals."

"Yeah. His name's the same." Clarence scratched his chin.

"Yes. He and I have talked many times. He's a believer. He couldn't abide the dishonesty."

Clarence surrendered. "Very well, Tipper. You do know he and Mattie are thick."

"You said she's not a criminal."

"True. She's hiding. Her new identity is all legal."

"So, what's the problem with them having a life?"

"None, I guess. I'm just a cop. Maybe I'm suspicious by nature. I do have it on good authority that we will have another fugitive in our midst."

"Who?"

"Can't tell you just yet."

As Clarence Dayton's family settled in, Amy Dent seemed a little displeased. "What's up?" Tipper asked her.

"Nothing. It's just Patsy Dayton. She spends too much time with Alain."

"Jealous?"

Amy grimaced. "It's not that. She's married. It looks bad for Alain. I don't think Clarence would be too tolerant of his wife spending so much time with another man."

"It's innocent. They talk. He didn't want Mattie, and now she's taken. Cut him some slack. He's an artist like you, only with words. Have you read any of his stuff?"

"Some. He's talented. He found a way to find humor even in his trials and ordeals. He wrote several stories about all of us that made me laugh. Yet, he didn't make us sound ridiculous."

"Patsy is talented too. Her children's books are good."

"If you insist. Let's talk about Gator and Sherry. They haven't been legally married all these years."

"That's changing, and you know the story is they're renewing their vows."

"Yeah. I have to say I'm proud of Miss Ina. My mother would have made her life miserable. I'm glad Sherry wants to acknowledge her."

"Me too. I wish I could acknowledge you."

"No! For the girls, no."

"I understand, Amy, but I want to tell at least Ma the truth."

"We'll see."

"Okay.

Many things happened in the short month between the time Clarence Dayton arrived and Gator and Sherry "renewed" their wedding vows with Amy and Alain standing up for them since Fester Munro had married them when he was a municipal judge. Clarence spent a few moments with them before they left on a real honeymoon. He gave them the heads up on what to expect when they got back, a new resident in witness protection.

After a conference with Gator and Sherry, he spoke with Alain. "Alain, is there more secrecy about Gator and Sherry than the fact that she was too young to get married?"

"Beats me."

"I think you know. I know Jacqui Fields is headed to prison for a long time. Her hitman disappeared when he went looking for Sherry years ago. Jimmy Joe Tillman has let people believe he killed the man. He's lying. Where's the body buried?"

Alain shook his head and turned down the corners of his mouth. "No unaccounted for bodies anywhere around here."

"Did Gator feed him to the hogs?"

"You don't know Gator Jones very well. He would never have the stomach for something like that."

"But you would."

Holding his hand up as if taking an oath, Alain said, "May God strike me with lightning if I ever fed a reprobate like Bilbo Jenkins to Gator's hogs."

Clarence looked smug. "I didn't tell you the man's name."

"I used to spend time at Jacqui's place."

"Alain, you know if Gator killed him, it would've been justifiable, I'm sure."

"That's a great big word for two letters, isn't it, Clarence?"

Clarence huffed in frustration. "Okay, Alain. The son-of-a-bitch deserved to die. I would've helped my best friend dispose of the body."

"Who's your best friend, Clarence?"

Clarence scowled. "Tipper, I guess."

"No, Tipper wouldn't have killed Bilbo; maybe Roscoe DuBlane, but not Bilbo."

"Is there another body missing?"

"Nope. DuBlane died in New York—AIDS. Did you ever consider that maybe Jacqui had Bilbo killed because he failed in his mission?"

"You don't trust me enough to tell me even though I fought Jackals with you. Why don't you use the info and write a mystery?"

"A whole book? I never tried that. It's an idea. Of course, anything I might write would be purely fiction, and I'd set it in the Ozarks or deep in Cajun territory and change the time period, as well as names."

"I look forward to reading it. What would you call yourself?"

"Caleb. It can mean a dog or faithful and loyal." Alain smiled.

"Damn! You are good. Oh, by the way, you're spending too much time with my wife."

Clarence walked away. Alain paid a visit to Amy Dent.

42

Witness Protection

John Mason and Mattie Boone eloped the last day of school and returned before Gator and Sherry exchanged vows. Upon their return, Tipper confronted him.

"It's all right, Tipper. I know," said John. "Mattie told me everything."

"Everything?"

"Yes. I know she's in witness protection."

"I'm beginning to wonder if all this city influx is bad."

"No. It'll be fine. You now have three real businesses in addition to the farmers and the Richter brothers. A couple of them are forming their own trucking company. That'll be four. You have two doctors and a dentist and lawyer coming. You should be happy."

"I am, but now we're getting another, um, fugitive."

"Who?"

Tipper folded his arms across his chest. "Not mine to tell."

"Clarence will control the situation." Mason laughed. "He investigated me."

"I know."

"Tipper, I'm not a criminal."

"I told him so." Tipper placed a hand on his former boss's shoulder, and the two walked their separate ways.

Many things changed in Possum Holler. Within six months of the Richter family's conversion, eleven of them were married, leaving only Alain, Fay and Polly without a mate. The toppers for Alain were when Robert Lee confessed he was the father of Lois Silsbee's child and married her, although the relationship had been consensual for years; when Dr. Jason Rockford who had come during the flu epidemic returned to stay and stole Glenda almost from the moment he came to town; and when Trish Jolson had walked into Possum Holler to accept Calvin's marriage proposal by letter. Alain laughed to himself, "These stories are stranger than fiction, Clarence. Yeah, I think I'll write about them."

However, with only three of them left at home, Royce Dent had designs on Fay. He had even asked Alain's permission to court her. Polly seemed unconcerned, even when she considered being alone at the farmhouse because Alain had bought the land behind the waterfall and planned to build a house comparable to Tipper's.

"Who's gonna share it with you?" Polly asked one evening when it was just the two of them at the house.

"You'll laugh."

"No, I won't, Alain. Are you still in love with Amy?"

"You're too young to even remember that."

"It's in your eyes."

Alain patted his baby sister's hand. "I always have been."

"I knew that. Alain, that new construction guy asked me to go to movie night with him."

Alain scowled. "Polly, I'm not sure I can give my blessing on that."

"Why?"

"Sweetie"—Alain took her hand across the table—"he's not what he says."

Polly smiled innocently. "I know what he is, Alain. He told me."

"His real name?"

"Jimmy Joe Tillman, but he's George Hicks now. The government set him up here with a new identity. He knows Sherry, and he knows y'all, well, you, Robert Lee, and Calvin."

Alain fiddled with the coffee cup he had. "Yeah, I know, honey, but…"

"Alain, he didn't hurt anybody. He testified against that Jacqui woman, and he doesn't care that Summer belongs to Simon."

Decisively, Alain said, "He needs to talk to me himself."

"Okay. Are you still mad about Simon and me?"

"I tried to teach you better. Tal would be so hurt."

"I'm sorry."

"Why did you do it?"

Polly got up and poured another cup of coffee and sat down before she explained. "Simon had that youngest Silsbee girl laugh at him when he was trying to get to know her. He was so hurt. She made fun of his limp and told him his whole family was reprobates. We were the only ones who hadn't coupled. Simon is an angel, Alain. He would never hurt a soul."

"So, comfort just went too far?"

Polly nodded. "Yeah. He apologized a hundred times, but he didn't force me. It was more me than him."

"It was the same for Fay and me. Okay. You tell George Hicks if he wants to court you, he's gotta face me first."

"Okay."

The next day George paid a visit to Alain. Alain laughed. "You must be serious about courting Polly."

"Yeah, I am."

"She's a lot younger than you."

"Fifteen years, I know; but she's sweet. I like her."

"Why did you turn on Jacqui?" Alain indicated a chair for the man to sit. The two sat at the rough-hewn dining table.

"Oh, Alain, when I first started as a bouncer for her, I was only a kid myself. I was just big—muscle. I was living on the streets and panhandling. There were times I resorted to scavenging trash cans. That's when Jacqui found me and offered me a job. She thought I was older than I was because of my size. I had no clue what I had accepted. I just knew it had to be better than being homeless and hungry. When I said something about her adopting baby girls, she had me beaten up. I was left with brain damage, but I ain't stupid or crazy. I took care of Sherry like she was my daughter, or maybe little sister."

George ran his fingers through his thick brownish-blond hair. Even though he was a good four inches taller and fifty pounds heavier than Alain's six-two, one-sixty, he felt small before the other man. His light blue eyes implored Alain.

"I knew when she snuck out; I knew you hadn't had but a couple of drinks and were faking. I was glad.

"About a year ago, Jacqui went to get some more babies. She wanted me to pretend to be Mr. Fields like Bilbo had done. I couldn't let her do it again. I went to the FBI, the organized crime unit. Jacqui's going to jail, but I had to have a new life. They wanted to send me out west, but I begged to come here because I know y'all, and y'all won't turn me over to crooks. Alain, I saw y'all the night you and Gator came to Jacqui's. I know about Bilbo. I wish I *had* killed him."

"Don't tell Clarence Dayton about Bilbo."

"Never."

Alain still hesitated. "You really like Polly?"

"Yeah. I'll treat her good, Alain. I'm a hard worker. After the building's done, I'll work the farm for you."

"You're staying in the old Reardon place?"

"Yeah. Dr. Mac said I could."

"You know about Summer?"

"Yeah. It don't matter."

"What about how Simon feels?"

"We already talked about it. Simon says he'd rather be Uncle Simon. He don't want her to know."

Alain let out a big puff of air. "Okay, but if you hurt her, you'll be seeing Bilbo."

"I would do the same."

"George, I respect your choice. It has to be hard to be in witness protection."

The big man nodded. "Alain, I couldn't have stood it if they had sent me where I didn't know nobody."

"Well, we take care of our own here. If you stay with Polly, that'll include you."

"Thanks, Alain. Being here actually makes me feel protected. I ain't felt safe in a long time."

43

Permission to Marry Your Sister

George Hicks had hardly left before Royce Dent knocked on the door. Alain had never had such a busy Saturday.

"Royce?"

"Hello, Alain. I need to talk to you."

"Something wrong?"

"No, something's right."

"You seem so serious. Come in and sit down. Coffee?"

"Sure."

The two men sat down to a cup of coffee before Royce began. "Well, I feel a little silly. I mean, I'm old enough to be your father. You're the one who should be doing this. I thought for sure you'd be pursuing Amy."

Defensively, Alain said, "We do stuff."

"Man-woman stuff?"

"What are you telling me, Royce?"

"Get off your ass and win the girl. You've loved her forever. Don't let her go this time."

"Whoa! Did Amy tell you to come?"

"No." He waved a hand. "I just know my daughter. Alain, she's too scared to admit she loves you, but she does. Don't give up on her."

"Royce, why did Amy really leave?"

"It's not mine to tell."

"More secrets?"

"I'm afraid so."

"Is this why you came—to encourage me to chase Amy?"

"Yes and no."

"What's the rest?" Alain indicated the coffee pot. "More coffee?"

"No, thanks."

Alain refreshed his coffee and cut to the point. "So, Royce is this about Fay?"

"Yes."

Alain laughed. "George Hicks just left after asking to court Polly. What are you asking, permission to marry my sister?"

"Yes."

Alain choked on the sip of coffee he had taken. "Seriously?" came out as a cough.

"Yes, Alain. I'd like permission to marry your sister. I'm crazy about her. I can provide for her. I don't care about the children. They're yours. I know that. I'll just be their stepfather, but I'll treat 'em well."

Alain rubbed his head as if he were getting a headache. "Will you and Fay be having some?"

"No."

"Okay? Why?"

"I can't."

"Amy?"

"Biologically, not mine. That's all I'm saying."

"You sure?"

"Yes."

Alain put his elbow on the table and covered his mouth momentarily with is hand. "Phew! Maybe Mac could help."

Royce shrugged. "Fay understands."

"Who's Amy's father?"

"Lucille never told me."

"But you know."

"Not mine to tell." Royce took a big gulp of coffee.

"I think I know."

"Could be. You're smart. No matter. She's my little girl."

"And you want to marry Fay?"

"I know she's the same age as Amy. Is that your objection?"

"I don't have an objection."

"Alain, I love her."

"Good." He slapped the tabletop. "Be happy."

Matthew Richter came in humming. Alain asked, "What has you so happy? You glad to have a stepfather?"

"Sir?"

"Royce."

"Oh, well, if it makes Momma happy. Actually, I'm going to town."

"Why?"

"Papa." He rolled his eyes. "Betsy."

"Tipper give his permission?"

"I'm going to ask."

Alain rubbed his head again. This Saturday was becoming excruciating. "You'll be leaving in August. Do you think you should ask to court her now?"

"Do you disapprove of Betsy?"

"No, but she has high school and then college. You have college."

"Yes, sir. I plan to come back here to teach."

"Then, she'll be leaving."

"Yes, sir. I'm not asking permission to marry her, just to date her over the summer."

Alain was doing his best to subtly convince Matthew to wait. "Tipper might think she's too young to date."

"Do you think Mary's too young to date?"

"Absolutely! Not until she's sixteen."

"Whoa! Okay."

Candidly, Alain said, "Go ask, but expect a great big *NO!* That's what I'd give you."

"Papa!"

"Matthew, you're a great kid, but Betsy's too young to date."

Matthew went to see Betsy anyway and asked Tipper if they could date over the summer. Tipper scowled. "Uh, no."

As they still stood on the porch, Matthew looked at the ground. "Why, Mr. Campbell?"

"Matthew, you're a fine young man, but Betsy is too young. Talk to me again when she's sixteen."

"Papa?" Betsy whined. She sat in one of the wicker chairs on the porch.

"No," Tipper repeated.

"It's okay," Matthew said. "Papa won't let Mary date until she's sixteen either. Mr. Campbell, are you sure it's not me— what I am?"

Tipper understood Matthew's dilemma better than the boy could possibly know. "No, Matthew. You're a good kid, and I like you. Alain is one of my best friends. When you come home from college for the summer in two years, talk to me again."

"I'm going straight through summers. I won't be back for three years."

"Perfect. What are you gonna do?"

"Teach math."

"Not engineering?"

"No, sir. I want to teach."

"That's admirable, but you know if you teach here after only three years of college time, Betsy will be a senior. You can't date until she graduates."

"What if she's not in my class?"

"Sunny would be better to ask, but when Betsy's sixteen, she can date. If she wants to date you, fine. Betsy, listen to me."

"Yes, Papa?"

Tipper pointed a decisive finger her direction. "You will *not* sneak out to meet Matthew like your mother did with Matthew's father when she was your age. Matthew, you would disappoint me if you did that."

"Yes, sir. I guess I'll go home."

"I'm not finished."

"Yes, sir?"

Matthew looked up at Tipper, and Tipper could not help but feel as if he were looking at Alain. Tipper took a deep breath.

"If you would like to do something with our whole family at our house, you're welcome."

Matthew's face lit up. "Yes, sir. I'd like that."

"We're having a barbeque tonight with Betsy's grandfather. I think you're expected."

"I am. Mr. Royce and Momma have an announcement."

"Oh," said Tipper. "Well, how's Alain handling that?"

"Just fine. Mr. Royce asked permission to marry his sister."

"Hmm. Where does that leave Amy?"

"Mr. Campbell, I know where my father would like it to leave her."

"Really?"

"Yes, sir. Would that change anything for Betsy and me?"

Tipper shook his head. "No. Your relationship would be the same. Has Amy indicated she wants to be with Alain?"

"She's very stand-offish, actually."

"Hmm." Tipper laughed. "I wonder if Alain will ask Royce's permission or mine."

"Sir?"

"Royce asked Alain permission to marry his sister."

"But why would Papa ask you that?"

Tipper sobered fast. "Never mind."

Matthew started to speak, but Tipper touched the boy's lips with a finger and shook his head. Matthew nodded. He had grasped the entire picture—Amy was Tipper's sister.

44

You Need a Man

Alain attended the barbeque at Royce's where Royce announced his engagement to Fay Richter. Amy walked away, and Tipper started to follow her; however, Alain beat him to it. Outside, Amy sat silently in the porch swing. She stared at the multitude of stars in the velvety black sky. Alain sat beside her.

"Amy, are you all right?"

"I knew it was coming. Daddy's crazy about Fay, but where am I to go?" Amy looked at Alain with tears in her eyes. "I love Fay too, but she won't want me underfoot."

Alain took Amy's hand and kissed it. "Amy, you need a man."

Amy snorted. "Nobody would want me."

Alain scowled. "That's quite untrue. I want you very much."

Amy let go of his hand and walked to the porch post where she leaned her head and laughed a little hysterically. "You want leftovers—tarnished goods?"

Alain sighed and stood, pushing himself wearily from the swing. He stood behind Amy and caressed her arms. "How are you tarnished? You're absolutely beautiful. Or is it because it's me asking? I slept with my sister and God knows how many whores. I made two children with Fay. I'd say I'm the tainted one. Still, God has forgiven me. If you can see past my background, I want to seriously court you."

She turned around and laid her head on his chest. He kissed the top of her head and held her tightly.

Amy sighed at the feeling of safety. "Alain, I can't make you any promises right now. I'm so jumbled up inside."

"One day at a time, that's all I ask. Give me a chance, no sneaking, no secrets, no lies."

Amy pulled back. Could she really tell Alain her secret? *Of all people, he would understand and not judge. Maybe. Maybe someone to share the burden would help.*

"Okay," murmured Amy. "Yes."

Alain bent to kiss her, but she put her hand to his lips. "Too soon."

"Oh, Amy." He exhaled his frustration. "One day, Amy Dent, I'm gonna kiss you."

She laughed at the thought of that phrase, but her reply came naturally. "One day, Alain Richter, I'll kiss you back."

The next day, Alain picked Amy up and drove to Wilmington to take her to a movie. Afterward, they ate supper at Amy's favorite Japanese steakhouse.

"The chef was new," she observed as they walked to the truck.

"They come and go," affirmed Alain.

Amy announced, "I want dessert."

"What would you like?"

"A banana split with two spoons. We'll share."

Alain chuckled. "Okay. There's Baskin Robbins, Dairy Queen, Maggie Moo's, and Ice Dream Heaven. You choose."

"I've never had anything at Ice Dream Heaven. Let's go there."

He took her to Ice Dream Heaven and let her order the banana split the way she wanted it. As they ate and talked about New York, a woman who could have been Amy's sister came to their booth. Her pin designated her as manager.

"Alain Richter?" asked the woman, unsure if this was the man she knew.

"Blanche!" he replied with honest delight. He stood and hugged the woman. "I'm so glad to see you're all right. I was concerned about you after Jacqui's closed."

"I went to community college for hotel and restaurant management. I'm the boss here."

"Good for you."

"You look different, real good."

"Thanks."

"I read about you in the newspaper. Way to go!"

"Thanks again. Blanche, forgive my manners. This is Amy Dent. Amy, meet my friend, Blanche Proctor."

"Hello," said Blanche. "So, this is Amy." She chuckled. "I was a poor substitute, Alain. By the way, it's Creel now. I got married a couple of months ago to one of the bartenders from Jacqui's. We're in the process of buying the place. We're opening a real restaurant, no dancers and no whores. You'll have to come for our grand opening."

"Nice to meet you," Amy said and looked at Alain strangely. "It sounds like your life is moving up."

"For sure. I gotta get back to work."

"It's good to see you," said Alain. "I'm happy for you, and we will come for your grand opening."

"Me too for you." Blanche winked at Alain and went back to work.

"Care to explain?" asked Amy.

Alain blushed. "Blanche worked at Jacqui's place."

"She was a whore?"

"Yeah."

"Your whore?"

"Not exclusively."

Amy jabbed her spoon into the ice cream. "When you came to Jacqui's place, did you see her exclusively?"

"Yeah."

"Why her?"

Alain scowled.

"I'm waiting," said Amy irritably.

Alain jabbed his spoon into the ice cream. "She looked like you. She even let me call her Amy if I wanted to."

"Whoa!"

"I told you I visited whores."

"More than her?"

"Not at Jacqui's place. At Fester's and other places."

"Did you ever catch a disease?" Amy asked snidely.

"Yeah. Chlamydia. Mac gave me antibiotics. It's gone. I haven't been with anyone in a long time."

"Did they all look like me?"

"No. Sometimes I wanted somebody with blonde hair and blue eyes so I wouldn't think about you."

Amy threw her napkin on the table. "I'm sorry."

"For what?"

"Asking you about women."

"I've been with several, but I only ever wanted one."

"Me?"

Alain took Amy's hand. "Yes."

"How?"

"Amy, you're not a bad person. Besides Roscoe, was there anyone else other than Tipper?"

"Don't mention Roscoe DuBlane. I hope he's burning in Hell."

"You *married* him."

"I don't wanna talk about that son-of-a-bitch. You think I need a man? Well, Roscoe was not a man—he was pond scum. Yeah, there was one other for one night, a guy named Rico, last name unknown. I met him when I saw Tipper and Jessica on their honeymoon in Miami."

"Okay, Amy. You don't need a man. You need *me*."

Amy huffed. "Did you enjoy Blanche?"

Alain threw his napkin on the table and placed both palms flat on the table. "Amy! Damn it! Blanche and I became friends. Sometimes we just talked. She was cheaper than a psychiatrist."

Amy laughed. "And sometimes?"

"What do you want me to say?"

"Do you love her?"

Alain shook his head incredulously. "Not like that. I care about her, and I'm glad she has a real life, including a man that apparently loves her."

"Okay. I accept that."

After a long silence, Alain ventured, "So? Are we courting?"

Mockingly, Amy replied, "Yes, Alain, we're courting. Maybe you truly are the man I need."

45

My Special Place

The day before Gator and Sherry planned to exchange vows to be legally married, although they told the general public it was a renewal of their promise of love, Alain showed up at Amy's door with a picnic basket.

"What a surprise," said Amy.

Alain grinned. "Do you know what today is?"

Amy puckered her lips. "The anniversary of a rafting trip?"

Alain gave her a playful glare. "Happy birthday," she said.

"I'd like to show you my special place. Nobody else knows about it. Will you go?"

"Of course."

"Bring your art supplies. I think you'll want to paint it."

Alain parked near the musketeer clubhouse. Amy laughed. "Alain, I've seen the clubhouse multiple times."

"We're not going to the clubhouse."

He looped the picnic basket over his left arm. "Give me your satchel." He draped Amy's art satchel over his shoulder and took her left hand firmly in his right. "Be careful. The rocks are slippery."

They picked their way up the side of the waterfall and slipped behind the cascading water.

"Oh, my!" exclaimed Amy as she took in the well-supplied little cave. "Is this where you hid so nobody could find you?"

"Yeah, especially when I was scared or upset. When I was afraid Pa would kill me; after Lucille caught us." He gave a one-shoulder shrug. "Many other times. I never told anybody, not even Gator, about this place. I'd like to keep it between you and me. I have another place to show you after our picnic. You can tell the whole world about it after you paint it."

"Where?"

"After you top the fall, there's a valley. I own it now."

"The whole valley?"

"All one hundred three acres. I've asked Felicia to look at it and design a house for me, one as nice as Tipper's. On the other side of the line of woods is a power relay station. I'll have electricity, running water, and a phone."

Amy laughed. "Tipper's house is enormous. Who's gonna share your special place?"

"I was hoping you."

"Oh." She fidgeted.

"Not tomorrow, Amy. I thought we could picnic and see the place today."

"Of course, we can. Tell me about your cave."

Alain spread the picnic, and they sat down. "This is my sanctuary. I found it the first time I stood up to Pa. He beat me because I kept Calvin from falling from the peach tree and getting hurt. I ran as fast and as far as I could. When I got up here, I saw a shadow behind the water that I had never seen before." He waved a hand back and forth. "This is what I found."

Amy picked up the foam pillow on the straw bed. "Is this the pillow I sneaked you?"

"Yep. The blanket too. I stored food in the white plastic chest."

"Your life must've been unbearable."

"No, because I got to see you. Seeing you made each day worthwhile."

"Alain."

"I know, Amy." He closed his eyes and heaved a great sigh. "I love you. I always have, even when you were married to Tipper."

"I never meant to hurt you." Amy hugged the pillow to her.

"I realize that. The choices I made in addition to your mother caused a monstrous chasm between us. I'm sorry."

"So much has changed."

"It has. When I would come here, I would write. You know, Sunny's trying to get my writing published."

"Wouldn't that be something! I knew your soul was romantic. You're an artist, just like me, but you paint with words. I read a couple of your musketeer anecdotes. Did you ever write about me?"

"Frequently."

"Will you let me read it?"

Alain sighed. "Some of it's dark."

"That's okay. Some of my art is dark. Let me read the best one or your favorite."

"I guess that would be 'Beauty Lost.' I wrote it when you left." Alain retrieved some papers from a second chest and let Amy read.

She brushed tears from her cheeks. "You're talented. You watched me with Tipper?"

"Yeah. Sick, huh?"

"A little."

"I would close my eyes and pretend it was me, just like I would pretend Blanche was you. I'm sorry. Both things were wrong."

"Forgiven." Amy laughed a little. "Actually, flattering. What's the worst thing you ever did? It was not helping Gator get rid of the scum that came after Sherry."

"I killed my pa."

"That was suicide."

Alain shook his head. "No."

"Tell me."

"Ma caught him screwing Fay, literally. Well, at least trying. She managed to stop him *that* time, but not many times before. She fought with him, and I came in. You heard the screaming."

Amy nodded. "Well, that's what was happening," Alain continued. "Ma sent Fay running with Polly. He was beating Ma black and blue. I jumped on him, and he turned his wrath on me." He held up his hand like a shield. "Okay—not the first time, but Ma had every intention of castrating him. She got the butcher knife, but he knocked her away into the wall. Then, he kicked her in the stomach. Blood gushed from her. Polly was not even two weeks old. He grabbed the shotgun and killed her."

Alain rubbed his face with both hands. "Her blood covered me. He turned the gun toward me. Amy, I grabbed the barrel and turned it back to point under his chin. I pressed his finger against the trigger. I knew what I was doing."

With her fingertips to her lips, Amy asked, "Did Mr. Jones know?"

"Yeah. He helped me cover it up. You know he and Ma were lovers. Polly is a Jones. I made sure Keenan knew that before I pulled the trigger."

"Yeah, she looks like Gator."

"She does. I'm glad."

"You look like your mother."

"I'm glad for that. I hated Pa."

"He deserved to die." Amy stroked Alain's cheek. "Oh, baby."

"Baby?"

Amy laughed softly. Alain leaned in to kiss her, but she stopped him. "Not yet."

"Why?"

"I have something to tell you. After that, you might not want to."

"Oh, Amy. One day, Amy Dent, I'm gonna kiss you."

"One day, Alain Richter, I'll kiss you back. Maybe today."

"Tell me, Amy."

46
Only You

Amy sat back on the straw bed and nodded. "Of all the people I know, only you will actually understand."

"What does it have to do with?"

"I'm gonna explain why I left."

"Okay. Amy, do you still love Tipper?"

"Not like that. I can't, but, yes, I loved him with all my heart."

Alain sat beside her and put her head on his shoulder. He could feel her trembling. "I'm listening."

"When Momma took you away from me, I turned to Tipper. He was willing. Alain, I'm devious."

"No, you're not."

"Yes, I am. I'm the one who initiated sex with Tipper. I knew sooner or later I'd get pregnant. I wanted to get pregnant. I knew Tipper would marry me and get me away from Momma. So, we had Betsy."

Alain gently rubbed Amy's leg. "And I had Mary because I sought comfort in the wrong place when you married Tipper."

"I'm so sorry."

"It was my mistake, not yours. Go on."

"You know Momma never accepted my children. I hated her for that."

"Why? Your girls are terrific. You know, Matthew is smitten by Betsy."

"Tipper told me, and Tipper's right."

"I agree, but continue your story." He gave a lopsided smile.

"Okay. Mac was so thoughtful. He sent Tipper boxes of condoms, so Callie wasn't right on the heels of Betsy."

"Yeah. Amy, what was with Roscoe?"

"I'll get there. Stop interrupting."

Alain held up his hands as if in surrender. "Okay. Sorry."

"Momma wouldn't even go in with me to have Callie. Roscoe did. Then, when I went back to Philadelphia, Roscoe raped me."

Amy could feel Alain's body tense in rage. "What? Dear, God!"

She tried to raise her head, but Alain held her tightly. "It's ridiculous because he was bisexual," she said. "He would rather have had Tipper."

"Amy! I knew it. I caught him watching Tipper just before you left. I should've killed him then. But why did you leave with him?"

"Yeah, well, he served my purposes. However, it was after Philadelphia that I realized how much I truly loved Tipper. Then, we made Laurie, and Momma got sick."

Amy lifted her head. Her face was stricken, and she fought the bile that rose in her throat, but she had to look Alain in the eye.

"Amy?"

"Okay. I'm okay. Here comes the hard part. I did the same thing you did."

"You didn't kill Lucille."

"No, I had sex with my brother."

"What?"

"Momma told me Nathaniel Campbell was my father."

"Oh, God! Did she lie?"

"No." She shook her head. "She finally told the truth. I had some DNA tests done after Laurie was born."

"Is that why you wanted to kill yourself?"

"Yes. I tried three more times, unsuccessfully."

"Thank God."

"Alain, I made three babies with my brother. I'm no different from you and Fay."

"Yes, you are because you didn't know."

"But I left them. I ran away. You have never deserted your responsibilities."

"I thought about it. A couple of times when I came up here, I brought the shotgun. I thought about killing myself, but I'm not a coward."

Alain smiled thoughtfully. "When Matthew put both his hands on my face and said, 'Papa, I love you,' nothing else mattered. When Mary sat on my lap for me to read to her, the world seemed better. I love my children. So do you."

"I do, but I don't want them to know."

"Of course. I would never say anything."

"Do you see me as less now?"

"No! Amy, it has always been only you. I love you."

"Oh, Alain! Baby, how can you?"

"You're easy to love. Baby? If you call me baby again, I *will* kiss you. You'll be lucky if I stop there."

Amy laughed. "You would stop because you love me." She threw her arms around him. "Baby."

"Oh, Amy." Alain held her body close to his and kissed her as he had wanted to for most of his life. The kiss took his breath away, his tongue tracing the outline of her lips ending with a soft nibble to her bottom lip. He stopped long enough to take a deep breath and inhale the scent of roses that she still wore. "One day, Amy Dent, I'm gonna make love to you. A kiss is not enough."

Amy stroked Alain's cheek. "One day, Alain Richter, I'll make love back to you, but today kiss me again before you show me your valley."

"Only you can share it with me."

Amy sighed at the thought. Could she open her heart to this man who had never closed his heart to her? Alain kissed her again, and both thought only of the moment at hand.

47
I Did It!

After Gator and Sherry's wedding the next day, Amy spent a great deal of time past the waterfall at the top of the hill. The valley was peaceful and calming. The stream wound lazily through the valley before it found its way, somehow, up the mountain to plummet into Crystal Cascade. Amy laughed at the name Betsy had given the creek, Cavalier Creek, as she pictured Alain as a swashbuckler, probably a pirate, albeit a likeable rogue.

Someone sat beside her as she painted. She was so lost in thought, she almost jumped out of her skin. "Felicia! You startled me."

"Alain wanted me to see this place again before I started my design."

"He told me he wants you to design a house. He wants it on that knoll." She pointed.

"I see it. I'll have to get a closer look another day. I just delivered the plans for the Easy Street Estates out Richter Road. The houses will all be modest, but modern. They're working on finishing the roads and getting water and electricity all the way out."

"Wow! Possum Holler for our children will be so different. Are you going to have a house there for when you visit?"

"I had planned to, but now I'm renovating the old Reardon place. You know, George Hicks will be marrying Polly and living at the Richter place. Ron likes Mac's old house so much he wants me to make it our 'bungalow.'"

"Will Alain's house be ready by the time George moves in with Polly?"

"I don't know. I'll make it a priority. How are you coping with Royce's impending marriage?"

"I'll be fine."

"Amy, do you love Alain?"

Pushy and intrusive. Amy scowled. "He's my best friend."

"Hmm. Do you still love Tipper?"

"No, not like that. I do love him, and I always will, but it's changed."

"Why?"

Amy gave her a look of scrutiny. "Felicia, I like you, but my personal feelings are my own."

"Sorry," Felicia said, standing.

"It's just that some things are better left unsaid."

"Secrets always come back to bite you in the butt."

"Do you have secrets?"

"Not from Mac."

"What does Mac have to do with it?"

"He's Chambry's daddy, but not his father."

"Oh!"

"Is that the secret?" Felicia pried. "Tipper is not somebody's father?"

"No. Royce is not my father."

"So?"

Amy squinted at Felicia. *She won't stop until she gets to the bottom of this.* "Okay, Momma told me on her death bed Nathaniel Campbell was my father." Amy began to pack up her art supplies, having finished her painting of Alain's Valley.

"Shit!" exclaimed Felicia.

"Now, do you understand?"

"Yes. My lips are sealed."

"Thanks."

"Amy?" a voice called from near the falls.

"Is that Alain?" asked Felicia.

"Yes. He sounds excited. Up here!" Amy responded.

Alain scrambled up the mountain. Breathlessly, he shouted, "I did it, Amy! Hey, Felicia."

"What did you do?" asked Amy.

Alain thrust two hardcover books into Amy's hands. One was entitled *Hillbilly Hijinks* and contained Alain's prose writing. The other, which contained Alain's poetry, was entitled *Hillbilly Valleys and Peaks*. "River Bankston sent me the first ones off the press. He got his company to publish my work. I've started a novel. Oh! River's company is in Boston. He wants me to come and do a book promotion at the end of the month. Will you go with me?"

Felicia laughed. "Congratulations, Alain. I'll leave you two to talk, and I'll buy a copy of each if you autograph them personally."

"I'll even write you a special note."

"What about a poem for me?"

"Second book of poems."

"Promise?"

"Yes, ma'am. It would be my pleasure. Maybe I'll entitle it 'No Longer Disgraces.'"

Felicia left Amy and Alain to talk.

Amy opened the book of poetry and read the dedication. "For Shirley Richter and Tal Jones, two people who found a way to love in a loveless world."

"How sweet," she said. "Alain, do you think the world is loveless still?"

"No. You just have to know where to find it. Read the other one."

She opened the second book and read, "For Amy, Gator, Tipper, and Mac, the best friends a boy could ever have."

Amy kissed Alain softly. "So, tell me about it."

"Well, Sunny is acting as my agent. Her brother, River, works for the publishing company, Dragon Publishing. Sunny says the company is really old, but still small. It's been around since the 1600s. The first book they ever published was called

Memoirs of Magic. Sunny found a copy at an antique bookstore. I've been reading it. It's…interesting."

"Okay. I'll read it."

"You'll love it. Sunny says they're really selective and only choose extraordinary writers. The company's owned by O'Rourke Enterprises. They own a lot of stuff all over the world.

"The last book they published was called *Lucky Thirteen*. I got a copy of it. It was written by a teacher, Larkin Sloan Reynolds, in a small town in Louisiana. It has been at the top of the *New York Times* bestseller list for most of the year.

"Sunny says the company has a knack for picking winners even though they only publish about five books a year." Alain finally took a breath. He was winded.

Amy laughed at Alain's enthusiasm. He seemed like the boy who had gone skinny dipping with her when she was thirteen. "You *are* a winner, Alain Richter. When will you have to be in Boston? What are the terms of your contract?"

"The end of June. Sunny negotiated a good percentage for me. She said the going rate for a debut book is eight percent. She got me twelve, and she gets two percent of my twelve. There was a hundred thousand dollar advance and a contract to write a novel and another poetry anthology. River is gonna be my editor. They didn't change a thing though in the poetry and only minor things in the prose, nothing that would change the stories."

"You're so excited. Let's go to the city to celebrate."

"Okay. Will you go with me to Boston?"

"Yes. Will Sunny be going?"

"She has to. She's my agent and promoter. Oh, but she's due to have a baby any day now."

"I guess that means Mac'll go with her."

"Maybe."

"Help me pack up so we can celebrate."

He helped deposit her art equipment. "Do you mind celebrating at Blanche's restaurant? Today's the grand opening."

"I had forgotten. No that's fine. What are they calling it again?"

"The Chicken Coop. They'll only serve chicken dishes as entrées."

"It sounds delicious."

Felicia Norton went to check the site where Alain wanted to build after Amy and Alain went to the city. When she didn't return at a reasonable time, a full search began for her. She was found in a hole in the mountain behind the fall with a broken ankle. Gator fell into the hole with her.

After a trying ordeal, Ron refused to allow Felicia to go home and care for their twins and Chambry. She stayed in Possum Holler to recover and commissioned Amy to paint portraits of her rescuers. While she was there, she drew the blueprints for Alain's house and oversaw the foundation and the beginning of Easy Street Estates.

As Felicia recovered and both Jessica and Sunny had babies, Alain and Amy read the two books he had from Dragon Publishing before he went to Boston.

Amy sat back. "Alain, do you think there's a world we know nothing about—a place of magic?"

"Who's to say? Whenever you paint on the canvas, you create magic."

"The same with your words on paper. I'd like to believe there is such a place."

Alain pointed to *Memoirs of Magic*. "Well, that author believed it."

"Yeah. However, the other book is definitely true, you know."

"It is?"

Amy nodded. "Yes. Without news here, you wouldn't know. I saw it on the news. That teacher told her own story, changing the names to protect the innocent."

"Then, she overcame a lot. That, too, is magic. That's what I've done to start a novel. It was Clarence's idea. I'm telling our story but changing the location and time period. I just can't seem to get past the first page though."

"Writer's block?"

He shrugged. "Maybe I just need a little infusion of magic."

Alain put his arms around Amy and held her close to him. "As far as I'm concerned, we can be magic," he said.

"You're a hopeless romantic."

"I love you, Amy. One day, you'll love me."

"We shall see."

"Maybe Boston."

MacKenzie and Sunny Reardon, along with baby Charlie, accompanied Alain Richter and Amy Dent to Boston. Alain appeared on several national talk shows and news programs. He had a book signing in Boston Common just before Independence Day and historical reenactments of battles of the Revolutionary War. He was scheduled to appear for book signings in several cities across America. Amy assured him she would fly to each place with him.

Alain visited Lexington and Concord. He stood where the Boston Massacre had occurred. "Oh!" he blatted. He swayed a bit as if he had been drinking and gripped the sides of his head.

"Alain?" Amy put her hand on his shoulder. "Are you all right?"

"I know what my first novel's gonna be about. Not the one I started—a different one. I'm gonna call it *Honor Bound*. It's gonna be about a young man whose punishment for fleeing battle in the fight for independence is to be reincarnated to fight again and again in war after war until he regains his honor."

"How will he do that?"

"There's only one way. He has to come to the place where he sacrifices himself for his fellow man. When he puts himself last, he will be free."

"How many wars?"

"The American Revolution, The War of 1812, The War Between the States, The Spanish American War, World War I, World War II, Vietnam, Iraq."

Amy shook her head as if to dislodge something. "That'll be a lot of research."

"I can do it."

"I know you can. How did you come up with this idea?"

Alain smirked and whispered, "A pearly white dragon whispered it to me."

Amy laughed. "I'm so proud of you."

"Do you love me?"

"Alain."

"One day, Amy."

"Hey," Sunny interrupted.

"Hey," said Alain.

"Is everything all right?"

"Yes. I have to tell you my idea."

"It's great—challenging," said Amy.

"Good. You won't be going home from here. You have thirteen stops before you get to go home, including this one. Amy'll be with you. Mac and I are leaving in the morning for home. I have to get back to the school. When you get back, your house might be ready. Felicia is really pushing the construction crew to finish your house first, but you have one more interview here tonight."

"Oh, yes, *The Salem Signal*, televised."

The interview seemed condescending to Alain.

"Mr. Richter, in *Hillbilly Hijinks* you write about a teacher embarrassing you because you had no underwear. Was that true, or did you embellish?"

Alain smiled. "Mr. Dormant, I grew up with thirteen younger siblings. My father was convinced I was not his child. He physically and emotionally abused me. When I write about the sweet girl who gave me underwear, it means more to me than the cruelty. But, yes, every word is true."

"You must have been so alone."

"Yes, but I want people to read this and see that just because a person is poor doesn't mean they're useless or not worth saving. I want poor children, abused children, neglected children to realize they don't have to remain victims of circumstance. They can overcome it through faith and education."

"You seem so certain."

"I am. I did it."

Alain took off the microphone and slipped into Amy's embrace. The interviewer followed him. "Mr. Richter."

"Interview's over."

The reporter scrutinized Amy. "Hello," said Amy. "I'm Amy Dent."

"The artist?"

"The little girl who gave Alain underwear. Let's go, baby."

"Wait, please?"

"Turn off the camera." Alain pointed at the camera operator who lowered the camera. "No. Your next question was gonna be about my relationship with my sister. Taboo topic. You read the book. My son is at Yale on full scholarship. I will not embarrass him on national television."

"How did you know I was going to ask that?"

"It was in your eyes."

"One question. Did you tell all?"

"No. Some secrets I will take to my grave."

"Criminal secrets?"

"Mr. Dormant," Alain crossed his arms over his chest. "Would you like to talk about the affair you had with your stepmother?"

"What? How?"

"Good-bye."

Amy grabbed Alain's arm as they exited the building. "How did you know?"

"I didn't, but he confirmed it by his reaction."

"Alain?"

Alain whispered, "I have to get out of Boston. I heard and saw that dragon again, the one that told me to write about the soldier, the one from *Memoirs of Magic*."

Amy looked terrified. "He'll think you're psychic."

"He'll treat his next interviewee with proper respect. Let's go. We won't talk about this, not here or anywhere."

48

Water and Electricity

Over the next several weeks, Alain went to New York, Philadelphia, Atlanta, Miami, New Orleans, Dallas, Los Angeles, San Francisco, Denver, Chicago, Washington, D.C., and Charleston, West Virginia, for book signings and television appearances. Finally, after six weeks, Alain and Amy drove into Possum Holler.

Both got out of the car. "Whoa!" stammered Amy.

"Lots of changes."

"Look at that." She pointed. "Lazy Susan Café?"

"A restaurant." Alain laughed. "Let's check it out."

Ina Campbell and Lauren Tomlin poured over blueprints with Felicia. "When are you opening?" Alain asked as he and Amy walked in.

Lauren clapped and squealed. Both older women hugged the couple. "Hopefully, the first of the year," said Lauren.

Alain asked, "You won't be teaching?"

"No. I've retired from that. I'll sub if they need me."

"What's the menu?" Amy asked

"Home cooking. Different every day. We'll be open from eleven until two, Monday through Friday, and five until nine, Friday and Saturday. Folks can have dinner and a movie on Friday. Sunny's agreed to run the videos twice. We'll be closed Sunday."

"Lazy Susan?" Alain asked.

Ina nodded. "Yeah. It'll be like a buffet, but with six large round tables with a lazy Susan in the middle to spin around to the desired food."

"I can't wait." Alain patted his middle.

"How was your trip?" Ina asked, rubbing the young man's arm.

"Tiring."

Lauren said, "Well, drive out Richter Road if you really want to see changes. Ina and I are a drop in the bucket."

"Whose idea was this?" asked Alain.

"Ron's," answered Felicia. "He says he's gonna get fat eating Miss Ina's and Mamaw's cooking if he doesn't share it with the world. I say he's gonna get fat anyway. He can't stay away from here, and he has gained twelve pounds. He bought a treadmill so he can exercise more."

Everybody laughed.

Amy unloaded her things from the car while Alain visited with Royce and Fay. "Set a date?" he asked.

"Yes," said Fay. "We were waiting for you to get back. August twenty-seventh."

"Soon."

"Alain, are you gonna marry Amy?" she asked.

"It would make me happy, but I don't know if she's ready. Royce?"

"You've got my blessing."

"Why are my ears burning?" asked Amy.

"Were they?" Alain grinned at her.

"Oh, yeah. Come on. Let's check out Richter Road."

They left holding hands. As they drove past the road to be called Easy Street, they saw a dozen houses in various stages of completion. The poles for power lines had been set, and it was obvious a good amount of pipe had been laid.

"Wow! Water and electricity," snickered Alain. "I wonder if we have it at the house."

"Polly's house?" Amy teased.

"Yeah, Polly's house." They drove on.

"I'll be damned!" Alain exclaimed. "Lights are on."

Amy shook her head. "I never thought I'd see it."

Polly and George came out holding hands. Polly said, "Alain, you're home."

"Did I miss something besides the water and electricity?"

"Well, yes. We got married."

"Polly! I was supposed to give you away."

Polly waved the comment off with her hand. "Do that for Mary."

"Are you pregnant?"

"What? No. You were just taking too long. Don't frown at me. At least we got married. Fay's moved in with Royce."

"What?" snapped Amy.

"Have you been by there?"

"Yes," said Alain. "They said August twenty-seventh."

"Okay. Fay didn't wanna stay here with us."

"Well, where shall *I* stay?" Alain growled.

"Your house."

"You throwing me out?"

"No, but it's almost ready."

"Y'all have really been working."

"Yeah," George confirmed, rubbing his back to indicate the stressful building regimen.

Amy sighed. "Polly, are any of the houses ready on Easy Street?"

"A few, but they're taken. Why?"

"I need a place to stay."

"You can share Alain's place."

Alain rubbed his head. Amy laughed. "Baby, you want some company?"

"Let's go see it. I don't have furniture yet."

"Oh." Polly beamed. "You can cut through off Easy Street and not have to drive all the way around."

"All the roads are paved," George said, "but they'll have to be redone after all the construction. Heavy equipment tends to tear 'em up."

A road had been cut around the waterfall, and it came up on the back side of Alain's property. The road turned into a packed gravel driveway that led to a three-car garage attached to Alain's house.

Alain and Amy got out and he looked around. He pointed up the slope to where the hole into which Felicia had fallen should be. "Did Felicia actually put a wishing well there?"

"Looks like it."

"How is that safe?"

"I'd bet you can't fall in. It's pretty. I kind of like it."

"Shall we go inside? The outside is what I wanted—stone."

"I like it a lot," agreed Amy.

Inside the kitchen door, Alain flipped the light switch. "Ha! Lights work." He flipped them off and on again like a kid with a new toy.

Amy went to the sink and turned on the faucet. "Water works." She picked up a note and read aloud:

Amy,

You choose the colors. You're the artist.

Love,
Felicia

Amy looked at Alain. "Why does it matter what I think?"

He laughed. "Felicia has decided this is *our* house."

"Really?"

"Amy, nothing would make me happier."

"You want me to share your house?"

"Among other things."

"Such as?"

"Oh, I don't know—my bed, my name, my life."

Amy frowned. "Was that a proposal?"

"Would you like it to be?"

"Just because your new fancy house has electricity and running water, doesn't mean you can buy me."

"Amy, I never thought that. How many times must I say I love you?"

"A million, and that might not be enough."

Amy laid the note back on the counter and went outside. Alain followed and turned off the light.

"Well," said Amy, "it needs to be painted, and you can't sleep on the floor. Let's get you set up tomorrow."

Alain took Amy by the shoulders and turned her around. "I don't want to live here alone. Damn it! I love you. I have waited my whole life for you. I want to marry you." He kissed her fiercely, and she responded. He pulled her close to him. "Amy, I want you so much it hurts. Give me a chance to truly love you."

Amy pushed away. "Alain, ooh! Let's get this place furnished. We'll talk. I need a lot more than water and electricity."

"Just a minute." Alain got the painting of the four musketeers and *The Queen Amy* from the trunk of the Camry he had bought. Amy followed him back inside, and Alain hung the painting over the fireplace in the den. "That was the happiest day of my life, Amy. It will be until the day you become mine."

49

Chasing Amy

The next morning, Alain picked up Amy early. "Good morning," he said as he kissed her gently.

"Morning." Amy yawned. "Have you had breakfast?"

"Yeah. Polly made hoecakes and sausage."

"Well, I need another cup of coffee before we leave. You want one?"

"Yeah. Sugar."

In the kitchen, Mary jumped from the table. "Papa!"

"Hey, precious." Alain hugged his daughter. "How much did you grow while I was gone?"

"Two inches."

"Good grief!"

"Momma says I'll be tall like you."

"Momma's not short."

"I guess I'll be real tall."

Alain glared at Fay. "We need to talk."

"About what?"

Alain kissed Mary on the forehead. "Don't you need to get ready for school?"

"Papa, it's summer for a few more weeks, but I can take a hint. I do need to get dressed before I go to Betsy's. Love you, Papa."

"I love you too."

Mary went to finish dressing. "What's on your mind, Alain?" asked Royce.

"Y'all aren't married yet. I don't like Mary living here."

"Alain!" snapped Fay. "I'll have you know I'm sleeping with Mary 'til we tie the knot."

"Okay. Sorry. I jumped to conclusions."

"The wedding is less than a week. I guess Mary can choose where she wants to live once you move into your house. Will you be living alone?"

Alain glanced at Amy. "I don't know, but I won't be living in sin."

"I see," said Fay.

"Excuse me," said Amy. "I need to brush my teeth before we leave."

Amy slipped from the kitchen. "My turn to leave," said Fay. "I'm chasing Amy for a minute."

Fay leaned against the door jamb of the bathroom as Amy brushed her teeth. "Don't hurt him again."

"What?" she muttered, spitting into the sink.

"I know your ma caused all the trouble for you and Alain the first time, but it almost killed him. Then, when you married Tipper, it was like pouring salt in his wound. Still, he loved you. He always has. When you left, I was so scared he'd hurt himself. Just being able to see you kept him sane. Now, you're back and free to be with him. Don't hurt him."

"I don't want to hurt Alain, Fay, but I'm scared myself. I just can't rush into something that might not work. That would hurt even more."

"Do you feel anything for him?"

"Alain is undoubtedly my best friend. That's what I know. I would be lost without him."

Fay sighed while Amy rinsed her mouth. "It's a start."

"A foundation that's solid."

"What are y'all doin' today?"

"Picking out furniture and paint colors for the inside of the house."

"Sounds like it's gonna be your house."

"Oh, Fay. Is friendship enough?"

"I can't answer that. I do think if you'd let down your guard, you'd find Alain is easy to love."

"You know, I loved him when I was thirteen, fourteen."

"Maybe it's still there, just hiding. Love is chasing you, Amy. Stop running."

"Hey!" Alain yelled up the stairs. "Girl talk can wait."

"Coming!" Amy responded.

"Amy, girl talk is asking you to be my maid of honor." Fay smiled. "If you're not mad at me."

"Of course, I will."

"It's gonna be a simple wedding. Pick out a dress while you're in the city."

"What color?"

"Blue. Royce's gonna ask Alain to be his best man. They both already have navy blue suits. I got a really simple ivory dress."

"I'll find something."

Amy and Fay came down the stairs arm in arm.

As they drove into Wilmington, Alain said, "What did y'all talk about?"

"Girl stuff. I'm maid of honor. I have to find a dress today too."

"I'm best man. Should we catch the paraphernalia?"

"We already did for Sherry and Gator."

"Not a real wedding, remember?"

"We know better."

"Others don't. I'm catching that damned garter. That'll be my third one. They say three's a charm."

"Why?"

"Amy, I'm chasing you. I'll do whatever I must to catch you."

"Oh, Alain!"

"Okay." Alain glanced toward Amy as he drove. She had crossed her arms over her chest. "I won't say anything else—right now."

They visited the home improvement store where Amy chose a flat beige paint for the walls in the entire house with a glossy trim that had a touch of gray and a semi-gloss ecru for the doors. Since all the floors were hardwood except for the kitchen and the bathrooms, she chose marble tile in a bluish-gray with flecks of rose, mauve, and beige with coordinating tiles for the kitchen and bath countertops and bathtub and shower stalls. The plumbing fixtures were already off-white porcelain. Neutral colors would not become outdated easily.

After arranging for the delivery of the paint and tile, Alain and Amy went to a furniture store. Amy said, "I'm actually glad the house isn't quite as big as Tipper's. Five bedrooms and three and a half baths are enough."

"I agree," said Alain.

The house had four bedrooms on the second floor with two bathrooms. For two of the bedrooms, Amy chose two daybeds with trundle beds in white wrought iron. She chose white eyelet bed coverings and curtains and white Queen Anne dressers and chests of drawers. She smiled softly. "That takes care of a place for all four of our girls to sleep and even have guests."

Alain smirked. "Does that mean your girls will be sleeping at my house?"

Amy just grunted and moved to choosing furniture for the other two rooms, which she decorated in a more manly fashion with black walnut twin beds and storage and bamboo window shades and tan chenille bedspreads.

Alain cocked an eyebrow. "For Matthew? Or if you slow down and let me catch you, would you consider having a child with me?"

Amy scowled. "Damn it, Alain! Too much too soon. I'll share the damned house with you. Now, let me furnish it."

Alain grinned broadly. "As my wife?"

"I don't think you'll settle for less."

Amy ran her hand over the post of a king-size four-poster bed in deep red cherry veneer. "I like this set for the master bedroom. What do you think?"

"It's big."

"Do you like it?"

"Yes. Is it the one you want?"

"Yes. We need the apricot patchwork comforter with the apricot sheers under the rust drapes." After that, she chose coordinating rugs for each room.

"All right," Alain said, "I guess we have the living room, dining room, den, and breakfast nook left."

"Yes. For the den I like that floral couch with the two rose-colored wing-back chairs and ottomans with the beige marble-top tables. There were the dark oak entertainment center and roll top desk, too. You can set your computer and printer up on the desk. Finish it off with the rose and gray Persian rug and rose drapes."

Alain nodded. "That room will be pleasant."

"Let's get the ivory couch and loveseat with the rose and burgundy stripes for the living room and the mahogany table set with the smoked glass inserts and the dusty rose Persian rug with the tiny rose pattern around the edge."

"I guess the kids won't go in there often."

"Nope. Probably, nobody will."

"Dining?"

"In the dining room I want the black walnut table and chairs with the crushed velvet seats and back in dusty rose for twelve. It has that matching hutch, china cabinet, and buffet."

"You'll need some china to put in it."

"I really liked that white set with the rosebuds and silver on the edge."

"With the crystal that has the etched rosebuds and silver rim?"

"Yes. That's perfect, Alain."

The salesclerk walking around with Alain and Amy was in Heaven. She wrote down every item.

"All right," Amy sighed. "We only have the breakfast area left. Felicia even put in the washer and dryer in the space off the garage and set up my art studio out back."

"Amy, I like that smoked glass dinette with the eight weathered-looking ladder-back chairs and four plain captain chairs for the bar."

"If that's what you want. You haven't chosen much."

"I want that."

"Okay.

"I also want two white rocking chairs for the end of the porch opposite the swing."

"That's good, but we need that matching table to put between them."

"Okay."

"Do you want to go ahead and get the patio furniture?"

"Damn! I guess." He shrugged.

"That rattan set with the big roses looks like you. And we'll take that gas grill and the black wrought iron table and chairs for six."

Alain paid cash for the furniture to the clerk's astonishment. "Deliver it next Monday. The inside of the house will be finished then."

Back in the car, Alain sighed. "What now?"

"Lunch. I'm starving."

Alain looked at his watch. "It's two o'clock. No wonder. What would you like milady?"

"Honestly?"

"Yes."

"A Wendy's cheeseburger, fries, and a Frosty."

"Works for me."

Alain and Amy ate lunch before Amy looked for a dress for Fay's wedding. "You get a dress," said Alain. "I need to do another errand. I'll meet you at the coffee shop. Okay?"

"Okay."

While Amy found a simple navy-blue dress of polished rayon that draped alluringly over her hips and crossed over the chest with two pieces that wrapped around the waist to tie in the back, Alain purchased a one-karat tiffany solitaire diamond with matching wedding bands in yellow gold.

"Who's the lucky lady?" asked the jeweler who showed Alain several rings.

"Amy Dent, but I'm the lucky man."

"Amy Dent? The artist?"

"Yep. Do you know her work?"

"I saw some when I was in New York. Congratulations, Mister?"

"Alain Richter."

"The writer?"

Alain looked up, cocked his head, and laughed. "I guess I am."

"I bought your books."

"Thank you. Now, I can afford to buy your rings."

Alain left the woman feeling as if she had met royalty when he promised to stop in the next time he came to town and sign her books.

"I thought you had left me," laughed Amy when Alain came up.

"I would never leave you. I met a fan."

"Are you ready to go home?"

"Yes."

"What did you buy?"

"You'll find out."

With only four days until Fay and Royce were to wed, Alain chased Amy relentlessly. She received flowers daily, and he dragged her somewhere every day.

Amy was at the house for the furniture delivery and found that Alain had also purchased everyday dishes and stainless steel and sterling silver and cookware, as well as linens and towels, all something she would have chosen.

The evening before the wedding, Alain prepared dinner for Amy in his new kitchen. After the meal, he handed her a box.

"What's this?" she asked.

"Open it."

Inside were a teardrop pendant and earrings of sapphire. "Oh, Alain! What's the occasion?"

"My sister's wedding."

"Thank you, but you've got to stop this."

"Stop what?"

"Spending all your money on me."

Alain carried the last of the dishes to the sink. "Amy, I love you. I've been chasing you my whole life. Do you have any idea how good it feels to be able to afford to give you things?"

"But what have I given you?"

"I only want one thing from you."

"What?"

"Your heart."

50

Mrs. Richter

Fay Richter looked lovely in her Victorian wedding dress. Tall and slender, the high-throated garment made her look regal. Alain knocked on the door where Fay and Amy waited for the wedding music to start.

"Alain?" Fay asked a bit alarmed.

"Relax. Royce's waiting for you. I have something for you. I found it in a small box buried under Ma's undergarments. It should be yours. It'll be perfect with your dress.

Alain handed Fay a cameo on a background of pale blue. "Oh!" breathed Fay. "I never knew Ma had anything so pretty. Pin it on me."

Alain pinned the brooch at Fay's throat and hugged her close. "I love you, Fay. I'll be here for you as long as I draw breath."

"I know you will. You're the best big brother anybody could ever have. I love you."

Alain kissed Fay's forehead. "I'll see you in a few minutes. Fay, I'm so happy a man like Royce Dent loves you." He handed her a tiny scrap of paper. "The brooch was pinned to this."

After Alain left, Fay unfolded the paper. It read, "*A lady for a lady. Tal.*" She showed the note to Amy, and both women had to fight tears. They could feel true love from beyond the grave. Fay touched the cameo. She felt blessed to have the item and to have found real love.

Leo Tomlin thoroughly enjoyed performing the wedding ceremony for Royce Dent and Fay Richter for he saw honest joy in both their faces. There was a characteristic Possum Holler reception in celebration as the populace shared their best food, serving pieces, and beverages with the couple. The new residents were amazed again at the feeling of family in this small community.

Although fall classes had just begun, Matthew Richter managed to get home for his mother's wedding and joined the group of single men when it came time to catch the garter. Alain leaned into him. "Don't even think about it."

"Papa, you've caught two."

"Three's the charm."

"Have you proposed to Amy?"

"Not officially, but I bought the rings."

Matthew laughed. "All right, Papa, if I can be your best man."

"Yes, indeed. Are you prepared?"

"What are you planning?"

"Stay and watch. If I fall on my face, I'll need you to pick me up."

When the garter hit the air, Alain proved he was in excellent physical condition as he leapt high to claim it. Amy laughed so hard she cried.

He pointed decisively at her.

"You better catch it," Sherry Jones whispered to her dearest friend. "And you better marry him."

Amy narrowed her eyes and set her lips in a fine line as she scowled at Sherry who shrugged. "The man loves you."

"I know he does."

"Do you love him?"

"I'm scared to, Sherry."

"Don't be. Don't let happiness pass you by."

"When did you become so wise?"

"I was born wise." Sherry kissed Amy's cheek.

Amy sighed. As she looked around, she saw she was the only woman waiting to catch the bouquet. "Oh, just hand me the damned thing," she snarled at Fay. Fay flipped the flowers a few inches so Amy could actually catch the small arrangement.

Alain spun Amy around and kissed her. "I love you, Amy Dent. Will you marry me?" He held out the rings he had bought.

The crowd, including the bride and groom, waited for her answer. Tipper nodded at her. Royce nodded at her. Sherry nodded at her. All eyes were on her.

"Yes," she said.

"Right now?"

"What?"

"You're wearing blue. That means you'll be true. Preacher Tomlin can sign the license in a matter of minutes, and we can file it Monday. My best man is here. In my periphery, I see half a dozen women who will stand up for you. Mac can do blood tests posthaste. It's August. I always wanted to be married in August because it's the only month without a reason to celebrate."

"Now?"

"Now. You even have flowers. Just say, 'Yes.'"

Amy looked around at the guests staring at her.

Leo cleared his throat and walked back inside the church to wait in the pulpit.

"Is it a conspiracy?" asked Amy through clenched teeth.

Betsy Campbell put her arms around Amy's right arm. "I would love to be your maid of honor, Momma."

"You're too young to sign a marriage license."

"I'm not," said Ina Campbell.

"Miss Ina?"

Ina kissed Amy's cheek and whispered. "It's right, baby girl. Marry the man."

"What about love?" Amy whispered back.

"You love him. You just have to admit it to yourself."

"You really want to do this right now, Alain?" Amy asked hesitantly.

"I do."

"All right. Let's do it."

Alain handed Amy the garter. "Put it on."

Amy devilishly put her foot on Alain's leg and slipped the garter onto her thigh.

The crowd returned to the church. Alain Richter married Amy Dent with Matthew Richter as best man and Ina Campbell as maid of honor. Leo Tomlin enjoyed this ceremony more than he had the last. He chose the simplest vows possible.

Leo looked from Alain to Amy and grinned wider than the groom. "Brothers and sisters, this might be the best wedding I have ever performed. It has been far too long in the making.

"Alain as we have already witnessed, you have a ring for Amy. Do you wish to become her husband?"

"I do," said Alain in sheer delight.

"Then, place the ring on Amy's hand and repeat after me. 'Amy, I give you this ring; wear it with love and joy. I choose you to be my wife, to have and to hold from this day forward for better or for worse, for richer for poorer, in sickness and in health, to love and to cherish as long as we both shall live.'"

Alain looked like a child at Christmas as he repeated the vows and slipped both rings onto Amy's finger.

Leo turned to Amy who looked more like a scared rabbit. He winked at her, and she took a deep breath. "Amy, you have been taken by surprise today. Do you wish to become Alain's wife?"

Amy looked from Leo to Alain. She felt Ina gently caress her back. "I do," she said after a great sigh.

Leo nodded subtly to her. "Then, place the ring Ina is handing you on Alain's finger and repeat after me. 'Alain, I give you this ring; wear it with love and joy. I choose you to be my husband, to have and to hold from this day forward for better or for worse, for richer for poorer, in sickness and in health, to love and to cherish as long as we both shall live.'"

Amy's hand trembled as she slid the ring onto Alain's finger. Looking into his eyes, she found a great part of her desperately wanted to say the words. "Alain, I give you this ring; wear it with love and joy. I choose you to be my husband, to have and to hold from this day forward for better or for worse, for Richter for poorer." She paused at her fumble of words. Alain winked at her. Leo nodded discreetly. There was no indication from the congregation they had even noticed she had misspoken. She took a deep breath and finished. "In sickness and in health, to love and to cherish as long as we both shall live." Amy never took her eyes off Alain's face.

Leo looked out over the congregation. "It there is anyone present who can show just cause why Alain and Amy should not be married, speak now, or forever hold your peace. Better yet—leave."

No one responded. "I hear no objections. It gives me great joy to pronounce Alain and Amy husband and wife. Alain, you may kiss your bride."

After the wedding, Leo filed the proper papers as soon as he could the first thing Monday morning, and the residents of Possum Holler celebrated again.

When Alain shot the garter, Matthew caught it, causing Tipper to scowl. Matthew laughed. "Don't worry, Mr. Campbell. It'll be several years."

Amy tossed her flowers over her shoulder with no intent. Surprisingly, the bouquet fell into Ina Campbell's hands. Ina shrugged. "It just goes to show that it's all superstition. I don't even have a fellow. I wouldn't dream of stealing Betsy's."

Royce and Fay finally left to drive to Nashville. Amy scrunched up her face at Alain. "You owe me a honeymoon."

"Where would you like to go, Mrs. Richter? We can leave right now."

"To my house."

"As you wish."

51

Separate Rooms

Alain scooped Amy into his arms and carried her into the house he had built with her in mind. He did not stop inside the door but carried her directly to the bed she had chosen. He untied the dress she wore and slipped it off her shoulders as he kissed her neck and ran his hand down her arms and up her back. "Oh, Amy. I love you. I have dreamed of this moment my entire life."

Alain laid Amy back on the bed and slipped off her bra. His mouth found her breasts, and his hand moved inside the navy-blue lace panties she wore. As his fingers gently probed into her, Amy shrieked, "Stop!" and pushed Alain with all her might. "Get off me! I'm not ready for this."

"Amy!" Alain called, dismayed as she snatched her dress and fled into the bathroom and locked the door.

Alain touched the door and leaned his forehead against it. "Amy?"

"I can't, Alain."

"Why? Talk to me. You know I love you. I won't hurt you. You're my wife. I want to make love to you."

Amy opened the door, but she was dressed. "No."

"No? I don't understand."

"I married you on paper this evening. I'll share this house with you. I won't change my name—not again. I'm not having sex with you. I'm not ready for that. You manipulated me into that wedding. I'm going to bed now. Good night."

Amy started out the door to one of the upstairs rooms. Alain grabbed her arm and pulled her back to him to kiss her. She slapped him as hard as she could. "Are you gonna rape me, Alain, like Roscoe did?"

Tears pricked Alain's eyes. "I would never hurt you." He covered his stinging, burning cheek with his hand. "Why can't you love me? My, God! You had sex with a total stranger in Miami, but not me. I would give you *anything*. I would die for you or kill for you."

Amy took a deep shaky breath. "It's not you, Alain. It's me."

Alain nodded. "Fine. You take this bed. You chose it. It's mighty big when you're alone."

Alain walked out the door and climbed the stairs to find a bed to sleep. He stopped at the top of the stairs. He muttered, "Damn it! Separate rooms? Right this second I wish I had never shown anybody my cave." He yelled down the stairs before he stomped down the hallway to the manly decorated room, "This is bullshit!"

Amy opened her eyes the next morning as she heard stirring. "Alain?"

"I won't bother you. My clothes are in this closet."

"Where are you going?"

"Church. It's Sunday."

Amy sat up in bed. "I don't think people will expect us today."

"Well, I have no reason to stay home."

"Are you mad at me?"

"Let me think." Alain leaned on his arm over his head against the open closet door. "Um. Yes."

"I'm sorry. I'm just not..."

"Ready. I heard you. Why didn't you just say, 'No?'"

"Everybody expected me to accept."

Alain sat on the side of the bed wearing a pair of khakis but no shirt. "Amy, I'm hurt." He tapped his chest over his heart. "I feel as if you stabbed me with a knife."

"You look awful this morning."

"I threw up three times last night. I couldn't sleep. I cried like a baby. I'm sure I look awful."

Amy brushed tears from her cheeks. "I don't wanna hurt you."

"Then, why are we in separate rooms? Why can't you make love to me? I have tried so hard to become a man you would be proud of."

Amy crawled across the bed and laid her face against her husband's back. Alain closed his eyes. "Oh, Amy, I can't feel you against me like that and not want you."

"Please don't go today? Stay with me. I'm just not ready yet."

"Amy, do you think I would hurt you?"

"No. I'm sorry I slapped you. It was like memories of Roscoe. I'm sorry. Please don't go? Please don't let people know? Please don't make me sleep alone in this bed? But sleep is all I can do right now."

Alain snorted. "Lady, you pack a wallop. My cheek is bruised."

"Sorry. Alain, I didn't sleep much last night either. Lie down with me. Let's sleep."

He swiveled on the bed so that one leg was up. "What are you wearing?"

"One of your shirts. My clothes aren't here."

Alain took a deep breath. "Amy, I have needs too. I'm not Tipper. I'm not your brother."

Amy gasped.

"Okay, we are very distantly related through the Munros, but far enough removed that even Preacher Tomlin wouldn't object. He was happy to marry us."

She opened her mouth to say something.

"Don't speak," Alain said. He held up a finger for emphasis. "Let me say what I need to. There's no legitimate reason for us to be in separate rooms.

"I'm not Roscoe. I will *not* force myself on you. If you don't want me, I won't be in this bed. I can't do that because I can't promise not to touch you.

"I'm not Rico. I won't fuck you and leave you. Until you can give me yourself, I won't sleep here."

Alain stood and started back to the closet for a shirt. Amy grabbed his hand. "Please?"

Alain heaved a sigh of defeat. He took off his khakis. "Alain?"

"Don't worry. I'm just hanging them up." He got a pair of pajama pants and put them on. "I don't do the tops, not even in winter."

Alain slipped under the covers and let Amy put her head on his chest. He ran strands of her hair between his fingers. "Are we gonna have separate rooms?"

"No. Just be patient with me."

"So? You won't change your name?

"No. I'm Amy Dent—artist. I need to keep my professional name."

"Okay. I can live with that. We're gonna sleep in the same bed, but not make love?"

"For now."

"How long?"

"Until I can tell you I love you as much as you love me."

"Do you love me even a little bit?"

"Yes, Alain."

"Best friends, huh?"

"Always."

"Are you sexually attracted to me at all?"

Amy sighed softly. "A lot, but I'm just not ready."

"One day, Amy Dent, I *will* make love to you."

Amy kissed Alain's chest, tugged gently on the sparse hair across his pectoral muscles and down his abdomen, and nestled into his arms. "One day, Alain Richter, I'll make love back to you."

"How do I always give in to you?"

"You love me."

"I'll stay here if I can, but if it gets too hard, I'm changing rooms. I do love you, Amy, but I can only take so much. I have a breaking point."

Alain and Amy fell asleep.

52

Sudden Impact

Alain kissed Amy on the forehead. Her eyes popped open. "Where are you going?"

"I have to go into the city. I thought you might want to pack your things. You can't wear my shirt forever."

"Is it Monday?"

"Yeah. We were both exhausted. I made breakfast—bacon, eggs and toast."

"Do you have to go today?"

"I'm going to see my lawyer. I have a few legal matters to attend, like my will."

"Don't talk about that! Don't you dare die on me!"

Alain laughed mirthlessly. "I promise not to die until I have fucked your brains out at least once. I definitely would like you to know what you're missing."

"Alain!" Amy gasped with her mouth agape.

"Too crude for you?"

"Unexpected. If anticipating that will keep you alive, maybe I'll wait forever."

Alain scowled and popped Amy's behind affectionately. "Come on. Breakfast."

Amy dressed in the dress she had worn for her wedding and came to breakfast. Having designated the trucks as a fleet for farm use, Alain had purchased a forest green Camry in which he drove Amy into town so she could pack. Matthew was packing to go back to Yale. Alain hugged him. "You be careful driving back into Yankee country."

"I will, Papa. I need to get on the road though. I saw Preacher Tomlin leave already." Matthew waved to Amy who waved back.

Alain walked her into Royce's house. "Get all packed up. I'll see you this evening."

"Be careful. It's pouring rain."

"I've driven in the rain many times."

"Still, be careful."

"Yes, ma'am. Do I at least get a kiss?"

"Yes."

Alain kissed Amy, and she held on to him as if she did not want to let him go. "Amy, let go."

"Alain."

"What?"

"Go tomorrow."

"You're being silly."

She kissed him again in desperation. "If I take you upstairs to bed, will you stay?"

"Amy, I'll be back." He pried her hands loose from around his neck. "If you wanna take me to bed tonight, I'll be ready. I love you."

Alain drove off into the rain.

Amy packed all her clothes and personal items. Then, she packed her art supplies. She heard the door open and hurried down the stairs. "Oh, Mary."

"Hey, Amy."

"I thought it was Alain coming back."

"No. School just got out. First day, you know. Where's Papa?"

"He went to Wilmington."

"Oh."

"You can't stay here alone."

"I can go visit Betsy. That's where I stayed the last two nights."

"You'll come with us. You'll love the rooms we have for you girls."

"I'd like that, Amy, until Momma gets back. She's scared I'll go live with y'all all the time."

"She doesn't want that?"

"No. She's already missing Matthew since he's gone off to college."

"Your papa misses you too."

"I miss him."

"You wanna bake some cookies?"

"Chocolate chip?"

"Sure."

Amy made cookies with her stepdaughter. She considered this girl who was slightly younger than Betsy. Of course, she looked like her father, or, maybe, her mother. Amy laughed at the thought. At least she and Tipper were colored differently. Betsy and Callie looked like her, while Laurie looked more like Tipper.

Mary walked to the window. "Amy, it's getting dark. When was Papa supposed to be home?"

"I would've thought by now."

"The weather's nasty."

"I know. Your papa's stubborn. I tried to get him to wait until tomorrow. Let's make supper. What sounds good to eat?"

Mary turned from the window. "Amy, does cooking take your mind off worrying?"

"No."

"Amy, are you worried?"

"Yes, Mary, I am. If he's not home by the time those cookies get done, I'm calling Clarence Dayton."

The minute the cookies came out of the oven, Amy called Clarence.

"Mrs. Richter, don't fret," teased Clarence.

"Don't patronize me, Clarence! Alain should've been back by now. You're the lawman. Go look for my husband."

"Amy, relax. I'll drive as far as my jurisdiction. If he's much later, I'll get Tipper, Mac, Gator, and Norman, and we'll really search."

An hour later, they really searched.

The rain poured in torrents while Alain drove back from Wilmington. There was no traffic on the two-lane back road.

"Damn," Alain muttered. "I need our raft." He flipped the windshield wipers to the highest speed. The low-beam headlights barely illuminated a few feet in front of the car.

As he seemed to poke along, a six-point buck darted into the road. Alain hit the brake. He struck the deer with enough force to deploy the Camry's airbags, and the creature crashed through the windshield, antlers like projectiles negating the protection offered by the safety device as they punctured the bag and tangled in the steering wheel. He lost all control as he hydroplaned on the newly paved road. He never thought he'd wish for the dirt road in which to bog, but he did. The last thing Alain remembered was careening down the ravine toward Cavalier Creek just outside Possum Holler.

Near midnight, Clarence Dayton's search light fell on the dark green of Alain Richter's Toyota Camry. After a great deal of maneuvering, the searchers were able to extract him from the wreckage, much of which was submerged in Cavalier Creek; the buck with a broken neck still protruded from the front of the vehicle.

Standing chest-deep in the water, Mac stabilized Alain's back and neck before the others helped to carry him to the new Dodge Charger Clarence used as his official police vehicle.

"Our little medical facility is closer than Wilmington. He needs attention *now*," Mac said. "He's been in the water a long time." Alain had been under water up to his chin for nearly six hours. "Obvious head trauma and hypothermia." Mac listened to the man's heart, ripping his shirt to show massive torso bruising.

"Chest trauma. Fluid buildup. This is bad. Move this crate, Clarence. I have to relieve the pressure on his heart."

He looked toward the vehicle. Clarence followed his gaze. The lawman said, "Hit the deer. Appears the antlers negated the airbag deployment and blocked steering. The driver's side door crashed into that large cypress. See the caved in door and the scarring on the tree bark."

Mac knelt on the floor of the backseat to do what he could as Clarence sped to the clinic.

53

Please, Wake Up

Amy sat at the kitchen table with her three girls, Ina Campbell, Jessica Campbell, Sherry Jones, Sunny Bankston and Mary Richter. Mary sat on Amy's lap, crying silently with her head on Amy's shoulder.

"He'll be all right," Amy comforted the child. "He has to be. We need him too much."

"I'm scared, Amy."

"Me too, sweetheart."

"Do you love my papa, Amy?"

Amy started to cry with Mary. "More than I realized."

Ina stood behind her former daughter-in-law and stroked her hair. "Have faith, darling. I know God didn't let you and Alain get together just to separate you."

"How can you be sure, Miss Ina? Look what happened with you and Ander." Amy began to sob. "And I'm so selfish. I haven't even given that to Alain. What's wrong with me? I love him so much. I just can't lose him."

Ina continued to stroke Amy's hair. "I had a dream when I was sick that I took care of my daughter. I didn't realize I had been doing just that with Sherry. I also dreamed that I took care of Nathaniel's daughter. I didn't know I had been for years. I love you, Amy. Alain loves you. He won't leave you. Have faith."

All eyes looked at Amy. "Is that why you left, Momma?" asked Betsy.

Amy nodded.

"So? We're just like Matthew and Mary?" Betsy continued.

Amy nodded. "We didn't know. Grandmother told me just before she died. I loved Tipper, but, God help me, I have loved Alain since I was a child. If Grandmother had never separated us when we were teenagers, none of us would have been hurt. Please understand?"

Betsy put her arms around Amy. "It doesn't matter. Please wake up, Momma. We're all family here, in one way or another."

"You are so grown-up." Amy kissed her daughter's cheek. "I love you so much, all of you."

Over the steadily drumming rain, the swoosh of multiple cars rushing into town could be heard. Amy jumped to her feet with Mary still on her lap.

The girl said, "I can walk, Momma Amy."

Amy loosened her grip on the child, and hand in hand they raced toward the clinic where the lights snapped on. Jessica followed closely behind, knowing her nursing skills would be needed.

The men carried Alain carefully into the clinic.

"Alain!" Amy screamed. "No! No!"

"Not now, Amy!" yelled Mac. "Tipper, keep her back so I can work."

Tipper held Amy and Mary firmly. "Let Mac work."

Mac ordered, "Jess, get Rocky here." He pointed Clarence and Gator toward the x-ray room. The two men carried Alain where the doctor ordered.

"What happened?" Amy gasped.

Tipper spoke calmly. "He must have lost control when he slammed on brakes to keep from hitting a deer. It didn't work. Deer's dead, and its antlers were through the windshield as well as jamming the steering wheel. The car was partially submerged in Cavalier Creek. He definitely has a head injury. He was wearing his seat belt, but the airbags were damaged by the deer's antlers. Mac said something about a chest injury causing fluid to build up around his heart. Mac's about to do surgery."

Dr. Rockford flew in the door. Within minutes, Mac came out. "Okay, Amy. The worst seems to be hemothorax, a massive chest contusion which has caused some fluid to build up around his heart. We have to relieve the pressure. We're gonna have to drain. He has a concussion, but it's not the worst. You have to sign the forms."

"Give them to me! Mac, don't let him die. Please?"

"That's the plan, Amy."

"Can I see him before surgery?"

"For a minute while we scrub. He's unconscious."

Amy went to Alain. He was deathly pale. His breathing was labored. Amy kissed his brow and stroked his hair. Tearfully she muttered, "Why are you so damned stubborn? I asked you to wait. Don't you leave me. I'm so sorry. I promise if you wake up, I'll be your wife in every way. I love you."

Mac said, "I heard that. You *do* love him. Let me work now, Amy."

Amy kissed Alain's lips softly. "I'll be waiting for you. Mary's with me. We need you."

While the sky lightened before dawn, Mac shook Amy as she dozed with her arms around Mary.

"Mac?"

"We drained the blood, and his lung is bruised. That was his only serious injury. He has a lot of abrasions and contusions, so he looks worse than he is. Keenan beat him worse than the bruises he has now."

"He's gonna live?"

"Yes. Go sit with him. Mary, you go see him for a minute too."

Amy took Mary with her. Each of them held one of Alain's hands, with Amy gently holding the one with the I.V. in it. Mary inhaled sharply when she saw her father. "Momma Amy, he has a tube in his side."

"It's okay, honey."

"Papa," said Mary. "Please wake up. I was so scared. I love you, Papa."

Amy kissed Alain. "Are you listening to your daughter? Please wake up, baby. You have so much to live for."

By sunrise, most of Alain's family was at the clinic. Mac said assertively, "I know y'all are worried, but there's not room here for everybody. Robert Lee, take Mary home with you. Make her sleep and eat. Amy is Alain's wife. She'll let you know when he wakes up."

"Is he gonna wake up, Mac?" asked Calvin.

"Yes, but call Matthew and Fay. Let them know what's happening."

Calvin's wife, the former Trish Jolson, who had walked to the Richters' door and asked for Calvin who had promised to marry her if she walked into Possum Holler, took Mary by the hand. "Come with me, darling. I lived. So will Alain." Mary left with her aunt Trish.

Mac peeked into Alain's room and listened as Amy sang "Time in a Bottle" to Alain. He continued to listen as she went through a list of songs, including, "If" and "Sometimes When We Touch."

Amy laid her head beside Alain's. "Alain Richter, wake up. I think you're faking it now because you like it when I sing to you. I'll sing to you every day if you'll just wake up. *Please* wake up? I need to tell you how much I love you. I can't do that if you won't wake up."

Mac entered and checked Alain's vital signs. He smirked and held up a finger to Amy and winked. "Well, Amy, it looks like I'm gonna have to insert another tube, a catheter. These things hurt like hell. Did you have a catheter with any of the girls?"

"No."

Mac got out a catheter kit. "See this? Imagine sliding this tube into Alain's penis. Ow! Ow! Ow! I wouldn't want one."

"Don't you use any Novocain?"

"No, not for this. If we used anesthesia, we wouldn't know if we inserted it correctly."

Alain grunted. "You just had to disturb my angel singing to me, didn't you?"

"Wake up!" Mac snapped.

Alain slowly opened his eyes. "Sorry, baby. I couldn't control my steering with the damned deer's antlers in the steering wheel. Did anyone get the deer to skin? It was a fair kill."

Mac chuckled.

Amy started crying. "Don't ever scare me like that again."

"Yes, ma'am. Mac, I need to talk to my wife. Alone."

"By all means. Throw your doctor out."

"When can I go home?"

"In a couple of days, probably."

54

I Want to Know What Love Is

"**What** do you want to say to me?" Amy asked after Mac left her and Alain alone.

"Say it. Say it now that I'm awake."

"I love you."

Alain closed his eyes. "The one song you haven't sung to me yet is Foreigner's 'I Want to Know What Love Is.' I might be a hillbilly, but I know more music than country and bluegrass. I do have a car radio."

"Maybe you could sing that one to me."

He opened his eyes. "Do you know it?"

"Yes."

"That's how I feel, Amy. I wanna know what love is. I want *you* to show me."

"I plan to as soon as you're able."

"I don't mean just sex, Amy."

"Neither do I. Scoot over. I've been up all night."

Alain scooted to give Amy room to lie beside him. He grunted for every muscle ached. She stretched out and covered Alain with her arm. Both slept.

Mac came in with a food tray for Alain. "Ahem! This is *not* a hotel. It's a hospital."

"This is good medicine, doc," Alain joked.

"Could be, but you need to eat right now. Amy, go home for a while. The rain has stopped."

Amy kissed Alain. "I'll be back later. I need to let your family know you're fine. I love you. You just keep remembering that."

"I'll try."

Amy made three trips to the new house to take her things. On the final trip, she took Elvis to his new home. She rubbed the Bassett hound's long ears. "Alain's just about perfect, Elvis. You are gonna love him. I love him. I love Alain Richter."

Amy hugged her dog. "Elvis, I think I've always loved him. I've just been so scared of being hurt again. I really wanna know what love is. Alain and I were meant to be. I feel so free."

Amy showered and changed into a bright red tank top and jeans before she went back to the hospital. Mary was with her father when Amy came in. She hugged Amy.

"That's nice," said Alain. "My two favorite ladies."

"Well," said Amy, "the younger lady needs to go with Uncle Calvin so she can get a good night's sleep and go to school tomorrow. He's waiting."

"Yes, ma'am. Good night, Papa."

"Good night, darling."

Mary went to get some rest. "Mm," sighed Alain. "Do I sense some bonding between you and my daughter?"

"She's wonderful. You've done a good job with her and Matthew."

"Thanks."

Mac came in again. "Are you gonna stay the night, Amy?"

"Absolutely."

"It's not necessary. Rocky has the night shift."

"Mac, I'm staying with my husband. I would be lost out there in the dark in that king-size bed all alone." Amy winked at Alain.

"I hear you." Mac snickered.

"When can I take him home?"

"A couple of days. I'll take his drainage tube out in the morning."

"Did anyone get Fay on the phone? I talked to Matthew. I made him stay at school."

"Thank you," said Alain.

"Jess talked to Fay," said Mac. "She convinced her not to cut her honeymoon short."

"Good," grunted Alain.

"Grouchy," teased Amy.

"I hurt all over," Alain complained. "I wanna sleep in my own bed with my wife."

"I get it," laughed Mac. "You *are* newlyweds. When I release you, there will be restrictions."

"Like?"

"Take it easy."

"Oh, come on! Surely sex will not be off limits."

Mac chortled. "We'll see." He handed Alain a couple of pills. "Take these and go to sleep. Amy, feel free to snuggle up with him. Good night. I'm leaving you to your brother-in-law. Rocky and Glenda still amaze me. They're like oil and water, but they seem to work, just like you and Amy."

Alain fell asleep quickly, and Amy stepped out. "Mac?"

"I'm leaving."

"Hold up. What restrictions?"

"No driving for two weeks. That's so the anesthesia can get completely out of his system. No operating machinery. He'll have to stay away from the brewery. You can have sex if he has no trouble breathing. I was teasing him."

"Good."

Mac laughed. Amy sighed. "We haven't."

"Why not?"

"Did Tipper tell you about us?"

"Yes, I know."

"Well, I guess I still feel dirty."

"Don't, Amy. It wasn't your fault."

She crossed her arms across her chest and rubbed both upper arms vigorously as if she were freezing. "Did he tell you Roscoe raped me?"

"That too. He was a bastard. Talk to Sunny."

"Why?"

"She was raped in college. You need support. You, Sunny, and Fay should sit down together."

"I need Alain. When we started to have sex, I had flashbacks to Roscoe. Is that normal?"

"Yeah, but Alain loves you. He would never hurt you."

"I love him too, Mac."

"So, go into the city and buy some sexy lingerie and knock him off his feet. Show the man how much you love him."

Amy hugged Mac. "You really are our homegrown healer, aren't you?"

"I suppose. I know this—you belong with Alain. Remember when we were thirteen and you told me you wanted Alain, and I pretended to kiss you because your mother was watching?"

"Yeah, I do."

"Even at thirteen, you loved him. Amy, honestly, did you ever think of him when you were with Tipper?"

"A few times."

"So, open your heart all the way. Take the plunge. It's worth the risk."

"I wanna know what love is, Mac. For me, only Alain can show me."

"And only *you* can show him."

55

A Real Marriage

Amy slept beside Alain that night. The arrangement was tedious, but she refused to leave. The next morning Mac examined Alain thoroughly.

"Well?" asked Alain impatiently.

"One more day at least. You still have a little rumble in your chest."

"I'm fine."

"Really? Take a deep breath and hold it."

Alain breathed as deeply as he could.

"Uh-hum," the doctor gloated

Alain let the breath out. "You sadistic bastard. Now I hurt."

"One more day if you can breathe well enough." Mac handed his patient a breathing machine. "Ten deep breaths now and ten again this afternoon and tonight. Take the pain meds I gave you."

"Stop arguing with your doctor," asserted Amy. "I want you healed."

Alain grinned. "Yes, Mac, this is a real marriage. She's nagging."

Amy folded her arms across her chest. "Mac, if I hit him and he gasps hard will that help him heal?"

"I wish it were that simple. *I'd* hit him."

Amy kissed Alain. "Listen to Mac. I have some errands. I shall return."

Amy drove into Wilmington. First, she met with Alain's insurance agent. The Camry had been totaled. She then set about finding a new car for Alain, settling on a red Escalade to be delivered that afternoon. Her reasoning was that the vehicle was larger, and red would be easier to spot in an emergency.

Next, she visited the attorney who had drawn up her divorce papers and got him to help her with a will. Alain's close brush with death made her aware of the need to have her affairs in order. As a part of putting her finances straight she visited a different insurance agent and took out three life insurance policies, one with Alain as beneficiary, one with her children as beneficiaries, and one with Tipper as beneficiary.

With the serious, yea, morbid, tasks accomplished, Amy turned to a pleasant endeavor. She booked her and Alain on a Caribbean cruise to sail in two weeks from Miami. By then, Fay and Royce would be back to care for Mary.

In anticipation of a belated honeymoon, Amy shopped. She bought appropriate clothes for the cruise for both herself and her husband. Then, she bought lingerie: a long, slinky, scarlet negligee; a teddy in royal blue with black lace trim; a pink silk baby doll pajama set; and a black leather bustier complete with garter belt, thong, fishnet stockings, stiletto-heeled knee-high boots, and riding crop made of satin. As an afterthought, she bought two long black silk scarves. She also bought silk boxers in red, blue, black, and green for Alain. She chuckled. "You wanted sex? Boy! Are you in for a surprise!"

The clerk commented, "That's a variety."

"Honeymoon."

"Congratulations."

"Thank you."

Amy got back to Possum Holler at dusk. "Where have you been?" Alain demanded. "I was worried a damned deer ran in front of you."

"Nope." She kissed him and handed him the tickets for the cruise. "I was arranging our honeymoon."

Alain looked at the tickets and read the brochure. "What if I get seasick?"

"Mac'll give us some Dramamine. We'll have fun and be back before Harvest Fest where I want a private hayride."

"Planning a trip?" Mac asked as he checked on his patient.

Alain passed over the brochure. "Amy wants to get me in the middle of the ocean."

"Looks like fun. You'll be ready by then."

Mac let Alain go home Friday afternoon. Mary accompanied her father and stepmother. Once to the house, Amy ensconced Alain in their bed and settled Mary in one of the girls' rooms.

"When will your girls come, Momma Amy?"

"Tipper and I decided to wait until Alain and I get back from our trip."

"Will we all be here at one time?"

"I hope so. We can drive your papa crazy with all kinds of girl stuff."

"Like painting fingernails and toenails?"

"That's just one thing. Betsy's starting to wear a little makeup. You should too. We can buy new clothes and have a fashion show. We can play girl games."

Mary laughed. "Are you and Papa gonna have a baby?"

"Maybe."

"Momma and Daddy Royce can't. Momma says he was sick. Is it because he's too old?"

"No. He had mumps when he was young."

"Then, how did he have you?"

"I was a gift he accepted."

"Is that what y'all were talking about the night Papa got hurt?"

"Yes."

"Momma Amy, is Tipper your brother?"

Amy was quiet for a moment. "There are no real secrets in Possum Holler, are there? Yes, he is."

"It doesn't matter. Betsy's my best friend, and, I think, one day she might be my sister-in-law because Matthew really likes her."

"That'll be just fine. I like you and Matthew."

"Momma Amy, do you think Daddy Royce and Momma might be able to have a miracle?"

"You know"—She patted her stepdaughter's hand—"Dr. Mac might be able to help. I'll talk to Fay when they get back. Mary, do you realize we never got to eat our cookies? Let's make some more and share with Papa."

Smelling the aroma of chocolate chip cookies, Alain ambled to the kitchen.

"What are you doing?" Amy scolded.

"Mac didn't say I have to stay in bed, just take it easy. I'm sitting in a chair. I'm waiting for a fresh, hot cookie."

While the cookies baked, Amy made BLT's for supper. Then, the three of them wolfed down a plate of hot cookies with cold milk.

Amy shooed Mary to bed at ten and forced Alain back to bed. "Alone at last," he said.

"Not quite alone. Mary's upstairs."

"Oh, no. You don't get off that easily. That door has a lock on it."

"Alain! You can wait for our honeymoon."

Alain scowled. "I'm so damned rusty, I need the practice."

Amy laughed. "Pouting will not work on me."

"Do you really want to wait ten more days?"

"You need a shower."

"I'll need your help."

"Uh-hum."

"What if I should get dizzy? Or have trouble breathing?"

"Oh, play it up." Amy held out her hand. "Come on."

Alain let the hot water beat on his back. "This feels good. Mmm. The vision before me looks good."

Amy scowled. "Take your shower. I'm sorry, but seeing those bruises reminds me of a rafting trip."

Amy lathered her hands and began to wash Alain. "Oh," he moaned when she touched him. "I remember when you did that on my fourteenth birthday."

Amy kissed Alain's chest. "I remember. Mmm." She smirked. "It appears the little worm grew."

"Worm? This worm needs a little tunnel to hide in."

"You must be a poet with all the metaphors."

They stepped from the shower. Alain maneuvered Amy backward toward the bed.

"Grab a towel," Amy said.

"No." Alain gently pushed Amy onto the bed. Once again, his mouth found her breasts and trailed down her torso until his tongue probed her soft folds and he found her throbbing clitoris.

"Oh, my God," breathed Amy as a warm tingling spread over her.

Alain's tongue found the perfect rhythm, and he added fingers to his seduction as Amy tilted to match his cadence.

Amy felt as if she were floating, and a meteor shower took place around her as she exploded with passion. She could hardly breathe as she stuttered, "Alain! Now!" And he was inside her. Each stroke intensified as the yearning of a lifetime came to fruition. Amy bit into Alain's shoulder to keep from screaming as her entire body jerked as if an electrical shock pulsated through her at the same moment Alain throbbed in climax and buried his face breathlessly in her neck.

Half an hour later, Alain lay beside his wife and caressed her body. "Am I dreaming?" he whispered.

"If you are, I am. Don't wake me. Nothing has ever felt so perfect."

"Mmm. I'd like to volunteer for seconds, but I'm exhausted."

"We have a honeymoon coming and ten days before that. You definitely need practice."

Alain chuckled. "I promised not to die before I fucked your brains out."

Amy gurgled, "I still have my brains. You have lots of work to do. I love you. Sweet dreams, darling."

56
The You I See

On Monday, Fay and Royce returned. Amy hated to see Mary leave for she had enjoyed sharing Alain's family.

As they ate supper alone Monday night, Amy commented, "I see so much of you in Mary and Matthew."

"That could be Fay you see."

"I don't mean physical appearance, although Matthew is your spitting image. You've instilled excellent qualities in them."

Alain chuckled. Wearing jeans and a green and black striped polo shirt, he pushed back from the table as Amy cleared the dishes. "Leave them. Come here." He patted his leg for Amy to sit on his lap.

Amy sat on Alain's lap and laced her fingers around his neck. He kissed her softly. "What do you see when you look at me? What would you paint if you painted me?"

"I plan to paint you on the beach in Jamaica. You'll have to wait to see."

"All right, but tell me what you see."

"A gift from Heaven crafted directly by the Hand of God. Your eyes are like emeralds, and when I look into them, I feel fresh like new spring grass. I can taste the delicate sweetness of caramel when my lips brush against your hair." She paused.

"Continue, please. You sound like a poet."

"You're my inspiration, my love."

"As you have always been mine."

"Your skin is like golden filigree on marbled muscle. Your lips are sweeter than honey and more refreshing than the early morning dew."

"Mmm. You're giving me ideas."

"Oh? Would this stimulate the process of those ideas into action?" Amy unzipped Alain's jeans and slid her hand inside. "My world explodes in a kaleidoscope of joy when I feel you inside me."

"That's it." Alain carried Amy to bed.

At the end of the week, Amy and Alain dropped Elvis at the Campbell residence and drove to Miami to meet their cruise ship. When the captain realized he had an internationally acclaimed artist and a best-selling author, as both Alain's books were on the *New York Times* bestsellers' list, Amy Dent and Alain Richter had dinner at the captain's table the first night.

Amy wore a crimson crepe evening dress to Alain's tuxedo. "My, you clean up well," Amy complimented.

"Thank you, ma'am, and I do like you in red. You set me on fire."

"Later. Let's get this over with. Did you wear the red boxers?"

"Yes, dear. I can take a hint."

"That way, we match."

"My love, we are a perfect match—period."

Alain struggled through the social nuances of dinner until he realized everyone at the table expected him to be eccentric since they thought most authors were, especially if the author was married to an equally eccentric artist. They had no idea that he simply did not know which fork to use. To escape people he considered downright weird, Alain escorted Amy to the dance floor.

"Whew! How many times have I stuck my foot in my mouth?" he laughed.

"They think you're charming. You *are* charming. Are you ready to make an exit?"

"As soon as I show you what Felicia Norton taught me." With the reggae music, Alain turned in an acceptable samba to Amy's delight.

Back in their cabin, Alain quickly doffed the tux in lieu of only a pair of silk boxers. Amy exited the bathroom wearing the scarlet negligee.

Alain's gaze raked over her. "So we match?"

"So I can set you on fire."

It seemed the room exploded with spontaneous combustion.

Not being tied to a social engagement for the rest of the cruise, Alain and Amy chose the casino and dressy casual clothes for one evening. Amy had laid out Alain's royal blue boxers and surprised him with the blue teddy. "Damn, woman! Do you plan to keep this up when we get home?"

"For the rest of your life."

"I pray for a long life."

They had a three-day stay in Jamaica in a private beach house. The first night there, Amy laid out the green boxers on the bed for Alain. "I could bypass these," he teased.

"But I like the way they feel against your skin," Amy said from the bathroom.

"In that case, I'll give up all other kinds."

"Mmm. Then, I won't be able to keep my hands off you."

Amy wore her pink baby doll pajamas. "Oh," breathed Alain. "Are you trying to project innocence?"

"Pink and green complement so well."

The next morning, Amy pulled Alain from bed early. "Up!"

"Why? Let's sleep in."

"I have painting to do."

"What do you want me to wear?"

"Your skin."

"Nude?"

"Yes."

"Are you gonna show it?"

"Possibly, but I'll never sell it."

Amy positioned Alain so the sunrise would be at his back. "Yes! Just like I envisioned it."

After an hour, Alain asked, "Do I get a coffee break? I'm starving."

"Don't move."

Amy brought a tray of croissants and fruit with coffee. Alain had not flinched. "How am I supposed to eat?"

"Take a break."

"Thank you, oh, slave driver."

After midday, Alain went on strike. He refuse to pose without payment. Payment took the rest of the day.

Amy re-posed Alain the next morning, but she had breakfast waiting. Afternoon brought payment. She lay in Alain's arms that night. He asked, "Is the painting finished?"

"No, but I can do the rest when we get home."

The three days back on the ship were spent by the pool. The last night aboard ship, Amy and Alain visited the karaoke bar. Alain kissed Amy's hand and bounded on stage. He selected Chicago's "You're the Inspiration."

He went into the crowd to kneel by Amy and serenade her. Caressing her thigh as he sang sent warmth over her body.

Alain stood and walked to the other side of his wife as the song progressed.

The crowd erupted with applause at the conclusion. As Alain returned the microphone to the stage, an older lady beside their table said to Amy, "That was sweet."

Amy nodded. "We're on our honeymoon."

"Congratulations. You should return the compliment."

"Yes, I should."

Amy kissed Alain as they passed each other. She picked up the microphone and started to scan the repertoire of songs but shook her head. In a sensuous á cappella she stood beside her husband and sang Roberta Flack's "The First Time Ever I Saw Your Face."

The bar patrons were perfectly quiet as she whispered to Alain at the end of the song, "I love you so much."

They left the bar wrapped in each other. "What do you plan to wear tonight to match my black boxers?" Alain asked.

"Just wait."

When Amy appeared in her mock dominatrix lingerie, Alain's mouth dropped. "Whoa!"

Amy forced him onto the bed and swiftly knotted one scarf around one wrist and tied the other end to the bed.

"What are you doing?" Alain teased.

"Having my way with you."

"The four-poster would be better for this."

"Scared?"

"Bring it."

Amy sighed as they drove into Possum Holler. "It feels good to be home."

"Wear the black tonight."

Amy laughed.

As Alain checked in at the brewery and came home to begin *Honor Bound*, Amy finished her painting of him. She propped it on the dresser and went to the den to wrap her arms around her husband. "I have something in the bedroom to show you."

"That sounds promising."

"Come see."

Alain stared at the painting entitled "The You I See."

"You can't be serious," he murmured.

"That's how I see you."

The golden glow of the sunrise on the Jamaican beach formed the background for a bronze angel with piercing emerald eyes and caramel hair. In the perfectly chiseled muscles could be seen fine, thin battle scars where the angel had taken the punishment for those he loved. The feathery wings added to the aura of warmth, comfort, and safety. Though the angel's body was bare, the connotation was not sexual, but ethereal.

"I am no angel, Amy."

"You are to me." Amy slipped Alain's shirt off his shoulders. With her index fingertip she gently traced one of the fine white scars from where he had frequently been beaten as a child and either the switch or the strap had cut the skin. She whispered, "'By his stripes we are healed.'"

"Those were not my stripes."

"No, but your love has healed my broken spirit. I can't imagine the suffering you endured."

"You upheld me so often. When you touch me, all my scars fade to oblivion."

"Then, let me touch you. Let me love you."

Softly and tenderly, Alain and Amy found a moment of Heaven.

57

On the Map

Ron and Felicia Norton drove in the week before Christmas.

Felicia wanted to check the progress of Easy Street Estates and deliver gifts for Chambry and her friends.

"Hey!" laughed Ron. "Did you guys know there's a sign on the highway showing the turn off to Possum Holler?"

"Truly?" asked Mac. "It wasn't there two days ago when I went to Wilmington."

"It is today."

"Where's Alain?" asked Felicia.

"His house with his wife," answered Sunny coyly.

"That's what I want to talk to him about. He did the deed without us."

Sunny laughed. "Yes. He sort of had to pin Amy down."

"And what about his wreck?"

"He's fine, Felicia," assured Mac.

"He deserves to be happy."

"Well, I haven't seen him without a smile since his accident."

"How's the construction going?" Felicia kept up her interrogation.

"Eight of the houses are ready to be occupied. Three are occupied." Mac sighed.

"Calvin, Robert Lee, and who else?"

"Simon."

"Has Betsy named the new road to Alain's house yet?" asked Ron, appreciating Betsy's imagination. He liked her logo design for Tipper's business so much he set up a trust fund with one percent of each bottle sold going into it for the girl.

Mac nodded. "Hideaway Lane, and the area by the clubhouse is officially a park, Hillbilly Haven. The clubhouse is being transformed into a play structure for kids."

Ron laughed. "When all is settled, we need to get an aerial shot and make a map of Possum Holler."

"Are you staying for Christmas?"

"I wish," said Ron. "Both sets of grandparents will be at our house. Felicia's folks are already complaining because this is your year for Christmas with Chambry."

"Too bad," said Mac.

As they chatted, Alain and Amy drove into town. Mac snickered. "Well, Felicia, the gang's all here."

"Ha, ha!" Felicia retorted, but she marched out to the Escalade. "New car?"

Alain rolled his eyes. "I guess you heard I totaled the Camry."

"And got married without sending me an invitation."

"Oops."

Felicia hugged both of them. "Please, tell me you have some pictures?"

"Yes, thanks to Sunny and her digital camera." Alain grinned. "You should see my portrait."

Felicia eyed Amy. "Is it nude?"

"Yeah. It's hanging in our bedroom. It's not for sale," Amy replied firmly.

"I'll drive out."

Amy smirked. "You'll be very surprised."

Matthew Richter drove home from Yale for Christmas break. He pulled into the visitor's center as he crossed into West Virginia for a rest stop. Just to stretch his legs for a moment, he looked at the gifts and souvenirs.

Matthew chuckled when he saw both his father's books for sale. "They're really good," commented a young blonde woman who worked at the center.

"I know," replied Matthew.

The girl extended her hand. "Bobbie Marley."

Matthew laughed out loud. "You poor thing. You must get teased mercilessly about your name."

"I'm a girl."

"At least you can get married and change it."

"Who says I want to?"

"Your prerogative. Matthew Richter." He tapped the book jacket. "My father."

"Really?"

"Yes. I'm headed back to Possum Holler right now for Christmas."

"Are the stories true?"

"In his book?"

The woman nodded.

"Yes, they are."

"So, you grew up like that?"

"Like?"

"Backward?"

"I'm not sure. We were poor, and we had no running water or electricity. However, we were loved. I have never doubted my father's or my mother's love. Can you say that?"

The woman looked taken aback. "I didn't mean to insult you."

Matthew inclined his head. The woman continued, "You might be interested in a new map of West Virginia."

"Why?"

"Possum Holler's on the map."

"No? Show me."

The woman unfolded a new map of West Virginia and pointed out Possum Holler. Matthew laughed. "It's barely a pin prick. I'll take a dozen."

Matthew pulled to a stop beside the Escalade. "Well!" exclaimed Alain, embracing his son. "Home for the holiday?"

"Yes, sir, and I brought a surprise."

Matthew handed a map to Alain, Mac, Felicia, Gator, Tipper, Leo, Clarence, and the rest to Royce since everyone seemed to be congregated. "We're on the map."

After a moment of finding Possum Holler in print, the group dispersed to their appointed tasks. Gator snagged Royce, "Hey, may I have one of the maps?"

"Sure, but why?"

"I'm sending it to Corky."

Matthew visited with his mother before he drove to his father's house. Once there, he viewed his father's portrait.

"Very nice, Amy." Matthew grinned. "I wonder if Betsy will ever paint me."

Amy popped him on the arm. He laughed.

Before she left for New York, Felicia made a trip to see Alain's completed house and portrait. She loved the way Amy had finished the house and gawked at the painting.

"Amy, it's better than Tipper's."

"Why?"

"I don't know. I don't see it as erotic. Tipper's portraits were, um, hot. Alain's is comforting. Is that how you see him?"

"And so much more. Felicia, I never thought I'd love again, but I can't imagine my life without him."

"I understand. I feel the same about Ron. You know, he wants to move here."

"Do it. You've helped to put this place on the map. You've practically designed Possum Holler."

"Things have changed, haven't they?"

"Some."

Felicia smiled thoughtfully. "I wish Grandma Newton could see it. She would be gloating."

"Yeah. She'd love to be on the map. She'd be so proud of Mac, Tipper, Gator, and Alain."

"And you."

Amy gave a one-shoulder shrug. "She knew about Tipper and me."

"Figures. She somehow knew *everything*."

"Then, I bet she knows we're on the map."

On Christmas Day, Gator's phone rang. When he answered the voice on the other end said, "Nice Christmas present, little brother. So, Possum Holler is actually on the map?"

"Yep, and you have a promise to keep now."

"Where would I live?"

"Easy Street Estates. The homes are quite nice in the subdivision Felicia designed."

"Subdivision? In Possum Holler?"

"Yep. It's out Richter Road."

"Yeah. Alain Richter has become a household name. I read the two books. Gator, I'm sorry I left you, and I'm so glad you didn't endure the hardship Alain did."

"Corky, I turned out okay. So did Alain, Mac, and Tipper. I told you we'd put Possum Holler on the map. We did. Now, will you keep your word?"

"What would I do if I were to come back to this little pin prick on the map?" Corky laughed.

"Work with me at Jones's Processing. Help me manage Jones's Hog Farm. Matlock's only running it for me. It's still mine. Be my partner, Corky. You did retain twenty percent interest in the plant."

There was silence on the line for a moment. "All right. Letha says she could be happy there; she's from a small hamlet in Germany. I have a little over three years left to retirement after thirty years in the military. You pick me out a house on Easy Street, and I'll come home."

"Will that be General Jones?"

"I hope I make general before I retire."

"You won't be going to Iraq or Afghanistan, will you?"

"I doubt it. They like me here in the Pentagon."

"Okay, then. Three years. You promise?"

"Promise. At least now I won't drop off the face of the map."

58

Have a Cigar

The third year for Tipper's New Year's Eve party took on a new direction as several smaller parties joined to make a community celebration. Moreover, Ron Norton came back for New Year's Eve rather than ringing in the New Year at one of his clubs.

Alain teased Tipper. "You created a monster."

"It's a good thing," Tipper argued. "Besides, I have no one to match-make for this year."

"Your matchmaking attempts were not wholly successful."

"Fifty percent."

"Relinquishing the job?"

"Yes. Mac's happy; you're happy; Gator's always been happy; I'm happy. Mission accomplished."

As the men congregated to discuss business and politics, the women jabbered about the children and the new homes.

Felicia poked Amy. "Hey! No glum expression. What's wrong?"

"Nothing."

"Uh-hum."

"Y'all seem so content. All of you here except Fay and me have given your husbands a son to carry on the family name. Unless Mac can help Daddy and Fay, they won't ever have a child together."

"Do you want to have a baby with Alain?"

"Can you imagine how excited he would be?"

Felicia watched the men talk. "Yes, I can, but do you want it?"

Amy was quiet for a time. "Yes, I do."

"Then, work on it, honey!" Felicia laughed.

"That's not a problem. As a matter of fact, I think I'll take my husband home at twelve-oh-one."

At twelve-oh-two, Felicia tapped Amy. "Take Matthew with you before Tipper turns around."

"What?"

Amy and Alain realized that Matthew and Betsy were wishing each other a happy New Year.

"Shit!" muttered Alain, and he strode to interrupt Betsy's first kiss.

Betsy waved as Alain dragged Matthew away. "Be glad Tipper didn't see that," Alain snarled in his son's ear.

"Relax, Papa. It was only a kiss."

"That's how it starts. Tipper already told you she has to be sixteen to date."

"Yes, but I can visit at the house."

"Matthew, I have no desire to be a grandfather any time soon."

"I promise there are no cigars in my near future. You're overreacting." Matthew smiled. "Amy?"

Amy glowered. "At least you weren't sneaking. You kissed her in the open."

Betsy slipped her arm around Amy. "We aren't hiding, Momma."

"You're too young."

"Okay. Relax."

"First kiss?"

"Yes, ma'am."

Amy led Betsy away. "How was it?"

Betsy giggled. "I liked it."

"You really like him, don't you?"

"Yes, ma'am. He's handsome and smart and sweet. He gave me perfume called Heaven Scent for Christmas."

"What did you give him?"

"A leather journal."

"Appropriate but be glad it was Alain that saw y'all kissing."

"I am."

"Don't get that boy in trouble."

"Yes, ma'am."

Amy kissed Betsy on the forehead. Then, she gave Alain the come-hither finger. "Let's go home."

Alain looked back at Matthew who had joined his mother. Amy rubbed Alain's arm. "He'll be along. I trust him."

A few days after the New Year, Amy popped into the clinic. "Mac, you got a sec?"

"Sure. Are you sick?"

"No."

"Do you need a doctor?"

"Maybe."

"Come on back. What seems to be the problem?"

"I think I'm pregnant."

"Do you want to be?"

"It will make Alain happy."

"Not what I asked."

She scrunched her face in thought. "I want to have a baby with Alain, but I'm still a little shaky and scared."

"Do you love him, Amy, I mean, completely?"

"I have always loved him."

"Then, let's see if you have a little gift. When was your last period?"

"Thanksgiving."

"So, you're a little over a week late?" He laughed out loud. "Jumping the gun, I'd say."

"Yes, but I'm never late."

"I want to do a blood test because it's so early. It'll be more accurate."

"Okay."

Mac checked Amy thoroughly and left her alone a few minutes. When he returned, he asked, "How do you feel?"

"Fine."

"Not sick?"

"No. So, I am?" She raised her eyebrows.

"Yep. You know your body. You're due the end of August."

"Anniversary baby?"

"Could be."

"How do I tell Alain? Don't you say a word to anybody. It's *his* news."

"I'm bound by oath, Amy. I have an idea. Give him a cigar."

"He doesn't smoke, and he quit chewing."

"Thank Felicia for that. Tie a pink ribbon to one end and a blue ribbon to the other. Your doctor is still in Wilmington."

"No, my doctor's right here."

"You sure?"

"Yes, Mac."

"I'd love to." Mac gave Amy a bottle of vitamins. "Are you still taking antidepressants?"

"No. They didn't help."

"That's because you were never clinically depressed. It was situational. Your whole life has found its course. Most of your stress has evaporated. So, you know the drill. I'll see you as your doctor in a month."

"Mac, did Fay and Daddy talk to you?"

"Yes."

"Can you help?"

"Oath, Amy."

"Gotcha."

Amy stopped by the store and bought a cigar. She passed Alain coming into the brewery and blew him a kiss. At home, she stared in the refrigerator. She realized she didn't know

Alain's favorite food. He never complained about anything she cooked.

"Oh, well," she sighed. She got out chicken breasts to roast in mushroom gravy, opened a jar of Ina's green beans, made banana pudding, baked biscuits, and made rice.

Alain came in as Amy pulled the biscuits from the oven. "Something smells good!" he called.

"I hope you're hungry."

He came into the kitchen and put his arms around Amy, kissing her neck. "I'm hungry for *you*."

She laughed. "You can have that after supper. I made a special meal."

"I wait with anticipation."

Alain devoured the meal. Amy laughed. "Is there any food you don't like?"

Alain thought. "I've never found one, except, maybe, beets. Oh, and oatmeal. I despise oatmeal."

Amy scrunched up her face. "Even oatmeal raisin cookies?"

Alain nodded. "Kinda. It was at Tipper's last New Year's Eve party that I ate something with oatmeal in it since Pa died. Mrs. Tomlin had made these little bite-sized fudge-looking things. She called them 'clean your teeth cookies' because they were so rich you have to clean your teeth after eating them. She started telling me the ingredients and suddenly stopped with a funny look on her face. I turned around to see Fay standing behind me with a sly grin on her face. Mrs. Tomlin said, 'Try one. They're only one bite.' I couldn't hurt her feelings, but I didn't trust Fay. So, I tried one, and they were delicious. Then I found out they had oatmeal in them, along with chocolate and peanut butter. I couldn't believe it. I muttered, 'They have oatmeal, disgusting, slimy oatmeal?' She nodded and then coerced me into taking three bites of a huge oatmeal raisin cookie." He held up his hands as if in surrender. "Okay. It was good. So, I'll eat dry, baked oatmeal, but I will *never* eat cooked oatmeal again. Pa used to force us to eat oatmeal and then drag us to the field with no more food for six hours. So, baby, if you want oatmeal for breakfast, feel free to eat it, but don't expect me to eat it with you."

Amy laughed. "What's your favorite?"

"Anything you make."

"Alain."

"I love lasagna, but I've only had it in restaurants."

"I'll give it a try next time. Did I just say that?"

"What are you babbling about?"

"This'll have to do this time." Amy handed Alain a long narrow box. "A gift for you."

"What's the occasion?" Alain opened the box to see the cigar with pink and blue ribbons. He looked at Amy strangely.

She grinned. "Why would I tell you to have a cigar?"

"Why would anybody? The things stink."

Amy put her hand on her head and laughed. "Why would you give your friends a cigar?"

"I wouldn't."

"Not even to announce the birth of a child?"

Alain put his hand to his mouth. "A baby? Us? Oh, my God!"

Alain jumped from his chair and knelt in front of Amy and caressed her abdomen. "When?" he asked in awe.

"The end of August."

"Oh, Amy, thank you."

"For what?"

"Making me the happiest man alive. I love you so much."

Amy lifted Alain's face to hers and kissed him. "I love you more than I ever knew was possible."

Sunday at the dinner on the grounds as they always had after church, Alain handed all his friends cigars. Mac cackled. "You're celebrating early, aren't you?"

"Oh, hush and have a cigar. I'll do it again when he or she arrives. It's not fair that you knew before me."

"I didn't say a word."

"I am excited." Alain noticed the chattering women. "I wonder if she's giving them cigars."

"They have bubblegum ones in pink and blue."

"Great idea! I can tell every citizen in Possum Holler to have a cigar."

59
Honorary Class Members

Sunny Reardon had been secretly campaigning since Alain and Gator had taken their high-school equivalency tests. She was determined that they be official members of the graduating class with Mac, Tipper, and Amy.

After petitioning, the school, the county superintendent, and the school board, she called Marvin Spalding and told him the runaround she had received.

"Mrs. Reardon," he said. "I'll take care of it."

"Thank you, Dr. Spalding. You know as well as I these two men deserve this. Both of them are working on college degrees online, as is Tipper."

"I've got it covered. I'll call you back."

"I look forward to your call."

Dr. Spalding did not call Sunny Reardon. However, forty-eight hours after their conversation, the county superintendent of education and the principal of the county high school drove into Possum Holler and went directly to Sunny's office.

"To what do I owe this dubious pleasure?" Sunny asked sarcastically.

"Mrs. Reardon," said the superintendent, "is there any way you can get Mr. Jones and Mr. Richter here?"

"Easily."

"Please do so."

"Why?" asked Sunny as she sat down and indicated chairs for the two men.

"We wish to present them with honorary diplomas and class memberships."

"I see." She gave them an insincere smile. "Would you like to make the presentation in public?"

"How so?"

"Mayor Dent could facilitate a brief ceremony."

"You're angry with us."

"What gave you a clue?"

"Your tone of voice and the scathing look."

"Just a little," she admitted. "I realize you can't do this for *every* dropout, but considering what these two men have overcome and accomplished, I would have thought you would have been enthusiastic. No, I had to go over your heads."

"Do they know what you've been trying to do?"

"No. Not a clue."

"Then, by all means, get your mayor and them outside the school in half an hour. We'll make the presentation in public. Marvin Spalding is ready to fire me."

"Good."

"He really likes Mr. Richter."

"Alain Richter is an exceptional breed. Have you read his books?"

"I just started."

"You'll see."

Sunny picked up the phone and called Royce, Alain, and Gator. Then, she called Amy. Sherry and Lauren. Within half an hour, a crowd had gathered in front of the school.

Mr. Bowden, the county superintendent, could hardly believe his eyes. "How did you do this?" he asked Sunny.

"This community is extremely supportive. So much has changed here."

"So it seems."

The two school officials approached Alain and Gator with Sunny. She said, "Alain, Gator, these gentlemen have something to say to you."

Bowden spoke loudly and clearly. "Mr. Alain Richter and Mr. Gator Jones, it is my pleasure to present you with honorary diplomas and class membership so that you are officially graduates with your friends, Dr. MacKenzie Reardon, Mr. Tipper Campbell, and Ms. Amy Dent. Congratulations."

Alain and Gator accepted the pieces of paper humbly. As the officials left, Alain whispered to Sunny, "Were you behind this?"

She shrugged. "You deserve it. They'll be having a fifteen-year class reunion in June. You need to be there."

"It wasn't necessary."

"Do you mind?"

"No. Thank you. I'd like to see the faces of a few of the guys I remember. We Possum Holler kids weren't very popular until Mac and Tipper hit."

"Well, you know I love Mac, but you and Gator have proven yourselves. I thought you should be a part of the class."

"Well, thanks a million. I imagine this means a lot to Gator. He always wanted to be a part."

"You didn't?"

Alain nodded. "I did, but I was…"

"What, Alain?"

"I always thought my skin was tougher. I endured so much, but being a part of this group means the world to me. Thank you for making sure we're honorary class members."

Amy slipped her hand into Alain's. "You just keep getting honors."

"The biggest is yet to come."

"What would that be?" asked Sunny.

Alain kissed Amy's cheek. "Being a father again."

Sunny shook her head teasingly. "I thought you were going to say winning a Nobel Prize for literature with your next book."

"I wouldn't turn it down. It's almost ready."

"I'll get it off to River as soon as you give it to me."

"A couple of more weeks."

"I can't wait."

60

Honor Bound

Tipper opened the small ivory envelope to find an invitation to his fifteen-year class reunion. Folded inside was a personal note:

Tipper;

I've been hearing good things about you. Have you achieved your goal early? If so, surprise me. I'll be in attendance at every function. It would also make me quite happy if you were to bring your lovely mother to the family picnic. I look forward to seeing you.

Eli Bounds

"Wow!" Tipper murmured. "I'm honor bound in ten years, but have I reached my goal? I'll have to get Ron to check."

Not only did Tipper receive an invitation, but Mac, Amy, Alain, and Gator received invitations. Alain's also included a personal note:

Alain,

Please, come and bring your family (your children) to the family picnic. I plan to be there. Once again, I'm pleased you proved me wrong. You make me proud to have come from Possum Koller. I hope to see you in June.

Daneen Butler Spalding

P. S.

Drag Gator and his family with you.

Alain knocked on Gator's door and handed him the note. "I suppose we're honor bound to go, huh? I mean, considering what Sunny did and all."

"I guess," said Gator.

"Well, I'm going."

"And you'll drag me along."

"You don't mind."

"Naa. I just wish Miss Stone would be there. She's the first one who cared."

"Maybe Mrs. Spalding can find her. I'll write her," Alain said.

"Yeah, do that. Let's drag Mrs. Tomlin with us."

"Good idea."

"I have work to do." Gator made a shooing motion. "I have a business to run."

Alain laughed and stood to leave Gator's office. "Me too. I have a book to write."

Amy slipped her arms around Alain as he typed. "How much longer?"

Alain hit a few more keys and the printer icon. "Finished."

"You have worked eighteen hours a day to finish."

"I was inspired."

"Well, you need a break."

"Yes, I do."

"Come on. I'll race you."

A man of his word, Alain entered Sunny's office the next morning with his printed manuscript and a disc of *Honor Bound.*

"Done?" asked Sunny.

"Yep. First draft, anyway."

Sunny flipped to the dedication page and gasped when she read:

> *For Sunny, my agent, mentor, and friend, and a woman who showed me I was honor bound to achieve.*

"Alain, thank you. This means so much to me."

"It's very little for such a wonderful lady."

"I didn't do anything."

"Yes, you did. You forgave me and gave me another chance."

"Alain, once I got to know the real you, it was easy to be your friend."

"Even with all the baggage?"

"Do you know how much I admire you? I don't think I could've dealt with all you have."

Alain laughed. "You dealt with being shot and your mother."

Sunny giggled. "You helped with Mom. What did you give her?"

"I passed a joint with her."

"Passed?"

"Yeah. Call it self-medicating."

"Does Amy know?"

"I haven't needed it lately."

"Amy was what you needed."

"Yes, ma'am." He gave a quick nod.

Sunny sighed. "As for being shot, Mac healed me physically and then emotionally. I know you're aware of what happened, but I'm going to share a little secret—I was in love with my principal. He was killed. So, you see, I do know what it's like to lose a loved one to violence."

"Secret?"

"Not from Mac or my family, but I don't share that with everyone."

"Thanks for considering me worthy." He gave her a radiant smile.

"Well, I'll get this to River. Alain Richter, I am richer for having known you." Sunny laughed.

"What?"

"Maybe you should write about your life, culminating with your vows to Amy. Rather than *For Richer or Poorer*, make it *For Richter or Poorer*."

Alain guffawed. "Sunny, that is the worst pun I've ever heard, and it's perfect."

"You will be honor bound to give me credit for the title, although Amy did make that slip in her vows."

"I'll gladly give you the credit. You know, I started a novel about Possum Holler. I decided to set it in the Ozarks and change the names. I think it's important to keep the time period present for it to have impact."

"Will there be deep, dark secrets revealed?"

"Only if you can read between the lines."

"Such as?"

"I'm committed to keep some secrets. Let's just say Bobo Jenks will be fed to sharks in the Gulf of Mexico, just to give you an example."

Sunny laughed. "I can't wait to read it. Paint the schoolteacher in a positive light."

"That won't be hard. Thanks for all you've done."

"It's been my pleasure."

Tipper read the financial statements before him. "I don't believe it."

"What don't you believe, partner?" asked Alain, poking is head into Tipper's office at Tipper's Bottling.

"Sit down. I'll explain."

Alain sat across from Tipper. Tipper said. "When I graduated, I told Mr. Bounds I would be a millionaire by our twenty-fifth-class reunion. I am, but so are a few others."

"Such as?"

"Okay." He ran his hand across the documents. "This is not cash on hand, but net worth. Our doctor's the poorest."

"Please, elaborate."

"Well, Mac has been investing. He's worth slightly over one million dollars. Gator's next at about one and a half million. I am worth three point six million. Then, there are you and your wife."

"Huh?"

"I guess, individually, I'm the richest, but the two of you together are worth right at five million."

"No way!"

Tipper showed Alain the printouts.

Alain laughed. "You promised to make me rich."

"Your books garnered more than the cider."

"But you got me started. Amy's paintings made her."

"Yep, and she's invested, just like you."

"So, this little hamlet is not quite so poor anymore?"

"No, and more money will be coming in. You know, John Mason and Patsy Dayton are both probably millionaires. And if I get Pa Dent, I mean Royce, some good investments, he will be too. Possum Holler will no longer be hidden and forgotten."

Alain crossed his right leg over his left, resting his ankle on his thigh. "That's a good thing."

Tipper leaned back in his chair. "I hope so."

"It is, Tipper, so long as we hold on to our values. We're honor bound to do so."

Tipper nodded. "Together we can."

"'All for one and one for all'—just like the musketeers."

"Yes, d'Artagnan."

Both men stood to go about the business of brewing and distilling. Tipper said, "Well, I've kept my word to Mr. Bounds. Now, I just have to show him."

61
Fifteen-year Class Reunion

The crowd in the park was loud and lively. Smoke billowed from a dozen barrel grills. Rows of table were laden with food. A voice called, "Tipper?"

A distinguished, lean, tall man with dark hair salted with gray and deep violet eyes made his way through the crowd.

"Mr. Bounds!"

The older man hugged Tipper Campbell. Before another word was spoken, Tipper thrust a financial analyst's report into the man's hands. The man scanned the document and broke into warm laughter. "I've had your moonshine. It's nice to see you're a man of your word."

Tipper said, "I learned to distill in science class, Mr. Bounds."

Mr. Bounds laughed again. The older man surveyed the group around Tipper. "It's Eli now that I'm not your teacher. Is this all of Possum Holler?"

"A good number. This is my wife, Jessica."

"I thought you married Amy Dent."

"Divorced."

"Ah. Go on."

"Amy's and my daughters, Betsy, Callie, and Laurie. This guy, Ander, belongs to Jess and me. Jess is Miss Langston's daughter who is over there and now Mrs. Tomlin."

"She married Mac's father, guardian?"

"Yes."

"Where's Mac?"

"Here he comes with his passel."

Mac came up. "Mr. Bounds."

The two men shook hands. "Mac, as I told Tipper, it's Eli. Introduce your family."

"I'd love to. This is my wife, Sunny, principal at Possum Holler School."

"Sunny? What happened to Felicia?"

"Divorced."

"The dreaded D.I.V. degree seems to have taken hold in Possum Holler. Nice to meet you, Sunny. I'd like to talk to you."

"Why?" asked Sunny.

"It's time for a change."

"A job? And I thought you were going to tell me a horrible secret about Mac."

"I'll rack my brain, but, yes, a job."

"Drive in. I do need a math teacher."

"Mac, it looks as if Sunny's outnumbered."

"These are my boys. This is Chambry. Felicia is his mother. Then, I have Abner and Zeke. Sunny and I adopted them after their family died in a flu epidemic. And this is mine and Sunny's. This is Charlie."

"Wow! Is that Amy?"

"Yes," said Tipper.

"Are you on good terms?"

"Very." Tipper motioned Amy, Alain, Matthew, and Mary to come over.

"Mr. Bounds?" asked Amy. "You look good."

"Thanks. So do you. Are you pregnant?"

"Naa. I just swallowed a watermelon—actually two watermelons. Mac here confirmed we're having twins, a boy and a girl, and I say this is caboose." She grinned at Alain.

"Silly girl. By the way, it's Eli. I met your daughters. Who's this?"

"This is my husband, Alain Richter."

"You're Alain Richter? It's a pleasure."

"Likewise. These are my two children, Matthew and Mary."

Mr. Bounds shook hands with Matthew and Mary before they wandered off with the Campbell girls.

"Are you divorced too, Alain?"

"No. Never married until Amy."

"Oh."

"Shocked?"

"Doesn't sound like Possum Holler."

"Actually…"

"Wait." Eli held up a hand. "Your stories. True?"

"Yes."

"Okay," Mr. Bounds said tentatively.

"Are you?"

"I can cope."

"Good because that's the past."

"Wise." Eli looked up beyond Alain and Amy. "Tipper, what am I seeing?"

Tipper followed the man's gaze. "My mother and my sister."

"The one you told me about?"

"Yes, sir."

"You'll have to tell me the story."

"I will." Tipper waved Ina, Sherry, Gator, and the Jones children over. "Eli, you remember my mother?"

"She's hard to forget." The two shook hands.

Tipper introduced Sherry. "This is my sister, Sherry Jones, and her husband, Gator, and their brood." Tipper winked at Gator. "Meet Fox, Rooster, Lily, Rabbit, Buck, Rose, and Iris."

"Is that the end?" laughed Eli.

"Yes." Gator and Sherry answered together.

Eli Bounds motioned for two teenagers. "These are my kids, Reagan and Gavin."

Heart fluttering as she recalled the first time she had seen this man who matched Tipper inch for inch and maybe a few pounds heavier brought on by age but still had a headful of black hair albeit flecked with gray and deep soulful violet eyes, "Where's your wife?" Ina asked as the teenagers joined the Possum Holler teens.

"She died ten years ago, cancer."

"I'm sorry."

"It's been hard raising two children alone, but they're good kids."

Several people began to lure the group apart, leaving Ina and Eli to talk.

Ina nodded. "Yes, it's hard alone."

"Ina. May I call you Ina?"

"Of course."

"Tipper told me about your daughter years ago. How did you get together?"

Ina shared Sherry's story with Eli. He listened without interruption. "You are an amazing woman," he murmured when she finished the tale.

"Not really." She shook her head.

"I think you are."

"Thank you. You raised two alone, and it looks like you've done a good job."

"Thank you, ma'am. Reagan had just been born when Tipper graduated. Darlene got pregnant with Gavin, and we found out she had breast cancer. She refused treatment until Gavin was born and lingered two years. It was hard to watch her suffer."

"You never married again."

"No." Eli laughed. "Only one woman ever even caught my eye after I met Darlene, and she was off limits."

"Too bad."

As Ina and Eli talked, Daneen Spalding found the group from Possum Holler. She and Lauren laughed when they saw each other. Daneen nodded. "You were right, Lauren. This scoundrel and this imp," she said as she put her arms around both Gator and Alain, "proved me wrong. I'm so glad." She looked around at the five children from Possum Holler that she had at one time taught. "Lauren told me years ago that this group would put Possum Holler on the map."

Alain laughed and held up a finger. He reached in his back pocket and handed Daneen Butler Spalding a new map of West Virginia with Possum Holler highlighted in bright yellow. She looked at Lauren. "Can I slap him? He made life hell that second year." She lowered her voice. "I lied about their attendance just to get rid of him. That's what you and Karen did, isn't it."

"Not to get rid of them, but to give them a chance."

"Yes, to give them a chance," said a very pretty woman accompanied by a tall distinguished man.

"Miss Stone?" asked Alain.

"Mrs. Jasper. This is my husband, Cole."

After a time of catching up, Mrs. Spalding said, "You two really went out on a limb for these young men. I'm glad you did. Alain, where are your children?"

Alain took the meanest teacher he ever had to meet his children, and she began to tell them the terrible things their father had done to her the second year she had him, leaving Matthew in stitches and Daneen giving the boy advice on what not to do when he became a teacher. As the younger folks wandered off, she turned to Alain. "I'm not your sister. I want you to know that my mother told me on her deathbed that I am also a product of incest. She changed her name to Butler, but she was a Bustin."

Alain sighed. "I knew that. Tal told Gator who told me."

She shook her head. "The two of you....always inseparable. I am still proud of you. You ended up making me a better person."

She patted his arm and went to find her husband while Alain returned to the group from Possum Holler.

A worn-looking woman with dark roots showing from a bad dye job walked up to the group who remained. "Hello, Mac."

"Susan?"

"Yes. You look good."

"Has it really been fifteen years since we went to prom?"

"Feels like fifty. So, you actually became a doctor?"

"I did, and you?"

"I work for a doctor in records."

"Transcription?"

"And billing."

Mac introduced his family. Susan talked a little longer before she moved on to greet other classmates.

"That was your prom date?" Sunny asked.

"Time has *not* been good to her."

"No, it seems time has treated the 'nasty little hillbillies that won't ever amount to anything' much better."

The picnic began to wind down around three. The class members and spouses or dates had a dance later, but the rest of their families began to return to a hotel or home. The people from Possum Holler drifted to their cars.

"Ina!" Eli Bounds called as he jogged across the park.

"Yes, Eli?"

"Um…"

"Yes?"

"Would you stay for the dance?"

"Why?"

"As my date?"

"You're asking me for a date?"

"Yes. I told you only one woman had ever caught my eye. It was you, but I was married, and you were suffering."

"Me?" She touched her chest and stretched her big blue eyes wide.

"You seem astonished."

"I am. I was so backward. I never thought I'd ever consider a date again."

"Will you?"

"I don't have clothes for the dance."

"We could go shopping before, kind of in between."

"Like another date?"

Eli blushed. "I guess. Yeah."

"Do you dance?"

"I do."

Ina thought for a moment. "I'll buy it myself."

Eli grinned. Tipper walked back to Ina. "Ma, Papa's ready to go."

"I'll be staying, Tipper."

"Ma'am?"

Ina kissed Tipper's cheek. "I have a date for the dance. I'll see you tonight."

Ina put her arm through Eli's, and they walked off.

Alain laughed behind Tipper. "Way to go, Miss Ina!"

"What just happened?" Tipper asked.

"Miss Ina just decided life begins at fifty. Fifty bucks says Ina Campbell is Ina Bounds before Christmas."

"My mother and my favorite teacher? No way. Not in a million years."

"Strange things happen at class reunions. Everybody else that I care about in my Possum Holler saga has found love. It's Miss Ina's turn.

"Yes, it is, Alain, but my mother and my favorite teacher? I don't believe it."

"Scared to take my bet?"

"What are you two bickering about?" asked Amy, slipping her hand into Alain's.

"Tipper's in shock," gloated Alain.

Tipper pointed. "Do you see that? They're holding hands. Oh, my God!"

Alain cracked up. "I raise the bet. A hundred bucks says they'll be married before Christmas."

"No way," countered Amy. "Miss Ina will put it off 'til Valentine's Day. She has a romantic streak. I'll take your bet."

Still looking bewildered, Tipper repeated, "My mother and my favorite teacher?"

"Mm," mused Gator joining the conversation. "I'll take your bet. I say the stroke of midnight on New Year's Eve."

"The pot is building," Alain said triumphantly.

Mac walked back to the group. "Did I just see what I think I saw?"

Tipper nodded. "My mother and my favorite teacher. Alain has 'em married before Christmas. He's taking bets."

Watching Eli's arm slip across Ina's back as he opened the car door for her, forcing his two teenagers into the back seat, Mac said, "I'm in. I'm with Alain. How much?"

"A hundred." Alain grinned. "Amy and Gator say after Christmas. What about you, Tipper?"

"My mother and my favorite teacher?"

The other four nodded. Alain quipped, "And you'll get a stepbrother and a stepsister."

Tipper shook his head in total disbelief. "I can't believe Ma would jump into something. If that date ends in a kiss, I'm with Alain. I can't believe I just said that."

They all laughed. Alain put an arm around Tipper's shoulders. "Tipper, that date will start with a kiss. Let's get ready for the dance."

Tipper looked back over his shoulder as Alain led him away. "My mother and my favorite teacher? Who'd've 'thunk' it?"

The five formed a chain of arms linked with Amy smack dab in the middle between Alain and Tipper while Gator and Mac formed the ends with Mac beside Tipper and Gator next to Alain and walked away laughing and speculating.

Epilogue

Ina Campbell wore a blue linen suit as she walked down the aisle on the arm of her son, Tipper, toward the altar and a man who had stolen her heart. She had never thought to love again.

Eli Bounds grinned, and his eyes danced. The woman that walked toward him to be his wife looked like a goddess. He could hardly wait to hold her in his arms.

The older couple had endured loss and tragedy. Ina had lost two men either directly or indirectly related to coalmining. Her husband had been killed in a cave-in at only twenty years of age. Her fiancé several years later had developed pneumonia, which was only aggravated by coalmining. The man, Tipper Campbell's high-school math teacher, had lost his wife in a battle with breast cancer. This union was a fairytale for both of them.

As Tipper laid his mother's hand in the hand of a man he respected, Dr. Leo Tomlin, the pastor who had encountered a third-world country when he came to Possum Holler, nodded with approval. He had seen much suffering in the community he had grown to love. He heard a few sniffles, but the tears were tears of joy.

Possum Holler no longer resembled a third-world country. The wedding Leo performed spoke volumes of change and foreshadowed only better things to come. Leo laughed inside as he almost said, "For Richter or poorer," as he spoke the vows to be recited. The funny thing was that the bride and groom would have gone along with a grin on their faces for Possum Holler was all the richer because of four young men and one young woman who had made bets on whether Ina and Eli would marry before or after Christmas. The five smiled mischievously.

Dr. MacKenzie Reardon, M.D., had brought a doctor and real medicine to the impoverished area. He was Possum Holler's homegrown healer. Mr. Tipper Campbell, whiskey entrepreneur, had begun the spread of business with his backyard distillation as it became legitimate. Mr. Gator Jones, businessman and Hog King, continued the growing business as the owner of the slaughterhouse that he had turned into a full processing plant. He shipped the best pork in the state. Mr. Alain Richter, brewer and author, had overcome abuse and neglect to become a bestselling author and partner with Tipper Campbell. And Ms. Amy Dent, artist, had fled the mountains only to return to become the bride of Alain Richter and staunch supporter of the others. The five had made bets at the group's fifteen-year-class reunion about whether Ina Campbell would marry Eli Bounds before or after Christmas.

Each placed one hundred dollars in a collection plate for the church as they headed for a Possum Holler wedding reception, an event no one wanted to change. None of them had won the bet. None of them had lost the bet. Yet, they were all winners. Ina Campbell became Ina Bounds *on* Christmas Day.

June 9, 2010

Word count—98,758

May 29, 2015

Word count—112,514

June 22, 2022

Word count—113,266

October 12, 2024

Word count—114,812

Final word count—116,813

June 25, 2025

About the Author

Like many of her characters, Janet is a history buff and loves anything of historical significance from old cars to old cemeteries. Get to know Janet and you'll see why she's been critically acclaimed at the Faulkner Wisdom Competition and why her writing continues to receive 4- and 5-star reviews. Her novel, *Spirits' Desire*, the second book in her *Legend of Draconis* series, won The Critter's, Preditor's and Editor's Award while the third book in *The Raiford Chronicles*, *Broken*, was a short-list finalist (top 20) at the Faulkner Competition. It could be that readers see so much of her in her characters: mother, grandmother, educator, author, editor, a leader in the Mississippi writing community as head of the Middle Mississippi chapter of the Mississippi Writers Guild; and board member of the Mississippi Writers' Guild, and a person who has overcome great obstacles and still holds on to her faith in her Lord and Savior, Jesus Christ.

http://www.janettaylorperry.com/

http://janettaylor-perry.blogspot.com/

https://authorcentral.amazon.com/gp/profile

https://www.facebook.com/Author-Janet-Taylor-Perry-299698950061301/

janettaylorperry@gmail.com

https://www.facebook.com/janettaylorperrybooks/

Instagram: @janettaylorperry & @jtaylorperry

X: Janet Taylor-Perry— @mom5kidz421

Goodreads: https://www.goodreads.com/author/show/7376480Janet_Taylor_Perry

Pinterest: https://www.pinterest.com/mumzy25/

https://www.youtube.com/results?search_query=janettaylorperry

Janettaylorperry.com—For a reading experience
EXTRAORDINAIRE!

MAP OF POSSUM HOLLER
Map not to scale

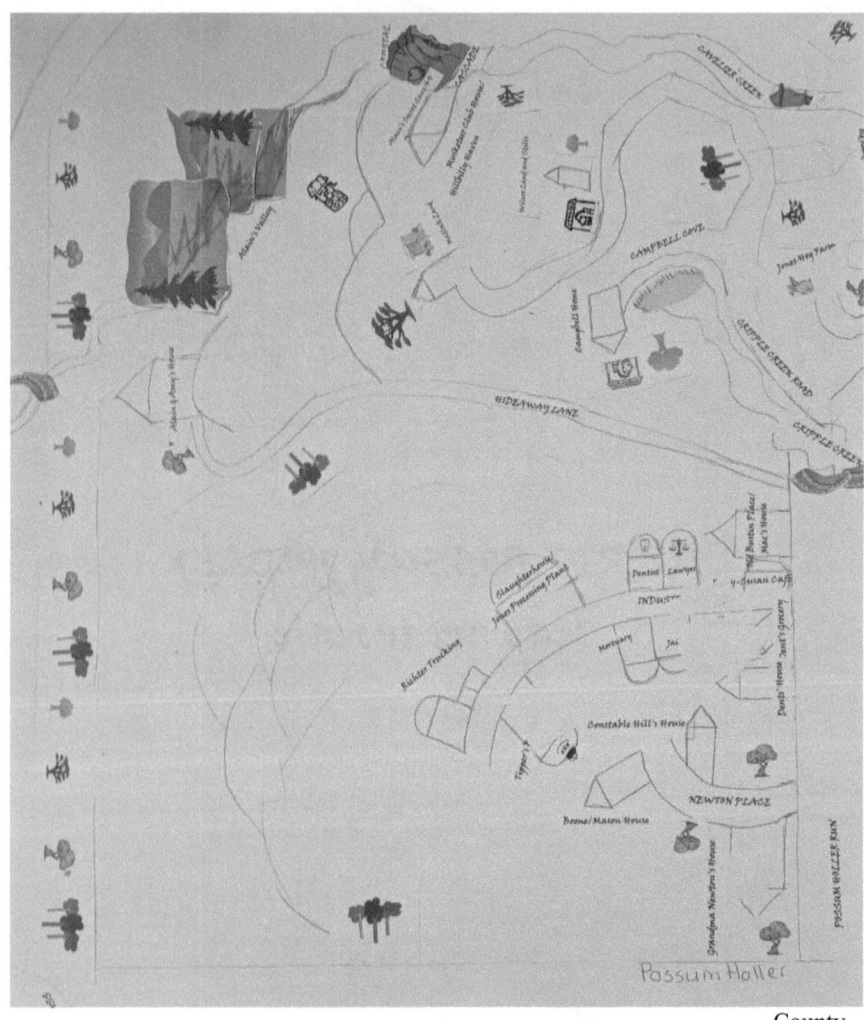

County
Map not to

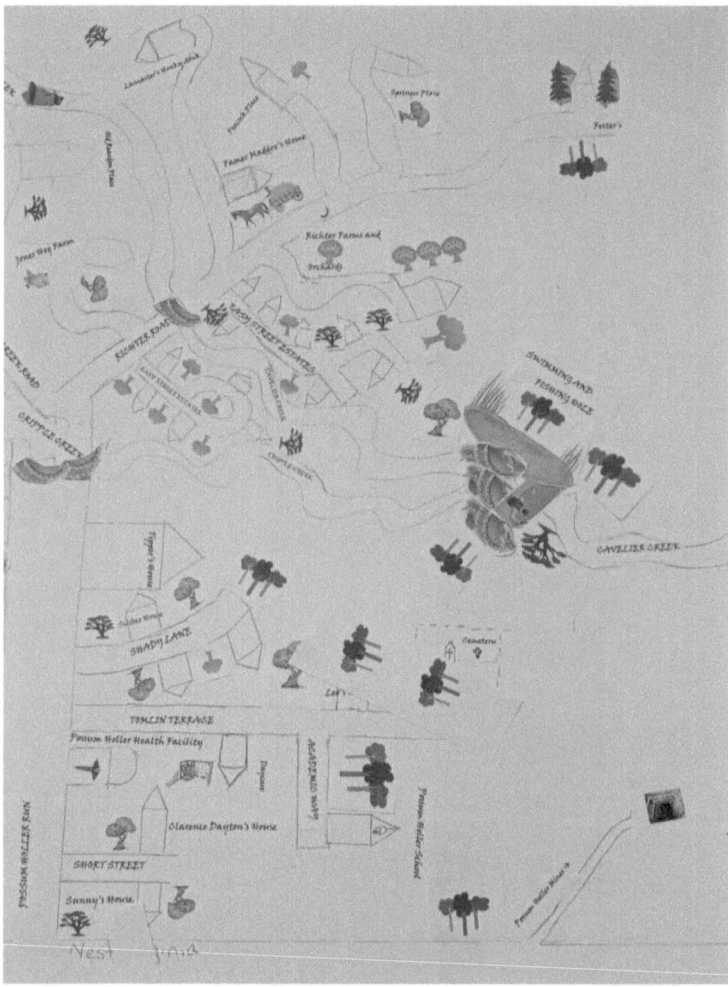

Road 13
Scale